One Good Knight

MERCEDES LACKEY
One Good Knight

LUNA™
www.LUNA-Books.com

LUNA™

First edition March 2006

ONE GOOD KNIGHT

ISBN 0-373-80217-X

www.LUNA-Books.com

Printed in U.S.A.

Dedicated to the memory of Andre Norton,
friend, exemplar, and mentor

CHAPTER ONE

Princess Andromeda stood on the very edge of a ledge three-quarters of the way up the cliff above the Royal Palace of her mother, Queen Cassiopeia of Acadia, holding out her arms to the wind. The same wind flattened her tunic against her body, and sent strands of her hair flying about her face as they escaped from the knot at the back of her neck. She raised her face to the sun, closing her eyes.

I wish I had wings—I used to dream about flying when I was little. It would be so glorious to simply step off this rock and fly, to escape the dreariness of being a Princess, with the din of "musts" and "must-nots," day in and day out, from governesses, tutors, her mother's ladies and, of course, her mother.

Especially the "must-nots."

There was an almighty number of "must-nts." You mustn't

laugh too loudly. You mustn't speak your opinion unless it's asked for. You mustn't talk to anyone below the rank of noble, unless it's to give an order. You mustn't be seen reading in public. You mustn't frown in public. You mustn't smile at anyone below the rank of a noble, and you mustn't smile at any young men, ever. You mustn't let anyone call you "Andie," nor refer to yourself by that name. You mustn't be seen moving at anything other than a graceful walk...the list was endless. It seemed that all she ever heard was what she shouldn't be doing. No one ever told her what she *could* do—aside from look decorative, wearing the serenely stupid gaze of a statue. No one ever came to her and said, "Princess, there is a task you and you alone can perform." One "must" along those lines would have been countered with a hundred distasteful "must-nots"—but one never came.

Surely that had never been her mother's lot. Cassiopeia had begun her life as Crown Princess and then Queen with responsibilities. In no small part because her husband, at least according to gossip, had been so good at avoiding them. That was why the old King, Andie's grandfather, had handpicked her out of the daughters of his nobles. He had wanted a girl with ambition, since his own son clearly had none, and a girl who would see that things got done.

Who ever would be foolish enough to envy the lot of a Princess with all of that hanging over their head? Nothing but restrictions without responsibilities. *I'm less free than a slave, and not allowed to do anything that has any meaning to it.*

She took a deep breath of the sea-scented air, and sighed

it out again. At least her mother was not going to be plaguing her with one of her unannounced inspections this afternoon, inspections that inevitably ended in well-mannered murmurings of disappointment and the appointment of a new governess. Queen Cassiopeia was holding a very, very private audience with the Captains of the Acadian Merchant Fleet, followed by another with the foreign merchants who plied Acadian waters, and the meetings were expected to last all day and well into the night. Trade was the lifeblood of Acadia. Without trade, this Kingdom would probably die. Anything that threatened trade and the taxes it brought in, threatened Acadia as surely as an army. Despite her mother's being asked, begged, by her daughter to be allowed to attend, Andie had been told to "run along." Under any other circumstances, she would have been happy about the freedom from her governess's supervision and the opportunity to get out in fresh air and to make a raid on the library. But being treated like a child put a bitter taste on the treat.

She pushed at the stiff wires crossing the bridge of her nose, part of a contrivance called "oculars," making sure they were firmly on her face, then curled the wires of the side-pieces securely around the backs of her ears. They were a bit of a nuisance, but she loved them, because without them, she'd be half blind. The Royal Guard's own Magician had made them for her when he'd realized, watching her try to hold a book right up against her tiny nose as a child, that she was terribly nearsighted. He'd been pleased enough to do so, though the Queen had been less than happy the first time she saw her daughter scampering about with the wire-and-glass-lenses contraption perched on her face. "It's unnatural!" she had complained. "It looks like a cheap mask! What need has a Princess to see clearly, anyway?"

She had finally given in only when it was made demonstrably clear that Andie's never-ending series of bruising falls came to an abrupt end once she could see where she was going.

Not that her mother cared if I fell, except that all the bruises were an embarrassment to her. Andie sighed again. *I can never please her, no matter what I do, so I wish she'd just get used to that and make use of what I actually can do.*

Queen Cassiopeia wanted a pink-and-white, sugarplum Princess, a lovely daughter who as a child would have been all frills and giggles, big blue eyes and golden curls, and as an adult (or nearly, anyway) would be the younger image of herself, immaculately groomed, impeccably gowned, graceful, lovely—not to mention quiet, pliant, uncomplaining and unthinking. A marriage pawn, who wouldn't argue about anything, or ask awkward questions, or want to do anything except to look as beautiful as possible. There had been nibbles of marriages over the years, but nothing ever came of them. Cassiopeia had enough ambition for two; she didn't see the need of it in her daughter.

Andie gave herself a mental slap. Maybe not *unthinking.* But—certainly more obedient than Andie was. And assuredly much prettier, much neater and much more concerned with her personal appearance than Andie could ever bring herself to be. So far as her mother was concerned, looks were one more weapon in the arsenal of a determined woman.

Cassiopeia never spent less than two hours in the hands of her maidservants before first appearing outside of her rooms. Andie could barely tolerate having the maid comb her hair and put it up, and she insisted on bathing herself, without all the oils and perfumes her mother seemed to think were necessary. Cassiopeia went through as many as six gowns before choosing one for the day, and it was always something so elaborate it took at least two maids to help her into it. Andie threw on whichever of her tunics the maid gave her, and if forced into a gown, made it the simplest draped column of fabric with cords confining it at her waist. Cassiopeia wore enough jewelry to finance an expedition to Qin for the most ordinary of days. Andie never wore any ornaments but a hair-clasp.

Cassiopeia had a lush figure that caused poets and minstrels from Kingdoms hundreds of leagues away to come write songs about her, and a face that had inspired fifty sculptors. Andie's figure was straight up and down and no gown could disguise that fact, and as for her face—well, as her mother often sighed, who would look past the lenses that took up half of it?

So how could the Queen ever be anything *but* disappointed in her daughter?

Andie had long since resigned herself to this, burying the hurt a little deeper each time Cassiopeia made some unconsidered remark. At least there was one area she could achieve success in—anything intellectual. And the Queen did seem to take some small pleasure in that, though she might bemoan the fact that Andie's nose was almost always in a book. The trouble was, she didn't seem to think that all of this study had any useful applications.

Even though I've quoted her facts and figures about Acadia until I've run out of breath. Every time she was going to have an important audience or meeting and I was able to find out about it, I did all the research on the subject anyone could ask for. Today at breakfast, Andie had detailed the revenues on import-taxes, given her historical background on inter-merchant disputes…but she might just as well have been telling her Godmother tales. The Queen just said, "How interesting, dear," as if she wasn't even listening.

She probably wasn't listening, actually. *She probably thinks I'm just reciting my lessons for her.* Once Cassiopeia had realized that her daughter was not going to develop into a miniature copy of herself, she'd left Andie's up-bringing to nurses and governesses, who mostly passed in and out of Andie's life without making much impact, for none of them had lasted very long. Not because Andie was a difficult child, but because even when they were compe-tent, and a shocking number were not, the competent ones sooner or later ran afoul of the Queen and were replaced. The incompetent, of course, were soon found out and sacked.

Not that it had ever mattered. The ones she'd had as a child, when it might have made her unhappy to lose a nurse she had become fond of, had, one and all, been rather horrible. Horrible in different ways, but still horrible. Some had been strict to the point of cruelty, some had been care-less to the point of danger, some had been neglectful, or had scolded and criticized until Andie was in tears.

If it hadn't been for her loyal Guardsmen and Guardswomen, she would have spent a lonely and very miserable childhood. But they had been everything that the nurses should have been and never were. The same set of Six had been standing watch over her safety since she was an infant, and when nursemaids were asleep, or drunk, or in the bed of their noble lovers, or lording it over the lesser servants, or off flirting with stable boys, the Guards were the ones who saw that she drank her milk, wiped her tears when she fell, and told her stories at bedtime.

Just as well that I wasn't the sort of child to get into serious trouble. They never had to get me out of anything difficult.

Not that she was spoiled. The nursemaids had strict orders from the Queen on that particular subject, and no few of them had taken great glee in loading Andie down with punitive punishments at every opportunity until she was as much of a model of correct and polite behavior as anyone would have asked. And her Six had too many children of their own to put up with nonsense from her.

From that faithful set of six Guards, she learned to know every member of the Guard assigned to the Palace as soon as her curiosity led her out of the nursery, Guard in tow. If she hadn't, she'd never have gotten her oculars.

Now she was something of a mascot for the entire Palace Regiment, and she did her best to help them whenever and wherever she could. Not that any of them had ever permitted the slightest slip so that the Queen learned of the peculiar attachment.

If Cassiopeia ever found out, she'd banish the lot of them to some awful assignments at prisons or remote Guard-posts, and put Andie in the care of even more horrible governesses.

One day soon, though, her faithful Six would be retired; Demetre and Leodipes were getting very gray, and the rest weren't much younger. It was only the fact that duty in the Inner Palace was largely a sinecure that kept them active. She dreaded thinking of that day, hoping their replacements would be guards she liked.

Andie looked down at the Palace and the city below it; from here, just below the lookout point for the Sea-Watch, it looked exactly like the model in the Great Library. The city of Ethanos was deceptively peaceful from here, its people reduced to little colored dots moving along the white streets, the striped awnings and banners too distant to show their stains and tatters, and none of its glorious, brawling untidiness evident from this height.

Which was, she reflected, probably the way her mother preferred it. Cassiopeia didn't like untidiness—not in her Palace, nor her city, nor her Kingdom, nor her daughter.

Unfortunately for the Queen's peace of mind, the only place she could keep untidiness from intruding was within the walls of the Palace—and then only within the places where she herself spent any amount of time.

Andie shook off her melancholy; after all, even if she was still being treated like a child, she had the whole afternoon to herself, without the intrusion of Queen *or* governess. She'd finished her set lessons, even the embroidery she hated, and knowing that the Queen was not going to appear in the Princess's Wing today and would be too busy to think of sending one of her ladies to do it for her, Andie's governess had gone off for a good long gossip somewhere, leaving Andie free to do as she liked.

She had seized on the opportunity to climb the cliff, and thought that while she was at it, she might as well take the Sea-Watch Guard's noon meal up to him. It was a long way up, and she always made a pause near the top, to survey Palace, town and harbor. Today for her lessons she had just been reading poetry, which made her wonder, perversely, why the poets always talked about the "wine-dark" sea.... *It's no color of any wine I ever saw. Nor the color of anything I'd ever feel safe drinking.*

She turned away from the sea and the view below, and scampered up the last few flights of switchback stairs cut into the rock of the cliff. The stairs ended in a platform planed as flat as a sheet of paper, with a three-sided stone shelter square in the middle of it, a shelter that kept the Sea-Watch Guard shaded from the sun and protected from the worst of the weather. On a gorgeous day like today, Sea-Watch duty was a pleasant thing, but in bad weather it was something only the strong of will and body would dare to undertake.

"Thesus!" she called, "I've brought up your rations!"

"Come around to the front, Princess!" came the reply. "I've got a sail in sight and I don't want to lose it."

"A sail?" She hurried around to the front of the shelter, where the big telescope was mounted—created by Sophont Balan, the Royal Guards' Magician who had created her oculars. "Sophont" just meant "wise man;" there were a lot of them, and most of them actually weren't magicians. Thesus—a powerful and sun-bronzed warrior whose fine body beneath the duty-uniform of sleeveless tunic and trews of brown linen gave the lie to the gray strands in his curly black beard and hair—had his eye planted firmly on the end of the instrument.

"What kind of sail?" she asked, as he showed no signs of looking up.

"Ah, now, if I knew that, I wouldn't be standing here with this be-damned thing in my eye, would I?" he replied. "There's nothing painted on the sail, and she's flying no colors I recognize. From her hull, she's a merchanter, and maybe come late to the Queen's meeting, but even if so, she's a stranger to these waters."

"What are you doing, then?" she persisted, curious. "Why are you still watching her?"

"I'm counting sailors to see if there are too many. I'm looking at the ones on deck, seeing what they do and if any are standing idle. I'm casting my eye over the ship, looking for armor, for a place where a ram can be fixed to the prow, and counting weapons' ports," he said. "If she's a seawolf in a dolphin's skin, I'll know it in a moment."

The port was large, but not that large. A single supposed merchant ship, if loaded with pirates, could raid it and make off with every other ship and its cargo in the harbor.

She waited, quietly, while he moved the telescope in tiny increments, and peered, muttering to himself. Finally he straightened and took down the horn hanging from the roof of the shelter. She tensed as he sounded it four times, then relaxed as he didn't add the fifth note that would have signaled a possible enemy approaching. Notes were only sounded for ships foreign to Ethanos's port. One for a small fishing boat, two for a large, three for a fast-courier, four for a merchanter, five for a "possible" enemy, and six for a ship approaching openly armed and apparently hostile.

"Simple merchanter—no armor, no ram, just enough hands to crew her and all of 'em scampering like monkeys, her captain's a fat ball of a man who'd probably pop straight to the surface if you pitched him over-side, and the mate isn't far behind him in blubber," Thesus proclaimed with a laugh, hanging up the horn and rubbing his hands. "Now, where's that grub?"

"Here!" she said, holding out the basket and leather wineskin. "I thought I would have a picnic on the cliff, and it didn't seem fair to make a boy climb up here with your ration since I was already coming."

"Ah, so that worthless stick of a governess of yours has taken herself off for the day?" Thesus asked shrewdly, the corners of his eyes crinkling with laughter as he sat down on a stone bench beside the telescope and unpacked what she'd brought, the standard soldiers' fare of olives, cheese, garlic sausage and a coarse loaf of bread. "Well, it's to be hoped Her Majesty has more of these meetings, then. You've been indoors too much—you're pale as this bit of cheese."

"A Princess mustn't get sunburned, or no proper Prince will ever look twice at her," she told him as she sat on the bare stone of the platform across from him.

He snorted. "Then I'd be saying that a so-called 'proper' Prince is no kind of proper man," he retorted, and though he kept one eye on her, and was making a quick and neat meal of his provisions, he never let his attention wander from the horizon where a new sail might appear. "But there you are, what do I know about royalty? Nothing, and there's an end to it, I suppose."

"Well, your advice is more sensible than anything I ever got out of a governess," Andie told him, feeling a twinge of concern. "Just be careful—"

"No fear of that, Princess," Thesus chuckled. "I've been with the Royal Guard, man and boy, a good forty years, and I've learned who to keep my mouth shut around."

"I'll leave you to your duty, then," she replied, scrambling to her feet.

"Best do that. This spot's a bit exposed, and we don't want someone to catch sight of those oculars of yours flashing in the sun and know who's bringing me my rations. No harm in you picnicking below, but plenty of trouble if you're visiting with riffraff like me. Thankee, Princess. You're a rare little lass." His blue eyes sparkled as he smiled, his teeth very white and strong-looking, framed in the black beard.

"And you are a true Guardsman," she said, giving him the Guards' salute of her closed right fist to her left shoulder.

He laughed delightedly, and the sound of his laughter followed her back down the stairs.

Now, there was no harm, no harm at all, in the Princess being up on the stairs themselves. They didn't *lead* anywhere but to the observation platform for the Sea-Watch. No one could get to them except through the Palace. So they were a safe place for her to be, and she was well known for spending entire afternoons up here, or rather, on one of the landings, sitting in the sun and wind and reading.

So once she was as far down as one of her known haunts she relaxed.

She glanced back down at the Palace again, and made note of the servants moving through some of the open courts. No one appeared to be looking for her and she relaxed a little more.

On the way up, she had left a few things of her own here, and now she collected them: a blanket, a cushion, and a basket containing a book and her own lunch. Short of being able to sneak down into the city itself, which, on a day when the port was full of foreign ships was simply *not* going to happen, this was the best place for her to spend the afternoon. Not even her friends in the Guard would let her slip out of the Palace when the city was full of foreigners. They might be anything in the guise of common merchants—kidnappers, assassins, spies. Whereas up here, no one was going to be able to get to her without going through several sets of Guards—and even then, she'd see whoever it was coming up the stairs in plenty of time to take refuge with Thesus.

Not that anything that adventurous was likely to happen. No one ever attacked Ethanos. No one wanted to. You'd first have to get past the harbor town and its regiment of Guards, then up the cliff to the city itself, where the City Watch would greet you with a hail of arrows and missiles. Then you'd have to fight your way through the streets, all of which twisted and turned like a tangled ball of yarn, to get to the Palace, which had its own walls and the Royal Guard to protect it. It was like a sea urchin; maybe the meat inside was sweet, but to get to it, you had to get past a thousand spines, all sharp, and all poisoned.

She spread out her blanket and flopped down on it, stomach against the warm stone, with arms crossed and her chin resting on her forearms as she stared down at the city.

It rankled that, once again, Cassiopeia had refused even to consider her presence at these meetings—and after she had gone to such pains to study the latest reports on every single merchant in the domestic fleet! She could quote import and export figures, tax revenues, profit margins and losses for the past ten years! Or—well, not exactly quote them, but she had all of it noted down and within moments could put her finger on any figure needed. And all she'd asked was that she be allowed to observe—not to participate, merely to watch and listen! After all, she was nineteen, and she still had very little notion of what it meant to rule. The only time she ever saw the Queen exercising her authority was in formal audiences that required the attendance of the entire Court. Those were as scripted as any play, and gave her no idea of just how Cassiopeia employed diplomacy, strategy and negotiation. The Queen wasn't going to live forever (even if sometimes it seemed as if she might) and when she was gone, Andie did not want to find herself at the mercy of "advisers" and "councilors" who did the actual ruling, while she served only as a figurehead on the throne.

It was all terribly frustrating. Maybe everything she knew was out of a book rather than real life, but at least she knew *something*. Her mother's Chief Adviser, Solon Adacritus, didn't even bother with *that* much; he depended on his secretaries to find out everything for him. That, by Andie's reckoning, was cheating.

Solon had been Cassiopeia's right-hand forever, though Andie could not imagine what her mother ever saw in him. Oh, he was handsome enough, in a rather limp and languid way, but he was the butt of a hundred jokes in the Guard for his manners and the superstitious way he hung himself with good-luck charms and amulets, fiddling with them constantly.

Not for the first time, she wondered if Solon was her mother's lover. Well, if he was, he was certainly so discreet and careful about it that there had never been so much as a hint of it her entire life. And there were plenty of people looking for information like that, she had no doubt. Information was leverage, and the game of inter- and intra-kingdom politics was played largely on the basis of leverage.

Acadia might be small and rocky, but it had the only protected, deep-water harbor for leagues and leagues, as well as one very good road that led straight to the heart of the Five Hundred Kingdoms and was safe and well patrolled, and that put it squarely on one end of an extremely lucrative trade route. Where there was money, there was power. Where there was power and money, people who didn't have it would be scheming to get it. Knowledge of who, if anyone, was Queen Cassiopeia's lover would be one more weapon to be deployed by those people. *Which is one more thing all my reading has taught me.* You couldn't read history for long without seeing the patterns.

Without that deep-water port, Acadia would have been the poorest of the Five Hundred Kingdoms. Although the sea did well by those who dared the waters to fish, the sea took as well as gave, and fishing was a dangerous profes-

sion. The rocky hills could not support grazing for much
except goats and a few sheep, the only fruits that flourished
were olives and grapes, and the grain harvests were just
enough to keep the populace fed without any surplus even
in the best years. There were pockets of richer soil, but not
the broad, flat pastures and huge fields of waving grain that
other lands boasted. Acadia didn't even have a Godmother—hadn't had one in so long that plenty of nobles
who never left Ethanos thought Godmothers were as mythical as centaurs and fauns.

There were pockets of all sorts of so-called "mythical"
creatures, little colonies in the wilderness that the country-
people traded with. Thesus had grown up playing with
centaur colts and faun-kids as his friends, before he'd come
down out of the high hills and joined the Guard. He'd told
her stories, and the tales had the ring of truth about them,
in no small part because they were not tales of great adven-
ture, but of the same sort of mischief that any children got
up to. The only difference was that when Thesus and his
friends teased a bull or a he-goat, his friends' parents could
grab him up and take him to safety on their backs, or speak
the same language as the goat and make the patriarch of
the herd back down.

Plus, the history of Acadia was full of treaties with the
"Other-folk," or Wyrding Others, treaties that were on file
in the library—and how could one write up a treaty with
things that were mythical? *I would so like to see some of
them…fauns, sylphs, centaurs, dryads and nymphs.*

She'd have liked to see a Godmother, too. But it was
clear from everything she had read that Acadia didn't have

one. Probably Acadia was too insignificant. After all, when had Cassiopeia ever hosted a ball? Or a masquerade? When had other Royals even visited? Not so much as a sixth- or seventh-son Prince had ever ventured across the border or into the harbor. Nothing of any consequence had happened here in more than a generation.

No wonder the Godmothers ignored them in favor of Kingdoms that actually *did* things.

But—if we had a Godmother here, I bet she'd see to it that Mother started educating me in my duties. Leaving me igno-rant like this is just making a big fat hole for The Tradition to stick an evil Prince into. Someone who'd come sweep me off my feet, then oppress my people. Or was the fact that she was already aware such a thing could happen enough to pre-vent it from happening? Maybe Acadia was so quiet and small that even The Tradition ignored it.

Acadians themselves ignored The Tradition. Of all the people she'd ever mentioned it to, only a few seemed even vaguely aware of such a thing. Maybe, again, because things were so quiet here that the only thing The Tradition did was to ensure that there were enough poor-but-honest peasants, worthy orphans, hearty fisherman, nosy gossips and that sort of thing.

Or maybe The Tradition is satisfied that we've got our quota filled with Queen Cassiopeia, beautiful and wise, she thought a little cynically. *It doesn't need to waste its time on anything else.*

There certainly didn't seem to be a great deal of anything you could call "real magic" employed in and around Aca-dia. Even the Sophont Balan, for all that he had the title of

Guard's Magician, seemed mostly to tinker with purely mechanical things like telescopes and oculars.

She turned over on her back and closed her eyes, listening to the gulls crying below, finally able to put a name to her restlessness. *I'm bored, but it's worse than just being bored. Nothing ever happens to me. Nothing is ever going to happen to me. I am going to sit in my wing of the Palace and do nothing for the rest of my life. Mother will probably even outlive me. Or else she'll marry some handsome fool who'll be happy to have the title of Consort with none of the work, have a son, and he'll become King—and then what? I'll still sit in my wing of the Palace, and the only thing that will ever change is that eventually I won't have to put up with governesses anymore.*

Would being played as a diplomatic marriage-pawn be any better? It would at least be a change…but it could be worse, she realized bleakly.

But before she sank into despair, she gave herself another mental shake. *There has to be a solution. Mother doesn't take me seriously—so working through Mother is no answer. So who else is there?*

And she sat bolt upright as the solution occurred to her. Much as she disliked the man, there was someone who might. Chief Adviser Solon Adacritus, who already relied on others to give him the facts he needed to properly inform the Queen. So what if she started writing up reports for him? It would be easy enough to do—easy enough to give them to him. Easy enough even to flatter his ego while she did it. Say something like, "You have your finger on the pulse of this situation, Lord Solon. Can you see if I've grasped it properly?" *I think it will work. He might even start to rely on me, give me access to information I can't now get. If he starts to take me seriously, it won't matter that Mother doesn't. If he starts to need my reports and research, he'll make sure Mother never marries me off.*

Besides, she didn't dislike him all that much. It was only that he was such a fop. It wouldn't be hard to *pretend* to respect him.

It was not only a plan, it was a *good* plan. Workable, logical. And if Solon was as ineffectual as she thought he was, as long as she acted the shy and mousy bookworm, he'd be likely to take what she gave him and look no farther than the surface, figuring that a word or two of praise would be all the reward she needed. *Huh. Maybe it's not so bad a thing that no one looks past my oculars.*

For that matter, this might pave the way to ridding her of governesses…because if Lord Solon wanted her to do research, he'd want her to have her time free, and to do that she'd have to do without all those stupid lessons in precedence, genealogy and the Royal Houses of the nearest Kingdoms. Not to mention the dance lessons, etiquette lessons, deportment and posture lessons, embroidery and so on…

This is better than a good plan. I'll not only have something to do, I'll be effective.

It was with difficulty that she kept herself from leaping up and running down the stairs to press the notes she had written into Solon's hands. For one thing, he would be with the Queen in those meetings. For another, she wanted to go over them and make fair copies before she gave them to him. This might be the most important bit of scholarship she ever did in her life. If she was going to convince him of her usefulness, she had to be sure that what she gave him was *better* than what he was getting from his secretaries.

So instead of pelting down the stairs, she sat quietly and ate her lunch while mentally reorganizing how she was going to present her work, and decided that a bit more digging in the library would not be amiss. For one thing, she hadn't included anything about the foreign merchants, and that would be a gaping hole in an otherwise presentable report, a hole that she could not, at this point, afford.

By the time she had finished eating, she felt she was ready, and she gathered up her things with a feeling of determination.

At least, in this battle, she was going in well armed. And as she headed down the stone stairs to take up her "weapons" of pen and paper, she felt herself grinning—because this was exactly the kind of battle she was best suited to win.

CHAPTER TWO

The Queen paid little attention to her luncheon, concentrating instead on the notes from yesterday's conferences as she ate. The morning had been occupied with purely Acadian concerns, but this afternoon she would be dealing with the Merchant Captains again. She hoped Solon's secretaries had managed to unearth more information, particularly on the foreign merchants. The men had been rather opaque and difficult to read, and had not been at all forthcoming with responses in the initial negotiations. Worse still, when she had made certain purposefully offhand remarks, there had been no reactions. The Merchant Captains were worse than professional taroc players. In her experience, most men let down their guard at least a little around a beautiful woman—but not these.

She heard Solon's familiar footsteps, as always, accompanied by the soft rattling of his myriad charms and amulets, and did not bother to look up. A stack of papers appeared beside her notes.

"I suggest you read this," said Solon, his soft and pleasant voice with a dry edge to it that told her there was something about this report that was of particular interest to him.

Still without glancing up, she shoved the notes aside and took his stack. At once, she knew this one was not from one of his usual sources. The handwriting was different from that in any other report she had seen—neat, precise, academic. Not an agent, then. A new secretary?

If so, this was the most competent secretary Solon had found yet. She did not permit her eyebrows to rise, since such incautious expressions made wrinkles in the forehead, but she did nod approvingly. This person, whoever he was, not only duplicated everything she already knew, he provided her with a few facts and figures that were new. Nothing earth-shattering, but useful, especially the information on the foreigners who had been so opaque to her.

"Well!" she said, when she had finished. She looked up at her Chief Adviser. Solon was not particularly tall, but he was well-proportioned—nothing like her muscular Royal Guards, but she happened to know that beneath his embroidered linen robe, he had a very fit body. His face was a little too long for classic beauty, but it was very pleasing to the eye. His hands, graceful and immaculate, and skilled, were the best features of a man who was widely considered one of the handsomest of her court. "I am impressed. Instead of merely competent help, you have conjured up someone quite clever! This will come in quite handy in my subsequent discussions. I hope you intend to keep him."

"Her," Solon replied; unconcerned with wrinkles, he did raise one immaculately groomed eyebrow. "And I am not at all certain you will be as happy when you discover that this report was pressed upon me at breakfast this morning by your daughter."

With great difficulty she kept her own eyebrows under control; true, her daughter was a scholar, too much of a scholar really, but Cassiopeia had not expected so…practical a turn to her scholarship. "Andromeda?" she replied, astonished. "All this? Was *this* what she was babbling to me about yesterday over breakfast?" She had long since gotten into the habit of turning a deaf ear to Andromeda's chatter. Perhaps she should have been paying more attention. Andromeda had evidently gotten beyond the peasant histories of Fauns and Centaurs (who were purely rustic creatures and of no practical importance). Now she was turning her mind to practical matters that had bearing on the governance of the Kingdom.

This could be either dangerous, or useful. If useful, Cassiopeia had no compunction about using her.

If dangerous, she had no compunction about finding a way to get rid of her. There were things that Cassiopeia did not want anyone aside from her and Solon to know.

Least of all Andromeda.

"Quite possibly." Solon's long and very handsome face remained sober, his blue eyes dark with thought. "I know she always has her nose in a book, but I was under the impression that she was reading poetry or mythical tales or something equally girlish. I had no idea she could put her finger on any fact or figure in the Palace library, but this—" he indicated the report "—seems to indicate that this is exactly what she can do."

"This could be very useful," Cassiopeia replied, tapping one graceful finger on the table. "She isn't someone we would have to pay, she doesn't leave the Palace, she is young and naive, she doesn't talk to anyone who matters and she should be easy to control. Much easier than some of your past secretaries." She smiled slightly. "Furthermore, she is as eager to please me as a puppy. If I begin paying attention to her, she'll work three times as hard."

"True, true." Solon ran a hand through his long, black hair. "Her eagerness to please her mother will certainly be a powerful hold over her. Attention from you—more to the point, direction from you, and an indication that you are pleased with this turn in her studies, would probably be more effective than any reward I could devise for the others. But I am still…concerned. I am not certain she will remain naive."

"Then you would be wise to see that as she gains in knowledge, she also gains in understanding just what a ruler is." She allowed herself a slight smile. "And the difference between the ruler and the ruled."

Ambition. That was what had gotten Cassiopeia here. And ambition—properly channeled and guided—might be a useful thing in her daughter.

"And if she persists in her…delusions?" Once again Solon raised an eyebrow.

Cassiopeia dismissed his question with a flick of her

wrist. "She is my daughter. If she is half as intelligent as you think, she will quickly come to the appropriate frame of mind."

Andie tried not to be impatient as the afternoon wore on, but it was hard. Solon had not only taken her report, he had begun reading it as he walked away. Surely he would be at least a *little* impressed, for she had included some anecdotal information about some of the foreign Merchant Captains from copies of ships' logs of Acadian merchants. Copies of all logs of domestic merchant ships were filed in the Great Library purely as a matter of historical record, although most contained little that was of historical interest. She had a notion that Solon's secretaries hadn't thought to look at *those,* and she had been right; from the slight layer of dust, it appeared they hadn't been looked at since they were put on the shelves.

But it wasn't until dinner that she received a summons from one of her mother's ladies to attend the Queen. Since this was not an evening when the Queen usually held a more formal dinner with the Court, it meant that Cassiopeia wanted to see her daughter alone, or relatively so. Although Andie had been ravenous, her throat closed and she lost her appetite.

With her maid's help, she changed from her tunic into a gown, and waited, twisting her hands nervously in her lap while her maid put up her hair, and consented to adding a simple necklace of gold and garnet beads, something she almost never did. Wishing now that she had taken lemon juice to the ink stains on her fingers, she made her way out of her own wing, through the marble Reception Hall and Great Hall, and into the Queen's Wing. At this hour, no one was in any of the public rooms except the Guards, one stationed at each doorway. The rooms were lit only by token lamps, otherwise in shadow, but the fact that most of the Palace was built from light-colored marbles made a little light go a long way. In winter, these rooms could be awfully cold and drafty, but now, in the middle of summer, the cool air flowing through was pleasant. When she was a child, she used to come here at night when she was too hot and just sit quietly in a corner while the heat leached out of her body.

Two of the Royal Guard were on duty at the bronze doors into the Queen's private quarters. They let her in with a wink and a nod of encouragement, and she stepped onto the first of the many thick, brightly patterned, imported silk carpets that had been her grandmother's dower when she came here as a foreign bride. The first chamber was a reception chamber for small audiences; softly lit by a few lightly perfumed oil lamps, it was empty of all except one of her mother's maids. As ever with any of the Queen's servants, the girl was flawlessly groomed, her simple linen gown spotless, not a hair out of place. Like most natives of Ethanos, she was dark-haired and dark-eyed. Many beautiful women preferred that their servants be plain; Queen Cassiopeia had always insisted on physical attractiveness in those who waited on her, and this maid was no exception to that rule.

"Please follow me, Princess," the maid said, without the faintly contemptuous tone her mother's maids usually used when they saw her. Evidently this time her appearance passed inspection.

With a nod, Andie obeyed, moving through several more chambers, also barely lit, until they came to the lesser dining chamber. This one, of marble beautifully ornamented with jewel-tone mosaic wall-murals made of millions of bits of glass depicting enormous baskets of flowers and fruit, held one large table. The Queen sat at the head of it; to her left was Solon, and to her right, an empty chair. Farther down the table sat three of her more favored ladies. Andie knew two of them by name; those two were young members of the Queen's regular Court, while the stranger was middle-aged or older. The young ones were dressed in a less elaborate version of the Queen's gown, with formfitting bodices, low necklines, full skirts, and tiny sleeves that left most of the arms bare. The Queen's gown was a pale blue silk with festoons of heavy lace, which suited her blond beauty. The young lady to the right, raven-haired and olive-skinned, wore cream color with a silk fringe, while the one to the left, also raven-haired but with a translucent complexion, wore pink with garlands of tiny ribbon rosettes. The older woman wore a somber gown of dark ocher with ornaments of jet and longer sleeves that covered her arms to the wrist.

"Andromeda, please join us," Cassiopeia said, with the slight smile that indicated her favor. She turned to look down the table at one of the three ladies, the one in cream. "Kyria, do you think you could manage something more attractive for those lenses than that wire frame?"

"Without a doubt, Majesty," replied the lady, whose

hobby was jewelry design, and whose talent for it was so formidable that the Queen would have no one else design for her. "The magician is a fine fellow, but his concern is function, not form." She tilted her head to the side and one attractive, raven curl brushed her cheek. "As the Princess is young, and her tastes are austere, I believe that a carefully wrought frame of white gold will suit her personality as well as her face best. And I believe that I will ask him to construct larger lenses."

"Larger? Surely not—" Cassiopeia objected.

But Lady Kyria smiled. "Majesty, larger lenses will allow one to see the Princess's eyes properly. Instead of being obscured, nearly eclipsed by small lenses, they will be enhanced. A little kohl, some malachite on her lids, and one will see the eyes first, and not the lenses. The oculars will become secondary to her face, not the first thing one sees."

Cassiopeia's blue eyes warmed slightly with approval. "I bow to your singular ability, Lady Kyria."

As the Queen spoke, Andie had gingerly taken the empty seat at the Queen's right, clasping her hands in her lap. She could hardly believe what she was hearing. Her mother was not only acknowledging her oculars, she was going out of her way to make them attractive? *Larger lenses? I'll be able to see so much better!*

"Now, Andromeda," the Queen said, turning to Andie. "It is time to speak of why I asked you to dine with us this evening. Solon gave me your report over luncheon, and I am pleased. It was useful to me this afternoon. I was under the impression that you were wasting your time with purely scholastic interests—I was favorably impressed to see that you have, in fact, been turning your intellect and talents to practical matters."

Andie couldn't help herself. She beamed. "Oh, Moth—I mean, Your Majesty! I hoped I could do something to help. I hoped that Adviser Solon would see that I—that I know that a Princess—is not free to choose her own interests. Not like ordinary people are." She decided to press her case while her mother was still looking interested. "I'm good at finding things out from books and records, and I think I can be useful to you. Please, Your Majesty, I *want* to be useful, I want responsibilities—"

"And you shall have them, child," the Queen interrupted with a throaty chuckle. "Tell her, Solon."

The Adviser coughed slightly. "Your report provided both an example of what you can do, and a reminder to us that, despite your outward appearance, which is that of a much younger person than your true age, you are not a child any longer. The fact that you wish responsibilities speaks well of your maturity, and the Queen has determined that we have been remiss in allowing your appearance to mislead us."

She blushed at his description of her. Well, so she was slight and flat-chested! And she didn't like to fuss over gowns the way the Queen's ladies did! Did he *have* to dwell on that?

But he wasn't finished, and her flush faded. "So from today, you are to provide exactly the kind of information analysis to us—that is, the Queen and I—that you provided in this report, and to signal the change in your status and responsibilities, there will be some significant changes in your household. Your governess will be dismissed—you clearly have no more need of such persons. If you determine you need a tutor in some subject, another language, perhaps, you will have the wherewithal to engage one yourself and dismiss him when you are through with him. You will have a secretary of your own appointed to serve you in your researches. Your personal staff will be augmented. Lady Charis will become your Lady of the Wardrobe, designing your clothing in accordance with both your personal taste and the needs of your new position."

The second of the two ladies present nodded at Andie in a friendly fashion. "The austere style suits you, Princess," Lady Charis said, and Andie suppressed a sigh of relief. "Columnar gowns will make you appear taller, and a very simple Gordian Knot hairstyle will suit your face. I will simply be making certain that any time you make a public appearance, you are not left to the dubious choices of an ordinary maidservant, and that your gowns will be kept in immaculate condition."

She hoped that Lady Charis would keep her promise of simple gowns. She didn't think she could bear to be laced into the things her mother wore as a matter of course.

"Your six current Guards will be retired," Solon continued. This time, it was a surge of dismay that Andie suppressed. Not that she hadn't been expecting just this for some time, but it was horrible to hear it voiced aloud, and so casually.

"They are good and faithful servants, and long overdue for retirement. They were fine for a child, but you will need young, strong warriors who will actually provide a visual deterrent to attack. You will have new Guards appointed, signaling your new importance to Her Majesty, and they will wear your own colors of—" He looked at Lady Charis.

"Silver and green," Charis said promptly.

Another relief. Those were colors she could live with. The Queen nodded her approval; her own colors were wine and silver.

"Yes. Silver and green. Your household servants will be augmented, and you will have your own household Steward appointed so that you need no longer concern yourself with the day-to-day trivia of your household." He smiled, his expression not actually reaching his eyes—but then, it never did. "You will no longer need to go anywhere that you do not wish to if you are busy. From now on, whatever you want or need can and should be brought to you, whether it be a pen, or a person."

"As is appropriate to an adult Princess," the Queen said approvingly. "Which leads me to Lady Thalia, who will be your household Steward."

The third lady nodded. Unlike the other two, she was gowned less for fashion and more for practicality. She did not appear to have been sewn into her gown like the others.

The Queen continued. "She has served us as the Steward of one of our estates for many years now, and I am very satisfied with her competence."

"The Queen is too kind," the lady murmured.

Andie didn't see anything in the woman's expression to cause misgivings, and her next words, and faint smile, reassured the Princess.

"As the Princess is not the sort given to extravagance, nor is she spendthrift and frivolous, I anticipate no difficulty in managing her household."

"You are more likely to have to join with me in urging the Princess to acquire a wardrobe commensurate with her rank and status than to have to curb her passion for gowns and jewels!" Lady Charis laughed. "I fear I have been present at one or two discussions with her dressmaker, if you will recall, Majesty."

The Queen sighed. "'But, Mother, linen is so much more practical than silk. Stains bleach right out and it wears so much longer!'" she quoted with a faint air of mockery, and Andie winced.

"She has a point, Majesty," Solon said unexpectedly, with a glance down at his own linen robes. Not that *his* elegant clothing had much in common with Andie's... "Especially for a—uh—young person who is hard on her clothing. As a young student myself, I chose black linen exclusively, not as an affectation, but because ink did not show."

Andie felt an unexpected surge of sympathy at that revelation, and she cast a quick, grateful smile at him.

"Indeed, she does, when it comes to everyday wear, *particularly* for someone who will be digging about among dusty books for most of the day," Lady Charis agreed. "Tunics and divided skirts of linen are quite suitable for such a duty, and practical, although I must insist that you are more than old enough to refrain from bare-legged scrambles about from here on, Princess."

Again, Andie flushed what she knew must be crimson. Her stomach kept turning over and over, the longer this interview went on. Pleasure that was half pain, followed by embarrassment that made her want to sink into the floor. Good things were followed by blows, so quickly she hadn't the time to recover before another hit her.

"However, Princess," Lady Charis continued, "your new responsibilities will include more Court appearances, as well as the occasional attendance at conferences and audiences, and your gowns will occasionally need to reflect your status. Silk there will be, and jewels, and other ornaments you would rather do without. You must look the part of a Princess when the Queen requires it. Think of it as armor. You are a kind of guard to the dignity of your nation and lineage, and you must wear the armor for that duty."

"On other occasions, however," Solon added, "we will wish for you, although you will be attending similar functions, to blend with the other secretaries and not stand out." He raised an eyebrow, and she flushed, realizing that *this* meant they were taking her very seriously indeed. "If there is no need for the Princess to be present, then it should not be obvious that the Princess is indeed in attendance."

"My beauty has consistently caused foreign princes and diplomats to underestimate my intelligence, Andromeda," the Queen said, unexpectedly, as Solon nodded. "It is a tool I have learned to use, and use well. That is *my* armor. If they look upon me, bejeweled and draped in costly fabric, and assume that is all I care for, that is all to the good. You have not inherited my beauty, more's the pity, but you have in your very ordinariness another sort of armor. You can make yourself overlooked and ignored, which is just as effective as being underestimated. I do not say these things to hurt you, child, but to educate you. The time for games and running about on the cliff steps is gone. You wish to be treated as an adult, and given responsibilities, I am doing so, and granting you the candor I give Solon."

Andie looked down at the hands twisting nervously in her lap. Maybe her mother didn't intend to hurt her feelings, but—but they were hurt, all the same. *I'm not that ugly, am I? Or no, she didn't say "ugly," just…forgettable.*

"Now, I believe we have said everything we need to," the Queen concluded brightly. "Tomorrow, the next phase of your life will begin. And tonight—we will have dinner."

She touched her knife to her goblet, making it ring, and suddenly the room was full of servants, bustling everywhere with food that Andie barely touched and certainly couldn't taste. There was no more serious talk; the Queen and her ladies and even Solon made light chatter that went right over Andie's head, seeing as she didn't know half the people they were talking about.

She did drink a little too much of the wine, though. Her mouth was so dry, the lamps were so bright, and she kept flushing for no real reason except an ongoing case of acute embarrassment, and the only thing to drink was the wine, at least until the dessert course came and she was able to cool her flushes with sherbet. She knew she was tipsy because she got light-headed, and after that she said even less and moved with great care. A fine thing it would be for her to spoil the impression she'd made by getting drunk!

Finally, after the dessert, she snatched at the opportunity to ask the Queen's permission to leave; Cassiopeia was deep in conversation with Lady Charis at that point, and simply waved a hand at her daughter. Feeling as if she was trying to balance on the edge of a cliff, Andie got up slowly, and just as slowly sketched a brief curtsy, and walked out, into the shadowed rooms beyond. The Royal Guards at the Queen's door stood like a pair of statues; she murmured a quiet good-night to them, and they nodded back. While she was within sight of them, she did her best to walk steadily, but once on her own, she felt her steps wavering a little, and she didn't bother to correct them until she came in sight of the Guards on her wing. The two Guards on her own door saluted her, and she nodded back, but neither she, nor they, spoke.

The cool breeze felt wonderful on her hot forehead, and it woke her up a bit, but she didn't feel safe until the doors to her own wing closed behind her and she was able to put her back against them, closing her eyes and waiting for the dizziness to pass.

"Princess?" She opened her eyes. One of her faithful Six, Merrha, was standing beside the door to the next chamber, holding a lantern and peering through the darkness at her.

"I'm afraid I had a little too much wine and not nearly enough dinner, Merrha," she said, her tongue feeling unnaturally thick.

"Thought as much. Come along, dear," the Guard said in a motherly fashion, coming to take her arm and guide her to her bedchamber. "I know you were on edge about that business you wrote up for old Solon. It seems to have done the trick rumor says, and you're coming up in the world, I heard? I think I might have a glass or two too many if I'd been sitting in your chair, having all that thrown at me."

She turned astonished eyes on the graying old Warrior woman. "You mean—you already know?" She had been dreading the thought of trying to figure out how to tell them—her head had been buzzing with the problem all during that strange dinner. But now—

"Of course!" Merrha laughed. "You can't keep anything secret from the Guard here in the Palace. Oh, we'll miss you like blazes, my darling girl, but we all should have been retired years ago and *would* have if we hadn't been worried about leaving you friendless with those hateful bitches Her Majesty set as your governesses."

"She's going." That, she was able to say with satisfaction.

Merrha laughed. "She's *gone*. Sent packing while you were at dinner. Now we won't have to worry about you anymore. You'll be the one in charge here, not them, you can pick your own people. And we've heard Lady Thalia is all right. It's about time you got a real household of your very own, and it's not as if you need us, old gray dogs that we are—"

"But I do need you!" she wailed, and to her own horror, burst into half-drunk tears.

The Queen and Solon lingered over their wine once the other ladies had retired. Not that there was even a hint of impropriety; she had ordered the outer doors to the Great Hall be opened "to let the breeze blow through," and her two Guards could see them both, if not hear them. Such painstaking caution was how she had kept her relationship with Solon untainted by speculation all these years.

Of course, no one knew of the other ways Solon could come to her chamber, once the last of her maids had been dismissed. They thought all of his amulets and charms were the sign of superstition and a timorous nature. If they only knew…

"That went well, I thought," she said, idly turning her wineglass around and around.

"I am cautiously optimistic," Solon replied, steepling his hands on the table. "The Princess is pitiably eager to please you. So long as we can keep her gaze directed only at what we want her to see, this may work out very well. Certainly giving her charge over her own household will resonate well with the people. And it won't hurt to trot her out for their inspection from time to time. Her physical immaturity will work on your behalf—no one would believe she is older than fourteen, especially not at a distance. That will eliminate those pesky rumors that you've been keeping her locked up because she's feeble-minded."

"She'll hate that," the Queen replied with a chuckle. "And it will certainly cure her of wanting to put herself forward in any way."

"I am concerned about possible marriage offers, however," Solon continued, with a sharp glance at her. "Apparent immaturity will be no drawback there."

This time the Queen's throaty laugh sounded like a cat's purr. "And therein lies the genius of assigning Lady Charis to her wardrobe. Lady Charis is much enamored of the styles from her cousin's land of Lytheria, the ones that emphasize waiflike proportions and pale skin. Obviously none of *us* is suited to the style, and none of us wishes to look like draped poles or famine victims, but Andromeda is the perfect model for such garments. Between Kyria's plan to give her oculars that will make her look like an owl, and Charis's Lytherian gowns in colors that will make her look like a ghost, any ambassador that comes sniffing about will think the child is about to fade away from consumption." She lowered her lids in satisfaction at his look of surprise. "I've told you a hundred times if I've told you once, Solon, that fashion is a weapon, and you never believe me."

He spread his hands wide. "Once again, you leave me dazzled."

"Once again, I demonstrate that our abilities are complimentary," she replied, sipping her wine. "On the whole, this evening has been entirely satisfactory."

"Should I put her to a task?" he asked. She shook her head.

"Not yet. She'll be busy with the setting up of her new household. Charis will appear first thing with fabric and seamstresses—she'll feel she has to know *everything* about her household, even though Thalia is perfectly capable of making it all run seamlessly and invisibly. And while I am at it, I believe I will send over some of the furnishings from the Dowager Queen's household that have been in storage, to replace everything that dates from Andromeda's childhood. This will serve two functions—having so much to think about will prevent her from recalling all the servants and Guards I am going to replace, until it is too late to bring them back, and organizing her rooms will keep her a little unsettled." She licked her lips. "I want her unsettled. I never want her to be comfortable or confident. I want her always to be a little unbalanced. While she is off balance, she will not think to look much beyond what she is told to look for. Ambition—in moderation. I want her ambition to go no further than to please me. I want her controlled."

"I think that can be arranged, Majesty," Solon replied dryly. "I am nothing if not an expert at keeping people unsettled."

"So you are," she purred, and flicked a curl back over her shoulder with one finger. "So you are."

When Andie woke the next morning, it was in a mixed frame of mind; she'd had odd dreams all night, reflecting her ambivalence. On the one hand, she was about to lose her six dearest friends and protectors, people who had been more nearly parents to her than her own mother. But on the other hand—

"Good morrow, Princess!" A brand-new maid dressed in a gown of green and silver swept into the room carrying a tray, which she set down on Andie's bed. Then she handed Andie the oculars from the bedside table, something the other maids had never done. Andie put them on and watched her, a bit taken aback while the maid went around the room, flinging back the draperies from the windows. The tray held herb tea, buttered bread, fruit and sheep's-milk yogurt mixed with honey, something Andie particularly liked first thing in the morning. It was, in fact, breakfast in bed. In her entire life, Andie had never had the treat of breakfast in bed…for that matter, in her entire life, Andie had never had exactly the breakfast she liked best without having to ask for it, and even then, more times than not, she hadn't gotten it.

"I am your new handmaiden, and my name is Iris," the girl announced, returning to the bedside. She was, truth to tell, a rather plain, freckle-faced girl, big-boned and looking more like a shepherdess than a maid. But she had an infectious smile, and when she added, "Merrha's my auntie, I've been working in the Palace where Lady Thalia's been the Steward. Auntie told me a long time ago that if Lady Thalia was ever sent for, I was to put myself forward to come along with her, especially if there was a vacancy in your household. Thalia's a good mistress, and when I did ask if I might be considered, she said she thought we'd suit, you and I."

Since the maid that had served Andie yesterday had been disinclined to do anything without being ordered, and was impersonal, cold, and as opaque as a stone wall, Iris was a definite improvement. Add to that, she was Merrha's niece—well, suddenly Andie didn't feel quite so alone.

"I can do hair in the Gordian Knot, the Kalliope Knot, the Centaur Tail, the Twisted Knot and Twisted Tail with sidelocks, but I can't do curls," Iris continued, putting the tray on Andie's lap, shaking out a napkin and laying it across the front of Andie's nightdress. "I can do makeup, but someone will have to show me what I'm to put where. I'm good with wardrobe, I mend, and I can make creams and lotions and apply them, and massage. I can't read, but I can tell stories, and I can play a shepherd's flute."

Andie blinked as Iris stepped back. "You already sound much more talented than my previous maid, Iris," she said, finally.

"Good. Then that's sorted," Iris said with immense satisfaction, giving another broad smile. "You suit me, and I suit you. Lady Charis is waiting with a seamstress and fabric as soon as you're done eating, Lady Thalia wants you to look over more servants while you're being fitted, and that's all there is for now. Would you like me to select a gown for the day, or would you prefer to?"

"Oh, pick anything," Andie said vaguely, feeling a bit overwhelmed. Fittings already? And servant interviews? What next?

She ate quickly, drizzling the yogurt liberally over her sliced fruit, and feeling very much as if she was going to need the extra energy. After rejecting several selections in the wardrobe, Iris brought out a plain ankle-length gown, in a blue that looked faded but actually wasn't, and an embroidered belt that laced up the front that matched. As soon as Andie was finished with her breakfast, Iris whisked the tray away, and briskly got her into her gown, then sat her down at the little stool in front of the dressing table. With fingers that were surprisingly deft and gentle, she brushed out and put up Andie's hair—not in a knot, but in some kind of tail on the top of her head, with a strand wrapped around the base of it. "Centaur Tail," said Iris in satisfaction, turning Andie to face the mirror. "Suits you."

It certainly did suit her. It got her hair away from her face and under control, but it was softer than the severe knot she usually wore. She looked at herself and smiled a little. This…was a surprise, as pleasant a surprise as the breakfast had been.

"Lady Charis is waiting, and Lady Thalia," Iris reminded her, and with a guilty start, the maid jumped to her feet.

"No slippers," Iris said, as Andie looked about for her favorite old sandals. "They're measuring your feet, too. Matching shoes to matching gowns. *And* new under-things, petticoats, under-gowns, stockings, underwear and all. Lady Thalia says yours are a disgrace."

"I suppose they are. I never think about them," Andie admitted guiltily.

"Your maid should have," Iris replied tartly. "*You* aren't supposed to have to. I'll salvage what I can in here—you go, Princess!"

Andie nodded and got up. Iris ran to the door to hold it open for her with a wink, and closed it behind her. Andie stopped dead, staring around her in shock.

Only three pieces of furniture were left in what had once been crammed full of old, outgrown, nursery furnishings: One low stool, one small table and a chair. The table and chair were already occupied by Lady Thalia; beside the stool were Lady Charis and another woman.

"Come stand on the stool, Princess, so we can measure you," said Lady Charis, when she didn't move. "That is a very good hairstyle for you. I believe that your new maid is a great improvement."

"I thought she would be," Lady Thalia observed with satisfaction.

"Where did all the furniture go?" Andie asked, feeling as if she had stepped into someone else's rooms.

"We've had that wreckage taken away," said Lady Thalia. "You're to have your wing properly refurnished. You aren't a child anymore, after all. You don't need nursery furniture."

"No," she said, feeling dazed. "Of course not…"

Obediently, she stepped up onto the stool, where the second woman, probably a seamstress, measured every possible part of her that could be measured, drew outlines of her feet, then made a rather good sketch of her face and took measurements of *that,* noting the measurements. Meanwhile Lady Charis held samples of fabric up to her face, making humming noises to herself, handing some to the seamstress, tossing most into a basket.

And while all of this was going on, a parade of servants came into the room to be interviewed by Lady Thalia. Some, she had seen about the Palace, others were total strangers. As each interview was concluded, Lady Thalia looked at her with a most penetrating gaze; after the first one, Andie realized that she was supposed to show approval or disapproval, and the realization made her feel dizzy. She had never been allowed to pick *any* servant before, much less all of them!

A very few candidates she liked immediately. Some she disliked even before they opened their mouths. Some seemed utterly unsuited to the positions they were applying for. On the rest—"I haven't the experience to judge," she said, deferring to Lady Thalia.

She was afraid that this would lose her the Lady's respect, but on the contrary, her new household Steward seemed to approve guardedly. It was altogether astonishing how many new servants it seemed she would need. She was going to have her *own* cooks and all of their helpers, her *own* housekeeping staff, her *own* gardener and his helpers, as well as maids and pages, footmen and Guards. Only with the

Guards did she feel on firm footing; most of them she knew at least on sight, and several she'd known almost as long as she had known her faithful Six. She was supposed to choose a total of eighteen; she had no difficulty doing so. All presenting themselves were young, and she thought it was going to be rather strange to see no gray hairs among them. She chose two-thirds male, one-third female, a ratio of which Lady Thalia also approved.

"The men will stand guard at the door to your wing, and in the garden," Lady Thalia announced. "The women will serve here within your rooms."

About the time that Lady Charis and the seamstress left and the interviews concluded, the new furniture began to arrive.

"Leave my bed!" Andie cried in alarm, when she saw serving-men heading into her bedroom with empty hands and a purposeful look in their eyes.

They stopped in their tracks.

Lady Thalia took a quick look in through the door. "The bed is the only piece of furniture in this wing fit to be used," she pronounced. "Take down the bed curtains, though, they're a disgrace. *And* the window curtains. Bring new, in the Princess's colors."

And in marched the servants; shortly thereafter, out they came, with every piece of furniture except her bed.

"Have you any particular desires as to how you want things arranged, Princess?" Lady Thalia asked.

Andie stood there uncertainly, then shook her head.

"In that case, I will have them follow my diagram and you and I can retreat from this madhouse to your new study."

My new study? she thought, dumbstruck. She followed Lady Thalia into what had been the nursery playroom and last night had still been stuffed full of worn and broken toys, child-size furniture, picture books and the like. Now—

Now the warm and sunny room was a study. A real study, like her mother's. The low bookcases, battered and tilting, had been taken out. In their place stood floor-to-ceiling bookcases, made for adult books and ornaments, and arranged on the bookcases were the books that had once been arranged in piles on the floor in what she had designated as her "reading room." There was a backless couch, with one high arm to recline against. There was a real desk, a proper-size one, already set up to take the best advantage of the light, with cubbyholes stocked with various sizes of paper, enough pens to have denuded a flock of geese, and three fat-bottomed, heavy inkwells, the kind you couldn't tip over if you tried, holding red, black and sepia ink. And sealing wax. She went over to it, feeling as if she *must* be in a dream, to see that there were even two kinds of seals, the kind for wax and the kind for ink. She picked one up. It was the escutcheon of the Royal House of Acadia, inside a lozenge to show it was a Child of the House rather than the King or Queen.

Her own seal. The seal of her House. It was real. It was all real—

She turned, still holding the seal in her hand, to survey the rest of the room. Beside the desk was a comfortable chair, not the backless stool she had been using. There were two other chairs beside the one at the desk, and a table with four more chairs around it, all at the farther end, near the fireplace. All of the furniture was made of bleached and waxed lime-wood, which dated back to her grandfather's day, but which she secretly preferred to the dark, fumed oak of her mother's wing. There were no carpets, either, but she was so used to that, she didn't think she minded.

"I will be giving you the household report here every morning," said Lady Thalia, "and asking if you approve of the menus for the day, as well as any expenditures from the household budget that I anticipate. I have looked over the budget allotted to us, and I foresee no difficulties. I take it that you prefer simple meals?"

She licked lips gone dry. "Oh, yes. Please. I used to eat whatever my servants ate—"

Lady Thalia chuckled. "There is no reason why that practice cannot continue, since the cook I have selected is both skilled and careful. It is not wise to be overindulgent in one's food at any age, but at yours, particularly, you should continue to eat simply. And a good cook can turn the simplest ingredients into a fine meal, while a bad one can utterly ruin the most expensive and exotic."

Andie nodded anxiously. "What do I need to know about my—my household right this moment?"

"I hope you approve of my choice for maidservant?" Lady Thalia asked, and nodded with satisfaction when Andie replied that she did. "Good. Iris is not the equal of even the handmaiden of one of your mother's ladies—"

"Yes, but I don't want to wear gowns like theirs, or have my hair curled and pinned up and tortured, or—"

Lady Thalia held up her hand. "Which is precisely why

I chose Iris when she presented herself. I was told by those I trust of your taste. I believe you value someone competent, trustworthy and certain in what she *can* do, and are not troubled if she is a bit rough-hewn."

"I like her," Andie said without thinking, then immediately wondered if that was the wrong thing to say. Were you not supposed to like a servant? But someone like Iris, who would be with you at the most intimate of moments, someone who would be the person to care for you if you were ill—

"Good. It doesn't do to make friends of any servant *except* one's handmaiden, and then only if one knows the girl is steady, has integrity and knows her place," said Lady Thalia firmly. "But if that is the case, as it is with Iris, then you will find having a friend in your handmaiden makes your path much smoother. She can and will tell you servants' gossip, and that is an invaluable source of information, and you can trust that she either will not gossip about you, or that she will tell nothing that is not commonplace knowledge. You can trust her with any delicate matter. You can trust that she will not spy on you. All these things are valuable beyond price to anyone in your position."

"I—I can see that," Andie replied, once again feeling overwhelmed. This was all so new—and the implications of what Lady Thalia was saying made her realize that perhaps it was a good thing that she had been a lonely child. Loneliness was going to be something that came with her new position, so it was just as well that she was used to it.

Not that she would have chosen differently. She felt that being lonely, or in any case *alone,* was not all that bad—at least now, she would have some useful work to do, and maybe a little respect.

"Let's take a walk around your wing, and you can decide if you want anything changed," Lady Thalia said, watching her expression keenly. "By then, I expect, Lady Charis will have a suitable gown for you so you can take your place at the Queen's morning audience."

Andie tried not to show her surge of panic.

In the end, she needn't have panicked. Lady Charis showed Iris what simple cosmetics to apply, and the gown was not a new one, but one of her old ones, in a jade-green, with the augmentation of some bands of bead-embroidery to the neck- and hem-lines. Similar augmentation in the way of jade beads on the straps had been made to her sandals, and she wore a jade necklace and bracelets. Her mother seemed to approve; she smiled slightly when she saw her daughter, and indicated to Andie that for the audience she should take a place next to Cassiopeia's own handmaiden just behind the throne. The one difference between Andie and the handmaiden was that Andie was allowed to sit on a low stool, while the handmaiden stood. The Audience Hall was a single large room, with frescoes of dancing nymphs (all discreetly clothed) on the walls, and the floor set with sand-colored tiles. Two lines of pillars painted with vines supported the roof, and to discourage loitering, there was nothing to sit on except the throne and Andie's stool. While this might be hard on the aged or infirm, it did keep people from crowding in to gawk and gossip.

Andie listened to everything as closely as she could,

making mental notes when Cassiopeia deferred some decisions for a later date. Andie intuited that her mother would want information about the families and situations involved, and that it would be Andie's job to find that before the continuation of the audience. After a while, she began to relax and enjoy herself. This was infinitely preferable to lessons with a dancing master that she would never use, or in the genealogies of the royal families of Kingdoms that had never heard of Acadia and would never give their realm a second thought.

There were more petitioners than there was time, which was the usual state of things; those waiting showed disappointment but no surprise when Solon stepped forward to announce that the audience was concluded for the day. Those who had not yet been heard would come back tomorrow, and the next day, returning as many times as it took before the Queen would get to their case. Andie was dismissed along with the rest, but at least she knew the protocols from all of her study of court etiquette; she made her bow and returned to her wing, with one of her new Guards in attendance.

It gave her a bit of a pang not to see one of her Six at the door, but she hid it as best she could, and gave each of the young men standing there an encouraging nod. One opened the door for her, and she went in, to discover luncheon was already waiting for her in her dining chamber, with Iris and a table-servant in attendance. Another shock: the only time she'd ever had a table-servant was when she'd eaten with her mother.

The servant presented dishes for her approval, served her

portions of the ones she indicated, poured her drink and kept it refreshed throughout the meal—somewhat unnerving for someone who had been helping herself all these years. Lady Thalia joined her, but only after asking permission!

But she had to admit she was beginning to find these shocks were more pleasant than otherwise.

"After your luncheon, you will bathe and Iris will give you skin treatments to smooth your wind-roughened complexion, and a massage," Lady Thalia announced. "This is the usual order of things for a lady of rank. It isn't done to rush straight into work after eating, it ruins the digestion. Then I have arranged for you to give a proper dismissal to your old Guards. I gather that they are the only ones of your former servants to whom you feel a friendly dismissal and a reward is due?"

Feeling a flush suffuse her face again, she nodded, grateful now to Lady Thalia that had the lady's inherent dignity not made such a gesture unthinkable, she would have leapt out of her chair and run to hug her.

"For future reference, Princess, when a good and faithful servant retires from one's service, it is perfectly appropriate to bid an affectionate farewell, and it is absolutely the done thing to include a monetary reward," Lady Thalia continued gravely. "Such rewards are part of the household budget. You, however, do not bestow them directly. That is my job. They are made up into packets in leather purses in your colors, and rank and length of service determines the amount. For your information, as you should know these things, although the usual reward for a Guard is rarely more than four thalers, in the case of those who have served as long as your six retainers did, it is appropriate to double the reward to eight."

"Is that good?" she asked hesitantly.

"Since a very good small farm can be purchased for six thalers, yes it is," the lady replied with a nod. "Such rewards are calculated on the basis of the worth of a small farm. This allows those who have not been provident on their own to purchase something that can support them in their retirement, and perhaps even acquire a spouse to share it with."

She blinked a little at that; the way it had been phrased, Lady Thalia made it sound as if the retiring Guards were going to stroll down to the next livestock market and buy themselves a husband or wife....

But then again, what did *she* know? Maybe that was exactly what would happen. Certainly the negotiations that attended the betrothals of any Royal had a lot of resemblance to a cattle-auction....

Well, at least she was going to be able to say goodbye properly! *And* make sure her Six were going to be all right. That made her happy enough that she was willing to put up with gowns instead of tunics, and makeup, and even truly torturous hairstyles—and no more running off to the cliff ever again!

CHAPTER THREE

"Well?" Cassiopeia asked, as she relaxed under the massaging hands of her servant. She took ample precautions with her body-servants; all were mute. Not *deaf*—that would have been exceedingly inconvenient. But mute. Most had been slaves, and silenced before she bought and freed them. It was prudent to purchase mute slaves that some-one *else* had rendered incapable of speech; they didn't blame you, and they were generally so grateful to be freed and treated decently afterward that they remained faithful despite the occasional beating.

Solon did not need to inquire what her subject was. "I am a little more optimistic," he admitted. "She looked suitably adult enough to satisfy the people and the Court, and suitably bewildered enough to satisfy me. So long as we can keep her off balance, all should be well. Your vanity will be pleased by the fact that she is being compared unfavorably to you."

"Not just my vanity. Anytime you have a potential heir on show, it is wise that people prefer you to her." Cassiopeia closed her eyes for a moment to judge if the twinge she had just felt was due to some stiffness in her shoulder, or the servant's momentary distraction. "A little more work to the shoulders, please," she said, and opened her eyes again.

Solon lounged on a nearby couch; his presence—and sometimes the presence of others of her advisers—at her daily massage was of so long-standing an arrangement that it had ceased to be anything to comment on.

Not that anything could or would go on. The presence of not less than three servants made sure of that.

"Why are you so concerned about keeping her off balance?" she asked. "I know why I am, but I am interested in hearing your reasons."

"Because, the girl has a formidable intellect, and we do not want her to exercise it in any direction save the one we choose," he replied, his nostrils flaring slightly. *"Ever."*

"I think you overestimate her," she retorted, feeling a bit annoyed. She knew ambition when she saw it and Andromeda had none. How could mere intellect be a threat? It was the possibility that Andromeda might one day develop ambition that concerned the Queen.

"I think she's her mother's daughter where intelligence is concerned, and I never underestimate her mother," was his response, which teased her out of her annoyance. "But Lady Thalia will keep her busy for a while learning the ins and outs of running a household, and by the time she feels equal to that job, I shall have something else equally petty and time-consuming for her." He sighed heavily. "It would have been so much easier if she had taken after her father in intellect and her mother in looks, rather than the other way around."

"Perhaps," Cassiopeia said, preferring not to contemplate the prospect of having a daughter who rivaled her mother's beauty, and had the advantage of youth on top of that. Then again—the answer to that would have been to marry her off to some provincial nobody or fur-wearing barbarian in exchange for a treaty as soon as she turned twelve. "Well, what approach are we to use with the captains from Thessalia this afternoon?"

"Ah." He brightened considerably. "Andromeda's report gave me some useful ideas on that score."

She listened attentively as he outlined his negotiation plans, thoughts about her daughter shoved to the back of her mind.

For now.

Andie's farewells to her Six would have been a lot harder, if they hadn't been so determinedly cheerful about it. As it was, she kept from crying only with an effort of will, and only because she didn't want to ruin their impression that she was going to be, as Merrha put it, "Snug as a queen bee in her own hive at last."

She was glad to turn her mind to something else immediately when they were gone, their rewards heavy in their belt-pouches, all of them looking distinctly odd out of uniform. The audience from this morning left her with a clear set of items to research, most notably, the origins of a dispute over some obscure salvage rights. With only one deepwater port for hundreds of leagues in either direction along the coastline, and plenty of treacherous rocks, shoals and reefs along that same coastline, there was no end to wrecks on the shores of Acadia, and salvage rights were valuable and jealously guarded. Half of everything came to the Crown, of course, but the rest could represent rich pickings indeed.

The trouble was, these rights could be subdivided and sold, inherited or given away. So when two petitioners came, both with apparently equal claims to "all goods come ashore to the Bay of Tralis, from Rocky Point to Oyster Rock," it was time to research all those old wills, deeds of assignment and bills of sale.

By the time she came to the rather surprising conclusion that the disputed rights were not held by *either* claimant but by a third party who had not even appeared, Lady Thalia was at the door to the library looking for her.

"The magician is here to fit your new oculars, Princess," she announced.

Recalling that the promise had been for *larger* lenses rather than smaller, Andie would have leapt to her feet and run out of the library at once—

The trouble was, she wasn't in a tunic. She was in a gown, which got tangled around her legs as she hastily shoved her stool away from the table at which she was doing her research, making her lose her balance and have to catch the edge of the table, then disentangle the cloth, flushing with acute embarrassment, while Lady Thalia watched impassively.

She said nothing as Andie finally sorted herself out, but Andie could practically hear that cool, composed voice making critical notes on her behavior. Her face heated, and only cooked when she reached the study and found the Guards' magician waiting there for her.

She gave him a bow of respect. *All* Sophonts deserved that show of respect even from the Queen herself, but Sophont Balan was something special in her eyes. He wasn't a Sorcerer nor anything like one of the sort who constructed remote towers and came to the aid of entire nations; like most of the magicians connected with the Acadian Guard, he might have been called a Hedge-Wizard. But he was a clever one, and intent on finding the most he could do with limited powers. Not content with merely repeating the spells he had learned from the various grimoires he had obtained, he was a researcher, always looking to find new and more ingenious ways of applying magic. It was his contention that the best Magician was not the one who displayed the most blatant use of power, but the one who used the least power the most efficiently. Which was why he never wasted a mote of magic if he could help it. He would carefully weigh his options when there was a task in front of him, to determine whether it was more efficient to perform it with magic or mundane means.

He didn't look much like a Magician, either. Instead of long, dark robes embroidered with mystic symbols and some sort of outlandish headgear, he chose to wear perfectly ordinary brown uniform trousers and tunics as the rest of the Guards wore, with a long canvas vest over the tunic that must have had twenty pockets sewn into it. Like most of the natives of Acadia, he was dark-haired and olive-skinned, with white flecking his curly black hair; he had a long face, and melancholy eyes that lit up when he saw her.

"Well, Princess!" he said, cheerfully, taking a new pair of oculars out of one of the inside pockets of his vest. "I must say this was one of my happier commissions from the Queen in the past few weeks! When Her Majesty summoned me to create new oculars for you, I was very much afraid she was going to ask me to reduce the size of the lenses yet again, but the Lady Kyria was very clear that she wanted me to make them as large as could be conveniently supported on your head!"

Having gone through examinations and fittings at least twice a year since he had begun to make her oculars, Andie went straight to the chair he had pulled out from the desk and sat, facing the piece of card-stock he had propped up on the table across the room. The pattern on it was of crisply ruled lines going both horizontally and vertically. He fitted the oculars to her face, and got out of the way so that she could see it.

"It looks quite clear, Sophont," she said truthfully.

"Well, this matches the last set I made you, but we might as well see if your eyes have changed in the interval. Now—" he muttered under his breath, something she didn't quite catch, and she sensed the glass of the lenses warm, just a little "—better and clearer, or fuzzier?"

"Better," she said decisively. The lines on the card were sharper than they had been before.

He muttered again; again the lenses warmed. "Better, or fuzzier and farther away?"

They repeated this three more times, until the lines got oddly distant and did get a little fuzzier. He reversed his last spell, which was subtly changing the shape of the lenses, exactly as he would have if he had been grinding them by hand. And, as a matter of fact, he once had done just that. As he had shown her years ago, he wasn't so much altering the lenses as matching them to sets he *had* hand-ground, when he first began making both telescopes and oculars down in his workshop. He had one master set of telescope lenses, and one of ocular lenses, which had taken him more than a year to make. Those were carefully stored away, but he had touched this set to every set in his workshop, and as he had explained to Andie, by the arcane Law of Contamination, that meant that these lenses "knew" how the others were shaped and could mimic that shape at his command.

"So," he said, taking out a scrap of paper and writing down the number of the lenses to which he had matched these new ones. "I'll have three more sets up to you by day's end. Lady Kyria has astoundingly sound design sense—you ought to go have a look at yourself in a mirror. She gave me the design she wanted, properly limned out, and it was a pleasure to cast the frames. Don't know why I didn't think to make *cast* frames before. They must be more comfortable than my wire frames."

"Uh—" she said, not wanting to agree because he'd been so good as to make her oculars in the first place.

"Never mind, I'll take that as a yes." He laughed. "Anyway, you're to have four sets—to match jewels, I suppose—white gold, pale gold, yellow gold and rose gold. Can't have your oculars clashing with your bracelets, I suppose. I'll send the 'prentice up with them later. I'm waiting for the frames to cool now."

"If the Princess is not here, you can leave them with her handmaiden Iris," Lady Thalia put in, and came around to take a look at the Sophont's handiwork. She blinked. "Good heavens. That is *much* more flattering!"

"Yes, it is," Balan agreed with a lopsided smile. "Now you can see what pretty eyes she has. Well, I'm off! Lady Thalia, it was a pleasure meeting you. Princess, a delight to serve you!"

As soon as he was out of the room, Andie was out of the chair. Picking up the skirt of her gown this time to keep it from tripping her, she ran to her bedroom to peer into the little mirror over her dressing table.

The difference was astounding. The old oculars had been small, vaguely rectangular, and had cut across her face like a slash mark. These were large, circular and, for the first time, did not obscure her eyes. If anything, they made her eyes look bigger, like those of a young animal, soft and giving an impression of innocence and vulnerability. The frame, of white gold, was very simple and polished, somehow less fussy than Balan's frame of twisted wire had been.

"Gracious!" Iris exclaimed. "What a difference!"

"You don't think they look—well—*owlish*?" Lady Thalia asked, a little doubtfully.

"Not a bit!" Iris declared. "Just look how big they make her eyes look! And *you've* heard all those daft poets, my

Lady, going on about a girl's eyes supposed to be like a doe's, or big pools of water! No, this suits her, it does. Lady Kyria knows what she's doing, and that's a fact!"

The same sentiment was echoed by Lady Charis, who arrived moments later with the first of the new gowns and a wardrobe full of new under-gowns, chemises, petticoats and all other such necessaries. This first gown was a high-waisted column of dark blue silk twill, with little, fluttery sleeves. The high waist was accented by a silk and silver cord that tied just under the breasts, the sides were slit up to the hip, and this gown was meant to be worn over an under-gown of cream-colored silk tissue.

"You'll be having dinner tonight with Her Highness the Queen, and two of her guests, Princess," Lady Charis told her, as Iris helped her into the new gowns, then sat her down to restyle her hair using cord that matched the gown. "This is not quite a state dinner but it will give the Ambassadors an opportunity to meet you under less formal circumstances than a presentation."

"Ambassadors?" Andie felt her stomach grow tense—was this going to be the situation every night?

"No one of great consequence. One is from the island of Sarmacia, the other from the island of Keles. There will be, at most, ten persons there aside from yourself and the Queen. You will probably be taking your dinner with Her Highness most nights," Lady Thalia said, confirming her worst fear. "Evening meals are an occasion, just like any other, to study one's courtiers and visitors, and learn from that study. In fact, it would be wise if you ate and drank as little as possible, in order to concentrate on them and take advantage of seeing them in a relatively unguarded state. Say as little as you can, and listen as much as you can. I have called for a pre-dinner meal of fruit and yogurt to sustain you, and I shall have your cook prepare something that will be awaiting you when you return to your rooms."

She started to nod—stopped herself, since Iris was in the middle of doing something with her hair, and said, instead, "Thank you, Lady Thalia. I truly appreciate your experience and advice."

For the first time, the rather formidable lady smiled. "It was not in my orders from the Queen to give you advice, Princess," she replied, resting her hand atop Andie's for just a moment. "But I hoped you would not think me forward to do so."

"Oh no! Please! Continue doing so!" Andie said hastily, and sighed. "This is becoming a great deal more complicated than I had thought it would be—"

"The business of a ruler always is, my dear," Lady Thalia replied. "Now, if you are not to be late, as soon as Iris gets your slippers tied, you must be away. Collect one of your Guards at the door. You must not travel even within the Palace walls without an escort anymore. You are a lady of consequence now."

And the unspoken words rang loudly enough in Andie's mind that Lady Thalia might just as well have said them.

"You are no longer a child. And you must never forget it."

As each day passed into the next, Andie slowly settled into her new roles. That of researcher and adviser was the easiest, and the one that gave her the most pleasure. Being

Princess was as restrictive, in entirely new ways, as it had ever been, but she found that having real work to do made the restrictions less irksome. Lady Charis and Lady Kyria did not reappear after the last of her new wardrobe was completed, but Lady Thalia was a constant companion, and somewhat to Andie's surprise, became a welcome one. She had been certain that Lady Thalia had been given charge over Andie's household purely to report Andie's failings back to the Queen. That might have been the case, but Lady Thalia had her own ideas of what she was to do, and that included patiently instructing Andie on the running of a royal household, on court protocol, and on how to watch other people, catch them in unguarded moments and learn something about them.

And Iris was a treasure—far more of a friend, because she was near to Andie's age, than Guard Merrha ever could have been. Between them, they turned what could have been an ordeal into something that was merely demanding, and could be quite interesting.

The one thing she didn't much care for was that she had to wear gowns now, instead of tunics and bare legs. But a great deal of the rest of what Lady Charis deemed needful to a lady was rather pleasant. The daily massages, for one thing. So she didn't miss running wild as much as she had thought she might.

The only problem was that she kept turning up odd things in the records…. Such as the oddity that in her mother's lifetime, a substantial percentage of the scavengers' rights along the coast had reverted to the Crown, and none had been parceled back out again.

Now, since such rights were a traditional way of rewarding good service, that was historically out of the ordinary. Even stranger, it seemed as if every one of the rights that reverted was always the center of a tangle of subdivisions, sales and inheritances that came out to favor a party who was either dead or vanished.

It was enough to send a shiver up her back as she thought about the old stories of cursed treasures, and ghosts taking revenge on those who profited, however obliquely, by their deaths.

When she looked back over the old records of her mother's reign, she discovered this had been happening, off and on, ever since her father died and her mother began to rule alone. It appeared that the policy of generations, to use scavengers' rights to reward those who in other Kingdoms might be given lands and titles, had been reversed. She wondered, though the Queen ruled in her own name and right, was this Cassiopeia's idea, or had someone advised her to it?

The source of the Queen's personal wealth, which had been puzzling her a little, was revealed in this, however. No wonder Cassiopeia was able to afford silk, where her predecessor had made do with linen!

Andie frowned a little and stopped herself just before she began chewing on her nail. Lady Charis would have a kitten—

It was true that this was a way—without raising taxes or harming anyone—for Cassiopeia to increase her "discretionary" income. Seen in that light, there wasn't anything to find fault with. And it was also true that since Andie had begun paying attention, there hadn't been much that *she* would have chosen to reward anyone for—or at least, nothing that would merit the sort of permanent reward that salvage rights represented. The Queen loved luxury, loved beautiful things, loved ornaments and extravagant entertainment; richer countries than Acadia had been bankrupt by such Queens and Kings. But Cassiopeia seemed to have found a way to indulge herself without bankrupting her country or impoverishing her people. Maybe she was going against Acadian custom, but in this case, it was hard to disparage her.

But then there was the other disturbing thing: the number of shipwrecks was also increasing. Thus, increasing the Queen's revenue…

Now, there always had been and always would be merchants who sought to bypass Acadian harbor taxes, unloading fees and inspections by bypassing the port at Ethanos altogether and meeting up with a caravan at some shallow or less-protected bay or river mouth or minor fishing harbor where there were no harbor officials, no tax inspectors matching what was unloaded with what was being declared, and no laws saying that they had to pay the longshoremen of Ethanos to offload their ship. And there were always smugglers who wished to bypass all Acadian taxes entirely, and elude customs officials to bring in items that had been banned. But it seemed that to an increasing extent, such scofflaws had found themselves facing storm and wreck, almost as if some divine hand was at work. Some, when not wrecked, found themselves driven into port before a storm, willing or not.

But there was something very troubling about those lists of wrecked ships, because there was another trend for which Andie truly could not find any sensible reason.

Not only were there more wrecks, but there were more wrecks every year from merchants and countries that had *never* traded out of Ethanos. Places where the sunken ships gave up corpses that had dark brown, black or yellow skin, where the cargos were things that had never passed through any market in Acadia, where no Acadian but a Sophont could read the lettering on the barrels and bales, and only then by bespelling the letters into something recognizable.

Where were they coming from? When Andie sorted through older and older records, she saw that such a prodigy would occur now and again, once every ten or twenty years at most for the entire length of the Acadian shoreline, and be talked about by the scavengers who found it for a generation or more.

Not now. Now the exotic ships were washing up once a month in the stormy season, as if some inimical hand had dragged them off course and then thrown them onto Acadian rocks. And it made no sense. This was like finding strawberries in winter, or a gryphon cub among the kittens in a farmhouse litter. Those vessels should not have been anywhere near Acadia—yet there they were, coming to grief, spilling their goods out onto Acadian shores.

More wrecks—wrecks from foreign lands…Andie had a hunch, and looked in still another set of records, to discover that, yes, the storms of the storm season were getting worse, stronger, lasting longer, and the season beginning earlier and ending later. Away from Ethanos, fisherfolk were suffering, unable to put to sea to make their winter catches, and farmers were suffering, too, as their growing season shortened. So although prosperity was coming to Acadia as a whole in the form of treasure, it was passing the people who formed the backbone of Acadia, the coastal farmers and fisherfolk.

She closed that book and sat staring into space for a moment. A horrible thought dawned on her.

What if the storms are being sent?

It was true that the wrecks were bringing a certain amount of prosperity to Acadia, but only to a few. The rest were suffering. Smaller harvests meant less to eat; so far, the difference hadn't shown up in the marketplace that she knew of, but the area around Ethanos seemed free of these prodigal storms. The rest of the coastline was not doing as well. And if there was one thing that Andie saw in history, it was that if you wanted to bring a country to its knees, you began by starving it.

Though, it might not be Acadia that was the target here. It could be some other land, whose merchants were being driven off course, whose cargos were being lost. Acadia could be both the unwitting victim of and benefactor from someone else's quarrels.

So, it was a theory. The question was, could it be done, or was all this some Godmother tale she was frightening herself with? *Can storms be sent? Can you perform some magic to bring them early, make them stronger and send them where they wouldn't ordinarily go?*

Only one person in the Palace would know.

Not long ago, she would have gone running down to

Balan's workshop herself. Now, with a sigh, she rang a little bell on her desk, and a servant appeared.

"Do you know where Sophont Balan lodges?" she asked the boy.

He nodded. Well, a boy would. Girls, many of them, at any rate tended to avoid the area of the Sophont's quarters because of the odd smells, sounds and occasional sights, and a fear that some *thing* would jump out and bite them. Boys, on the other hand, tended to linger for precisely the same reasons.

"Then take the Sophont my compliments and ask if he can spare me a moment."

The boy nodded again and ran off, probably eager to be granted a task that would allow him inside the Sophont's door. Who could predict what he would see?

Since Andie knew precisely what he would see, despite her concern she stifled a smile. In Balan's workshop, which was so neat that even the most exacting housekeeper would be unable to find fault with it, he would see nothing much more exotic than he'd see in the housekeeper's still-room. Unless he happened to look up. Then he'd see the stuffed crocodile Balan kept hanging in the rafters.

She'd asked him why years ago, and he'd laughed. "Tradition!" he'd said. "Tradition says that Acadian Sophonts have a stuffed crocodile hanging from the rafters! I never wanted one—I threw the first one I had away. In the morning, it was back up there. So I gave it away. In the morning, it had returned. I pitched it in the ocean. It was back the next day with a drape of seaweed across its back and a glitter in its glass eye. Finally I burned it. The next day—

that was hanging up in the rafters, twice as big as the first! I gave up. There are just some things it's not worth trying to fight The Tradition over."

She hoped fervently that she wasn't interrupting some experiment, because as polite as he was, Balan would come whether he could spare the time or not.

She was quite relieved when, following the boy, Balan arrived looking as relaxed as if he had been doing nothing more than a bit of light reading when she'd asked him to come. And she saw no stains on his fingers, and no burn holes in his vest, which argued the same conclusion.

She gave him the bow of respect, then launched straight into her question. "Sophont, is it possible for a magician to change the weather?"

His brows wrinkled. "It depends on what you mean by 'change,'" he said, finally. "Can they make weather vanish? No. Weather patterns have a lot of force behind them. The natural world is one of the hardest things for a magician to alter, because it resists change. Weather can be called, or sent, but that's still tricky, and it takes a great deal of power. More than I'd have, unless, for instance, The Tradition decided to reinforce me to make weather behave the way The Tradition dictates for a particular time and place."

It was her turn to wrinkle her brows. "Why?" she asked.

"Because weather is *part* of The Tradition," he explained, waving his hand at the clouds outside. "Take Ethanos, for instance—in all the songs and stories about Ethanos, the Royal Family, and the port, you'll never see one where the weather is bad, so The Tradition tends to insist that we have many more fine days than wretched ones. Every single song sung here talks about rainbows after the rain—and rainbows we have, after every single rain. We've got something of a reputation for it, in fact. So if I were going to try to *change* that, I'd have the entire weight of The Tradition mustered against me."

"But a strong enough magician could still make the weather go where he wants it to go?" she persisted.

He sighed with reluctance. "A strong enough magician, and an area that doesn't have a lot of Tradition dictating the kind of weather it gets, yes. He could. Why?"

She told him, and when she was done, his eyes were narrowed in speculation. "Interesting," he said, chewing on his lower lip. "The thing about the open ocean is that you *aren't* burdened with a lot of Tradition about what kind of weather should go where, and that's more than half the battle. Very interesting…"

"Do you think it's sent at us?" she persisted anxiously.

He shook his head. "I think it's far more likely we're getting tangled up in someone else's fight. See, that's the other reason you don't mess with the weather. You don't know who, or what else you'll be affecting. They might take offense. *You* might actually hurt or kill someone. The Tradition might take a hand when someone else's land is getting weather it isn't supposed to, and the next time you try a spell, it could snap back at you. But I'll look into this. If it *is* someone causing it, there are some countermeasures I can take, and if the weather patterns really are worsening, it might be enough for The Tradition to help me out."

She sighed with relief, and smiled up at him. "Thank you, Sophont," she said earnestly.

He shrugged. "For what? I'm the Guards' Magician—that's part of my duties, and if you hadn't brought the situation to my attention, since I almost never leave Ethanos, I might not have known about it until something enormously bad happened. I'm in your debt."

"No, now that's *my* duty," she responded with an embarrassed smile. "Noticing things and making sure people know about them."

"Then we'll call it even," he replied. "Now if the Princess would excuse me?"

After he was gone, she wondered for a moment if she ought to report this to Solon. After all, it wasn't what she'd been told to research…

Then again, telling someone when she found something odd, or an unexpected pattern, was part of her duties.

So she uncapped the bottle of black ink—for the "not urgent" reports—dipped in a quill, and began.

In researching salvage rights, I made note of what seemed to me to be an unusual number of foreign wrecks from unknown lands washing up on Acadian shores in the past decade or so….

CHAPTER FOUR

Solon thanked her gravely for her report about the strange weather. More importantly, as far as Andie was concerned, the Queen also took her aside just before the Morning Audiences.

"Solon and I are very glad you noticed this trend in the winter storms," she said, with the slight downward turn of the corners of her mouth that was all she ever permitted by way of an expression signaling unhappiness. "I have asked not only Sophont Balan, but other Royal Sophonts to investigate this situation. If it is the effect of magic, and not some freakish trend in the weather itself, they will soon let us know and we will do something about it."

But a horrible thought had already occurred to her. The Sophonts were not especially powerful magicians, those few of them that even *were* magicians. What if this was magic, and it was too strong for them? And besides, what could they do if this was due to some action in some other land?

"Majesty," she ventured, "if it is magic—shouldn't we find a Wizard or a Godmother and ask for his or her help?" Surely, since Acadia had no Godmother of its own, it was the duty of any Godmother hearing of the troubles to do something about them? Or a Wizard—they were equally obliged to set things right when magic was involved.

"One thing at a time, dear," the Queen said indulgently. "First we should determine exactly what is going on, and decide what our actions should be. Winter will not be here for months, yet. If we need one, Wizards are not particularly hard to find, especially not for a Sophont. But I wouldn't like to trouble a Wizard if it turns out we don't need him. It isn't wise to annoy a Wizard." She smiled a little. "I doubt that Balan would relish being a toad."

Andie had to be content with that. Well, what else could she do? She wasn't a Sophont, and she couldn't send anyone to look for Wizardly help. She certainly didn't have the right to issue commands to anyone, even if she knew who to issue the commands to.

And it wasn't as if she didn't have plenty to do now, she thought as she worked at her desk later that day. In fact, Solon had asked her to research so many things that she was actually spending as much, if not more, time in the library than she ever had in her useless studies.

She was hard at work, when Lady Thalia entered her office bearing a bowl full of flowers. Distracted for a moment, Andie looked up. Lady Thalia frowned.

"How long have you been here, bent over those books?" the Lady demanded.

Suddenly conscious of a stiff neck, Andie rubbed it distractedly as she tried to remember when she had started. "Uh—just after luncheon, I think," she ventured.

"You look like a mushroom!" the Steward declared. "I am aware that young ladies are supposed to have delicate complexions, but you look as if we have been keeping you in a cave for weeks. There's a crease between your eyebrows, and you're squinting, and both of those expressions will give you wrinkles. I very much doubt that you ever spent *this* much time cooped up indoors before Her Majesty began giving you responsibilities."

"Uh—well, no, I didn't, but—" Andie began.

"Even the Queen doesn't spend the entire day working." Lady Thalia crossed her arms over her chest and leveled the kind of stare at Andie that her governesses had used when she had been particularly obtuse. "This report is not going to be harmed if you take some time in the garden, but *you* might be harmed, or at least your eyesight might be, if you don't. Do you *want* your eyes to get worse?"

Lady Thalia could not have chosen a better motivator than that. Her eyesight was bad enough now....

"If you think it will help," she replied, still reluctant to abandon her duty.

"I think if you don't, you will be harmed. Go." From the look of her, Lady Thalia was not going to leave until Andie did as she wanted.

It was a worrying thought, that her eyes might get worse. So worrying that it didn't even occur to her why she had avoided the garden in the past until she got there, and then it was too late to turn back.

There were fundamentally two kinds of people who came to the Court: those who came with a purpose, and those who came to be amused.

Of the first sort, there were those like Solon, Lady Charis, Lady Kyria—working members of Cassiopeia's household, acting as advisers or with household functions—and there were those who came because they might have to wait some time before Her Majesty could hear a petition or act on a problem. Then there were those who came with the singular intent of making some alliance *within* the Court— a marriage, a trade contract.

But there was, of course, the second sort. Members of the noble houses who had nothing particular to do with themselves, and, obliquely, those attached to the ones with a purpose, such as spouses and offspring or other relatives. They were here looking for amusement, or at least, entertainment of a sort they couldn't get at home. By its very nature as the center of Acadian society, the Court attracted better musicians in a greater variety, better actors and players, better poets. Ethanos was the capital, and as such also had a wider range of entertainments, from the public speeches of philosophers and politicians at the Academias, to the playhouses and, yes, brothels (though Andie wasn't supposed to know about *those*). If you had money, the markets had plenty of things you certainly wouldn't see at home. If you didn't, you could still spend hours being housed, fed and entertained at the Queen's expense.

It was those latter, the folks that had no real purpose here except to see and be seen, who thronged the gardens whenever Court was not in session.

This, Andie remembered as soon as she was a few yards into the gardens, her eyes adjusted to the light, and she saw dozens of eyes fixed on her as the newcomer. There was a strange hunger there, as if they would devour her if they got the chance. They were watching intently, looking for any crack in Andie's armor, any sign of weakness.

A few weeks ago, none of these folk really knew her by sight; in her usual plain tunic, she could have passed herself off as a servant sent to get flowers, broken off a few blossoms and left.

Not anymore. Now she was known, and if she turned and fled, tongues would wag. She would be watched, as a cat watches a mouse, more than they watched those that were already familiar to them. She was, at this moment, an unknown quantity. They hadn't yet categorized and measured her. All they knew of her was that she had begun appearing at the side of the Queen, looking infinitely more adult than she had a few weeks ago, and suddenly being treated by her mother and Solon as an adult. Although the court had made no formal announcement, the tacit understanding was that the heir had been "accepted" in a way she had not been until this moment. And the tongues must have begun to wag. Had she a lover? Would she take one? Was she only what she appeared to be on the surface, studious, serious and sober, or was there a hidden side to her? That was another common amusement among these folk—gossip. And if she was going to attain any level of respect, she was going to have to walk right into the nest of vipers with her head high and face them down.

So she smiled blindly at the inquisitive faces, and kept right on walking, nodding in greeting as she passed people who saluted her.

Those nearest the entrance to the garden were the oldest, and probably the worst of the gossips—they had positioned themselves so they could see everyone who came and went, and were gathered into pairs, trios and quartets. They were mostly women, though there were a few dyspeptic-looking men among them.

Several benches were arranged under the shade of the ornamental trees, some even built around the trunks of those trees. None of them, however, were directly lining the path, so at least she didn't have to run a gauntlet of those avidly staring faces.

Once out in the garden, the snoops were not quite so evident. Instead, she found herself among the purely idle and mostly young. "Young," that is, when compared to the first lot. They ranged between her mother's age and her own.

There was a musician with a harp under one tree, and a half dozen ladies, some with embroidery or some other form of fancy-work in their hands, though by the number of stitches they took, they would be old hags by the time the pieces were finished. Not far from them was another group, listening to one of their number reading. These girls were probably either safely betrothed, already married or unlikely to make any catch at all. Those who were actively looking to ensnare a husband were otherwise occupied.

A number of games were being played—bowls, ring toss and lawn tennis, though the word *played* probably conveyed far more of a sense of motion than was actually going on. The young women were hampered by long skirts and petticoats, not to mention that they appeared to possess no athletic ability whatsoever. The young men spent all their time, it seemed, in returning errant balls and rings that somehow found themselves in the flower beds or shrubbery. There was a great deal of flirtatious laughter, fluttering of eyelashes, and coy blushes on the part of the females. On the part of the males, there was indulgent laughter, would-be witty remarks and some exchange of jealous glares.

All of them watched her covertly as she passed, the girls with speculation, the men with assessment. She fought down a flush, realizing why the men were watching her. After all, the young men were here to make an advantageous marriage right along with the young women, and what could be more advantageous than to wed the Princess?

It made her feel a little ill.

And of course, the girls all knew this, and they were jealous, because no matter how stunningly beautiful they might be, nothing they could offer could compete with a crown.

Desperate now to find someplace out here where she wasn't going to be stared at, she finally remembered a spot she used to use to hide from her governesses and nurses. It would do, provided that she could get up into it wearing a gown rather than a tunic—

She hurried, attempting to look as if she was not hurrying, toward the bottom of the garden near the edge of the drop-off that separated the Palace gardens from the Palace

kitchen-gardens, and some huge, ancient apple trees, so old
that the fruit they bore was usually inedible, hard and
woody. The trees were allowed to remain because they were
sturdy and provided a good windscreen, as well as a visual
screen for those in the privacy of the Palace garden. With
a quick look around to make sure she wasn't being watched,
she used the long, double-wrapped cord-belt at her waist
to tie her skirt up above her knees, then removed her sandals, tied them together and slipped them through the belt
at her waist, and began climbing.

Only when she was safely settled in the huge fork halfway up the tree, hidden from below by a mass of foliage,
did she breathe easier. From here, she could see without
being seen, and no one ever came down here for flirtatious
courting. The trees were too leafy for grass to grow under
them, but the ground was also too dry for moss to grow, either, so unless you brought a cloth to spread (and what
noble of any age, accustomed to servants doing everything
for him or her, would ever think to do so?), it wasn't a surface conducive to sprawling at one's leisure without a certain amount of planning. The view of the town was good,
but there were equally good views elsewhere. It was too
open for conducting a torrid love affair, not open enough
to supply a good backdrop for a stroll designed to display
clothing or personal attributes.

But from up in the fork it was possible to observe without being observed. One thing she had definitely noticed—
the new oculars were much more secure on her head than
the old ones. Lady Kyria was, without a doubt, a master de-
signer.

She never used to come up here without a book, but after a moment of regretting that she hadn't snatched one in blatant disregard of the fact that she was supposed to be resting her eyes, she decided to make the best of the situation and see what she could learn by studying these hangers-on to her mother's Court.

The one thing that struck her immediately was that among the flirting couples were a few who seemed genuinely fond of each other—even in love. It was easy enough to pick out which they were; there was an absence of calculation in the way they moved, looked at each other, interacted. The others sensed it, too; even if they weren't aware of it consciously, they responded to those little signals that seemed to bind the couples together with reactions that were as varied as the individuals. Some put on airs of superiority, as if they were above such a display of emotions. Some acted as if they found it amusing. Some showed every sign and symptom of raw envy, but only when they thought they were not being observed.

She was surprised to feel a surge of sympathy for the latter. Yes, certainly, they should know very well that so far as the game of alliance and political maneuvering went, no one was going to take feelings into consideration. But that didn't stop people from seeing that once in a while it was possible to marry for love, or at least, with affection. And even if you wished both parties well, when such a thing was out of *your* reach, it was hard on you....

And it was even harder to keep from thinking, "if only."

She recalled crying out with frustration one day, after yet another long lecture on the duties and responsibilities of her royal birth, "If people are supposed to marry each other for politics, why did God create love?"

The answer her governess had given her was devastating in its cynicism and blunt cruelty. "Love," she had said crisply, "exists so that peasants will put up with their miserable lives and willingly pair up to create more peasants to perpetuate the workforce. It has no place in the considerations of a noble or royal house."

Of all the things that a governess had said, that one remained in her memory to haunt her. She had wondered then, and she wondered now, was the woman right? Were love and affection nothing but illusions?

If Cassiopeia's court was anything to go by, it certainly seemed so. Andie couldn't recall her father, but the Queen didn't seem to miss him in the least, and although she never spoke of him in a deprecating manner, she also never mentioned him with any more affection than she would have for an ornament that had been broken and thrown away. And yet, it was Cassiopeia who had been elevated from the ranks of the nobles to marry the Crown Prince, and not the other way around.

Really, the only people who ever *did* talk about caring for someone had been her loyal Six…who were, of course, of that peasant class her governess had alluded to.

And yet that just felt so *wrong*, as if there was something missing, a component necessary to life, or at least, to living.

It was with a feeling of grim resolve that she turned her attention away from the happy couples, and refocused it on the unhappy singles. *Watch and note,* she told herself. *You never know what you might find out—or when you'll need it.*

But she couldn't concentrate on them for long. They were like dolls, or like the shadow-puppets Merrha had brought in to amuse her when she was very small—flat, artificial, and without a very wide range of expression. She couldn't hear them from here unless they really raised their voices, so that made it obvious that they kept doing the same little stilted actions over and over. Take the people playing bowls—one of the young men would knock over several pins. The young ladies would jump up and down and clap their hands. The other young men would posture, probably boasting that they would do better. Most of the young ladies, with the exception of the one or two who had designs on the current bowler, would simper. The rest would gaze with feigned adoration on the object of their desires. Then a young lady would bowl. She would miss, or perhaps knock over a pin or two. The young men would smirk and commiserate; she would pout and be comforted. Then a young man would bowl and the actions would repeat. Maybe that was just Court manners, but it still didn't make for very interesting watching.

Her attention wandered, and she began staring at the clouds, dreamily watching them drift over the city. When she was little, she wished she could fly up there and play, or even, when things were particularly miserable, stay there forever. She'd never told anyone, but she used to daydream about trapping one of the flying horses that were supposed to live in the mountains, or finding some other way of getting up there. The idea of living in a place where you were never above the same landscape, that in fact, you could see the world without leaving "home," was enchanting.

In fact it wasn't anything that she learned, nor anything any adult said that ultimately persuaded her that this might be a bad idea. Partly it was that she couldn't think of any way of bringing enough food and drink up there with her to keep from having to find a way back down to the ground eventually. And partly it was because eventually she observed for herself that clouds didn't just *stay* lovely, puffy, soft-looking things. No, they grew—and they also dissolved.

The dissolving business would be no problem, she had reasoned, while she was awake. She could just jump to another when she noticed the cloud she was on beginning to shrink in size or use whatever means she'd found to get herself up there in the first place to move to a new home. But if she was asleep when it happened, she might suddenly find herself plummeting to earth in the dark…. Not so good, and the realization was reinforced by a dream of doing just that, from which she woke up with a *thump* on the floor beside her bed.

Still, she thought lazily, *I wonder what it would be like to be up there? Would it be like running through acres of fleeces, or bouncing on acres of pillows? What are they made of, anyway? There's water up there, or there couldn't be rain, but where does lightning come from? The old myths say it is the gods, and the priests still say God is responsible for it, but it seems altogether too random for that. Balan swears it's a natural phenomenon, like rubbing a cat with amber, but—*

She frowned, her attention caught by a tiny, winged thing among the clouds, moving very quickly, and very high. *What on earth is that? It's too big for a bird—*

It moved a little nearer. The wing-beats were…odd. *It's too big for an eagle.* Could it be one of the flying horses from out of the mountains? She thought it looked as if it might have four legs as well as the wings. But the neck seemed awfully long, and as it drew nearer, it just didn't look horse-like.

It's not a flying horse, and it's not a bird—

Then the vague shape resolved itself, and as she realized what it *was*, horror washed over her like a flood of ice-cold water. At that moment, she was paralyzed; she tried to shout, and nothing came out of her mouth but a tiny squeak, not even a word—

Dear gods.

She tried to scream, but it was exactly like being in a nightmare, seeing the horrible thing coming and being un-able to *do* anything—she felt her whole body go cold as she struggled against the paralysis. The thing was impossible! It couldn't exist!

And the impossibility was approaching on ponderously beating wings.

In the end, it wasn't she who gave the warning, it was whoever among the Guards that had Sea Watch above on the cliff that began frantically sounding the horn, in des-perate blats and honks. At first heads swiveled toward the harbor, but by that point, the thing was close enough that the movement caught their eyes, and someone, some man, was the one who finally screamed the word in a voice as shrill as any girl's.

"Dragon! DRAGON!"

In the garden, the pretty little tableaux dissolved into a

chaos of screaming, fleeing bodies, and with a few rare exceptions, it was pretty much every man (and woman) for himself. Andie stayed where she was—partly because she was still held in that paralysis of fear, and partly because some tiny little crumb of rational thought reasoned that the dragon probably couldn't see her in the tree, and if it went after anything, it would go after the people running around like frightened rabbits with arms waving, go after the people announcing themselves with screams of panic, and not after someone that wasn't drawing attention to herself. Maybe it was rabbit-reasoning, but rabbits were pretty good at surviving.

It seemed like forever, but it couldn't have been very long before Guards appeared in the garden, rushing out of the Palace doors. Some began herding the senseless idiots toward the Palace, picking them up and carrying them when their legs failed to hold them. Others lined up with bows along the highest retaining wall and began firing arrows at the beast.

The beast completely ignored the arrows, which bounced off its hide and wings without harming anything. It didn't seem particularly concerned or annoyed by them, but approached the Palace in a leisurely manner, for all the world as if it were King here.

Finally it hovered just below the top of the lookout cliff, regarding the buildings and inhabitants below. The Guard on the top of the cliff had stopped blowing the alert. God only knew what he was doing now. The Guard on Sea Watch wasn't armed with anything more lethal than a knife.

The dusky-bronze dragon stretched out its neck and

peered down at the bowmen, tilting its head to one side. This was too much for some of the Guards. They broke and ran.

The rest, however, stood their ground and drew their swords, which looked about as useful against the huge armored beast as toothpicks against a war chariot.

It seemed to dismiss them, then looked around on the same level with itself. Then it stretched its neck out and Andie held her breath, so terrified now that there was only room for one thought in her mind.

It's going to flame!

She had never seen a dragon before—no one in Acadia had—but every story she had ever heard or read warned of that indrawn breath, that long pause, and what it meant. And if it directed that flame down on the poor Guards—it would be bad.

From where she was, she could hear the creature taking in a long, deep inhalation, heard the pause as it held its breath for a moment—

Then it whipped its head around, pointed its snout at the unoccupied bell tower of the Palace chapel, opened its mouth, and with a roar like angry surf in a killer storm, a fountain of flame burst out of the gaping jaws. She couldn't even hear her own screaming over the roar of the dragon. She clutched the trunk of the tree as a hot, sulfurous blast of air hit her, feeling as if she were standing too close to a forge.

It didn't last long. One moment, there was a cone of white-hot fire gushing from the thing's mouth. The next, it had snapped its mouth shut on the flame, cutting it off.

And the bell tower wasn't there anymore. There was a stump of charred wood and stucco, but no tower.

The dragon turned its head, and that was when Andie noticed another peculiar thing. It was more than near enough for her to make out its features perfectly, and she would have expected to see the cold, unemotional, unintelligent eyes of a snake or a lizard in its head, unwinking, and unfeeling-looking.

Instead its smoky-dark eyes were warm, bright, intelligent, round-pupiled and very nearly human. And they looked—sad.

It didn't flame the men. Why didn't it flame the men?

The dragon snorted, and with a couple of wing-beats that made the branches of the trees around Andie thrash as if in the midst of a winter storm, it arced away from the Palace and down toward the town. It hovered there for a moment, while screams and cries came up from below, and then it folded its wings and dove.

Andie emitted a horrified gurgle.

It rose again, and in each taloned foreclaw was a limp form. One was a donkey. The other, a cow.

She heard that sound of intaken breath, and cowered against the trunk of the tree—and again, the dragon whipped its head around, opened its mouth and flamed. This time, it was the marble statue of Victory atop the column in the center of the Public Forum that was the target, and when the flame cut off, poor Victory was looking very damaged indeed, black as a cinder, with her bronze spear melted and her wings mere shattered stumps.

This seemed to satisfy the dragon. With another snort,

it propelled itself upward in surges, with every beat the wings making the snapping sound of a sail filling with wind. Andie watched in stunned fascination as it lost itself among the clouds.

Only then did she shake off her paralysis, slide down to the ground, slip her sandals back on and shake down her skirts. Then she headed back into the Palace. The Guards still on the garden grounds ignored her, or perhaps they just didn't notice her, since she was the only person walking quietly back into the Palace amid a horde of screaming, weeping and fainting courtiers, servants and hangers-on. They clearly had their hands full.

All *she* could think was that she had something she needed to research with a lot more urgency than any of Solon's requests.

The Queen and her advisers stared at one another. Cassiopeia was on her throne, with Andie on a low stool beside her. The advisers had been granted the unusual concession of low chairs, since this was going to be a very long meeting. All six of them faced the Commander of the Guards to hear his latest information.

"There are reports coming in from all over the countryside, Majesty." The weary Guard Commander looked as if he had personally collected every one of those reports himself.

Andie felt terribly sorry for him. He looked as if he was taking the failure of the Guard to protect people from the monster as his own responsibility. There were dark rings under his eyes. His curly black hair had been flattened under a helmet for hours, and his face and uniform-tunic were slightly charcoal-smudged.

"The creature can't be stopped. It doesn't even notice arrows, and doesn't come down to the ground long enough to be attacked with spears or swords. It seems to have an insatiable appetite. Everywhere it goes, it's been seizing livestock and devouring it. So far, it hasn't set fire to any occupied buildings, but that may just be luck."

"It is difficult to imagine the word luck in connection with that monster," Solon said dryly. "Precisely how bad are things, do you know?"

"Bad enough." The Guard Commander shook his head. "The people are terrified. Those people in the city are fleeing into the country, the ones in the country are trying to get into the city. It's a madhouse out there, especially at the gates. No one seems to know what to do, but they're all trying to do *something,* and if the monster wasn't so horrible, I'd say that the mere effect of his presence is far worse than the actual damage he's caused. So far he's burned a couple of high ornaments and eaten some livestock—but everywhere he goes, people trample market stalls, foodstuffs, and each other. There's been some looting in the chaos, fighting has broken out, and when people catch sight of him, they just go mad with terror."

"But if he starts burning crops and devouring entire herds," Solon pointed out, "I doubt that you'll be able to say that for much longer."

"Not to mention the sheer chaos that's being caused," the Queen put in. "Nothing is getting *done* while people are milling about, trying to find a way to flee from the beast.

Businesses, crafts, farms—it may be a race between all of us starving to death or being killed by the dragon!"

"I wish I could argue with that assessment, Majesty," Solon replied. "As our good Commander has explained, our usual weapons don't seem to be affecting the beast. We *must* find a way to kill it, or at least drive it away—and I hope Princess Andromeda has some information for us on that score."

All heads in the Audience Chamber turned, and all eyes stared at Andie.

She swallowed hard, and surreptitiously rubbed her sweaty palms against her gown. Yes, she had gleaned every bit of information on dragons that there was in the Great Library. Not that there was much. And none of it was very comforting. Still—

"If everything I've found in the Library is correct, there is a way to be rid of it. First, we need a Champion," she said carefully. "Every single document is quite clear on that. Only a Champion will have the weaponry and the magic to defeat a creature like a dragon. Champions generally belong to Orders, and each Order has a Chapter-House. The nearest is—" she consulted her notes "—the Kingdom of Fleurberg, the Chapter-House of the Order of the Glass Mountain."

Cassiopeia turned her gaze upon the Guard Commander, who looked happier than he had since this meeting started, and nodded. "Inland and north of here. It's farther than we usually trade, but I've seen it on the maps. Messengers will be dispatched immediately, Majesty."

"But until the Champion can be found?" Solon asked, persistently, turning his penetrating gaze on Andie while her nerves stretched thin. "Is there a remedy to keep this monster from ravaging the countryside? As the Queen has said, if we cannot keep it in check, we will starve before help can come."

Andie felt sweat trickling down the back of her neck. "Well, yes," she admitted reluctantly. "The Tradition is very—very strong on this point. There *is* one way to keep it from raging everywhere. But—but it's not very nice—"

"My dear child!" one of the other advisers exclaimed. "What is going on now is a great deal worse than 'not very nice'! Come, what it is?"

She bowed her head over her notes. "You have to give it an offering. Mostly The Tradition says that it has to be once a week, although some records say it has to be more often. Once a week is probably right." She felt the words forced out of her against her will. "But it has to be a very—very special sort of offering, in order to make the thing work. It has to be something that's a real—sacrifice." Finally the last of it came out in a rush. "You have to offer it a virgin to eat. A girl. A live girl, once a week, left tied to a stake where it can easily find her."

Her words fell into the silence like leaden pellets.

Then, everyone began talking at once.

Andie remained numb, listening to them. She could hardly believe what she was hearing. Not one of them asked if there was some other way of dealing with this dragon. Not one suggested a different approach. They simply, and without argument, and with no hesitation at all, accepted this preposterous idea, and began putting forward ways of implementing it, immediately.

"Slaves—" said Lord Hira, who was something of a slave trader. "We can bring in slave girls to feed it. I can have my factors contact the slave fleet—"

"I believe that the sacrifice was specifically to be a *virgin,* Lord Hira," Solon said dryly. Papers rustled in his hand as he looked over the copy of the notes Andie had made for him. "Yes. A virgin, and nubile, *not* a little girl. So trying to get around the stipulation by using a child won't work— and when have you ever brought in a nubile virgin, eh?"

Lord Hira mumbled something, but he knew, as Andie knew (though she wasn't to say so, as she wasn't supposed to be aware of such things) that Acadia was the end of the corridor of the slave trade. Technically in fact, the slave trade was illegal in Acadia; any slave purchased was supposed to be freed immediately, and allowed to work off the price of his or her freedom from the master. In practice, this was impossible; a master would set the value of the slave so high, and wages so low, that it would take a miracle to work the sum off. Only someone like Cassiopeia, who chose to buy her slaves' loyalty with their freedom, would actually follow the spirit as well as the letter of the law.

But because of this, it was unlikely that Lord Hira would be able to purchase a dozen virgins or even one virgin at short notice, at this end of the trading corridor. Virginity had a very high value, and a correspondingly high price tag attached to it in the southern kingdoms across the Lesser Sea, and by the time a girl arrived here, that price would certainly have been met long ago.

"We should ask for volunteers!" said Lord Cheon insistently. "For the good of the country!"

"You don't really believe that any girl is going to offer herself to be eaten by a dragon, do you?" Lord Hira sneered. "At least, not a sane one! I suppose we might get some poor wet fish of a girl who wants to kill herself who will offer, but surely not more than one!"

"Well, then, offer to enrich her family if she volunteers!" Cheon said desperately. "Offer a fat reward!"

"Then we will not be getting volunteers," Solon pointed out. "We will be getting young ladies whose families have no use for them, or who value gold over their offspring. And what is more, I should doubt their virginity, as well."

Andie wanted to clap her hands over her ears. This was awful, but there was worse. None of them wanted to say it—the only possible solution, if they were really going to go through with this horrible thing… It was up to the Queen to say it.

Andie knew her mother. Cassiopeia had a gift for seeing straight to the heart of a matter, facing it without flinching, and saying the things that no one else would say. After listening to her Advisers wrangle for a few moments, she ended the entire argument. "A lottery," she said, the sound of her voice sending them all into silence. "A lottery. It is the only fair way."

"You do realize that there is a simple way for girls to evade their duty, don't you?" Cheon said, sounding sullen.

"I can do nothing about a girl choosing to dishonor herself before being chosen," Cassiopeia replied, serenely. "And no doubt, many will consider the risks attendant on lying with a man less than those of taking the chance on the lottery. But as for afterward—well, once the selection is made, the girl who is chosen must be placed into protective custody to prevent such a thing. Comfortable custody, but the simple expedient of using female Guards should ensure that she doesn't find a way to render herself ineligible."

After that, there seemed to be no other choice, or at least, there was no other choice that the Queen was willing to consider.

It made Andie feel absolutely ill. If the decision had been hers to make, she would have gone into the countryside, hunted high and low for some other solution. She was certain there must be one! And the dragon had killed no people yet. Maybe the Sophonts could do something—drive it into the mountains, make it hole up in a cave until the Champion could be found, or present it with something other than human beings to eat. She wanted to say this, but she knew no one was going to listen.

She knew that her nightmares were going to be haunted by this—and it would be worse once the sacrifices started. She couldn't possibly sit in the Palace and pretend it wasn't happening. She would have to force herself to attend the ceremony and be a witness, but her own conscience demanded that she not ignore it, nor pretend it wasn't happening.

"There should be some solemn ceremony, of course," Solon was saying. "Something to show that we aren't taking this lightly. Something to honor the girl. And some compensation for her family. Not enough to make it seem as if we are paying them for their daughter, of course, but enough to make it clear we value what they are losing."

And then, even more horribly, they began calmly discussing just how much was "appropriate." She glanced at the Guard Commander. He looked suitably appalled.

Then again, this was a complete violation of everything he stood for. His duty was to protect the people of Acadia, not offer them up to monsters. But he wasn't going to be given any choice in the matter, either.

Finally the long, dreadful meeting was over, and she was able to flee back to her wing. Once there, she waved off offers of food or drink, to go out into the clean and open air of her terrace-garden.

But once she was outside, she happened to look up—and there, in the distance, she saw it. Unmistakable, having seen it once…

The dragon.

She fled back into the sanctuary of her rooms, and once alone, clasped her hands together, shut her eyes and began to pray, fervently, that a Champion would come.

And soon. Very soon.

CHAPTER FIVE

Iris pulled back the heavy bedroom curtains, letting in the thin morning light. "What does the weather look like this morning, Iris?" Andie asked, without moving out of bed. If she had not woken up knowing what day it was, the sad, gray light would have told her. On these days, she put off getting out of bed as long as she could—

"Cold, damp, overcast," Iris replied. "You can't even see the sun through the clouds. Not like yesterday."

Of course not. The Tradition was working in full force today. You couldn't have a brisk breeze, full sun and a cloudless sky today.

"No chance of a storm, though," Iris added, taking garments out of the clothespress and the wardrobe. "Not like last time. This one drank the potion, and they say she was quiet about it even before she drank."

Andie winced, and slid out of bed. She wasn't sure which was worse, on a sacrifice day—the ones who screamed and wailed and wept, who had to be tied to a stake in a cart and taken to the sacrifice grounds that way, or the ones who drank the drugged potion that Balan always offered them and went to their death quiet and dreamy, carried in a sedan-chair bedecked with flowers or ivy. The fighters brought storms with them, real tempests, with wild wind and lightning striking the tops of the hills; the quiet ones invoked bleak, heavy overcast skies, with a sad drizzle of rain, or a mist.

In the beginning, there actually *had* been a brief influx of volunteers. Some were clearly insane, viewing the dragon as some sort of manifestation of God to which they had been called. Some came from homes with a father so abusive that in the minds of these girls, death was preferable to remaining under the same roof. Some actually stepped forward bravely out of a sense of duty.

Not all of them had been accepted. Some had been rejected because, on inspection, they no longer had the necessary "qualification." But after that first lot there had been no more volunteers, and the other option became a necessity.

It had been six months since the lottery began, and there was still no sign of any Champion, nor word from the messengers. Once a week, Solon plunged his hand into a bag of tokens and condemned another poor girl to death. They had been as young as twelve, and as old as fifty. The fifty-year-old had been a Sister at a convent in the hills, who had prayed and sung the entire time. She'd actually been the easiest for Andie to bear; the twelve-year-old had been the worst. The girl had not been told she had been selected. Her parents had given her the potion themselves, and she had looked like a sleeping angel in that sedan-chair....

Iris helped her into her gown of fine black lamb's wool, with heavy black cords and embroidery of black silk acanthus leaves around the hem. She sat down at her dressing table while Iris bound up her hair in a severe knot, then arranged a black mantle over it and pinned it in place. "Are you sure you won't have something to eat, Princess?" she asked anxiously.

Andie's gorge rose at the mere thought. "Positive," she replied. She never could eat on sacrifice days.

"You don't have to be there," Iris said tentatively, touching her shoulder, before helping her push her feet into soft black leather boots, suitable for the cold of the day and the rough track they would have to climb.

"Yes, I do." Though Iris would never understand, Lady Thalia did, and approved. Andie had to be there because not only was Andie the heir-apparent, it was at least partly Andie's fault that these poor girls were being sent to their deaths. If she hadn't found the passages that described how the virgin sacrifices would keep the dragon pacified—

Maybe someone else eventually would have, but she didn't know that. What she did know was that she was the one who had. To attend the sacrifices was to acknowledge her guilt and the part she had played in this.

She glanced at her face in the mirror; pale, swathed in black, she looked properly in mourning. There were dark circles under her eyes that not even her oculars could hide.

The echo of muffled drums sounded all through the Palace, and Andie stood up to go. Iris opened the door for her, and with the servants lined up, watching her with solemn faces, she moved out of her rooms and into the Great Hall, where one of the Guard fell in behind her as her escort without a single word being exchanged. She generally tried not to talk before a sacrifice, because talking often made her cry.

Outside, at the front of the Palace, on the graveled area in front of the two enormous double doors leading into the Great Hall, the procession had already begun to form. First came the sacrifice in her sedan-chair; this morning, the girl was already there, waiting for them. Or rather, she was sitting passively in the chair; from the look on her face, she was off in her own dim little world. She wasn't a pretty one this time; that would make it easier on the other people who came to watch. In fact, with her sallow skin, dull dark hair and slightly receding chin, she was distinctly plain. What little expression was left to her after drinking the potion made it look to Andie as if she was the timid sort, accustomed from the moment of her birth to obeying orders. Not all the pampering and preparation in the world could change the red, chapped condition of her hands, nor the brittle state of her hair, nor the pinched, half-starved look of her. This one was poor. It shouldn't have made a difference, but of course, it did. Most of the people in and around the Court found it easier to shrug off a sacrifice when it was a poor girl, as if being poor made them somehow less human.

"Well, not so bad!" Andie had heard one woman say.

"She'll never have had food that fine, nor baths, nor clothing as lovely, and never would have in her whole life."

That was just wrong. There was something more pathetic about the fact that the poor girl's entire, short life had been nothing more than a lead-up to a single feast, one nice gown, a warm, soft bed for the night, then a horrible death.

She was dressed in a flowing white gown, with a crown made of ivy, and there was ivy woven all around her chair. In the dead of winter it was hard to find any flowers or greenery except ivy. The gown was thin, but it didn't look as if she felt the cold. She sat very still, her eyes wide and fixed on nothing, her mouth a little open. *The potion must have taken her hard.* With luck, she wouldn't even see the dragon coming.

Usually behind the sedan-chair came the parents, but in their place was a single priest, reading silently from a prayer book. Her parents probably couldn't bear to watch—when they were so cold as to not care, they always showed up, and reveled in being the center of attention, usually carrying on with theatrical weeping and wailing that would have made a bad actor ashamed of himself. It was the parents who cared the most that kept away from the procession, who sometimes had to be drugged into insensibility themselves. Or maybe the poor thing was an orphan.

Andie shuddered at that, because it somehow made it all that much more horrible, that this poor girl's sad and deprived life should end like this, before she even had a taste of any kind of happiness. And once the day was over, she would be utterly forgotten. No one would mourn her. No one would even remember her name.

Behind the priest, Cassiopeia's chair waited; it was empty, but her ladies were clustered around it, all in black. Andie joined them. They knew enough, or were sensitive enough, not to say anything to her.

To give her credit, the Queen never kept them waiting for long on an occasion like this one. Even the most restless of them had just begun to fidget when she appeared. Like the rest, she was all in black, enveloped in a black wool cape, but unlike the rest, she was veiled. Without a word to any of them, she took her seat in her chair, nodded to the Guard Captain in charge of it all, and the procession began.

It wound down from the Palace, out into the quiet, deserted streets of Ethanos, until it came to the main road. First came a priest, reading prayers aloud, followed by the girl in her chair, carried by four burly men. Another priest followed in the place where her parents would have been, then all of the Queen's advisers, Solon leading. They, too, were dressed in black and afoot. Then two men playing muffled drums, followed by the Queen's chair, also carried by four men, and flanked by two Guards. Behind Cassiopeia's chair came her ladies-in-waiting, with Andie among them, more priests, another pair of drummers, and whomever of the court wished to attend. In the beginning, there had been a fair number of courtiers, drawn by curiosity, but now, unless a courtier was related in some way to the sacrifice, there generally weren't more than a handful. Last of all came a full troop of thirty-six Guards. The only people not afoot were the Queen and the sacrifice.

Ethanos might have been deserted; there was no sign of

life or habitation until they reached Tavern Street, the main street that led from the docks to the city gates and the trade roads beyond. There, at last, were the citizens of Ethanos, lining the street like two ranks of silent statues.

No one spoke. Today, no one wept, either. But they did look sad and solemn, as if they felt the same guilt that Andie labored under. Strangely enough, no one had ever ordered them to do this; they had turned up for the first sacrifice, and had continued to show their faces and their feelings every week since. In that they were far more faithful and respectful than the courtiers, and Andie never felt their presence to be mere show.

They passed down Tavern Street to the outer walls of Ethanos, and went out through the Old Willow Gate, which was barely big enough to accommodate the cart they sometimes had to use. There was no trouble today, of course, since the girl was in the sedan-chair.

It was a long way to walk, and it wasn't over yet. They moved along the Trade Road for a while, until farther on, an old track branched off the main road and headed up into the hills.

It led to what Balan and the other Sophonts had deemed the most appropriate place of sacrifice, so up the track they went. A horse-cart could never have made it up this track; the few times a sacrifice had to be brought here in that manner, the cart had been pulled by a donkey.

Last night, the victim had been at least treated like royalty. She had been luxuriously bathed, scented, massaged and perfumed. She'd been fed on every delicacy available to the Queen's own table, and had slept—if she could sleep—in the softest eiderdown, on silk sheets, under a fur coverlet. This morning there had been more of the same pampering. From the moment she had been chosen, she would have been offered Balan's potion as often as she cared to drink it—and about half of the girls accepted it at that point. Balan had told Andie that it was a euphoric, and it clouded the memory, until by morning, the sacrifices generally had no idea why they were in the procession or what it was about, nor did they care. He swore to her that it made them happy, that they were unafraid and mostly lost in a kind of dream.

In Andie's eyes, that didn't make it better.

She'd suggested arming the sacrifices and, needless to say, that particular notion had not gone down well. She had suggested having the Guards attempt an ambush, and that had been ignored. No one so far had even been allowed to try to defend the sacrifices.

Behind her came the drummers, their slow cadence setting the pace of the procession, their drums muffled in mourning. The drums weren't just a symbol, or a part of the pomp and show. They had a purpose. The sound of the drums told the dragon that they were coming. By now, Andie knew, he would be waiting, perched on the top of a crag overlooking the place where they would leave the girl. He never moved, from the time they entered the little cup of a valley to the time they left it—though Andie had, once or twice, caught a glimpse of him flying off with a limp figure in one fore-claw. The victim looked like a doll in the hand of a child; the dragon must be enormous.

She looked up as they entered the valley, and there he

was, black against the dark sky. In the sunlight he was a kind of dark bronze with gold touches here and there. As usual, he didn't move, and the sacrifice must not have seen him before the priests surrounded her in her chair and flung a thick white veil over her head. They led her to the stake and gently pushed her back up against it, then pulled her hands around behind her back and tied them there. One of them gave her the Last Rites; like most of the drugged ones, she was oblivious to what was going on, though she went through the motions readily enough, or at least, as well as she could with her hands tied behind her back. If there had been loved ones there, this was when they would have taken a final farewell.

And at that point, it was over. There was nothing more to do, except to leave her to the fate that perched above the valley. The procession formed up again and filed out of the valley, heading back to the Palace.

No one looked back.

Not even Andie.

The life of a Fairy Godmother was generally not the easiest in the Five Hundred Kingdoms, and that of a Godmother with not one, but several Kingdoms to administer as well as a myriad of other duties tended to be as crowded as a swarm of bees in a too-small hive.

But Elena would not have traded it for another life. Not even the one of the princess she would have been, had The Tradition had its way with her and had "her" prince not been a toddler at the time they "would" have met. Unfortunately, for every scullery maid with a Fairy Godmother who went to a ball and enchanted a prince, there were dozens for whom that particular happy ending never came. Elena had been lucky, in a sense. She had not gone off and married someone else, and although The Tradition had built up enough magical potential around her to flatten a palace, it had not driven her mad nor attracted the attentions of something evil. Instead, she had been taken as a Godmother's Apprentice herself, and learned how to use the magic of The Tradition, steering The Tradition in ways *she* wanted it to go. It was a challenging job. It could be a very, very exciting job. It was always a rewarding job.

There were, however, moments…

Such as this one, which had brought her to the Library of the Castle of Glass Mountain, which was now the Chapter-House of the Order of the Champions of Glass Mountain in Fleurberg. Not that she ever minded coming here, since the Head of the Order was her own beloved consort, Champion Alexander. But there was work to do, fairly urgent work. There was a pair of homicidal children in the Witch-wood of Nestoria. They had already tried to murder one poor old biddy, who had escaped being shoved into her own bread oven only because she knew a spell to make herself temporarily fireproof and had read the signs of what was coming. There were twelve more witches in that same wood, all Good and not Evil, and they were in danger; sometimes, when The Tradition got its metaphorical hands on malleable humans, it was working with severely flawed material. This was *certainly* the case with that brother and sister.

The Traditional story featured a pair of quite innocent

young children, sent by a poor mother whose patience had been tried once too many times, to gather mushrooms or berries in the forest after they had ruined the only food in the house in their play. It would be an Evil witch that found them, captured them, and was about to transform them or devour them outright, when through cleverness, they turned the tables on her, killed her, broke the spell on other children being held there and were reunited with their frantically worried parents.

Not this pair. They were in their teens, though they looked much younger, and rather than being gentle and innocent, they already had a history of torturing animals and tormenting younger children before they decided to make a career for themselves as murderers. It appeared that they had decided it would be safe enough to kill someone who was a witch, since even the purest of Good Witches was often regarded dubiously by her neighbors.

Elena had to put a stop to this—but she had to do so in a way that The Tradition would recognize, and work to reinforce. So right now, she was investigating brother-and-sister tales to find one that would at least incapacitate the pair. The selection, alas, was not a large one. Granted, she could have used her own library, but it had occurred to her that the former owner of this place had been a Wizard, not a Godmother, and his library might have a few volumes hers did not.

Besides it was another good excuse to spend time with Alexander. As the Head of the Glass Mountain Chapter-House, he spent every other month here besides being on call when he was at the Godmother's Manse. Luckily, there was a private Portal to use anytime he needed to be there instantly.

In addition to the problem of the two "children," there was an outbreak of minor curses in Florinia; all the symptoms pointed to a young wielder of magic suddenly coming into his or her power, but she couldn't seem to pin down the source.

And now this delegation of shepherds from—where was it, exactly?—had sought her out *here*.

She ran the fingers of both hands through the hair at her temples and marked the place in her book where there was a promising beginning to a Traditional Tale. "I'm sorry," she said, hoping they believed her apology was sincere. "I wasn't attending. You are from—?"

"Acadia, Godmother," said the shepherd, twisting his woolen hat in his hands so hard that if it wasn't shapeless already, it was certainly going to be shortly. "South of here. On the coast."

She frowned a little. "I'm sorry," she said again, "but that is not one of my Kingdoms. Shouldn't you be going to your own Godmother?"

"Strictly speaking, mum," said another, a shepherdess who looked about as much like one of the little pink-and-white porcelain figurines (the sort that the wealthy in Elena's Kingdoms liked to display in their parlors) as a wolf looks like a lapdog. She looked, in fact, as tough as briar, weathered as a crag and quite capable of hauling a full-grown ram up out of a ravine, never mind a lamb or two. "Strictly speaking, Acadia don't belong to any Godmother. Haven't had one for a dog's age."

Elena tried not to groan. This was, after all, the sort of thing she was supposed to handle. She might be young in years, but she was old in power, a senior Godmother. If there was an orphan Kingdom with a problem anywhere near one of hers, it became hers to deal with.

"Ye see," said the first shepherd, still twisting his hat. "We got a dragon problem."

As he outlined the "dragon problem," she listened in growing astonishment. Because there shouldn't have been a "dragon problem" in Acadia. Acadia was a very small Kingdom, bucolic in nature, and dragons just didn't turn up in places like that. Dragons could be good or evil, just as human beings could be, but the evil ones didn't bother with half-sized Kingdoms like Acadia, they went for the places where they could heap up treasure-beds of stolen gold and gems piled higher than they were tall. If there was enough gold in Acadia to fill more than a couple of small-ish chests, she would be surprised.

As for the good ones—they just didn't *do* what the shepherd had described. And they certainly didn't accept virgin sacrifices.

And where in the name of all the Powers of Good had they gotten that idea from, anyway? she wondered. What idiot would think that a dragon could actually live on one skinny little girl a week? Dragons needed food, and a lot of it. Maybe this beast wasn't burning down buildings anymore, but he *was* helping himself to flocks in the hills, with or without virgin sacrifices.

Virgin sacrifices…well, there's one way to escape that fate. She wondered wryly how long it would be before the population explosion started—

"So we need a Champion, Godmother," the shepherdess

said, interrupting her train of thought. "The Queen was s'p-
posed to have sent here for one, but we hadn't heard nothin'
about it, so we decided to come ourselves."

"Quite right," she replied, standing up. "I will look into
this right now, and before you leave, I'll have an answer for
you." She picked up a handbell and rang it, summoning a
squire. Squires went with Chapter-Houses, just as Brownies went with Fairy Godmothers. There seemed to be a
never-ending supply of young men and women who could
think of nothing better than to serve Champions, in hopes
of one day becoming one. However, as she had rapidly discovered, none of them could cook, and their idea of proper
housekeeping was less than satisfactory. So, there were
squires on show at this Chapter-House, but behind the
scenes, there were Brownies keeping the place comfortable
and tidy, and everyone fed.

As Alexander had discovered, there were a great many
advantages in being married to a Fairy Godmother.

"If you would take these postulants to the guest chambers, Squire Hakkon?" she asked politely. "They are probably famished and definitely tired and road-weary." She
turned back to her visitors. "You won't leave here without
an answer in hand, and probably a Champion, if not with
you, then on the road behind you," she promised.

The nervous fellow looked ready to faint with relief. The
tough shepherdess just dropped her head forward and
heaved a sigh. "Thankee, Godmother," she said fervently,
and the squire led them all away.

Which did not make the problem go away. If a Champion had been sent for, why hadn't one *gone?* Certainly if

something bad had happened to him, they would not only know, but the Chapter-House would be making plans for a full-scale assault by now.

There was one person here who would know the answer to that, and he would be in the practice arena at this time of day. Normally she didn't like to interrupt anyone at training, but she had promised a quick answer and she intended to keep that promise.

But communication in a Chapter-House was as swift as in a Godmother's Manse, as she discovered when she tentatively pushed open the doors of the arena. Word-of-mouth at her Manse spread from one end of the property to the other in the blink of an eye, and it appeared to do the same here. Alex was just pulling off his helm and had already turned to face the opening doors; the squires had taken his and his opponent's arms off to the side, and his opponent was being unarmored.

Despite a black eye he had picked up in the course of his training bouts—because he took his job as Chief Champion very seriously, and trained with all of the single-minded determination anyone could ever have asked of a Chapter-Head—he was a delight to the eye of any female with warm blood in her veins. His wavy brown hair, thick and shining, was now pulled back into a tail, where it helped to pad and protect the back of his neck. She loved that hair…though at times, she was a little jealous of it. And those long, curly eyelashes. What did a man need with lovely eyelashes, anyway?

As for his face—he looked every bit the Champion. Square chin, chiseled cheekbones, broad brow—it was saved from perfection only by his nose. *He could plow a field with that nose,* she thought, amused, as she so often had. But she loved that nose, and she wouldn't trade it for another. It gave him character. It also gave fair warning that he was at least as stubborn as she was. When they clashed—

Fortunately, this was probably not going to be one of those times.

"Acadia—" she said, and then experienced one of those delightful moments of accord that only occurs between two partners who have come to know each other so well they can speak in a kind of code.

"Liam's just back," he replied, knowing that *she* knew Liam was the newest of the Champions, a true virgin knight, and thus absolutely the best to send after a dragon. The Tradition would have such force behind him, he would probably be shining like a young sun by the time he closed in battle. "Been at the Acadian Border for a month, trying to break through."

That brought her up short. *"What?"* she replied, quite certain she hadn't heard him correctly.

"They sent merchants, farmers, a whole delegation to ask, and of course, we sent a Champion along immediately."

"But?" she prompted.

"There's a barrier at the Border." Then he elaborated. "Magical, probably—that's more in your line than mine. Anybody who isn't a Champion has no problem getting across. But Liam tried everything he could think of and still couldn't get in. Asleep, drunk…he even had his squire knock him unconscious—it didn't matter. Finally he gave up, and reported to me about the same time that those shepherds showed up. If I'd known they were from Acadia, I'd have seen them myself. I was waiting until you'd done with them before coming to ask you what we could do about the situation."

"We can find out what sort of barrier it is, for one thing," she replied. "Let me try the most direct route first." She turned and started for the door, then called back over her shoulder, "And you had better get that eye seen to while you can still see out of it."

The next morning, she summoned the shepherds to the library. It seemed the logical place for her to speak to them. It was grand enough to impress them without being so regal that it made them uncomfortable, and it would remind them that she, despite looking young, had plenty of experience. The books all around her would remind her to be very careful about what she said, because it had been someone in Acadia that had erected that magical barrier, and she suspected it was someone high up enough to be in the Queen's very Court. No one else would have the motivation to prevent a Champion from getting through. Particularly not after what she had learned.

She sat at one of the tables, a massive thing of light-colored wood. They lined up in front of her, like schoolchildren waiting to be told what to do next.

"You're getting your Champion," she said, cutting their inquiry short. "But I can't tell you who it is. There is something very peculiar going on in Acadia, and it is best for us to send the Champion across the Border in secret. So, other than reassuring your immediate friends and family, you are to tell no one that the Champion is on the way."

They nodded earnestly. She had not one iota of faith that they would be able to keep their mouths shut, but they wouldn't need to—because the Champion had already started for Acadia at dawn and, on a powerful horse, would certainly cross the Border long before the shepherds were halfway there. She *wanted* them to tell. Whoever was preventing the Champions from crossing should know that Glass Mountain was sending another, and get himself prepared to repel the invader. His eyes would be on the Border, and not inside Acadia, where the Champion would be waiting to attack the dragon when the next sacrifice came due.

She cut short their effusive thanks—but graciously—and sent them on their way, to be provisioned before they made the return journey.

Once the door was closed behind them, Alex came out of the shadows beside the cold fireplace where he had been lurking, and joined her.

"I didn't mean to usurp your authority," she began. He put a finger on her lips, hushing her.

"They petitioned you, not me," he pointed out. "And besides, you were the only one who could have found the one person here who *could* pass that barrier."

"True." She frowned. "Still, what I want to know is, who made it? There's mischief afoot there, and it's going to get worse before it gets better."

"We sent the best possible choice for the job. It's up to

our Champion, now," he pointed out. "You've done everything possible to pull things onto the Traditional Path *you* have chosen. You can't do anything more for the moment, so concentrate on your other problems."

"Argh. Don't remind me," she groaned. "I wish I could send a dragon to eat those homicidal little—" As an idea struck her, she stopped in mid-sentence.

"I know that look," Alex said, with mingled amusement and alarm. "I think, if you don't mind, my love, I'll go have a few practice rounds—"

"Go, and try not to get too bruised," she said absently, hunting for parchment and pen, and beginning to hum— because it had occurred to her that there were *plenty* of mothers' tales of terrible ends coming to naughty children, and mothers' tales were just as Traditionally valid and powerful as any other. All she had to do was go interview a nice cross-section of mothers and grandmothers. "This could take some time."

CHAPTER SIX

Cassiopeia closed the door of her chamber behind her, carefully and quietly, then whirled, picked up a vase and flung it against the wall. "*Damn* that girl!" she swore. "How can anyone be so ridiculously—" She groped for a word.

"Good?" Solon suggested mildly. "I did warn you. Though what I cannot fathom is how someone like you ever gave birth to someone like her."

"It's her father's blood," Cassiopeia said sourly, as one of her mute servants carefully picked up the shattered bits of the vase. There was a scuffed place on the mosaic of the walls, showing that this was not the first time an ornament had gone hurtling across the room, and it probably would not be the last. "He was just like that, only not nearly as intelligent."

"Too intelligent for her own good. First, I had to head Balan off on his investigation of the weather by deflecting him into looking into the past for similar spates of storms. Then, somehow, she has ears down in the marketplace, though I don't know how. She's noticed how often the daughters of those who speak out against the Queen's policies end up as sacrifices. She's said as much—thinking I wouldn't hear of it." He smiled. Cassiopeia knew he had ways of "hearing" things that little Andromeda couldn't imagine. "She may have ears in the marketplace, but I have ears everywhere."

The Queen started to grit her teeth, and stopped herself. "She thinks too much."

"And she is too dangerous to be allowed to live." Solon gave her a hard stare, but she was prepared to sacrifice a great deal more than her daughter to implement this plan.

"If there are murmurs in the marketplace that those who oppose the Queen lose their daughters to the dragon," she said smoothly, "I imagine those rumors will die when the Queen herself loses her only child to the beast. And you're right—not only is she too intelligent, she is also too tenacious and far, far too caught up in notions of honor. I had thought I could bring her around to a more acceptable mode of thought—" The Queen shook her head. With Andromeda dead, the Queen would have to find a new heir…well, she would worry about that when the time came.

Solon laughed mirthlessly. "And the rumors that the lottery is a sham will also die," he replied. "Which will leave the dragon itself as the only enemy here. Soon people will be demanding you take new measures to keep them safe."

"And they will be willing to give up just about anything

to have that safety." From the moment she had taken the throne as the sole ruler, the one thing she had wanted above all others was to have the means to disband the Concord, the monthly gathering of common folk and noble alike, that ratified her decrees. Nothing became law unless the Concord approved it, and the Concord had stood between her and her will far too many times over the years. It was due to meet again shortly. Unless she did something drastic, the questions that Andromeda was posing would echo between the benches. But if Andromeda went to feed the dragon before the next meeting—

I will be a grief-stricken mother, and there is nothing that they won't give me. By the time they realize they gave me too much, it will be too late.

"How tragic for poor Andromeda," she said, practicing a sad, brave little smile on Solon. "To have all of her promise and potential just cut off like that, in the bloom of her youth."

Solon bowed. "I will see to it, Majesty."

It was lottery day.

Andie stood beside the Queen's throne, overlooking the Forum of the Concord, which was where the lottery took place. Between the benches for the Members, and the galleries for observers, there was plenty of room for anyone who wanted to be here. Most people did; she supposed it was easier to be here and hear the bad news at once, than be waiting tensely at home, never knowing if the next set of footsteps was that of the priest come to take your daughter away.

Once again, she wore black. The Queen, however, did not. She wore gray with a hint of rose-pink in it. Not exactly frivolous, but not full mourning, either. There was an interminable wait while the old man from the Concord who was next to choose the sacrifice hobbled to the cauldron that held all the names of the women and girls that met the criteria—or at least, all of them that could be identified. There were probably some hiding in the mountains, and maybe more disguising themselves as boys. But there were more than enough to fill the cauldron, and there was always the pressure of the neighbors whose girls' names *were* in the lottery, to keep too many young women from escaping their duty.

Finally the old man stood beside the huge iron vessel, bit his lip and plunged his arm in as deep as it would go. The crowd went as still as only a group of people, all holding their breath, could be. Then he held out the bit of paper to the presiding priest without glancing at it himself. He looked as if he was going to weep, as if he felt personally responsible for what was about to befall some poor, unknown—

"The name—" the priest's voice sounded unnaturally shrill "—the name is—Princess Andromeda, daughter of Queen Cassiopeia."

For one, incredibly strange moment, Andie literally could not understand what he had said. *Princess Andromeda—who is that?*

And then every head in the Forum turned toward her and every eye in the place was fixed on her, and her mind snapped into understanding, and from understanding, into horror.

And she did something she had never done in her life. She fainted.

"Are you sure you won't have the potion, Princess?" the priest pleaded. Andie shook her head, beginning to be angry with him. As a concession to her rank and birth, she had been allowed to stay in her own rooms in the Palace, but she had had to send most of her attendants away because they just wouldn't stop weeping and falling into hysterics.

"I am sure," she said, with the peculiar cold calm that had settled over her once she had been revived. "And I would appreciate it if you would please go away."

The importunate priest finally did take himself off; she heard the *click* of the lock as he left. As if that would stop her if she intended to run away...

That left her alone with Iris, who was as white as snow on the mountains, but looked just as determined as Andie felt. "You aren't going through with this, are you?" the handmaiden asked.

"I am, but not the way they think." Of that much, she was determined. "Iris, I am *not* going to wait tamely for that thing to eat me up. If there's a way I can kill it, or at least get away from it, you and I have to figure it out!"

Iris hesitated. "But—if you escape from it, won't it be angry? Won't it come after the town again, or even the Palace?"

She grimaced. "They won't know I got away, and if it's angry and starts attacking things again, I bet they'll find a way to get a Champion here quickly!"

A little more color crept into Iris's face. After all, she was the one who had brought Andie the rumor that no one was really making a great effort to find a Champion as long as it wasn't costing anyone more than the lives of a few worthless girls.

She was also the one who had brought Andie the rumor that it was the daughters of those who objected to one or another of the Queen's policies that were being selected a little too often for chance. And her eyes widened.

"You don't think—" she began, and swallowed. "You don't think that your own mother—"

Andie felt tears stinging her eyes and angrily brushed them away. "My own mother—no. But Adviser Solon would happily sell me into slavery to a pirate if he thought it would gain him a political or trade advantage," she said harshly. "Throwing me to the dragon to quell the rumors is exactly what he would do."

Iris was a smart girl. "It's a good thing I'm not a virgin," she murmured, as if to herself, then focused on Andie. "And if they can diddle the results to get *your* name, they can easily have been doing it all along."

Andie nodded. "So this whole thing has been a sham, and a fraud, and I am not going to feel one bit guilty about trying to bring it crashing down. But I need your help, and somehow, before dawn, we need to figure out as many ways as we can for me to do that."

"I'm going to get my aunt," Iris said instantly, then hesitated. "Do you trust Lady Thalia?"

"I'm going to have to," Andie said, after a moment of hesitation.

"That's very good, child, because otherwise I should have to force myself on you," said Lady Thalia from the shadows of the doorway. "For instance—do you know how to pick a lock? I do."

Andie gaped at her.

Thalia smiled mirthlessly. "Believe it or not, it is a skill that comes in handy for a Keeper of the Household. People are always losing keys, or locking themselves into places *with* the keys, and one grows tired of sending for the locksmith to do a relatively simple task one could do one's self. I am never without at least one set of lock-picks." She reached up into the severe knot of hair at the top of her head, and pulled out something, gazing at it meditatively. "Amazing, how they look so very much like hairpins. Especially when one has little decorative knobs crafted onto the ends."

Andie blinked. And dared, for the first time, to hope.

If she had not been so keyed up with fear, she would have been perishing to sleep. She had spent the entire night learning how to pick locks. Merrha had confirmed what she thought she had remembered; the pliant, drugged victims were tied to the stake, but the lively ones were locked in chains. So Iris had spent a goodly part of the early evening sharpening one edge of an ornate ring, so that she could use it to slice through rope. They tried it with her hands tied behind her, and she freed herself fairly quickly. Merrha had brought as much of the poison that the Guards used to kill rats in their barracks as she could lay her hands on, and Lady Thalia sewed it into the hem of the sacrificial victim's gown that the priest had brought along with the potion.

So at least, if it eats me, I might have some revenge....

Merrha had brought a long, slim dagger that Lady Thalia sewed into the back of Andie's chemise, down her spine. Recalling the size of the dragon, Andie tried not to think of how it would be like trying to kill someone with a needle, and instead concentrated on listening to what Merrha was telling her about the weak spots where a stab would do the most good. She'd love a sword, if only she knew how to use one. Then again, where would she hide it on her person?

But the big hope was this: the rest of the Six were out tonight, hiding real weapons among the rocks of the sacrificial valley. And by now, she knew every rock and landmark in that valley. If she could just get away, she'd have her hands on something useful in a very short period of time.

"But your real hope isn't to kill it," Merrha said, over and over. "Your real hope is to make it more trouble than it's worth for it to eat you. Look, I don't know dragons, but I know lions, and lions won't go after anything that gives them too much grief. If you can just hold it off long enough to make it irritated, it'll go away and find some better quarry. Which is what you want, anyway."

She noticed that no one had made any plans beyond that—

Maybe because none of them really expected her to survive this. They were distracting themselves with these plans, but in the back of their minds, they really didn't think any of them were going to work.

Well, *she* did. And she knew exactly what she was going to do. She was going to cut her hair, get hold of some boy's clothing, somehow, and make her way into the mountains. They always loaded the victims down with gold jewelry to appease the dragon's other appetite, and they'd probably deck her out with even more. She could hammer off bits of it to pay for what she needed.

I am going to survive this.

Finally, Merrha slipped away, out the window. And as dawn began to gray the sky, the expected knock came at the door. They all started. It was loud, and rang hollowly through the rooms. It sounded—final.

She had long since donned her gown and Lady Thalia had put her hair up with the lock-picks. At her own insistence, Iris had added a heavy belt of gold links, a matching necklace and two bracelets. As the procession of priests came in, she was once more offered the potion, and once more, she refused it.

The priest who seemed to be in charge noted the jewelry as he placed the flower-crown on her head, and seemed to approve of it, though he said nothing. Then, it was time.

Outside, the drums began.

Now it was her turn to make that long, lonely walk, flanked by priests on all sides—to step into the litter and take her place in the seat.

Her mother was not in the usual position for the victim's parents. In fact, her mother was not in the procession at all.

Well…if her mother was not aware of what Solon had done, she would probably be prostrate with grief. And no one would blame her.

The journey that always had seemed to take forever before, now went far too quickly. Her heart was beating so fast that she thought for certain those carrying the chair must hear it, even over the chanting of the priests. It all seemed horribly unreal, like a nightmare. Part of her was paralyzed with terror, numb—and yet, her mind was racing. It felt as if she were two different people in the same body—

And when they reached the valley, she might just as well have drunk the potion after all, she felt so helpless. Obediently, in a kind of fog, she let them assist her from the chair, up the path to the stake, and chain her hands to a ring at the top, above her head. She accepted the Last Rites, and watched in dazed and shaking horror as they all left her, walking out of the valley to the cadence of the muffled drums, and no one looked back.

And only then, as the last of them vanished, did she look up, to the crag above the valley.

Where, patient as death itself, the dragon still perched.

Waiting. But not for long. Only until it was sure they were alone.

The dragon fanned its wings wide against the dark gray sky, then pushed off from the cliff, spiraling down in a lazy fashion, its eyes fixed on her. It didn't seem in any great hurry to get down to claim its meal— *Well, of course not! It knows this is one meal that can't fight back or run away!*

When she jolted out of her paralysis, her hands began writhing in the shackles over her head, trying to get to the lock-picks in her hair, and only at that moment did she realize that although she had practiced picking the locks on the shackles in this position, she had never even considered that she might not be able to reach the picks them-selves. When she'd had her hands bound above her head, they'd been resting practically on the top of her head, not stretched far above it. She strained her fingers toward the ends fastened in her hairdo, but no matter what she tried, she couldn't even feel her hair, much less the picks fasten-ing it all up. She fought her panic, and felt herself losing, as the dragon drew nearer.

She stood on tiptoe, trying to bring the top of her head nearer her fingers. She scrabbled about with her feet for some support to raise her higher—and all the while, the dragon kept circling nearer—and lower—

And then it landed. It regarded her thoughtfully, its head to one side, and took a slow, deliberate step toward her.

And she couldn't help herself. She screamed in sheer, weak-kneed, hysterical terror.

The dragon snorted and backed up a pace. She screamed again, hopelessly, certain that it was going to flame her, and she began to thrash, all thought of trying to get to the lock-picks gone, and nothing in her but the fear and the mind-less need to *run*, get away, somehow hide from the horrible, horrible death that was approaching her.

And at that moment, as if this was a tale in a book—

Something clad in black armor leapt down out of the rocks above the dragon, landing on its back. A knight! An incredibly agile knight, because he managed to keep his balance as he stood on the dragon's shoulders, pulled a sword from a sheath at his back and swung for its neck. With a little more luck on the knight's part, and less on the dragon's, the contest would have been over then and there.

But the dragon, *really* startled now, reared and bucked like a horse and managed to toss the knight off before he could connect with that sword.

The knight landed in a controlled tumble, rolled, and came back up on his feet. Somehow without losing the blade. He faced the dragon, standing between the monster and Andie, sword in both hands. The dragon eyed him, snorting in alarm, but before it could make up its mind what it was going to do next, the knight charged.

Now, much though Andie wanted to watch the fighting, two things prevented her from doing so. The first was that within moments, as the knight continued to rush the dragon aggressively, the fight moved up the valley and out of sight, at least as far as Andie was concerned. And the second was that if she was going to watch the fight, she wanted to do so someplace other than chained to the sacrificial stake!

After a moment of contorting her body in every direction she could, she realized that there was just enough slack in the chains that she could get herself turned around to face the stake. If she could do that—

She gathered herself, took a deep breath, thrust herself sideways as hard as she could—and bit back a scream.

She felt like she'd wrenched her shoulders out of their sockets, and the thin dress hadn't protected her skin from the rough wood of the stake—it was on fire where she'd scraped it. And she was still only halfway around, one shoulder jammed into the stake, and forced up on the tips of her toes as the chain holding the manacles twisted—

Don'tstopdon'tstopdon'tSTOP! With a scream, she wrenched

herself all the way around, now sure she'd dislocated one or both shoulders, and landed with her cheek against the stake.

She rested for just a moment, panting, but the sounds of combat coming from up the valley reminded her that there was no telling when the dragon would win the battle and come back for her.

If. No, when. No, if. Never mind. Concentrate!

Still on tiptoes, she braced herself, gritted her teeth against the pain and wrapped her hands around the chains. Using the manacles, she pulled herself up off the ground as tears ran down her face. She wrapped both legs around the stake and hitched her way up it. Once her legs were holding most of her weight, it was easier.

She didn't have to go far—just enough so that she had the slack to get at the lock-picks in her hair. And once she had them, she could actually hitch herself up a little farther, until she could *see* the locks she was picking. It wasn't as if she hadn't climbed trees and poles like this in the not-so-distant past!

She lost one of the picks, but that was why she had several hidden in her hair. She tried very hard to ignore the sounds of battle as she worked; she concentrated only on the lock, and the "feel" of the pick on the inside. Right hand first—that was her dominant hand, and if she could get it free, she could get the left off in half the time.

Finally, with a reluctant *pop,* the lock yielded and the manacle fell open.

At that moment, the knight and dragon came ramping down the hillside toward her. The knight had lost his sword. She watched in awe as the knight dodged a blow from the dragon's fore-claw, rolled away, and came up with a boar spear in his hands. She blinked, wondering, for a moment, where *that* had come from.

Then she realized what it was—one of the weapons her own friends had seeded around the valley. And how had the knight known it was there? *He must have been here for hours. He must have watched them hiding every bit of it.*

So, not only skillful, but *smart*.

As the dragon made several little wing-assisted backward leaps and the two of them tumbled out of sight again, she returned to freeing herself.

Finally the second manacle opened. With a yell of her own, she slid down the stake, hauled her skirts up out of the way with both hands, and sprinted for the shelter of a pile of enormous boulders.

Just as knight and dragon came tumbling back…and the knight was definitely losing.

From the way he was tumbling, he had been swatted over the rocks, and he didn't look nearly as agile now; the parts of his armor that were plate—the helmet, shoulder-protection, and knee-, elbow- and ankle-guards—were dented and battered. And as he landed on the path, the dragon leapt over the rocks between them, did a half turn and swatted him into the air with its tail. He landed farther down the valley—and didn't move.

Her heart in her throat, Andie waited for the dragon to flame, to leap on the knight and tear him apart, or to spot her.

Instead, the dragon gave a snort, shook itself all over and

leapt into the air. With heavy wing-beats, it labored into the sky, got over the rim of the valley and vanished.

Andie ran for the knight, her own pain forgotten.

He was just starting to move as she reached him, and as she knelt down beside him and put out a hand to take off his helmet—

—he swatted it away.

"Ow!" she said indignantly, overbalancing and falling to one side. "You hit me!"

"Leave me alone," growled a high tenor voice from inside the helmet. "I didn't ask for your help."

If this was a Champion—he certainly was a rude piece of work! "I just wanted—" she began.

"I know what you wanted," the knight said rudely. "The Tradition is going to make you fall in love with me, because I rescued you. And the last thing I need is some lovesick girl trailing after me. So go away, leave me alone. You've been rescued. Now go home."

"Why? So they can tie me to the stake again?" she retorted, rubbing her sore shoulders. "I lost the lottery. If I go back, I'll still have lost the lottery." In that moment, the vague ideas she'd had before knowing she was going to live through this came together. "I'm coming with you. You rescued me, so you're responsible for me."

"No, you're not!" The objection had a bit of a yelp to it.

"Yes, I am," she replied. "You can't stop me."

"I won't feed you," he growled.

Whatever happened to all the chivalrous *Champions?* she wondered. "In case you hadn't noticed, I'm wearing a Princess's dower in gold," she countered. "I'll buy my own food."

"I have a horse. And I won't hold him back so you can keep up." This time he sounded smug, and it made her want to slap him.

She snorted. "In these mountains? A horse will have a hard time keeping up with *me*. You'd be better off buying a donkey, which is what I am going to do." *Then we'll see who can't keep up.* "And I can pay you, you know. Reward you. It's not as if you'd be taking me on for nothing."

"My job is only half done. I have to track down that dragon, and I have to kill it. I don't want your pay, I don't want your gratitude, I don't want you to fall in love with me and I don't want *you*. Now *go away*."

She sniffed, and had started to climb stiffly to her feet when she realized that it wasn't only her shoulders that had been scraped raw. She sat back down again and hiked up her dress. So he didn't want her? Fine. That meant he wouldn't be bothered by—

"What are you doing?" This time, it was a yelp.

"I have splinters in my thighs!" she snapped back, not looking at him but at what she was doing, picking them out and wincing every time she did. At least they were sharp slivers, and weren't leaving anything behind. "They hurt, and I'm not going another step till I get them out. Ow!"

"You could have had dragon-teeth in your rump. Forget the splinters and go away!"

She ignored him. There were fewer of the things than she had thought, it had just felt like more. To make sure, she ran her hands along the skin of her thighs, ignoring his outraged gurgles, and only then stood up again. She looked around, spotted the formation of rocks where Merrha had said she was going to hide some clothing and provisions, and clambered over the formations until she got to the place. Meanwhile, the knight was moving at last, very slowly, and wincing and grumbling a great deal.

She wondered if he had broken any bones, then wondered how he had *avoided* breaking every bone in his body. He must have flown for yards when the dragon hit him with its tail. *Why didn't it kill him? Why didn't it kill us both?*

Maybe it was a miracle. Though why she should deserve a miracle, and not one of the other girls, made no sense to her. In fact, it made her feel horribly guilty....

Merrha hadn't made any attempt to conceal anything— why should she? In the cache, as promised, were a cloak, an old canvas skirt to go over the flimsy dress and a pack. Inside the pack were a pair of her own old shoes (sturdy ones, good for hiking on rough ground), a knife, a belt-pouch for small things, a belt, a fire-striker, a water-skin, and some bread. And one of her favorite books. As she caressed the leather binding of the book, she had to fight to hold back the tears. Iris had put this together while she was learning to pick locks; Iris, at least, had believed she would live, or she never would have placed the book and the bread in there.

And she would probably never see her friend again.

The dress made a poor garment, but a reasonable chemise, once she got rid of the trailing over-sleeves. There would be no mistaking her for a peasant, but at least she wouldn't be so obviously a Princess once she got the skirt and cloak on. The sandals, studded with gold rivets and gems as they were, could be broken apart to sell or barter the bits; she shoved them, the rest of her jewelry and the discarded sleeves into the pack, slung the cloak over her shoulders and went looking for the knight.

She found him at a sketchy sort of camp, well off the trail and out of sight of where the dragon perched. He was just hauling himself into the saddle of a handsome black destrier, a muscular horse with a braided mane and tail, and big, feathery feet. To her mind, the beast looked like an elegant version of a plow horse, but then the Acadian Guards didn't have a cavalry or mounted knights, so she didn't have much to compare the destrier to. The knight groaned and rattled as he got himself in place. The helmet turned so that the eye-slits pointed in her direction.

"You might tell me which way the dragon went," he said.

She indicated, knowing he wouldn't be able to follow so vague a direction. "I might point out that you're going to need a guide."

"You're a guide." The words dripped contempt. "As if you could find your way out of Ethanos without help."

She narrowed her eyes and gritted her teeth. "I have studied every map ever drawn of Acadia." Which was the truth. "I have committed them all to memory." Stretching the truth a bit. "And I'm the best guide you're going to get." Marginally true, if what she suspected was the case. If it was…he was going to have a hard time finding *any* guide.

Without waiting to hear his answer, she stalked off in the general direction that the dragon had flown. But if her memory was correct, as they exited the valley she was heading in the specific direction of the same village that Merrha's family was from. They probably wouldn't get there until tomorrow morning, but she had bread, water and a cloak. She wouldn't starve or sleep too hard. And it might be possible to find other provisioning along the way.

The destrier stepped carefully along in her wake as the knight followed her up the rocky path deeper into the mountains. This was not the sort of trail that a horse cared for at the best of times, and it had been drizzling this morning, making it slippery. She took a grim satisfaction in getting so far ahead of her reluctant companion that she often had to pause for the horse to catch up.

This was goat country, goats being the only livestock you could successfully raise here among rocky, tall hills, tough grass, weather-beaten trees that were mostly acacias, weather-beaten bushes that were mostly gorse. It had neither the advantages of the coast, nor of the mountains, and it was very hard to find your way here. Things you thought were trails turned out to be goat-tracks that thinned away to nothing, then vanished altogether on the rocks. Afoot (though she badly wanted some ointment for her legs and the skin on her shoulders) she was able to scramble ahead, find out if they were on one of those dead-end tracks, and scramble back before the knight had gone too far along it. If the frequent backtracking made him doubt her boasted ability as a guide, he didn't say anything, and the contempt for her that oozed from him was more than enough to cover every possible defect in her character twice over.

She almost regretted attaching herself to him. The gray clouds were clearing off, the weather was rapidly improving, and she could have enjoyed hiking out here—slowly—without him. But she needed the protection he represented.

Short of being able to do something clever, or lucky—and she thought she had probably used up her store of good luck for the next decade—she would never be able to defend herself against an attacker. And at least she *knew* the knight was safe to be around.

Though, every time a little contemptuous sniff or an exaggerated sigh came out of that helmet, she regretted her decision.

They made their way into the mountains in silence right up until about noon, when the knight said, as reluctantly as if the words were being pulled from him with tongs, "If we see a stream, we should stop. My horse needs to be watered."

"All right," she replied. "There's a stream in the next valley." *And more than your horse needs tending to.*

Actually, since they had found their way to one of the regular trails that appeared on maps, she knew that there was a stream and a habitation in the next valley, but she wasn't going to tell *him* that. Two could play at the "surly" game.

Truth to tell, even though she didn't strictly need a rest, she wanted one. And more to the point, she wanted what she might be able to get at the manor-farm that she knew was there. Like ointment…

So when they edged their way down the steep slope to the lushly grass-covered banks of the stream, she waited just long enough to be sure that the knight really *was* going to dismount and stay for a bit, then followed the stream down to where she knew the farmhouse was. Or at least, where the map she remembered said there was a farmhouse.

Farmhouse was a little bit of a misnomer, because this was an estate, but the absentee-owner lived at the Court of Ethanos, and the place was run by a Steward who never saw the Court and wouldn't recognize her. He *might* recognize her as an escaped sacrifice, except that no sacrifice had ever escaped before. And she had a good story ready to explain why she had gold to barter—though she took the precaution of twisting off three links from the chain she had worn as the maximum she would bargain with, and hiding the rest. No point in making whoever she met greedy by showing too much gold. Each of those links was worth three gold thalers, and she now knew that much gold would buy a good farm hereabouts.

It was a big house, indeed; surrounded by a low stone wall, meant mostly to keep livestock out of the gardens, it was made of more mellow, old stone, with a fine red-tile roof. It looked big enough to support a staff of twenty, more or less. Plus the owner and his family, when they chose to visit. She slipped around to the back of the house, by the kitchen garden, and found the kitchen door. The good smells coming from the place nearly knocked her over, and her stomach growled, reminding her she hadn't had much appetite last night nor this morning.

But as she had hoped, lunch was over for the workers, the household servants and the Steward, and now the kitchen staff was just sitting down to enjoy their own meal when she tapped at the door frame.

There were six people sitting around the big wooden table in the kitchen, and all six heads swiveled to look at her. She tried not to stare at the food, but her stomach growled again.

"Don't need kitchen help, girl, if that's why you're here," the woman at the head of the table said. She was plump and red-faced, with a big floury apron tied over her skirt, her sleeves rolled up to the elbow and her hair bundled up under a cap. She looked stern, and there was a frown line between her brows, but the staff didn't look overly cowed and they were all well-fed. So as long as Andie trod carefully, this was probably someone she could work with.

"Don't need to hire on, mistress," she said, bobbing a curtsy. "Goin' home. Tarrant Three Pines village, up west in the mountains. Just need some provisions, mistress."

The cook's frown deepened. "Turned out, were you?" she began, but Andie shook her head, and let some of the tears she'd been holding back flow.

"Been serving House Tarrant in Ethanos. I was the five-year servant to the daughter of the house. They brought me up from there when the young milady came out of the nursery," she said, naming the family of last week's lottery loser and keeping her eyes cast down. "She lost the lottery." Watching through her lashes, she saw the disapproving expression on the cook's face fade, turning into embarrassment. A five-year servant was a girl who contracted to serve for five years in order to build up enough money for her own dower; often, a family from far away from the capital would hire a five-year girl out of one of their villages to be their daughter's handmaiden when she was in that in-between stage of "old enough to leave the nursery" but not "old enough to consider for marriage." It was reckoned that such girls were "safer," didn't have haughty airs, and were less susceptible to wheedling and bribery.

"So, they don't need me anymore. Paid me my five years with some of mistress's dower-jewels, so I'm off back home." Most people didn't keep a great deal of actual coin money around, and under the circumstance she had just described, that was a reasonable thing for a family to have done in order to pay five years' worth of wages at once. She fished in the pocket of her skirt and held out the three links of gold where the cook could see them. "I'm needing a few things...." she began. "I turned up with just the clothes on my back, and that's pretty much how I left them, except for my pay."

The cook smiled slightly.

Andie trudged back up the bank of the stream with a full stomach, and a very full pack with a rolled blanket tied atop it. In the pack was a real chemise (not new, of course, but clean), a wooden spoon, a small clay pot to cook in, a wooden pot of ointment and another of pine-sap liniment, a wedge of homemade soap, a wooden comb, a pot of soothing scented lotion, a wax-covered round of goat cheese, a second loaf of bread, some dried figs, a bag of dried peas and a little bag of salt. Strictly speaking, she did not *need* the soap, but it was one of the cook's little specialties, scented with rosemary, and it had smelled so good when she passed where it was sitting out to cure that she'd asked for a wedge of it, too. The cook had looked sharply at her, then at her hands, which, while not as fine as Cassiopeia's or any of the other ladies Andie had been with, were certainly not all that dissimilar to Iris's. A lady's maid had to keep her hands softer than those of other servants; she gave her mistress massages, tended her hair and skin and handled her fine clothes.

"Ha. Aye, you've been a lady's maid, right enough." That

must have clinched the story in the cook's mind, because the cook was a great deal more sympathetic after that. While some servants might run away from a bad master, a lady's maid was generally treated so well that at least half of them elected to remain after their five-year term, rather than going home with a dower, and turned into full household servants with yearly fees, two suits of clothing, bed and board, and a raise in pay every year.

But no one would want to keep the girl who only reminded them that the daughter of the house, rather than the servant, had lost the lottery. The cook had thrown in the little wooden pot of rosemary hand-salve as a gift. Andie thought, rather wryly, that she was going to need it.

Actually, there were a great many things she was going to need, but that could wait until they got to Merrha's village, Rocky Springs in the holding of House Kiros. If Merrha had thought there was *any* chance that Andie would survive the dragon, she would have known that was where Andie would go next.

In fact, if Merrha came to check after the dragon was gone, she would find the signs of fighting, the empty manacles, the pack gone. She would probably try to get a message out by heliograph.

Andie wouldn't dare stay at Kiros Rocky Springs—especially not if some of what she suspected turned out to be true—but there would be people warned she was coming and prepared to sell her what she needed and not talk about it afterward.

When she got back to where she had left the knight and his horse, she found the latter tethered and grazing, and the former with his helmet and some of the pieces of his armor finally off. Not the mail shirt or trews, but the bits of plate, which he was inspecting with a frown. The frown deepened when she entered the clearing.

"Damn," he said ungraciously. "I thought you'd run off."

Irked, she threw the packet of bread and cheese she'd gotten for his lunch at his head rather than in his lap as she had intended. Quick as a snake, he snatched it out of the air before it could hit him.

"You're welcome," she said sarcastically, before he could utter a word. "I told you I could fend for myself."

The frown became a full-fledged scowl. Which was rather sad, since underneath that sour expression, he wasn't bad looking, if you liked the androgynous sort—absolutely beardless, so he was probably no older than she was, with somewhat angular features, which was a bit unsettling to someone used to softer, rounder faces, but by no means was he ugly. He looked exotic, and he had a generous mouth that unfortunately was set in an ungenerous expression. His hair was reddish brown with a wave to it, and his eyes were green—which was also a little unsettling to someone used to brown eyes and black hair.

"Why didn't you fend yourself into a job, then?" he demanded. "Get yourself out of my life. I told you, I don't need you, and I don't want you!"

From the sudden sharp whiff of liniment that wafted to her when he matched an emphatic gesture to that statement, she suspected that he *did* need her, even if he didn't *want* her. He was bruised all over at the least, and at the worst, might have cracked bones. He hurt now, and in the morning he would be hurting worse, and he'd be stiff to go along with the pain.

Idiot.

Now that she saw him, and saw how young he must be, there was at least a partial explanation for his rudeness. He probably hadn't grown past the "girls are stupid and useless" stage. Or even if he had, he wasn't going to let one get in the way of "his" quest.

"And just where, exactly, am I supposed to go?" she demanded. "Don't you know who I *am?*"

"The Queen of all Acadia, I presume," he sneered.

"Close, you dolt," she retorted. "You don't think they bedeck every lottery loser in enough gold to buy a noble estate, do you? I'm *Princess Andromeda!* And if anyone ever figures out I wasn't eaten, knowing what I know, they will make certain I never get a chance to tell anyone about it! There is nowhere safe in this entire country for me! Or—well—" she amended, "almost nowhere safe. If I can get to the centaur settlements in the heart of the mountain forests, in the Wyrding Lands, I might be all right. But I'm going with you for now. I'm not stupid, and I can fend for myself, but I can't protect myself."

"And I have a job to do!" he shouted in exasperation. She noted absently that he was very lucky; his rather high voice clearly hadn't broken when he'd begun to mature, because it didn't crack when he yelled. "I have a dragon to track down and kill, and then I have to go back to Glass Mountain and make a report to my Chapter-Head!"

"Good!" she replied sharply. "Because I have plenty for you to report!"

So much for not speaking to him. Now that she had an opening, she wasn't going to let him get away without hearing everything she knew, or guessed. She told him all that had happened to her since she'd begun making those reports to Solon, filling the silence while he sullenly ate the food she had brought him. She told him what was in those reports while they continued to walk in the direction she had chosen for them. She told him all about her beginning suspicions and speculations, and the altogether-too-well-timed arrival of the dragon. She told him about the lottery, and her suspicion that it had been rigged to silence those who most opposed the Queen's current policies. By the time she was close to being done, it was late, the sun was going down, and the landscape had changed from goat country to forested mountains. She'd never been here; had only heard of the forests, and in the back of her mind, she was wishing she could stay for a while. To see trees that were so tall and so thick that they blocked out the sun, to hear birds she didn't even recognize—she wanted to explore this place. And she knew she didn't dare.

He didn't say a word until they made camp—and to his credit, he helped her gather firewood and he himself built and lit the fire. For a long time he only spoke in occasional monosyllables, until she finally ran out of things she wanted to tell him and he stopped responding at all.

By then, it was fully dark, the moon was up and the night sounds of birds, animals and insects that had always seemed so pleasant and soothing coming in through her open window were distinctly unnerving when coming from all around her. She had never spent a night in the open before, and the sounds that might have elicited a sleepy "Oh, I wonder what that is" were instead making her react with *"What was that?"* as she tried not to jump out of her skin.

He sat on one side of the fire, with his blankets neatly unfolded and his saddle and saddlebags arranged at one end of them. He was still in his armor, which was a bit unnerving. She sat on the other side, having made a pile of pine needles under her blanket to pad out its meager comfort. *Now what? You'd think he would see the wisdom of letting me come with him by now.*

"I suppose you must be the Princess," he said suddenly, making her startle. "What with those people in Acadian Guard uniforms hiding things in the rocks in that valley. Glad they did. I needed those weapons."

No, really, you don't have to thank us, she thought sarcastically.

"So?" she said, when he didn't add anything.

"So it doesn't change anything. Actually, it makes things worse, Traditionally speaking. If you're a Princess, you *have* to fall in love with the Champion who rescues you." He sounded so arrogant, and so sure of himself, that she was mightily tempted to slap him. "I told you, I've got no use for a female, and especially not a Princess. I'm a virgin knight—"

She started to giggle, and he glared at her. "That does *not* mean what you are thinking!" he spluttered.

"I know what it means, I'm not an ignoramus!" she countered. "It means you've just been knighted, probably just been made a Champion, too, and you're on your first Quest. Traditionally speaking, you will never be at your strongest, purest or most powerful unless you are working with a Godmother or someone equally powerful."

"Which is why the last thing I need is a moony female!" He was shouting again. "I just don't need to be distracted right now!"

"And what makes you think I'm a 'moony' female?" she demanded.

He just shook his head, threw the twig he'd been stripping the bark from into the fire, and lay down.

She stared at him in amazement. "You're not going to sleep like that—"

"It's more comfortable than what you're wearing," he said, closing his eyes. "Dwarven-forged and dwarven-enchanted with protections, *and* with comfort-magic put on it precisely so I *can* sleep in it. A Champion needs to be able to leap up from sleep into instant combat. Our Chapter-Head is Champion of and married to a Godmother. She takes care of us, she does."

"Which is how you know about The Tradition," she mused aloud. "Most people go their whole lives never even hearing of it."

He just grunted, and turned on his side to face the forest.

Idiot. Handsome idiot, but—

She suddenly recognized the tug of The Tradition in her last thought, and countered it fiercely. *And I do not need to have to housebreak an arrogant pup!*

To occupy herself, she filled her little clay cook-pot full of dried peas and water, and buried it in the hot ashes and coals. By morning—if the books she had read were correct—she would have something edible there. She thought about refusing to share it, then shook her head. That he was rude and insufferable didn't give her the right to be the same. *Champions come from all classes. He's probably just a peasant, and doesn't even realize how rude he's being. It's ignorance. He'll learn.*

But he wouldn't, if she didn't give him a good example.

With one eye warily on him to make sure he didn't roll back over and get offended, she pulled the chemise down off her shoulders and daubed the ointment on them, then did the same for her maltreated thighs. Then, with the discarded outer sleeves of the gown wadded up to form a marginally comfortable pillow, she rolled herself in blanket and cloak, and put her back to the fire—

Which was the last thing she remembered until dawn, when a crow yelling in her ear woke her.

CHAPTER SEVEN

The pea soup, or pea porridge, or whatever it was, turned out to be edible. Not what she would have called more than that, but it was hot and filling and (so her books had told her) cheap. It needed salt; fortunately, she had bartered for some. There was a variation with lentils, too, if she recalled correctly....

"Needs sage. And thyme. And basil," said the knight, who at least hadn't rejected her offering, nor made a rude remark about it. "Garlic wouldn't go amiss, either."

She squashed flat several of the sarcastic comments she wanted to make. "You can cook?" was all she said.

"Champions have to. Mostly, we're off in the wilderness alone, or with a squire, and generally we're the ones who have to teach the squires how to cook when they first come along with us. Unless they're professional squires," he added thoughtfully. "There are some who just don't want to become Champions—they prefer being the support for the Champions. You should see them—off on a Quest with a pack-mule, and you never have to think about anything, because whatever you want, you know they'll have it on that mule. So yes, I can cook."

She felt crestfallen. "I'm sorry, I didn't know to ask for herbs, I only remembered that you can make this pea porridge from a book I read, so all I bartered for was the bag of peas."

He raised his head and looked at her in blank astonishment. When he wasn't scowling, he had nice eyes.

"You mean, you've never cooked anything before?"

"Princesses don't, usually," she reminded him dryly. "I just tried the simplest thing I could remember, bar sticking meat on a spit over the fire. I can probably manage that, too."

"Huh. You're either extraordinarily lucky, or you have an extraordinary memory for what you've read." He shook his head. "All right. You've impressed me. You haven't whined, you haven't complained more than you've a right to, you've done your share, and you've tried things you've never done. If you'd burned it, would you have eaten it?"

She made a face. "No," she admitted.

"And you're honest...." But then the scowl came back. "But I still do *not* want you falling in love with me."

She flushed, and anger smoldered inside. "I know about The Tradition, too! And I don't intend to fall in love with you! If you were the last man on earth, I still wouldn't want to fall in love with you! Look—knight—"

"My name is George," he interrupted her.

"Right, George then—I had an idea when I was waking up." She had awakened with a lovely golden haze over her thoughts, out of dreams full of sinking into the knight's tender embrace, then had realized where the dreams and the euphoria had come from, and fiercely driven that moony feeling away. "I went over every possible thing I could do to make it hard for The Tradition to muck with us. I thought, 'I'll dress myself up like a boy and be his squire,' then I remembered three plays and at least as many minstrel-ballads that have a girl doing that to get *close* to her knight. Then I thought, 'We'll each swear true love to someone else!' then I realized that if it wasn't true, it would do nothing, and if it was, well, we might just as well ask for a forest spirit to come along with a handful of love-in-idleness or a love potion to slip into us, because there are ballads, tales, plays and an entire school of farce founded on that plot. But then I thought of the one thing we could do to thwart it." She smiled tightly in triumph. "We have to swear to be blood-siblings."

"Whaaat?" he spluttered, taken completely by surprise.

"If we swear to be blood-siblings, there is *nothing* in tale or song or anything else that The Tradition can get hold of to force us to fall in love," she pointed out. "The only time siblings fall in love with each other, Traditionally speaking, is when they don't know they are brother and sister. And in fact, devoted siblings rescue each other from peril all the time in tales. So?"

He reached up with one finger and scratched his head just above his ear. "It sounds reasonable. It's got the benefit of being logical."

"Good." She had been cleaning her knife in the fire, and now she took the sharp blade and sliced it shallowly across her palm. As the blood welled up, George did the same with his dagger, and they slapped their palms together.

"Blood is mingled. Sibs forever," she said, using the simplest version of the oath. With The Tradition, the simpler, the better. Simplicity made it strong and hard to unbind.

"Blood is mingled. Sibs forever," George agreed.

And both of them raised their heads at the same time, like horses scenting something odd, as there was a sensation of something silently popping, and the release of pressure they hadn't been aware of until it was gone.

They blinked at each other. "Was that what I think it was?" she asked, cautiously.

George shook his head. "Don't know. I'm not a magician, and I never had The Tradition trying to force a path on me before. I hope so, though. I—"

Whatever he was going to say was interrupted by a huge shadow passing overhead. They both froze. Andie felt her heart pounding, and clapped both hands over her chest in a vain attempt to muffle the sound of it. Fear washed over her, and she fought off dizziness.

But the dragon didn't seem to notice them. It just kept right on in the direction it had been heading, which was roughly the direction they were going. They watched until it passed out of sight, and gradually Andie's fear ebbed.

"Do you think it's going out to hunt, or—" The sight of the beast had made her mouth unbearably dry and her knees still felt weak.

"It's going in roughly the same direction it was yesterday. That's good enough for me," George stated. Then he glanced over at her. "You're kind of low on supplies, and you have gold. Why didn't you barter for more?"

"Because I didn't want to arouse suspicion," she sighed, rolling up her blanket. "But—" She paused. She had been intending to go to Merrha's village without telling him, but now that didn't seem fair. "One of my friends, the one that arranged for all those things to be hidden around the valley, will probably have figured out I got away. Her home village is half a day in our direction, and I'm sure she has told someone there that I'm coming. She could have sent a runner, or she could have paid for a heliograph. Either way, a message would get to her relatives long before we could. I can barter for a lot more there and know that no one is going to betray me. If you don't mind stopping."

He gave a one-shouldered shrug, then something that was almost a smile. "I'll tell you what to get when it comes to food. I only have enough for myself, and it's all journey-bread anyway. I have to admit I wouldn't mind cooking something a bit different, and—" he coughed "—I thought you'd slow me down, but now that I've seen this countryside, it's going to take me longer to hunt this beast down than I thought anyway, and you're something of a guide, I suppose. Can you exchange some of that gold for real money too?"

"Probably. Would that be safer?" Then she shook her head. "No, don't answer that, obviously it would be safer. And I'll get a donkey to ride, or a mule, so I really, truly won't slow you down."

He nodded. "All right. You're along until we find the dragon and I get rid of it. After that—well, we'll see."

* * *

Oh dear, Andie thought, looking down on the village in the valley below them. *I'm not sure I'm as prepared for all this wandering around in the wilderness as I thought I was.* From here, it was clear that Kiros Rocky Springs was nothing like Ethanos, and in her mind's eye, she had somehow pictured something a lot bigger. Oh, Merrha had said it was a tiny little place, but Andie hadn't visualized it correctly. It was, in fact, little more than a cluster of houses around a well. There was no marketplace, just a village square with the well in the middle, where (Merrha had mentioned now and again) a market was held once a week, and since it was empty, that day was not today.

How could anyone ever get word here that I was coming? she wondered, feeling her heart sink. All her confidence evaporated, and with it went any expectation that she would be able to get what she needed here.

She steeled herself against the disappointment, and straightened her back. No matter what, she was not going to give Sir George any excuse to be rid of her. She would buy what she could, and do without what she couldn't.

They made their way down the track; there was still a long way to go before they actually reached the village, and if Merrha had gotten word there, the sight of a weary maiden with a fully armored knight in foreign-looking gear was surely more than enough to tell them who she was.

They passed a couple of farms on their way down into the valley, and from each of them, Andie had spotted a child running off toward the cluster of houses in the distance. When she and the knight entered the village square she was nearly faint with relief, when they were intercepted by a matronly looking woman with gray hair and a strong family resemblance to both Merrha and Iris.

"Are you Merrha's friend out of Ethanos?" the woman asked, with a glance aside at her companion.

"Yes, and this is my *brother*, the errant knight Sir George," she replied, telling what was the truth, just not all of it. "As you said, my friend Merrha of Kiros Rocky Springs sent me here. I hope we can get supplies to continue our journey."

"We've been expecting you," the woman replied with a smile. "Please, follow me."

A thousand blessings on Merrha. A hundred thousand. I don't know how she did it—and I don't care.

After only a day and a half outside of the Palace, Andie was woefully aware of just how unprepared she was to *be* outside. A few weeks ago, if you had asked her if she could go off on a journey like this one, she would have confidently said that she could. Now—well, now she knew very well that without George, she'd be absolutely helpless.

Their guide took them out of the village itself, to yet another farm on the farther side. George sat warily on his horse, keeping a sharp watch on both of them through the slits in his helmet. He still hadn't said anything, but at this point, she really didn't want him to. Let him think she was more in charge than she really was. But when they reached the farmhouse, he finally spoke.

"If I may water my horse—?"

For answer, the woman whistled sharply, and a curly-haired boy poked his head out of a cow-shed.

"Timon! Bring the knight some hay for his horse, then

come to the house and I'll give you something for him to eat," she said.

"You don't—" George began.

The woman laughed. "Oh, Knight, you'll be paying for it, rest assured! We won't fleece your sister, but she doesn't expect to get anything for free from us."

"Not a bit," Andie replied, feeling herself relax at last. This, she understood, and finally she was in her element. The wealth of Ethanos was built on trade. She was the daughter of a long line of merchant-kings. She would have felt uneasy about being given anything, especially from people as so far from wealthy as the folk of Kiros Rocky Springs were. But a good, sharp bargain—that was different.

It might not make George comfortable, but she was on her home ground, now. Before the elevation in her status, she had slipped out of the Palace and gone down to the marketplaces of Ethanos countless times. There, when she'd had money, she had learned to haggle just like any other child of the city. Now she settled down at the kitchen table in the immaculately clean farmhouse, with her list and a glass of coarse, resinous wine at one side, feeling more at ease than she had in days.

"Now, understand, I can't supply what you need by myself," the woman said, sitting down across from Andie. "I'll be acting as factor for my neighbors, and as we make bargains, anything I can't sell you, I will send one of my children after. They know only that my cousin Merrha has sent travelers from the city who need supplies and didn't want to be fleeced by sharpers in the big-city markets."

Andie nodded. "I don't have actual coins," she began.

In answer, the woman got up, went to the cupboard and brought out a tiny scale and a bag of barley grains. "It won't be the first time I've been factor for bargains with a mercenary or mustered-out Guard," she said simply. "We're the last big village before the mountains."

When she was done, and the bargain was concluded, they were well into the afternoon. Each time they concluded the bargaining for a particular piece of merchandise, and the links of chain were weighed out, the woman either had a child bring the article out and set it beside George and his horse, or she sent one with the gold off to the neighbor for whom she had acted as agent, and within a short time, the child would return with precisely what had been requested.

Last of all, when the matter of a mount for Andie had been settled, came a tiny little girl riding a mule. That was when George put his oar in.

"I'll look at this creature, if you don't mind," he said, and without waiting for permission, lifted the tot out of the simple riding-pad, and began a thorough inspection of the beast.

Andie was going to protest—then thought better of it. After all, what did she know about horses and mules? Merrha's cousin wouldn't cheat her, but what about the unknown neighbor? She watched as George looked in the mule's mouth, inspected its eyes and the insides of its long ears, then felt each of its legs, picking up the foot for a complete inspection of each hoof.

When he finished, he stood up, and patted the mule's

shoulder with one armored hand. "Older, but not elderly." That was directed at the woman, who nodded.

"A sturdy fellow, if you expect endurance rather than speed, and don't overload him. Good tempered—my youngest can handle him." The woman patted the mule herself, and it flicked an ear at her. "My neighbor breeds good donkeys and mules, but this is one he's kept, waiting for someone a little out of the ordinary to take him—someone we know will be kind to him. If I were going on a long journey, he's the mount I'd pick."

"You're sharp, but fair, Mother," said Andie, who was actually quite pleased with how things had come out. She still had most of the belt, all her rings and half the bracelets. They had everything George had asked her to get, plus more bedding, a large piece of canvas that could serve as a tent or a rain shelter, and she had more clothing and some medicines. And she had taken the opportunity to get the woman—whose name she still did not know, and did not want to know—to help her bandage her shoulders. The pain of the scrapes was already less, and she wasn't as concerned about infection anymore.

"Thank you," Andie said, once she was mounted up on the saddle-pad, nicely balanced between the shoulderbags holding some supplies in the front of the saddle and the panniers holding the bulk of their purchases behind. For someone who was not a rider, this was very comforting.

"You are very welcome," the woman replied. "We wish you all success in your Quest."

And with that reserved farewell, she withdrew into her

house. George gazed after her, his body language register-
ing puzzlement and surprise.

"Let's go—I'll explain," Andie urged. "We need to make
as much distance as we can before we camp for the night."

George shrugged and clucked to his horse. The mule followed, and as soon as they were out of sight of the farmhouse, and well on the trail leading upward out of the
valley, he held his horse back for a moment so that they
could ride side by side.

"I don't know her name, so that if we are questioned
about who sold us what, I can honestly say I don't know,"
she said without preamble. "I don't expect us to be caught,
but both that woman and I know it could happen, and anyone who helped us *knowing* that I was a lottery-maiden
could be severely punished. So if someone were to question her, she only knows she sold things on behalf of her
neighbors to a girl sent to her by her cousin in Ethanos, and
to the girl's brother George, who is a foreign knight. She
doesn't know the girl's name, and the girl was dressed like
an ordinary sort of person who could have been a shepherdess, or a farmer, or practically anything. She doesn't know
where I come from, whether it's Ethanos or outside of it.
And I don't know who she is. Do you see now?"

He nodded. "And I can see that, since you took the time
to bargain with them, they have no reason to consider us
fugitives."

She nodded somberly. "And from now on, we need to
avoid people as much as we can. Sooner or later, someone
will realize that you rescued me. And if you haven't slain
the dragon by then…"

"Even if I have, if what you are afraid of is true about the involvement of someone among the Queen's Council, at least one person in the Royal Household is going to be angry and want to be rid of you," George pointed out. "You won't be safe until you are out of Acadia."

There it was—bald and unadorned—the one fact she had avoided thinking about. She didn't want to leave Acadia. But she couldn't see any way around it. She would have to, if she wanted to live. Not even the centaurs could hide her forever.

But if she left Acadia, nothing would have changed, except that she alone would be safe. All the things she feared for her people would still be hanging over them.

That—that was not acceptable, either. But right now she was quite out of ideas.

This was true mountain country, now, and true wilderness. Valley meadows, leafy trees halfway up the slopes, then evergreens gradually taking over at the higher altitudes…their road wound its way up and down through tree-tunnels that only intermittently allowed them to see the sky.

It would have been a lovely journey under other circumstances. The weather remained fair, and remarkably pleasant, even if the night was going to be cold. She had only read about the wilderness, never experienced it for herself, and she found herself liking it a lot. Or—parts of it, anyway. The way it was never entirely silent, but simply *quiet*— birdsong and insect noises, the rustle of leaves, the distant sound of water. She had never before realized how noisy people were. And the forest was so beautiful. She wasn't at all used to deep forest; it was like being inside a living cathedral, with beams of light penetrating the tree-canopy and illuminating unexpected treasures, a moss-covered rock, a small cluster of flowers, a spray of ferns. These woods were *old,* too, the trees had trunks so big it would take three people to put their arms around them, and there was a scent to the place that somehow conveyed that centuries of leaves had fallen here and become earth.

Those were the good parts. The bad parts were that as tiring as walking had been, riding the mule all day used an entirely different set of muscles, and by mid-afternoon they hurt. A lot. She wasn't looking forward to a bed on the ground.

They camped that night among evergreens, and George showed her how to make use of her herbs for a lentil stew for breakfast. She already was thinking longingly of the food back in the Palace—though, she was ravenous enough to have eaten almost anything. But their fare was plain in the extreme and even though there was quite enough to keep her from feeling hungry, still, images of roast fowl, lamb, bowls of ripe fruit and yogurt, fresh bread and honeycomb, and sweet wine kept intruding between her and her plain flatbread and crumbled goat cheese and olives.

She didn't say anything about her cravings, though, because she was fairly sure George would take it as just another sign of weakness. So far as she was concerned, she was already showing enough of those as it was—because when she'd gotten down off the mule, she had discovered her legs hurt so bad she could hardly walk. The muscles on the inside of her thighs and calves were screaming by the time they had stopped for the night. She had *thought* she was in good physical shape, good enough to face just about anything....

Evidently not.

And when she'd gone off to the nearby stream for a wash, she had realized on splashing her face that the water was so cold it would make her very bones ache. There would be no bath; she'd be lucky if she didn't end up too cold to get warmed back up again just doing a quick wash. And at that moment, sitting beside the stream, she wept, pining for a hot bath to ease away the aches. A stupid thing to cry over—hadn't she escaped death? What was there to cry for?

But she was just so sore, so aching, so tired, and felt so alone—

George was no help. The occasional moments of friendliness he showed toward her always turned to indifference or even what seemed to be barely concealed hostility. It was no use turning to him for any kind of comfort.

At least she hadn't been anywhere that he could see her crying over wanting a bath, and the cold water had erased the traces of her tears. His raised brow as she hobbled around was bad enough. His earlier thaw had turned chilly again. Perhaps he was having second thoughts about having her along, doubting her ability to serve as any sort of a guide, questioning her usefulness.

Perhaps he still didn't trust her solution for keeping The Tradition from mucking up their lives.

Certainly he was watching her carefully for any sign that she was becoming a burden. And she knew, she just knew, that the moment he could point to anything and say "You are holding up my progress," he would find a way to be rid of her. He must be certain that as a princess she couldn't take care of herself, and that shortly she would be demanding things of him that were impossible. Like, say, a hot bath.

It was horrible, because she got an occasional glimpse of someone who could be a pleasant companion, and then it was as if he dropped the shutter over that part of himself, closing it off from her.

At least Merrha's cousin had been more solicitous. On learning that she wasn't much of a rider, she'd insisted that Andie buy a bottle of sharp-scented liniment. It was effective, at least, and her legs had healed enough that she didn't send herself into paroxysms of pain rubbing it into the places where she'd been pulling out splinters that first day. She took the opportunity when George went off into the woods to hike up her skirts and deal with the situation.

George lapsed back into his usual unnerving silence once he'd finished helping her with tomorrow's breakfast. It was something of a relief to crawl into her blankets and close her eyes. At least she didn't have to watch him staring into the fire with that faintly disapproving look on his face.

Of course, maybe that was her imagination at work. Maybe the scowl didn't have anything to do with her. Maybe, given how poorly he'd fared in combat with the dragon the first time, he was trying to figure out a way to kill it all by himself. Certainly she wouldn't be of much use there. Maybe the second thoughts he was having were about taking this Quest in the first place.

Or maybe not. Maybe he figured that her solution of declaring themselves brother and sister would only force them down another, equally noxious Traditional path, and he was trying to figure out what that would be.

Maybe he just doesn't like me.

He certainly was a prickly sort. She had gotten the impression from tales and histories that Champions were a good bit more amiable than Sir George. This fellow acted as if he was afraid to let anyone near him.

But what do I really know about Champions? Like Godmothers, there hadn't been one in Acadia in a very long time. It wasn't as if there was any real need for them. Nothing had ever happened that required something as potent as a Champion—until the dragon appeared....

She shrugged and pulled the blankets a little closer. *I have some suspicions about exactly why that dragon appeared when it did,* she thought, clenching her teeth. She wasn't going to share them with George just yet, though. *Maybe not ever.*

The tip of her nose began to grow cold, and with a sigh, she pulled a corner of the blanket over her head.

At least tonight she had enough blankets. Last night there hadn't been quite enough coverings; it hadn't been bad while she was falling asleep, but once she was unconscious, she'd moved about and bits of her had been sticking out in the cold all night. She must have half awakened six or eight times, with cold feet, or her neck and shoulder going stiff and cold, or the blanket slipping off her back. No fear of that tonight.

Of course, George didn't need much except a saddlebag and his cloak. Or so he said. *How he sleeps in that armor I will never know.* Maybe there really was magic on it to make it comfortable, but it didn't look like anything she would want to sleep in. And it must keep him pinned in one position all night long, since when she'd looked over at him, it hadn't seemed as if he had moved at all. Lying on his back, with the cloak draped over him and his hands crossed over his chest, he had looked like an effigy on a tomb.

She shuddered at that thought, and fleetingly wondered if the Champion might *not* be able to defeat the dragon. What then?

Ruthlessly she shoved the thoughts and image from her mind for now. She needed to make some plans, and the first would be based on the assumption that George would do what he had come to do.

I need to decide what I'm going to do next. Go with Sir George when he left Acadia, of course—that was the immediate future. She couldn't do much about what was going to happen when he actually caught up to the dragon, but until then, she really was helping him negotiate the countryside, even if he wouldn't admit it, not even to himself. Without her along, the country people would be less friendly, and though she might not know where the beast's lair was, she did know the roads of Acadia and what was in the kind of countryside they were passing through. But once he killed the dragon, she would become exactly the useless burden he thought her. When that happened, she would have to have a plan, a reason for him to take her along.

I could tell him I need to talk to the Chapter-Head. It wouldn't be a lie, either; she did need to speak directly to *someone* about her suspicions. Surely the Godmothers and the Wizards should look into the situation, at least. Even if they didn't interfere directly, they might find a young hero with the right Traditional background who could go to Acadia and set things right. Or they could tell her that her fears were groundless, and she could go home again.

But what if he doesn't survive? Again, the unpleasant thought intruded. And she finally admitted to herself that was a situation she probably ought to plan for. If he couldn't kill the dragon—

If he's hurt, I will need to find someone to take care of him; I am not a physician nor a Healer. If he's dead…someone will need to be told—his Chapter-Head, at least. And in either case, I am going to need to find a new Champion for Acadia. If there had been anyone capable of taking the dragon in Acadia, it would have been dealt with months ago; The Tradition would have seen to that.

That would mean getting out of Acadia on her own. Well, she could do that a lot faster, now that she had a mule. Once outside the borders, she supposed, it should be possible to find her way to the Chapter-House that Sir George belonged to—Glass Mountain. Surely one could ask to be directed to these things. It stood to reason that if a band of Acadian farmers and shepherds could find the place, she ought to be able to.

It isn't as if Champions are trying to hide themselves, she reminded herself. What would be the point of that? They were *supposed* to be accessible. How could you find them to get them to handle a monster or lead an uprising against a cruel tyrant if you couldn't get anyone to tell you where they were?

No, it stood to reason that people knew where the Champions' Chapter-Houses were. And if George was defeated, she would just have to go and bring back an older and more experienced Champion.

Not to mention more pleasant. Those were her last thoughts as she finally drifted off to sleep with the sounds of the night around her.

George was just as silent in the morning, though he did at least have a couple of pleasant words to say about the lentil porridge left cooking in the coals overnight. And at least he helped her with her mule's saddle and harness, utterly foreign objects to her that she had fumbled off the poor beast anyhow last night. The trouble was, he was the most difficult person to read. If eyes were the windows to the soul, his had the shutters closed and barred where she was concerned.

The one thing that *was* clear, however, was that this morning he was uncertain about something. Finally, when they had been riding for half the morning, as he grew visibly more restless, he came out with it.

"I have a concern," he said. "I thought when I took on this Quest on, I would easily find the dragon's den. I *thought* it would be near where the girls were being sacrificed. I mean, that only makes sense, doesn't it?"

She nodded vaguely. A lifetime of reading had not given her much insight into picking the proper site for maiden sacrifice.

"When I realized the dragon *didn't* den anywhere nearby, then I thought I would be able to just ask people where to find it," he continued, sounding aggrieved. "But I hadn't counted on all this—this—this wilderness!" The last words came out fraught with frustration. "Where are the villages? Where are the people?"

"Um—" she said hesitantly. "For one thing, this is very poor farming country. The soil is thin, and it doesn't support a lot of people. For another, they're there. At least, they're supposed to be there. They just probably won't let you see them. Not the inhabitants, and not their villages."

Now he turned to scowl at her, and she hastened to add, "Because they aren't human."

She had been a little afraid he wouldn't believe her, but to her relief, the scowl eased. "Elvenkind? Fay?" he asked.

She shook her head. "Centaurs, Satyrs, Fauns, Nymphs mixed about half and half with humans. Those are the friendly ones, that live in small villages with humans. There's others. Harpies and Sphinxes. Minotaurs. The Cyclopses. No one ever sees those, or at least, when they do, the people who encounter them generally don't survive. But there aren't a lot of the bad ones, and they know better than to let themselves be seen, because there would be hunts for them again. They were nearly wiped out in the Wyrding Wars, and they don't want to take that chance again."

Now he looked intrigued. "But why won't we see them? The friendly ones, I mean."

She shrugged. "Just because they're comfortable with *certain* humans doesn't mean they've lost their suspicions about *most* humans. The Wyrding Wars didn't end all that long ago, and the hunters weren't always very careful about what they killed. My grandfather's time, I think, was the last of the Wars. The Wyrding Others don't forget things like that quickly."

They might show themselves to a single young woman alone, but they aren't going to show themselves to a foreign knight, and doubly not a dragon-hunter, she added to herself. Because the dragon, after all, was a creature that had more in common with the Wyrding Others than one might think.

"Anyway, we signed a peace, and part of that peace was that some of Acadia was to be given over to the Wyrding Others and those humans who chose to be with them. This is it." It was her turn to indicate the land around them with a sweep of her arm. "They're shepherds for the most part, rather than farmers, so this land suits them."

He sighed. "Then I don't know how—" He paused.

Because his horse had stopped, and it was staring at something in the middle of the road.

The something looked rather like an odd-shaped plate; it stood out in stark contrast to the path, because it was dark and quite shiny. It seemed to be translucent, and the same general color as a dark smoky-quartz crystal.

George dismounted and walked over to stand above it, looking down at it. He didn't move to pick it up, which she thought was odd.

"What is that?" she asked.

"A dragon-scale," he replied. "And the question is, what is it doing here, now, at this moment?"

She licked her lips. "The Tradition does tend to put wild coincidences in your path," she suggested.

He shook his head. "This is more than a coincidence."

He looked up at the leafy canopy overhead. "To lose a scale and have it land right here, I would have had to hit the beast hard enough to have damaged it, and I happen to know I did nothing of the sort. It would take a catapult to crack a scale the size of this one. Furthermore, the dragon would have had to be flying directly above this path to have it land here, and that's not a coincidence, that's a miracle."

"So?" she prompted.

"So this has to have been planted here for us to find." Now he turned and looked at her, as if expecting her to come up with some answers. "You're the guide—"

Oh dear. "The first thing that springs to mind," she said, stalling for time while she thought, "is that the Centaurs or the Nymphs are just as unhappy about the dragon being here as we are. Maybe it ate one of them—"

"It's more likely to have eaten a herd or flock. Did you say that these Centaurs are shepherds?" Now he knelt down beside the scale to examine it more closely. "I don't see any hoofprints or footprints nearby, but it could have been tossed here from farther away."

"It's the sort of clue one of them might give us." She felt a bit more cheerful at that thought. "To show us we're on the right road without having to show themselves."

"Or to distract us from the right road," he countered. "If they're working with the dragon, this could be to lead us away from the beast, or into a trap."

He stood up. She blinked at him, because that hadn't even occurred to her. He was right, of course, but from what she knew of most of the Wyrding Others, she wouldn't have thought they would be that duplicitous. "Are you always so suspicious?"

"My father taught me that a Champion can never let his guard down because The Tradition likes tragedy as much as happy endings," he replied. "He said there are two kinds of Champions—the ones who think ahead, and the ones who are dead."

She swallowed, but felt oddly comforted. At least Glass Mountain hadn't sent someone who was reckless and stupid!

"What this means to us is that someone wants us to go in this direction," he continued, looking up the path through the tunnel of ancient, gnarled trees. "Whoever it is could be a friend or a foe, and we can't know which until we end up wherever the trail is taking us. But we *are* going in the same direction that we saw the dragon flying, and I really don't care how I get to the dragon so long as I do so." He looked back at her.

The visor was up on his helm, but she still couldn't read whatever expression was on his face.

"A trap you are prepared for isn't a trap anymore. And the worst thing that can happen out of following a string of clues is that we are led away from the dragon."

"What will you do if that happens?" she asked quietly.

One corner of his mouth twitched. "Then I do what I should have done in the first place. I find a Witch or a Hedge-Wizard and get him or her to give me a charm that will show me where the dragon is." He shook his head. "No matter what, we don't lose much by following our unknown 'benefactor,' and we might gain a lot, even if he doesn't intend it that way. Hindsight, and all that, but I really did think that the dragon's lair would be where the sacrifices were, and that the beast would stand and fight. I guess that just proves I didn't think enough and I need to start following Father's advice better. I'm just glad this little wake-up came at a time when we were not in danger."

And with that altogether astonishing statement, he got back on his horse and started off again.

"Aren't you going to take the scale?" she called to him, as the mule eyed the scale and sidled around it.

He shook his head. "Magic can work for or against us," he pointed out. "Maybe the only reason for dropping that scale was to leave something we would be sure to pick up—and from that moment on, the dragon or its allies would have a way to track *us* or affect *us*. No, we'll leave it there. If nothing else, the one leaving the clues for us can go pick it up and leave it farther along the trail to show us where to go."

He certainly does think ahead, she reflected somberly. *None of that would have occurred to me.*

"Don't feel too badly if none of this occurred to you," he continued, in an uncanny echo of her thoughts. "You've been a sheltered Princess all your life—you've never been required to be this suspicious." He looked back over his shoulder and the corner of his mouth twitched again. "I've been trained by some of the best, Princess. And this is much more than just my job. It is, when all is said and done, my life."

And on that somber note, they rode on, under the deepening gloom of the trees.

* * *

That night when they camped, he surprised her by being very talkative indeed. But he wasn't simply chatting; he interrogated her thoroughly on all the Wyrding Others that she had ever heard or read of, their strengths and weaknesses, their general attitude toward humankind. More than pleased by this turn, since it meant he was treating her as something other than a burden or a Traditional trap, she expounded on the inhabitants of this quarter on as great a length as he asked for. At least now all her reading was paying off!

When he finally ran out of questions, he stared into the fire with a look of intense concentration on his face. Finally he looked up at her, raised an eyebrow and asked, "And how likely do you think is it that *any* of these creatures are allies of the dragon?"

"Honestly—not very," she replied. "There hasn't been a dragon in Acadia for—" she shook her head "—for so long that the writings I found were a matter of legend rather than record. The Wyrding Others have long memories, but not that long. A dragon wouldn't be seen as another ally, but as an interloper."

"Not even the bad ones?" he asked.

"Not even the bad ones. In fact, *especially* not the bad ones." She ticked off the reasons on her fingers. "The dragon will draw attention to the Wyrding Lands and might start the Wars again. At the very least it's brought in a Champion. The dragon is competition for the available food—I cannot even remotely imagine that a beast that large can subsist on a single girl once a week, it *has* to be eating more. The dragon is competition for available hiding places. And lastly, the bad Wyrding Others are not exactly cooperative by nature. The closest you can get to that is the Cyclopses, and they only cooperate with each other. The rest are as ready to fight other bad Others as they are to prey on the good ones or the humans."

He nodded.

"Now, I have been told that there are a few self-appointed spokespersons among the Wyrding Others who would take the tactic of trying to protect *anything* that might be called Wyrding, but the moment the dragon helped itself to someone's sheep, the rest would quickly turn their backs on that idea," she said, thinking of the earnest little man who came to Ethanos and stood in the marketplace for weeks, lecturing anyone who would listen on the topic of "The Wyrding Others Are Your Friends." He usually lost his audience right about the time he got to the Kyryxes, a nasty little blood-sucking insect the size of a bird. Most people might not know much about Wyrding Others, but everyone had either a friend or a relative who had encountered a swarm of Kyryxes, if they hadn't themselves. There wasn't much good to say about Kyryxes, except that they didn't discriminate in who or what they attacked, so they were as likely to fell a Chimera as a Centaur or a human.

More than one hero of the Wars had turned the tide by leading a swarm of the wretched creatures into the enemy's side of a battle.

"Hmm." He brooded into the fire some more. "I hadn't realized that there was that much competition for resources here. It seems so open and unclaimed."

"Acadia is not a wealthy land," she pointed out. "We don't have a lot of rich farmland. It takes a great deal of acreage and careful management to support sheep and goats, when the soil is as poor as this is. And—" she drew ruthlessly on Sakrete's book *On the Natural Historie of Greate Beastes* "—a large predator like a Chimera needs a huge territory. They have to hunt a great deal just to keep fed."

"That may be why the woods are so quiet," he said, as if he was thinking aloud. "The game is wary, and possibly over-hunted." He nodded with resolution. "Princess, I owe you an apology. I thought you were worthless, and I find instead you are a fund of knowledge. As long as we can keep The Tradition from mucking about with our lives, I believe you will be a valuable companion."

Somewhat to her discomfiture, she found herself blushing hotly. "I've always been one for learning things," she said awkwardly. "I'm just glad you're finding it useful."

"Does your learning extend to the natural world around us?" he asked. "Such as what things might be poisonous and what might be edible?"

"Poisonous—yes," she admitted, thinking about the frantic research she had done hoping to find some substance that would poison the dragon. "Edible, I am afraid not."

"Ah well. One cannot have everything," he said philosophically. "A Champion's education generally runs to just enough about the natural world to allow him to hunt and feed himself, and about the people and creatures he will meet to avoid offending anything or getting himself too deeply in trouble."

She laughed. "I suppose it wasn't likely you would have gotten into trouble with the Wyrding Others. The good ones would have avoided you if you had been alone, and if any of the bad ones had attacked you, they would have deserved what they got."

"Let us hope that they do not elect to do so," George said with a faint smile. "We have enough on our plate as it is."

CHAPTER EIGHT

"A Champion!" Queen Cassiopeia practically spat the word, and her eyes flashed with a dangerous show of temper. "I thought you had promised me that no Champion could pass our Border?" She glared at Solon from the lofty vantage of her throne. She was still in black, in mourning for her daughter, of course, swathed in filmy ebon veils that made her look mysterious and tragic.

In mourning for a daughter who had, most inconveniently, not died. She clutched the arms of her throne so hard her knuckles turned white.

"Will it help to say I have no idea how the Champion got into Acadia?" he asked, keeping his posture still, his expression aggrieved and puzzled. The Queen did not require a great deal to provoke her when she was in this state.

The Queen's glare was all the answer he needed. He

sighed, and altered his expression a trifle so that the puzzlement won out over aggravation.

"It is entirely possible that the Champion was here all along," he pointed out. "My informant did not get a particularly good look at him. It is well within the parameters of The Tradition to have produced an Acadian Champion from some unlikely candidate within a relatively short period of time. One tries to manipulate The Tradition, but once you set certain forces in motion, The Tradition has a way of seizing them for its own use. I pledge you, Your Majesty, I did my best to be sure there were no likely 'hero' candidates within our borders, but obviously I couldn't search every village and hamlet for impossibly brave boys with their fathers' swords hanging on the wall."

The Queen abandoned her throne, rising with a rustle of silk to pace the dais dramatically—Solon noted with a heavy sense of irony that she did not descend to his level for this purpose. He had to give her credit for style, however. The veils fluttered and billowed as she moved, and she managed the long train perfectly at the end of every turn. She never once, no matter how angry she became, made a single movement that was not graceful. How such beauty had produced a little nonentity like Andromeda was a mystery of nature.

She paused in her pacing to fling another question at him. "So your informant did not even see if this was an Acadian or not?"

My informant could not have told the difference between an Acadian shepherd boy with his father's rusty sword and a bucket on his head, and the Head of the Chapter of Glass

Mountain. He spread his hands wide, in a gesture of apology. "No, Majesty, I am afraid he did not. His vantage point was not the best, and obviously he would not have wanted to get too near the dragon when it moved down onto the valley floor. All he saw was that a warrior of some sort interposed himself between Andromeda and the dragon, fought it until it flew away, and released the Princess. The Princess herself accompanied him out of the valley. We can probably assume they are together. My informant is following them."

The Queen made another two sweeps of the dais, then again turned toward him with a dramatic swish of her train, and pointed a long finger at him. "They must not leave Acadia!"

"I do not believe that is their current intention, Majesty," he said soothingly. "The direction in which they went leads them deeper into Acadia, not to any of the roads leading to the Border. The Champion has more than a Traditional obligation to free the Princess, he has a Traditional mandate to slay the dragon, and whether he is a bumpkin-hero, an old Guardsman, or an actual Champion who somehow crossed the Border or was here before I closed it, he must fulfill that mandate. I expect that is where they are going, tracking the dragon to its lair."

Cassiopeia crossed her black-swathed arms over her chest and tapped her foot as she considered that. Her eyes narrowed, probably as the same solution occurred to her that he had already considered and dismissed. "I don't suppose you could arrange for them to be ambushed?"

He shrugged with every evidence of helplessness. "If I

knew where they were going. I don't. I don't even know where the dragon's lair *is* except that it is within the treaty lands granted to the Wyrding Others. I do have some…contacts among the Others who would take on the task, but first my informant has to come back to tell me where they are going. There are a great many trails through the Wyrding Lands, and unless the ambush is set up on the right one, it won't catch them."

That is the last time I use a fox. They're as bad as cats for twisting orders around to suit themselves. Trying to bind a fox or a cat to a task they don't want to do is like trying to catch an eel with your bare hands. He had not been able to obtain a vial of dragon's blood in order to allow him to speak to all animals, so he had had to expend a great deal of time and concentration finding a wild beast that would serve as his eyes and ears in that valley and bind it to his service as a Familiar. He had thought the fox was perfect—the right size to be inconspicuous, clever, agile and intelligent. But, alas, not obedient. Even the geas he put on it was not enough to make it obedient. And the geas itself depended on the fox of its own accord thinking that the dragon was a menace to the countryside.

"And these contacts of yours—what are the odds of them succeeding if you do find a place to set an ambush?" she asked. Then she raised her eyebrow. "The priority is to silence the Princess, of course. I don't like the cost of having to summon another dragon if the Champion kills this one, but if Andromeda escapes outside Acadia and tells her story, we will have a true disaster on our hands. She was already suspicious enough on her own, and any half-competent Godmother or Sorcerer would certainly put the facts together quickly once she lays them before her—or him."

You will have a disaster on your hands. By the time any-one figures out I was the one who summoned the dragon in the first place, I will be on a ship halfway to the Fortunate Islands. "You are quite correct, Majesty," he said aloud. "So long as Andromeda is silenced, the most important issue is taken care of." He groped for the Summoning charm just around his neck. Made of dragon scale (and how lucky he was to have found the scale from a living dragon!) it was warm to the touch. So the dragon that had lost it was still alive. "We might not in fact need to summon another dragon. The populace is sufficiently cowed, and sufficiently in sympathy with your sacrifice, that the murmurs of discontent have stilled. I believe that just on the basis of having been forced to give your own daughter to the dragon for the good of the Kingdom, the people's sympathies will remain with you no matter what else happens."

If that damn Champion kills the dragon, I don't know how I'm going to Summon another one…although a Chimera might do. Or if I could get that fox to steal me a Hydra's tooth. Or perhaps a sea-monster? There were a number of possibilities he had not yet explored, but on the whole, he wondered if it was worth his time looking into them. If the Champion managed to slay the dragon, unless the wretched man died in the attempt, there was still the possibility that Andromeda had already told him all she knew. Why shouldn't she? He had been her rescuer. Traditionally speaking, she should be head-over-heels in love with him now and pouring out her heart to him.

The Queen went back to pacing, and evidently came to the same rather grim conclusion. "Not if Andromeda tells him what she knows. She may be the most naive child in the Five Hundred Kingdoms, but we can't count on this Champion being that naive. Especially since we don't know anything about him. He could be another ignorant shepherd boy, but he could just as easily be a shrewd old warrior, suspicious and all too clever, especially if he was *not* once in the Acadian Guard but has actually been a mercenary instead. Those men know a trap a hundred leagues away, and can smell out anything that might threaten them. She must be silenced, and so must he!"

"First, she must be found," he reminded her. "And trust me, Majesty, I am working on that."

The trouble was that once they had gone into the Wyrding Lands, he was going to have the devil's own time tracing them. Much to his silent fury, he had discovered that by the time he knew of the Princess's escape, her room had been completely stripped of everything that had ever been owned by her or touched by her. Her miserable attendants had told him, with many protestations of sorrow, that they had felt it would ease the Queen's grief sooner if all reminders of her child were whisked away out of her sight. There was not so much as a hair of the Princess left to be used to find her. So far as her rooms went, she might never have existed. Nor could he find any hints of her outside her rooms. The old furniture that had once decked those rooms had been broken up, given away, or disassembled and stored with other pieces exactly like it. The reports that she had made were gone when he went to look in the archives for them. Or rather, the reports were still there, but they were scribes' copies. After the initial one that had so intrigued him, her own secretary had made the fair copies from her hasty ones, and where her originals had gone, only heaven knows.

The only things left that he knew with certainty that she had handled were books, but such ephemeral contact faded quickly and was confused with the traces of everyone else who had handled them. He had tried anyway, but it seemed that between the last time that Andromeda had touched the books and when they were put away they must have passed through the hands of twenty different people. She could not have been more effectively erased, magically speaking, if someone with knowledge of magic had gone about trying to obscure her presence.

So he could not trace her by her personal essence, and he did not dare try a broad magical sweep in the Wyrding Lands. Too many creatures of magic existed there, and no few of them would sense such a sweep and retaliate without hesitation for something they considered an intrusion.

He had made the fundamental mistake, once the fox had reported that the Princess was rescued, of telling it to follow her, lure her into the dragon's talons if possible and report to him. In that order. He hadn't thought then that he himself would be unable to track her, and he hadn't thought that the fox would take his orders so literally as to completely fail to report back at regular intervals. Now the blasted beast was somewhere out there, and while he might be able to track the fox, he would be able to see only what the fox saw, which probably would not include the Princess and her Champion.

"Majesty, I believe I have the situation on the way to a solution," he told the Queen mendaciously. "But I will need time and work. If I may withdraw?"

It was dangerous to make such a request at this moment. But she was clearly still in such a state of anger that it would do neither of them any good for him to remain. It was his good fortune that he had gauged his moment correctly; she was caught up in her own thoughts, and dismissed him with an angry wave of her hand. He did not ask twice, but backed out of the Throne Room with a bow. He pitied the next person to come under her hand. Not that she would do anything overt—no, she would just find the worst possible task to assign him, or her, something that had little or no chance of success. Then, when the poor fool failed, she would, with a falsely compassionate smile, administer a cruel punishment in such a way that the wretched victim would feel he or she deserved it, and worse.

She was a past mistress of the manipulation of just about everyone around her. Even, on occasion, himself. She was good enough at it that he could even see her doing it and know what was happening, and she still managed to manipulate him. There was no question of how she had become the ruling entity here in Acadia.

He retired to his own rooms, to ponder his options.

His own suite here in the Palace was second in comfort to none, not even the Queen's, and yet that comfort was not of the visible sort. He had selected with care the craftsmen who made his furnishings, which were all deceptively plain. He did not require inlay work, nor frescoes, nor hangings

of silk. But when you sat on one of his chairs and discovered yourself embraced by supple leather and plush
padding, when you reached for something on a nearby
table and understood that the table was at the perfect height
for a man precisely of his size, and above all, when you
slipped into the silk sheets on the bed, under the blankets
of lamb's wool, atop the feather bed stuffed with the finest
eiderdown, the level of hidden luxury here became clear to
you. What appeared to be plain leather and wood furniture,
a starkly simple bed, were anything but. He maintained this
illusion even in his clothing; what seemed to be simple
wool was the finest of lamb's wool, and what seemed to be
linen was, in fact, silk twill. Next to his skin he always wore
silk, though that was as much out of need as out of a love
of luxury. Silk was a magical insulator, and he had a certain need to be insulated from magic.

The foolish thought that he was superstitious, because
he was hung all over with what they thought were amulets.
He knew he was frequently the subject of jests for all of his
"trinkets," which ran the gamut of carved bits of bone and
amber to what appeared to be simple stones with water-
worn holes through them.

In fact, they were something far more potent. He had
found a way to store magical power and purpose in an object. And sometimes, to keep from inadvertently activating
one of his objects, he needed to be able to insulate himself
from it. Using the carved carnelian amulet that summoned
a Demon Lord, for instance, would be very bad. Aside from
giving the game away, it would waste the amulet that had
taken a year and a day to craft.

And the Demon Lord would not be particularly pleased about it, either.

One problem that most magicians had was that they were limited by their own power—or that which they could steal from others. Their own power was limited by their capacity to store it—power regenerated, but if your capacity had been filled, you did not generate any power over and above what you had. Solon had found a means to take an object (things made of metal or stone seemed the best), and store a spell and the power to make it work in that object. Releasing and targeting the power was a trivial exercise. So far as he was aware, he was the only Acadian magician to have discovered how to do this, though, of course, he could not speak for Mages outside of Acadia.

He honestly did not care what the Mages outside Acadia could and could not do. He had never had much interest in moving outside the bounds of his own Kingdom.

The simple fact was, Solon was the most powerful Magician in Acadia, not counting the Wyrding Folk, but Acadia was a very small Kingdom. That might have irritated some Magicians with wider ambition than Solon had, but Solon was a man who carefully weighed and measured every action before he took it.

And to his mind, this was of no matter. It was better to be the King Frog in a small pond than just another green jumper in a larger venue. No one would move to take Acadia away from him *because* it was so small. Solon was, he flattered himself to think, no fool. He had a fine, luxurious life here, he was the power behind the throne, and what more could he ask for? Untold riches? For what purpose?

There were only so many fine meals one could eat, grand vintages one could savor, luxurious beds one could sleep in, and so forth. Now, before he had begun his work with Cassiopeia, the Acadian ruling family had not been nearly this wealthy, but between the wealth from the ships he was wrecking with his weather magic, and the taxes he and Cassiopeia were extracting, there was enough gold and silver flowing into the Royal Exchequer to give the two of them an admirable style of living.

Cassiopeia was very well aware of the source of her wealth. That was why she was unlikely ever to attempt to punish him. However much she might rage at him—and she had, in the past, said many harmful things to his face—she would never actually do anything to harm him, not physically, and not in regard to his position at Court. She might withhold her favors from him for a time, but that approach hurt her more than it harmed him. No, this was a good situation, comfortable in every way, and stable. He had everything he could want, and avoided a great deal of unpleasantness that came to Magicians with broader ambitions. Who wanted heroes riding up to your door every other week looking to slay you, younger Mages challenging you, or thieves trying to break in to steal some powerful object , the loss of which, would, Traditionally, be your ultimate downfall? Oh no. This was much better. Eventually he would claim the throne, but not now, and not for some time.

Move slowly, that was the key. Be careful how you use magic, so that you don't attract the attention of greater Mages, or of The Tradition. Do things as indirectly as possible—using weather-magic to wreck ships, for instance. Even if he was caught at it, he could plausibly say he was trying to use it to weaken the storms, not make them more powerful.

It was a great pity none of this had prevented the Princess from becoming suspicious about what he had done.

Because calling the dragon had been a stroke of genius.

He'd had the dragon-scale for a while; he had known it had come from a living dragon when he had investigated what it was, but he hadn't *particularly* had a purpose for it until complaints started coming about the increasing taxes, as well as a few other minor matters that concerned him, personally. Now, there were always options in handling widespread complaints. One was to ignore them. Another was to make plausible excuses. But the third was to distract attention from the cause of the complaints and make people focus on other issues.

The best way to distract attention was to start a war; unfortunately, Acadia was ill-situated to survive such a war. With only a minimal army and without the ability to pay for mercenary troops, a war, regrettably, was out of the question. Regrettably, because a war could be used as an excuse for a great many things.

That was when it had occurred to him the next best distraction would be a—well, call it a "natural disaster." All he had to do would be to use that dragon scale to summon and control the behavior of the original dragon—child's play, since the behavior he would be dictating was *very* Traditional for a dragon—and prevent any Champion from coming to the rescue. In fact, to be on the safe side, rather

than merely specifying "Champions" he had worded the
spell as "Any Godmother, Wizard or Sorceress, or man capable of and inclined to meet the dragon in mortal combat
and defeat it" when setting the magic in place on the borders of Acadia. That way the Champions of Glass Mountain could not sneak one of their own inside by sending
someone technically only a *candidate*. And it would (or so
he had thought) eliminate any possibility of a wild card
coming in from outside.

I wonder if this is really an Acadian Champion? The more
he considered the situation, the more certain he was that
that was the answer. He cursed himself for not taking some
other way to eliminate the Princess. He had probably set
the whole thing in motion himself. It made perfect sense—
a Princess in peril, an unlikely hero, who probably *was*
some burly Acadian shepherd-boy with a bucket for a helm
and his father's old sword. How could he not have seen that
he was setting himself up for a Traditionally iconic rescue?

Well, he would have to be very careful how he handled
things from now on. Anything he did, he would have to
make certain he was not cueing up The Tradition for some
other inconvenient solution.

But first, he would have to find out where the Princess
and her rescuer were.

"Curse that fox," he muttered, and went to his workshop
to see what he could think of to do.

The Princess and her rescuer were staring at a dragon
scale in the middle of the road.

"It can't be the same one?" she asked doubtfully. "Can it?"

He got down off his horse and walked all around it, carefully not touching it, then drew his sword and, with the tip, turned it over. "It's the same," he said with some satisfaction. "There's a chip here, and a crack running from it that passes across these growth bars—" he used the sword-tip as a pointer "—that I made note of. So, we have a benefactor who is marking our way for us, or a villain who is leading us into a trap."

She blinked. "How can you be so calm about this?" she asked, finally.

"Is it going to make any difference either way if I'm prepared for both possibilities?" he countered. "No. If it is a benefactor who intends to lead us to the beast so that we can dispatch it, I'll be prepared for a cautious approach. If it is a trap, I will be prepared for ambush once we are into territory where so large a beast can ambush us." He looked around at the dense trees and foliage. "This is not the place. So for now we can simply be ready for more ordinary perils."

"As ordinary as they get in Wyrding Lands," she muttered. He must have heard it, though, because he smiled.

"Believe me, I have often been in places with a high population of creatures that weren't human. They're either evil, or they're not. If they're not, they either dislike or avoid humans, or like them. It's just a matter of watching for signs and being ready to act on what you learn." He mounted his horse and touched it with his heels. It moved off, Andromeda's mule following. "Really, this is just another aspect of learning to fight. You have to be prepared for every move that your adversary could make, and have a counter ready in advance for it. A fight is not like—like a dance. A dance follows a pattern. A fight creates a pattern that you can see only after it is over. In a fight, or in planning strategy in advance, it doesn't help to get agitated. You have to be calm enough to anticipate most moves, and you have to be trained enough to be able to make counters without having to think about them first."

That just made her dizzy to think about, and certainly didn't match what she had always *thought* warriors did. They just hit things, and tried not to get hit. Oh, there was training involved, of course, but it had all seemed quite random to her.

Then again, she had never actually watched training in progress. All of that was kept quite out of the way of a Princess, even one known to escape from her confinement from time to time.

Actually—she'd never seen a real fight until she saw the Champion fighting the dragon.

"How long does it take to learn to become a warrior?" she asked, thinking now how naive her own ideas about escaping from the dragon had been.

George laughed. "How long does it take to become a dancer?" he asked. "Or a musician? It takes as long as it takes. Some people are naturally suited to it and are competent in a matter of months. Others are not, and it can take them years. Champions tend to be in the first category, and in, say, the highest ten percent of that category. We are very good, naturally. Then we train intensively. Kings and Princes and Warlords have offered untold wealth for our services but—" He shrugged. "What would be the point of being a Champion if our services were for sale? There are plenty of mercenaries for that, many of them good."

Unspoken, the words *not as good as we are*, finished that sentence. And yet it didn't feel boastful. If felt more like a simple statement of fact.

Well, she had no way to judge, really. Except by reputation, which was that Champions were who you turned to when all was lost. Champions were the rescuers of the hopeless, the protectors of the innocent and, above all, the warriors no amount of money could buy.

She wondered what The Tradition would do to one that did sell his services to the highest bidder.

Probably something nasty.

"Do you factor The Tradition into your strategy?" she finally asked, tiring of looking at his back.

"It's one of the first things we learn to allow for or use," he replied without looking back. "There is a Fairy Godmother associated with our Chapter-House who is always happy to advise us on these matters. A good thing, too. Working with The Tradition behind you is a powerful factor for success and trying to work against it is going to be an uphill battle."

"And what if *both* you and your foe have The Tradition working for you?" she asked.

Now he turned and looked at her. "That," he said slowly, "is one of my worst nightmares."

Dinner tonight had the addition of some fresh meat, courtesy of George's bow. He had scouted ahead and discovered there was no good camping spot that they could reach by sunset, so they had stopped earlier than usual, and he had gone out hunting. In her turn, she had done her best to make their camp a little more comfortable than usual; she had gathered thick beds of bracken, had found a few things like watercress to add to their food, and had added stones to the fire that they could put at their feet later as a source of all-night heat.

There was a curious dreamlike sense to this journey. Yes, they had begun it in fear and some pain. Yes, eventually they would find the dragon, and then the real difficulties would start. But for right now, they rode through a mountainous landscape of stony peaks and heavily wooded valleys, one of which was full of life but seemed curiously uninhabited. "Curiously" because it was unusual in Acadia for neighbors to be unable to see the next farm or shepherds' cot over. The landscape itself did not vary a great deal. They followed the road, a mere trace, over rocky mountainsides, down into the cool of the wooded valleys and back out on the other side. If it were not that some distinctive landmarks arose, were passed and receded into the distance, Andie would have had the uneasy feeling that they were on a circular, never-ending path, doomed to wander the Wyrding Lands until they died and became sad, restless ghosts.

Or perhaps they were already dead and on that journey.

But reassuringly odd things—boulders, ancient trees— came and passed with enough variation to make her feel certain that they were not caught in a dreamscape.

There was a stream nearby, and she decided it was more than time for a bath. And to wash all the spare clothing she had. She'd have washed George's, too, except that he never got out of that armor.

She wondered what he looked like in ordinary clothing. She knew what he looked like in it, but with the helm off—beardless, androgynous, chiseled and altogether like some idealized statue of the Young Warrior.

As they settled down for the evening and shared out the rabbit he had killed, he waited until her mouth was full before saying in a quiet voice, "I believe I have seen our benefactor."

She paused, mouth open, rabbit leg poised just under her chin. She recovered quickly.

"Who?" she asked.

"More like a 'what'—it is a small, furred animal. I saw it running off with the dragon scale. My guess is that it is a fox."

A fox! Foxes often played roles in Traditional paths. She nodded. "The question would be, who is using it, or is it doing this on its own?" she whispered back.

"I don't know, but since I started watching for it, I have seen signs of it several times. The end of a tail, eyes in the bushes, a pair of ears—when you know to watch for it, you can catch it without a lot of difficulty."

Well, maybe *he* could. Spotting hidden foxes in the undergrowth was not the sort of thing a scholarly Princess had ever trained for.

"It is definitely watching us," George continued, "but I do not think it is overlooking us at the moment. It knows that once we camp for the night we aren't going to do anything interesting, so I expect it goes hunting then."

She nodded. "I suppose we should pretend we don't see it—"

"Exactly so. Because at some point we might want to try to catch it."

And that would hopefully signal the end of the Quest.

She woke with a start. They were not alone in the camp.

Somehow the interloper had managed to get close enough to stand between them, staring down at them. It was hard to read his expression—

It was always hard to read the expressions of non-humans. But his body language, so far as she could tell, showed a combination of tension and exhilaration.

And if she was going to put a name to the expression in his eyes, it would be "rapture."

"Oh!" he said with delight. "*Oh!* Two of you! I can't choose!"

And the male Unicorn continued to stare at them both as if he had found his own personal paradise.

Her mind was always slow to wake up in the morning, and having a male Unicorn standing beside her wasn't making things any easier. Part of her just wanted to stare back at him with the same rapturous delight that he was showing. Because—well, because he was a Unicorn, of course! Magical, unbelievably magical, Unicorns practically breathed magic. He was to a horse what a horse was to a pig. Four tiny cloven hooves shone like burnished silver, slender legs as graceful as an antelope's led to a slender body, a delicate neck with an arch like the stem of a lily-blossom and a head like the blossom itself, crowned with that glorious pearly horn. And the eyes—big golden-brown eyes you could fall into and never come out of—

It's a male Unicorn, Andie. Her brain prompted her with that information. *Male Unicorns are attracted to female virgins, female Unicorns are attracted to male virgins. And what did he just say? "Two of you, I can't choose—"*

Two of you...

She sat bolt upright. George was glaring at the Unicorn as if the Champion was seriously contemplating doing something un-Champion-like like drawing sword and lopping his head off.

"You're a girl!" Andie blurted.

George growled and pulled off her helmet. Yes, George was definitely a girl. Despite short hair and a firm jawline that a lot of young men would really have liked to own, now that she knew the truth, there was no doubt. The Champion was a young woman.

"I guess you don't have to worry about me falling in love with you now," Andie said faintly.

George—and *now* what was she going to call her companion?—transferred the glare she had been giving the Unicorn to Andie.

"I could have done without that particular remark." She glared at the Unicorn again. "You. Go. Now."

The Unicorn stared at her for a moment, then drooped all over with dejection. His head went down, his ears went flat, his whole body sagged and some of the light went out of his eyes. His lower lip quivered.

"You don't like me?" he said forlornly.

"Only in stew," George growled, and reached for her dagger.

The Unicorn gave a squeak of alarm and leapt up in the

air, somehow turning in midair and coming down on all four hooves, but facing the opposite direction. He tore out as if George had set his tail on fire. Andie stared wistfully after him.

"That wasn't very nice," she ventured.

George gave an exasperated sigh. "The wretched thing could destroy in a heartbeat everything that allows me to be here. The spell that has been keeping Champions out of your land is very specific that no *man* intending to slay the dragon can pass the borders. Fairy Godmother Elena unraveled that, and that's why I'm here. But if whoever set the spell finds out that's how the Chapter got a Champion across the spell-barrier, the Magician can correct it and I'll be forced out."

Andie kept looking wistfully at the spot in the woods where the Unicorn had vanished, and George made an exasperated sound. "I don't want to interrupt your reverie or anything, but we need to pack up our things and get out of here."

She suited her actions to her words, and after a moment of hesitation, Andie followed suit. The Champion was right.

"Look, I know he was pretty," the Champion continued, "but the blessed things are the worst nuisances in the world! They follow you around like lost puppies, keep wanting to put their heads in your lap, moon over you, sigh at you and just generally get in the way. You know, the whole Traditional force for 'if it's pretty, it must be stupid,' was never better exemplified than in a Unicorn. I can't think of anything more useless than a Unicorn, unless it's *two* Unicorns. And I won't get into how their mere presence tells the entire world that you're a virgin, which under some circumstances is something you might not want someone to know."

"I—suppose," she said reluctantly, and turned back to the Champion. "So if your name isn't George, which obviously it isn't—what is it, then?"

"You'd better remember to call me George in public," the young woman warned. "Absolutely you had better. Unless you want the dragon to continue to have free rein here."

Andie shrugged. "I'm not stupid," she pointed out, nettled. "I can remember. But your name obviously isn't George and I'm not going to call you that, all right? What is it? Georgette?"

The Champion winced. "Georgina," she said, and added hastily and crossly, "Call me Gina if you want. Just remember to—"

"Call you George in public, yes, I perfectly well understand that," Andie replied just as crossly. "Try to look on the bright side, will you? At least now you won't have to sleep in that armor."

But Gina barked a laugh. "Firstly, if the dragon decides to come after us in the middle of the night, it would be a good idea if I didn't have to scramble after the scattered bits and hope I can dodge him long enough to get it on. And secondly, I wasn't lying, it *is* more comfortable to sleep in this than it is to make up a bed in a pile of leaves." But she paused, and added reluctantly, "I will admit to you that I'll like to be able to get a bath and a change of clothing without hiding from you."

Andie shrugged. "If it's that comfortable, then by all means—"

"It is. I'm not the first Champion that's had to hide his or her identity by any stretch of the imagination," Gina replied, and looked around nervously. "And hopefully our little spy doesn't know enough about the differences between men and women to tell that I'm not a man."

"If it's a fox, I shouldn't think so," Andie said reluctantly. "A thing used to living in the wild isn't going to get enough close views of people to be able to do that. The biggest difference so far as it can tell is that you're in armor and have weapons and I don't. For all I know, it might not even recognize that *I* am female."

"I hope you're right."

The two of them made short work of the camp, and were back on the trail again in no more time than they usually took, Andie half on fire to ask questions, but at the same time afraid of being rebuffed. Gina was no more talkative than "George" had been on the long ride. But the questions were nearly eating her alive by the time they stopped for the night.

Once again, they set up camp early, but this time for a very different reason. "I want a scrub," Gina announced, in a tone that suggested that "want" was, perhaps, not nearly strong enough a term. "We might just as well take turns, if you think you can set a reasonable guard."

"I can at least warn you if something is coming," Andie said, irritated at feeling so helpless. Odd that when it had been "George" who was on guard, it had not seemed to matter that Andie was about as helpless as a child when it came to defending herself, but now that it was "Gina," she was chagrined and annoyed that all she knew about fighting and weaponry was "the pointy end goes in the enemy."

Gina regarded her thoughtfully. "You can't be everything, you know," she said abruptly. "No one can." And with that, she turned her attention to unpacking and setting up the campsite. "Let me scout out a place to bathe. I want you to get hobbles for the beasts and bring them along when I find a good spot."

"Why?" she asked curiously.

"Well, for one thing, I don't want them left alone at the camp," Gina replied. "And for another, their senses are better than yours, and if something approaches, they'll know before you do." She ran her hand through her hair and scowled. "And stay alert. If ever there was a Traditional disaster waiting to happen, it's this setup."

"What?" Andie heaved the packsaddle off the mule and stared at Gina.

Gina rolled her eyes. "Please, don't tell me you're that naive. Lady Warrior taking bath in open pond 'guarded' by a slip of a girl? That's the fodder for at least a hundred lecherous—" She stopped and stared at Andie's perplexed expression. "Good gods. You *are* that naive. Maybe I ought to call back that Unicorn."

"No need to call me back, maiden!" said a swooningly eager voice from behind both of them that made them jump. "I am already here, and so is my brother, my uncle and my second cousin twice removed."

Four stunningly beautiful Unicorns stepped out of the underbrush. Andie stared at them, entranced. If one had been gorgeous, four were overwhelming, the more so as they stepped daintily toward her and surrounded her. Unconsciously, she clasped her hands together and began to breathe heavily, Gina completely forgotten.

That is, however, until one of them glanced to the side and said, "Cousin? Why is the Warrior Maiden beating her forehead upon the tree?"

CHAPTER NINE

A bargain had been struck with the Unicorns. They could come along so long as they stayed out of sight on the trail and played guard at night or when Gina and Andie were taking baths. In return they were allowed to accompany them on the journey and to come into camp at night for petting and grooming and virgin-adoration.

"I'm not going to ask you to help us with the dragon," Gina said. "And once we are out of your herd's territory, you don't have to come with us any farther."

The first of them, predictably called "Florien," bobbed his horn. "Thank you, Warrior," he said. "It will be grief to leave you, but we are not much use against a dragon. Rapacious men, yes—dragons, no."

It was a good campsite. A cliff at their back had a series of ledges going down it that were rather like terraces. At the bottom was a stream that supplied a large pond that watered the valley immediately below the ledge they were camping on. With four Unicorns standing watch, even Gina let her guard down, though she didn't do so enough to let Andie have a bath at the same time.

As they switched places, Gina in a clean gambeson, vigorously toweling her hair dry, Andie asked Florien, "Why did you follow us? And why bring your friends?"

"Alas," Florien said mournfully, "these are the lands of the Satyrs. Virgins are exceedingly difficult to find."

Gina choked.

But even Gina conceded that the Unicorns were very welcome once the sun went down and the temperature plummeted. They arranged themselves on either side of the two bedrolls, providing not only something to lean against, which apparently put them in sheer bliss, but a source of gentle warmth.

With the Unicorns playing guard, Gina elected to wear only the body-pieces of her armor, keeping the helmet and gloves off. And for the first time since the beginning of this journey, Andie was able to look at a face across the fire. Gina was a girl Andie would have called "handsome," rather than pretty. Her features were strong and striking, though hardly unfeminine. Her short hair was cut in the "bowl" fashion favored by many Warriors who had to wear helmets; it was curly and rather unruly and a chestnut-red in color, a hue that Andie had only ever seen on one or two foreigners before. She had greenish eyes and a boyish figure, but was clearly quite strong.

Very clearly. After all, Andie had seen her fight.

Still, Andie had never heard of a female Champion before....

"Bet you never heard of a female Champion before," Gina said, giving her a shrewd glance from across the fire.

Andie started. "Can you read thoughts, too?" she gasped.

Gina smirked. "No, but the look on your face was fairly clear. There aren't many of us. Some Chapters simply won't accept them, and to be honest, there aren't a lot of female Warriors willing to put up with the hardships of a Champion's life. The ones that are fighters out of necessity know that they can get very good pay working for men who want their wives or daughters guarded by people who won't seduce them. The ones that are fighters out for some other reason are generally following a lover or acting out of loyalty to a liege. That leaves very, very few interested in becoming Champions." She stretched, and popped her neck in a way that made Andie wince. "We are something of a secret weapon. This is not the first time that someone has created an exclusionary spell that specifies 'no *man* will do such and such.' In fact, at this point, it just might be a Traditional path." She chuckled. "Though, another way to get around it is to have someone give up his real name and be dubbed 'Noman.' That works, too."

"But in this case they sent you?" Andie asked.

Gina nodded. "It's because young women were involved, Princess. Godmother Elena has strong feelings about young women being forced down the Traditional path of falling in love with their rescuers. Though I must admit, you were clever with that oath of blood-siblings. That was one I hadn't thought of, nor had she. When I get back to the

Chapter-House, I will have to make sure that goes into the record books for future reference."

"Please don't call me 'Princess,'" Andie said, as Gina speared a roasting mushroom with her knife, looked at it and took a bite. That was another area where the Unicorns were proving handy. It didn't matter if the mushrooms so abundant in this part of the forest were poisonous or not. A Unicorn's horn could purify every sort of poison. So Andie had gathered up as many as she could stuff into a sack and one of the four had dutifully touched each one with the tip of his horn before they were arranged around the fire for roasting. "I'm Andie. At least until this is over."

Gina nodded, mouth full. "These are really good," she said, after swallowing. "Never thought of this aspect of having a Unicorn along. I take back all the nasty things I said about you four."

"We don't mind, Warrior Maiden," said Florien, his eyes misting over with stupefied devotion. "You can say any-thing about us that you like."

Gina rolled her eyes but did not comment.

"How did you end up a knight?" Andie asked. "I mean, you *are* a knight, right? I thought all Champions were knights."

"I am and we are," Gina replied. "And it's not very com-plicated, really. My father was a Champion, out of the Chapter-House of Earendell. When he started feeling him-self going stiff in the knees he knew it was time to think about settling down. He really didn't want to retire to the Chapter-House—he wanted to raise a family. So he started looking for the right opportunity, trusting, oddly enough, that The Tradition would put something in his path. And sure enough, he got one of those 'save the Kingdom from the rapacious beast' jobs. It was a tiny little Kingdom and the reward was small enough that it didn't tempt any of the mercenary types. So they asked for a Champion, and he answered. It was an easy task as such things went and he was offered the reward of a title and a little bit of land and the hand of the Princess. It was exactly the situation he had been hoping for, exactly the right size Kingdom and reward. And—" she added with a smile "—exactly the right person to settle down with."

Something about that smile prompted her to respond, "But not the Princess."

Gina shook her head. "The Princess he'd been offered was only six. Her personal guard, however…that was another story. He's quite famous in our part of the world, though I doubt you'd have heard of him here. Sir Septimus of Galenstein."

Andie shook her head.

"Didn't think so," Gina said cheerfully. "Godmother Elena hadn't heard of him, either, so I doubt his fame would have spread this far. Anyway, the lady he settled down with, my mother, was the Princess Iselda's bodyguard, and Poppa found her a lot more to his liking than a six-year-old. The King was a bit put out about having to find a new Guard but—well that was just his bad luck. She wanted lots of children, he wanted lots of children and—" she laughed "—wouldn't you know that was just what they got. With Mama being something of a sword-bearer herself, he never saw much reason to keep his girls at their embroidery frames if that wasn't where they wanted to be. So we all got good educations in whatever we thought would be our life work."

Andie listened to this with envy, thinking how much easier her life would have been if her own parents had been like that....

"I'm the middle of fourteen children," Gina continued. "The only Champion, though. There are too many of us to inherit what's really a pretty small estate, and Poppa had some ideas about that, too. Whichever of us shows the most aptitude for running the duchy, the most love of the land and the most care for our liegemen and farmers, is going to get the lands and titles. So all of us chose things that would support us. I've got a couple of siblings in the clergy, a couple in the King's service, one that's a Wizard, two that are Sorceresses—let me tell you, that kind of startled my parents, they had no idea that there was magic in their blood, but the sibs in question are the seventh born, the ninth born and the thirteenth born, so that probably explains it."

Andie nodded.

"As it happens, I'm a good fighter." Gina shrugged. "And I like it. So did Christine, Michael, Gabriel and Raphael. So father trained and knighted all of us. On top of that, I really believe in the ideals of the Champions, so I went looking for a Chapter-House that fancied me once I was knighted."

"What an enlightened fellow your father is!" said an interested voice from above. "I'd like to meet him!"

Andie didn't even get a chance to blink before Gina was

instantly on her feet, sword at the ready, with one hand throwing something on the fire that made it flare high, revealing the cliff-face at their back.

A dragon perched above them on a ledge well out of reach. It was big—Andie had forgotten just how big dragons were. The ledge where it perched was easily of a size to support a large farmhouse and gardens and the dragon overflowed all of the edges.

The four Unicorns bleated, scrambled to their feet and bolted, leaving Gina facing the beast alone. Not that Andie blamed them. Against a creature that size, their horns would scarcely be of much use, and they would merely serve as appetizers.

It was hard to tell what color the dragon was in the shadows and firelight. Something dark, and there couldn't be that many dragons about, so it was probably "their" dragon. It craned its neck down along the rock, peering at them, eyes gleaming redly in the fire.

"My dear Sir Gina," it was saying. "Please put that away, I have no intention of—"

But Gina was already moving, jumping up the slope with the agility of a cricket, and halfway to him by the time he got the word *intention* out. It looked absurd, but there was no doubt that she was going to reach him in a moment.

He uttered a yelp and leapt up, flapping heavily off into the night sky. Which was equally absurd—he had the highest position and he would have no difficulty in picking her off the cliff, and yet he acted as if he was afraid of her.

"Come back here, fell beast!" Gina screamed after him, shaking her fist and waving her sword. "Coward! Scum!

Wretched thing of evil! Come back here and taste my steel!"

The dragon evidently had gotten more than enough of a "taste" of her steel the last time, and wanted no part of her. His shadow crossed the moon, wings flapping hard to gain him height and distance, and it was obvious from the speed he was going that he had no intention of coming back.

Gina stood on the ledge he had vacated, waving her fist furiously in the air.

It took her a long time to calm down enough to descend again, and it was quite clear that their Unicorns had abandoned them altogether. Not that Andie blamed them.

She strapped on the rest of her armor, made sure it was secure, and remained sitting on a rock staring into the fire, her expression furious, long after Andie crawled into her bedroll.

For her part, Andie was confused.

The dragon, this horrible creature, this rapacious beast that had devoured maiden after maiden, had sat above them on a ledge and listened to their conversation. And it wasn't as if what they were talking about was the strategy of how they were going to deal with the dragon, either. It could have plucked them right off the cliff wall. They had no defenses against it. The dragon had the advantage of height and stealth. If it hadn't spoken they would never have known it was there.

Gina's stony expression and rigid posture told Andie that she was furious. Andie, however, was thinking hard, and coming up with a great many things that made no sense— because the dragon had not attacked, had not attempted to defend itself, had, in fact, flown away with a yelp that would have been more appropriate coming from a dog than a dragon.

Gina didn't have any sort of mystical dragon-slaying sword, Andie was relatively certain of that. It had looked absolutely ordinary, and Andie was sure that Gina would have mentioned something if she *had* possessed something like that. After all, that would have been one more way to invoke The Tradition on their side. *Fear not, for I have in my hands, the mighty blade Wyrm-slayer, known throughout the Five Hundred Kingdoms!* That sort of thing turned up in tales all the time, and as versed in The Tradition as Gina was, she would have made sure to get something like that said aloud.

So why would the dragon flee like that?

And why, back when she herself had been rescued, had the dragon been defeated so easily? At the time, she had just been terrified out of her wits, sure they were both going to die, and ready to faint with relief when they didn't. Now, in retrospect—

Looking at those claws, Andie knew there was no way that Gina should have escaped without a puncture or gash. She had barely even had scratches. It hadn't bitten her once, not once—and teeth were one of its chief weapons. It hadn't flamed her, either, using the other chief weapon.

In retrospect, it almost appeared that Gina's injuries were accidental, the result of her doing something stupid, or of the dragon misjudging its own strength. That made absolutely no sense unless you posited that it hadn't wanted to fight in the first place, and…

She went to sleep with the puzzle churning over and over in her mind.

She woke up just as puzzled, and Gina was clearly just as furious. Their road took them upward today, far upward, above the green valley into the rocky cliffs and stony tops of the mountains. The road, clear though in poor repair, wound around and through crags like a snake writhing through rocks—a dust-covered snake. It was warm and very dusty up here.

Gina's back was all that Andie could see. The Champion had been silent all through breakfast and pack-up, and now her back looked as rigid and angry as her face had. Gina was taking this personally.

Andie felt duty-bound to at least try to posit some of her own theories, however. She coughed. "Uh, Gina?"

No answer.

"I was wondering—I mean, we could easily have been picked off last night—"

"Because I was stupid," Gina growled. "I let it get right on top of us. And, yes, it could have grabbed us at any point."

"But what if it didn't want to?" she asked. "And I suppose it must have used magic to sneak up on us, but all it did was talk."

"Use magic? A dragon *is* magic, in the same way a Unicorn is," Gina replied, each word sounding as if it had been bitten off. "But it was my—"

She paused, as if only now taking in the rest of Andie's words. "What do you mean, it didn't want to?"

Before Andie got a chance to answer, they had rounded the bend, and—

There was the dragon.

Tucked into the side of the mountain was an ancient fortification, now ruins, at least in part, but probably livable with work. There was a wall about it, and a gatehouse, which *was* thoroughly ruined, all of the same gray-brown stone. The dragon was sitting there, atop the gatehouse, looking down at them.

Part of Andie just stared, feeling like a mouse looking up at a ferret. But another part of her was taking all of it in—

First, the dragon. He wasn't a dull charcoal gray, as she had assumed. His scales were actually rather translucent, and reflected in part the colors of things that were near him. Where a half-squashed bush protruded from under his flank, for instance, there was a faint tinge of reflected olive-green to the scales. He had twin frills, one at the hinge of each jaw, that looked something like ears and fanned forward and back as he stared at them. His eyes were a brilliant ruby color, and his head was crowned by twin twisting horns.

But it was his posture that was more than a little startling. Because—because it didn't look to her as if he was poised for an attack. His head was held alertly up on his long neck, his fore-claws folded neatly one over the other, and he reclined, rather than crouched.

Then again, that was probably because he wasn't alone.

He had a bodyguard.

Between him and Gina, who had reflexively drawn her sword at the sight of him, stood a phalanx of young women, all of them armed in a motley assortment of weapons and armor, most of it looking at least as old as the building behind them, though in slightly better repair. Most of them held their weapons as if they had no idea what to do with them—which was probably the case. At least one of them had a bowl-helm on sideways.

But they all looked angry, and from what Andie could see, perfectly ready to defend the "monster" with their lives.

The one closest, who appeared to be in charge, also looked as if she had at least some idea of how a weapon should be held and armor donned. She brandished her spear with determination; she was kitted out in gear that mostly matched and mostly was strapped on correctly, she had a full helmet that even retained part of its old horse-hair crest, and had kilted her skirts up above her knees, the better to move.

"Go back where you came from and leave Adamant alone!" she shouted.

Something about that voice… The accent was cultured, the voice one she had heard before. But where?

And a moment later, it hit her. She would have recognized it sooner if she hadn't expected that the owner of the voice was dead months ago—one of the few maidens of wealthy or noble houses to be sent to feed the dragon. Andie didn't know her well, but she had seen the young woman enough to recognize her voice.

The voice of one who was supposed to have been dragon-food. Then again, wasn't she herself supposed to be dead?

"Kyria?" she gasped.

"Princess Andromeda?" Kyria gasped back. "What are *you* doing here?"

"I ought to be asking you the same question," Andie replied, as the other girls looked startled and caught off guard. The points of weapons began to droop, and some of them pulled off helms and helmets. Andie thought she could recognize, at least vaguely, some of the faces.

She did a rough head count, and came up with about the right number. These were the virgins that the dragon supposedly had carried off and devoured. All very much alive, looking healthy and well, and clearly ready to defend the monster that had supposedly devoured them.

Now it was Gina's turn to look stunned. The point of her sword dropped, and she stared at Kyria, dumbfounded.

"Ah," the dragon said, sounding pleased. "So you do know each other! I had hoped so, it does make things easier."

They might have continued standing there in the hot sun, dust-covered and bewildered, except that something else interrupted their tableau of shock. The sound of a minor scuffle behind Gina and Andie—the sound of talons on rock, cursing in a deep and echoing voice, and then a shriek. They turned to see a smaller, darker dragon behind them. This one was greenish in color; its horns and frill were not as ornate as the other's. Its eyes were red also—and did not look at all fierce or intimidating despite the color.

It was holding a fox by the scruff of the little beast's neck. "You seem to have brought a spy, ladies," the new dragon replied. "One wonders why—"

Gina sheathed her sword, pulled off her helm and looked the beast straight in the eyes. "It's not ours," she said slowly. "And I think we all need to talk."

"That," said the larger dragon, "is *exactly* what I have been trying to tell you!"

"I can't begin to tell you how long I've been trying to find someone who would listen to me," the big dragon said plaintively.

They had moved their discussion to a less-ruinous part of the fortification, a courtyard nicely shaded by the cliff behind it. The two dragons, with their captive, took up most of the center; the maidens distributed themselves around the periphery, claiming whatever seats they could find. As Andie and Gina took their places, Andie was looking around the courtyard and finding it inexpressibly sad. Why had this place been abandoned? It had been built well, before it had fallen into ruin. Horrible, really. Truly horrible. Had this once been a fortress guarding the road from the Wyrding Folk? That would at least account for its having been abandoned. The Wyrdings had no use for such things, but would not allow anyone else to occupy the place and threaten the road.

This was a courtyard not unlike some at the Palace, a colonnade surrounding an open space. But half the columns were broken, as was the roof they supported. No one had yet moved the rubble away. The maidens perched on mounts of broken stone or sections of columns.

The dragons were polite to a fault, making certain everyone had a seat, that the seats were comfortable, or at least as comfortable as stone got, that everyone could see, could hear.

It was surreal. These were two giant carnivores of a species known for eating humans, acting like a pair of maiden aunts with unexpected visitors.

When everyone had finally settled in place, the larger of the two dragons took control of the situation by starting with introductions. "Greetings, Champion, Princess," he said. The voice was deep and remarkably human-like for someone who didn't have lips. "I am Adamant, this is my brother Periapt, and I believe you know most of the ladies here."

Well, yes and no. Yes, because she had branded their names and faces in her memory at the time of their sacrifices. No, they knew her only as a distant shadow standing behind her mother at audiences. And she really didn't know *them*—not even Kyria.

The fox had been confined in a wooden crate; the smaller dragon, Periapt, had brought it, as well. And as soon as everyone settled, the courtyard filled with the buzz of low-voiced conversation. The dragons sat on their haunches, looking gravely at the gathering. Finally when the initial chatter died down, the smaller dragon made a sound like clearing his throat and got instant silence.

"We need to begin at the beginning," Periapt said. "And that is with my brother. And, we think, a lost scale."

Adamant nodded. Had they learned such gestures from humans, or was a nod just universal in nature? And despite the red glints visible, their eyes were—very human.

"We don't often lose scales," he said gravely. "And most of the time when it happens, the thing just vanishes and if anyone finds it, they generally don't know what it is. A lost scale loses its color pretty quickly, so I suppose that people who find one generally think it's some kind of odd stone. But as youngsters we are warned that if Magicians get their hands on a lost scale they can work some real mischief with it. And I suppose that's what must have happened. All I knew is that one day I suddenly found myself flying here to Acadia, completely against my will. I tried fighting the compulsion, but I couldn't. As soon as I would go to sleep, I'd start flying here. Finally I had to give in, and Periapt came with me."

"Couldn't let you go alone," the small dragon murmured, and the siblings exchanged an affectionate glance.

It astonished Andie how quickly she was learning their body language. She *knew* the glance was affectionate, and not annoyed or merely questioning.

"Once I got here, the compulsion changed, and I started ravaging the countryside. That, I managed to fight a little. I kept it from making me hurt humans or do very much real damage."

The nature of the dragons' faces made it difficult to read their expressions but Andie thought she heard a great deal of tension in the big one's voice. Adamant? Yes, that was the right name. Another word for "diamond."

Periapt looked away. Andie guessed that meant that Periapt was not at all sure that Adamant had been able to mitigate the damage nearly as much as Adamant thought he had. Remembering the dragon's attack near the Palace…well, it was true that it was only property damage but…

And probably a dragon would not consider the loss of a flock of sheep or a herd of cattle to be "too much damage"—but if you asked the shepherd or farmer in question you would get a very different answer.

Instead of adding to that, Periapt looked back to them. "You know that all dragons collect treasure of one sort or another, correct?" he asked, looking straight at Andie.

"That's The Tradition, of course," she replied. "I don't know how you could possibly escape that particular compulsion."

"Well, our family does that, too, of course," he said. "But our treasure is a bit different. We're librarians."

He held up his fore-claws and she saw that they had been blunted; looking closer, she saw that what was covering the talons were sheaths of some sort with blunt tips. Well, if they were librarians...they'd have to keep from damaging the books, wouldn't they?

"Librarians," she said aloud, then grinned as she got it. "Good gods. You are Bookwyrms, aren't you?"

Gina stared at her a moment, then groaned as she got the pun. The Tradition loved puns.

"Yes, we are," Periapt said proudly. "Very much so. Adamant is straight out of our maternal line of fighting dragons, but I'm a pure Bookwyrm from the tip of my snout to the tip of my tail. My library is cataloged and cross-cataloged and I have read every book in it at least once. I also collect all manner of information and I have created books of my own. Without the talon-sheath, a claw makes a fine pen, and I also have Bookwyrm magic to help me write human-size tomes."

"Don't get me wrong, I like books, I like to collect them and I like people to tell me things, but I don't read much myself," Adamant said, arching his neck and looking a little uncomfortable. "Besides, the pure Bookwyrms need someone to defend them, right? There are always nasty Magicians trying to steal things out of the hoard."

"The library," Periapt corrected him.

"Um, yes, the library." Dragons couldn't shrug, but Adamant certainly was giving the impression of that gesture. "Anyway, the point is that Peri knows how to look things up, where to look, and has a pretty good hoa—uh—*library* of his own. So he knew how to look up what was happening to me."

"I fairly quickly realized that someone in Acadia had decided that there was going to be a landscape-ravaging dragon wreaking havoc here, that he had probably gotten hold of one of Adam's scales and that it was only a matter of time before someone in the populace decided to start offering up virgins." Periapt nodded wisely. "We still don't know who, or for what purpose all of this is happening, but at least we knew what to predict in the short term, and I will get to the long term in a moment. The point is, that when the first virgin—"

"That's me—" said a sturdy-looking girl off to the left, raising her hand.

"—showed up tied to a stake, we knew what was going to happen and we worked very hard to keep him from— from doing anything socially unacceptable," Periapt finished.

"Like eat her."

Andie had to smother a chuckle at that. Adamant was clearly not long on tact. Periapt had tried to be diplomatic, and Adam had blundered right into what could have been an uncomfortable moment.

But the girl in question just laughed and the awkwardness passed.

For a moment Andie sobered. Because the way that Adam had so bluntly blurted "Like eat her," reminded her that these were *dragons* after all, and there were as many "bad" dragons as "good" dragons. And, yes, if the compulsion had been strong enough, they would have eaten the maidens. They would have felt dreadful afterward, but—

But they *were* dragons. This was what dragons sometimes did.

She had to chuckle a second time, because after so short a time with them, the two were now "Peri" and "Adam" in her mind, and they already showed distinct personalities.

"Well," Adam continued, "we pretty quickly figured out that as long as I carried off the sacrifice, I didn't have to do anything else to her. The thing was, the magic wouldn't let me let her go, at least not at first. So we had to bring her back here."

"Which was where things got—difficult," Peri added.

The girl laughed. "I'm Amaranth, Champion, Princess. And difficult isn't the half of it. I was hysterical."

"I wouldn't have called you hysterical," Peri said diplomatically, his tail twitching.

"I would," Adam said abruptly, and the rest laughed. "You were horrible. I never heard such screams. You carried on till you were hoarse *and* you gave us both headaches. Why human females have such shrill voices—" He shook his massive head. "Anyway, we had to lock her up in the tower with one of us curled around the base at all times."

He nodded at a near-windowless spire. From where she sat, Andie thought the tower looked impossible to get out of, since the only windows were mere slits near the top.

"After three days I finally believed them," Amaranth said, when she had stopped laughing. She looked as if she had been a hardworking girl in her previous life, though there were no real signs of rank on any of the girls. It was mostly that Amaranth had good muscles, and the air of someone who *did* things, rather than had things done for her. All of them were dressed pretty much alike in sensible short tunics over long dresses that could be belted up above the knees, the sort of thing that Andie favored when she wasn't in trews.

Well, hardly a surprise, that, given the flimsy gowns they'd been carried off wearing.

"When they kept feeding me and finally brought me something to wear besides the rags I was in, I finally believed them. It was the tunic that did it, actually. I mean, why dress something you're going to eat?"

"Sensible answer," Peri said, gaping in what Andie suspected was a draconic smile. "And after that, since each of the previous girls was here, alive, well and ready to verify our explanation, of course it became easier to get the victims to believe us."

"I'm Thalia," said a willowy girl with raven hair. "I was the third and it was about at that point that we all began to wonder if it was going to be safe for us to go back home."

"I did not think it would be," Peri said, as Adam and Amaranth nodded. "After all, some Magician had set all of this up for a purpose. If the maidens began returning unharmed, suddenly the ravaging dragon becomes less of a threat. I was very much afraid that whoever did this would then feel compelled to ensure that the maidens died…one way or another."

"Nothing easier," Thalia agreed. "Slow poison in our last meal."

"So they all decided to remain with us, with a few exceptions." Peri tilted his head to the side. "The religious woman, the child, and two girls. The religious woman took the child with her off into the mountains to become a hermit. Of the girls, neither was particularly happy with her family about being chosen as the sacrifice. Both asked to be taken across the Border, where I put them down near the town of their choice with enough valuables to be able to set themselves up in some fashion. We dragons have a knack for acquiring treasures, and when I go searching for lost books, I often find other gewgaws put in with them." He shrugged. "I'll admit, we're like magpies. If it's shiny and valuable, we're inclined to pick it up."

"If it's shiny and valuable, I'll *always* pick it up," Adam admitted cheerfully. "But since there's Bookwyrm blood in me, I don't mind giving it away afterward."

Peri nodded. "And meanwhile I thought it best to see if I could find some means of determining who was behind all of this. Once we knew that, we could move to deal with him—and everyone else could go home."

"When I was set up—I'm Myrtle—I knew by then that a Champion had been sent for," said a plump little brown-haired thing with melting brown eyes. "I told them as much, and then we knew we had to come up with something to deal with the Champion, as well."

"We actually thought for a while that this whole business was a plot for some person to come in and pretend he was the Champion, kill Adam and marry the Princess," Thalia put in.

"That would have been a very logical idea to gain control over Acadia." Peri nodded gravely, his tail twitching again.

"Well, we weren't having any. We actually trapped the whole fortress and waited for a Champion to appear, but when he didn't, Peri said he thought that there must be some other plan afoot." Amaranth made a face, and smoothed down her tunic with one hand.

"I'm Cleo. By the time I got here, it looked as if any Champion that appeared was going to be real, so we needed to deal with someone who was going to have his heart in the right place, just all the wrong information." This was a girl who could easily have been Andie's sibling in looks; the only difference was that she was a little more feminine, and Andie still wore her oculars. "And Adam and Peri are so kind-hearted—they got us basically anything we needed or wanted. It's really comfortable here. And since there are a lot of us, it's not lonely."

"Speak for yourself," muttered a dark-haired, sultry-eyed lass with an impressive figure. "I could stand a few men around here." The others laughed, in a way that seemed to indicate that this was a joke of long-standing among them.

"Believe me, Mel, if I could find a way to convince some

handsome young men with good muscles to move up here, I would," Peri replied, in a half-joking tone. "Especially stonemasons. But they keep trying to kill me when I approach them."

"Ha. You ought to take me with you, then, and let *me* do the approaching." Mel stood up and walked a few steps in a way that made Gina chuckle and Andie blush.

"I'll take that under advisement," Peri replied.

Thalia continued. "The thing is, we figured that if there were a couple dozen former sacrifices standing between him and Adam, that would be enough to give even the densest Champion pause. Plus, if we were armed and looked like we were serious about defending our friends, a Champion would have to fight through a mob of girls to get to the dragons. So Adam and Peri have been finding us armor and weapons, and we've been trying to train with them to at least look convincing for a little bit. And that's where we are. Although—" she looked curiously at Gina "—the one thing we didn't count on was a lady Champion."

"And that is where we all stand," said Peri. "So. Your story?"

CHAPTER TEN

"Well," Gina began. "You know that a Champion was sent for. And the nearest Chapter-House to Acadia is Glass Mountain, so that is where the people who were looking for a Champion came. As it happens, though, this Chapter-House is rather intimately associated with a Godmother. Godmother Elena to be precise."

Peri held up his head alertly. "Ah. Now I begin to see the start of an explanation. Godmother Elena is clever enough to have several Kingdoms in her care."

"Well, we sent out the Champion as requested," Gina continued. "And—he came back. He couldn't get across the Border. Just couldn't. No matter where he tried to cross, he found himself back on the other side. He was angry at first, but then started to get alarmed and came straight back to the Chapter-House. Godmother Elena herself looked into the situation, and sent her consort, a virgin knight and a squire to try to cross, just to see if there was some peculiar twist to The Tradition that was requiring a particular kind of Champion. But no one could, and Godmother Elena discovered that it wasn't a Traditional problem at all. Someone had spell-set the Border so that no man who had come to slay the dragon could cross it."

"No man," repeated Peri, then nodded. "Of course. No *man*. And you are no *man*."

Gina nodded. "Godmother says that this is probably a case of The Tradition working against the spell-caster. He probably intended to say 'no one,' and may even still think that he did. But when he set the spell he set it as 'no man'— and so here I am."

"And very happy we are to see you." Peri nodded at her. "And that leaves us with only one unanswered question. Why were you being followed by a fox?"

"It isn't the Godmother's doing," Gina assured him.

"Then it is someone else's. Foxes do not spy upon humans for the fun of it." Peri snapped his jaws together smartly. "So. I suggest that we ask the fox what precisely it is doing here."

Andie could only stare at him, perplexed. "Ask it how? Foxes don't speak—"

"Of course they do," Peri replied a little impatiently. "They speak Fox. The only difficulty is that humans don't understand Fox. Unless, of course, they've drunk dragon's blood."

"Drunk—" Andie couldn't help herself. Her first and unconsidered reaction was "Ew."

"Do you want to be able to interrogate this fox, or are you going to take our word for what he says?" Peri asked reasonably, his tail curling back and forth.

Much as Andie was revolted by the idea, she also, on consideration, didn't want to hear things at second hand....

"Well, I've downed worse things than a little blood," Gina said with a shrug. "And since we seem to have a ready source for it at hand—"

"I'm told it's rather nasty," Peri said apologetically.

"It cannot possibly be worse than my aunt's medicinal tea," Gina said, shuddering.

It was Periapt who, in the end, provided two small wine-glasses with a few drops in the bottom of a maroon liquid the consistency of thick soup. "It's the blood of a Book-wyrm," Peri said helpfully. "That makes it much more potent for Understanding than ordinary dragon's blood. That's why you only need a taste." Gina and Andie looked at each other with some misgiving, but at that point, Andie suspected, neither of them was going to back out. *She* certainly wasn't going to balk unless Gina did, and she suspected that Gina was not going to, because she felt she had to live up to being a Champion. So the two of them toasted one another and—

And it was *horrible*.

Andie had no idea what that medicinal tea tasted like, but at the moment, as the liquid choked her throat and made her tongue want to leap out of her mouth in disgust, she would happily have drunk a gallon of the stuff to get the taste of *this* out of her mouth.

One of the girls had brought pitchers of water flavored

with mint, and when she had managed to force the *wretched* stuff down her throat, Andie snatched up the pitcher and tried to wash the vile taste out.

"Rinse and spit," Peri suggested in a kindly tone. "I'm told that works."

It wasn't very ladylike, but at this moment, being ladylike was the furthest thing from her mind. And rinsing and spitting out the contaminated water repeatedly did seem to help. What helped even more was when another of the girls brought her a bunch of mint and a bunch of parsley to chew.

"Now what?" Andie asked.

"Now," said Adam cheerfully, "I make it quite clear to this little beast what he has to lose if he refuses to answer us." And with that, Adamant picked up the wooden crate, grabbed the beast by the tail and popped the fox into his mouth. But he didn't entirely close his mouth. The fox stared helplessly out through the "bars" of the dragon's bared fangs.

On the one hand it was comical. The dragon looked as if he were grinning. Actually, he probably was. This looked like a situation that perfectly suited Adam's sense of humor. On the other hand, the fox was terrified, and Andie was starting to feel sorry for it.

"You'd better answer our questions," Periapt said with perfect calm. "He can swallow at any time."

Every hair on the poor fox was standing straight out. "I was just sent to make sure the dragon got the Princess!" the fox said hysterically, his nose shoved between two of the teeth. "I mean, if the dragon doesn't get the Princess, he's going to ravage the countryside! Right? We can't have the dragon ravaging the countryside? Right?"

"Well, the dragon has the Princess," Periapt said reasonably. "Your orders were only that the dragon should 'have' the Princess, correct? You were not told to make sure the dragon *ate* the Princess? I want to be quite clear on how your orders were phrased."

"An ah ih im ou eh?" asked Adam, which Andie interpreted as "Can I spit him out yet?"

"Not quite," Peri said, and repeated his question to the fox. "Your orders were that the dragon should 'get' the Princess, and not 'eat' the Princess, correct?"

"Yes!" the fox yelped. "The word was *get!* Definitely! Positively! Not *eat!*"

Adamant spit out the fox. "Bleah," he said. "Next time I do something like that, wash the prisoner first. What were you rolling in?" he asked the fox.

"Just some dead leaves," the fox said absently, staring up at the dragons. But it didn't seem in a hurry to go anywhere. "Nobody told me about a Champion," he said doubtfully. "I thought it was just some random would-be hero. Not a Champion. I can see you are a real Champion, female human—only a real Champion would not have slain these dragons without seeing if there was something more going on here. I don't like this. Something about this doesn't seem right."

"Well, the things you've been overhearing should have made *that* obvious," Gina said with irritation. "I thought foxes were supposed to be intelligent."

"Clever and cunning, not intelligent," the fox corrected absently. "Not the same thing at all."

It was carefully looking all of them over. "I don't like this. Most of the geas-spell on me is in force because this is all supposed to be—Traditional. Dragon ravages countryside, dragon eats virgin, dragon stops ravaging countryside until it's time for the next virgin delivery. Only...only you didn't eat the virgins, you don't want to ravage the countryside, and I can feel the geas breaking down. This is *not* Traditional."

"You can say that again," muttered Gina.

"This is *not* Traditional," the fox repeated obediently. Gina rolled her eyes.

"I think we had all better put our heads together over this," Andie put in.

"Over dinner, please?" Adam pleaded. "Or...after dinner?"

"After dinner," Amaranth said pointedly. "You two have terrible table manners."

Considering that the dragons ate entire sheep at a gulp...

It turned out that they had an arrangement with the Centaur hunters and Cyclopsean herdsmen. When Adam was not being compelled to "ravage" the countryside, he and Peri bought their dinners with some of the "baubles" they had collected. So they went out to collect (and eat in private) what they had bought, while the maidens—Gina and Andie now counted as part of their company—got together their own dinner. The fox trailed along, looking hopefully at the preparations.

A great deal of what they were eating was gathered or grown there. The guess about Amaranth being a hardworking lass was true. She had been a dairymaid, and had a flock of goats to provide milk, which mostly went into cheese. Andie chose to believe that the dragons had bought the goats rather than stealing them.

The girls had a good vegetable garden, a flock of hens, several beehives, the dragons brought back flour and other things they could not grow or raise themselves, and there was much they could collect from the forest in the valley below. Nuts, berries, wild olives. Cress and other edible greens and herbs. Mushrooms. They had discovered the same thing that Gina and Andie had about mushrooms, and a castle full of virgin girls was to Unicorns what a beehive was to a bear. They wouldn't come near the dragons, but they were only too thrilled to meet the girls in the forest and purify their mushrooms in return for being petted and being fussed over. But they kept the secret of the girl, and the dragon from all other Unicorns in the forest. Reluctantly, true, but they were afraid of the dragon.

The fortress's original kitchen was in ruins, but the girls had improvised a fairly good one in what had once been a storage room. Having no source of water at hand meant a lot of hauling for the cooking and the cleaning, however. Especially the cleaning. Since Andie was no use at all in the kitchen, she was delegated to haul water.

And this was certainly a first. It wasn't long before her arms were trembling with fatigue and aching worse than she ever remembered. Gina had taken her bow and gone hunting, and come back with rabbits that she proceeded to clean and skin out of sight of the others. So that was the Champion's contribution to the meal. Andie was glad when they told her she had fetched enough water for the moment and she could go and sit down again.

Preparing a meal, she was just learning, was a lot of hard work. Even when it didn't involve much "cooking."

After much discussion of portions, the designated cooks—who were, Andie was told, the ones who could reliably be trusted not to burn anything—decided on a kind of stew as the way to stretch the meat the furthest. The fox finally got his hoped-for handout, when Gina presented him with the pile of entrails, heads and feet. Shortly afterward, there was a wet spot on the stone and a round-bellied fox dozing happily beside the kitchen fire.

One girl made flatbread, another cleaned and sliced greens, cucumbers and mushrooms, and a third made dressing of olive oil, vinegar and herbs. So while they waited they had greens and mushrooms tossed in the dressing with crumbled goat cheese on top to eat on the folded-up flatbread.

There was more flatbread to sop up the juices of the stewed rabbit and vegetables, and the dragons appeared, as they were finishing the meal, with yet more flatbread and honey. By this time Gina had unbent enough to take off her armor and put on one of the tunics that all the girls seemed to wear. She wouldn't wear a longer gown, though. She looked uncommonly leggy and rangy without the bulk of the armor and the padding underneath it.

"Time for a council of war!" Adam called cheerfully as he landed. Peri rolled his eyes, but made no comment.

Once again they all gathered in the courtyard, though as the sun set, the air was quickly growing cooler, and the girls had all brought woolen mantles with them. Andie had the cloak she had gotten in the village—it seemed a lifetime ago—and Gina had the cloak that went over her armor.

"Well," Peri said, once they had all settled in. "The list of things that we know is sadly short and most of them come with questions. We know that someone put a geass-spell on Adam to make him come here and become a villainous monster. But we don't know who, and we don't know why."

"What about some random evil Magician?" Amaranth asked. "Don't they just do that—come in and cause misery just for the sake of it?"

"Actually, no," both Peri and Andie said at the same time. They looked at one another, and Andie laughed.

She gestured to him. "You're the lore-scholar."

"Evil Magicians are like any other sort," Peri explained. "It costs them in terms of power to be able to work magic, so they aren't inclined to spend it just for the sake of spending it. They're also as impelled by The Tradition as the rest of us are. The Tradition requires that they have reasons for everything they do."

"And," Andie added thoughtfully, "it's not as if they're *insane*. At least most of them aren't. People who are not mad always have reasons for what they do."

"And that's the problem here in a nutshell," Peri said, putting his head down on his fore-claws with a sigh. "So far, no reason for this has come to light. No one has come forward to say, 'Make me King or I'll see to it that the dragon turns this land into a blackened cinder.' No one has demanded gold to make the dragon go away. No one has come forward to slay the dragon except one genuine Champion. When the Princess was offered up, that would have been the time to do so, as well. The Tradition would have put all of its force behind it, even if the motives were evil. Slay the dragon, rescue the Princess, wed the Princess, rule the Kingdom. All very Traditional."

Andie brooded over that. "The thing is," she said slowly, "no one with a motive has turned up. In fact, if it weren't for the geas on you, Adam, and the magic spell keeping Champions out of the country, *you* would just be the Traditional, mindless, ravening monster that is supposed to awaken a hero for the people." Solon might have rigged the lottery, but he couldn't have summoned the dragon. All he'd done was take advantage of the situation. Plus, if he'd wanted the Kingdom, all he would have had to do was arrange to marry Andie.

"No heroes," said Adam. "And though my brother might disagree from time to time, I'm not entirely mindless."

"That's another thing. Why the spell?" asked Gina. "It doesn't even seem to have a purpose. Unless the purpose is for Adam to lay waste to the country until it can fall to the first outside force that crosses the Border."

Andie snorted. "Nobody *wants* Acadia," she pointed out. "Look at us! We're not particularly fertile, we have no wealth. All we have is a convenient port that a lot of traders can and do bypass. We're too small even to have a standing army. So if anyone really wanted to invade us, it wouldn't exactly be difficult."

The courtyard was entirely in shadow now, and the last of the sun was sinking behind the mountains. The cloudless sky overhead had turned to a soft, dark blue; only in the west did some deep crimson light linger. And in the farthest east, the first stars had begun to emerge.

"And I am not exactly ravaging the countryside, either," Adam said, raising his head. "We've been buying our meals, thank you. What's more, we never did all that much 'ravaging' in the first place. People were still coming to market days—we watched them. People were still raising crops, building things, making things."

"He has a point," Peri sighed. "Begging your pardon, maidens, but sacrificing one virgin girl a week does not ruin an economy."

"Might even improve it in some areas," Adam observed dispassionately. "Anti-lottery charms, fireproof roofs, dragon-repellent..."

Both Peri and Andie leveled glares at him, which he probably didn't see.

"And the Queen doesn't seem to be doing much, either, not even when her own daughter was selected," one of the girls put in.

The fox trotted in and joined them at that moment, perhaps because he wanted company, perhaps because he was hoping for a snack, perhaps just because the fire had died out in the kitchen and company was better than cooling stone. He sat down with his tail wrapped neatly around his forepaws and listened to the conversation with all the interest of an observer at a sporting event.

Andie thought with guilt of the Queen's reaction to her selection. Cassiopeia had gone into immediate mourning, secluding herself, dressing in black.... She wished there was some way she could let the Queen know that she was all right. It didn't seem right that her mother should be left to grieve over something that hadn't actually happened.

Granted, probably every one of the other girls here felt the same, but still…

"My mother was absolutely stricken," she said quietly.

"Stricken is one thing, but wouldn't you have thought she'd actually *do* something?" asked one of the other girls. Thalia. "She is the Queen after all. Couldn't she have mustered up an army or something?"

"Such as? She'd sent for a Champion," Myrtle reminded them.

"Well, something. That adviser of hers is supposed to be so clever, you would be more than clever enough to find a way to save the Princess." Thalia looked unconvinced. "Why didn't he try to find a Wizard or a Sorceress? A powerful one. There are Wizards that can defeat dragons. Why didn't he look for a Godmother? Why didn't he realize there was a spell on the Border?"

"Because," Andie said with a touch of scorn, "Solon might have a reputation for cleverness, but quite frankly, I think he's too timid to ever go outside the Palace walls. Most of the powerful Magicians that I have ever heard of want you to come to them in person to prove your sincerity. I've never even seen Solon go down to the marketplace himself—he always sends a servant instead. As for mustering an army—" And there she had to pause because she couldn't think of any good reason why her mother had not put at least a small army together to hunt the dragon. After all, if a single Champion was supposed to be able to beat it, why shouldn't several hundred men?

"Oh, he's not such a weak-necked creature when there's no one around to see him," the fox put in casually. "And he does go outside the Palace walls, a great deal in fact. He's the one that sent me, after all. There I was, minding my own business, and the next thing I know, I'm living in a cage in his rooms. I don't even remember how he caught me. And suddenly I'm stuck obeying his commands, he's promoted me to Familiar and stuffed all sorts of things in my head no self-respecting fox really needs to know." But the fox seemed crestfallen, rather than proud. "Then, as if I'm just something to be used and thrown away, he sends me out chasing you to be sure you get into the dragon's claws. He's probably using that stupid toad now. The humiliation! Passed over for a toad!"

"Wait—" Andie stared at the fox in astonishment. "Are you saying that Solon is a Magician?"

"A good one, if I'm any judge," the fox replied. Then he added, "But then again, you know, he's the only one I've ever seen, so I'm not sure I'm that good a judge. Still, he does do quite a bit. He can keep track of people and know where they are, for one thing. He can send birds and animals to find things out for him. He can turn some things into other things."

"The Queen's Adviser is a Magician. And no one knows." Periapt stared off into the darkness. "You know," he said after a long pause, "Traditionally when one's Adviser is a secret Mage, he's generally a bad one, and generally intent on stealing your throne."

"Well, he's the one that sent me with the dragon scale to

keep leading you to the dragon," the fox pointed out, as if he assumed they had already known this rather crucial fact.

"He sent *you* with a dragon scale?" Periapt yelped. The dragon reared up to his full height, dark against the rising moon, his wings half mantled in surprise.

His reaction made Andie jump; truth to tell he looked terribly dangerous at that moment.

The fox leapt back, startled, landing on all fours with his fur bristling. "Of course. Where did you think I'd gotten it? Or didn't they tell you they were following what they thought was a trail of scales?"

"For the record," Gina said tightly, "I *never* thought I was following a trail of scales. I knew it was the same scale being moved. But I knew someone was watching us and I didn't want to betray myself or what I knew. So we acted as if we thought that there was a trail of scales to follow."

"*You have one of our scales?*" The otherwise mild-mannered Peri was not going to let the fox off this particular hook. The voice was that of a roaring fire increased a hundred times.

And the fox knew perfectly well by the reaction that Peri was not going to allow him merely to brush this off. Not when flames were curling around Peri's nostrils and flickering at the corners of his mouth.

Not when his eyes had begun to glow an ominously darker red.

He began to edge his way out of the courtyard. Backward, which is difficult for a four-legged creature. "I'll—uh—be fetching it then, shall I? Right away. Don't mind at all. Know right where it is—"

He was snatched off his four feet and into the air by Gina, who held him up by the scruff of the neck. He hung limply from her grasp as she shook him slightly. "You will be getting the scale, of course," she said pleasantly. "But not just yet, I don't think. First you'll be telling us everything you know and observed of the Queen of Acadia's Chief Adviser who just *happens* to be a Magician. Won't you."

It wasn't a question.

And it turned out that the fox knew a lot more than anyone had ever dreamed possible. In fact, he was a veritable cornucopia of information.

Some of the other girls had gotten torches, lit them and stuck them in the rusted sconces still attached to a few of the pillars around the courtyard. There was plenty of light to see by, and now that the fox knew he wasn't going to be incinerated, he had regained his aplomb.

"Cats," he said succinctly. "You two-legs think they're so inscrutable. They are the world's worst gossips. And they are everywhere."

Andie had to agree to that statement. The Palace was full of cats. Lean, hardworking cellar cats, energetic kitchen cats, pampered, aloof darlings of Cassiopeia's ladies—you couldn't walk ten feet without seeing a cat somewhere. The Queen didn't mind, because cats didn't demand attention the way dogs did, nor were they noisy, and as long as her maids could keep her gowns cat-hair free, she tolerated the creatures.

And as if they understood the limits of that tolerance, they kept their territorial squabbles and amorous serenades out of earshot of the Queen's Wing.

"I'm not a dog, but I'm not a cat, either, which makes me a kind of neutral party," the fox went on. "So they like to come to me and gossip about each other, and I nod and make all the right sorts of noises in the right places, and that kept me from going crazy with boredom, locked up in that little cage in Solon's quarters. But as well as gossiping about each other, they like to gossip about the humans." He tilted his head to the side. "Oh, did you know there's a hidden passage that connects Solon's rooms with the Queen's? I bet people have been wondering for years if they were lovers." He made a kind of snickering sound. "They are. Oh, yes, indeed they are. Have been for years as far as I can tell."

Andie nodded numbly. Her mother and—Solon? *Nasty.* She shook her head. *Just—nasty.*

And then, suddenly, she wondered. How long had that been going on? Because it would not be the first time that a lover had killed an "inconvenient" husband.

She did not like where that thought was going and resolutely shoved it aside. It was no business of hers if her mother took a lover. Her mother had every right. It wasn't as if she was being untrue to anyone.

"Now Solon is under the impression that he is a very cunning fellow. And you have to admit that he's cunning enough to have made all of you underestimate him," the fox continued with relish. "The thing is, he is not really prepared to be the power behind the throne. He wants to be the power *on* it."

Andie started at that, and stared at the fox. The fox gave her an odd look. "I thought for certain you must know all about this, Princess. You are not only a human, you were raised in the Court."

She shook her head. "Never an inkling," she said, feeling horribly naive, not to say stupid.

"Well, he talks to his Familiars. Or rather, he talks *at* his Familiars, since we really can't answer him back, and even if we could, he's never drunk dragon's blood so he wouldn't understand us. Not that he would listen." The fox sighed theatrically. "He's tried to get dragon's blood, but every time he bought what he thought was the right stuff, he was cheated."

"Not surprising," Adam rumbled. "We good and decent dragons don't give ours up except to those we trust. And the blood of the slain…well, it's really hard to kill a dragon, and harder still to collect the blood of a dead one."

The fox nodded. "Well, to make a long story far too short, he wants to sit on the throne. To do that, he first has to marry the Queen, then get rid of her somehow. Which, given that the man has more bottles of potions and ingredients than I have hairs in my tail, makes me think that he would not have a lot of trouble doing that. Then he has to get people to follow him. That is likely going to be the hardest part, if he's as disliked as the cats think."

"In every coup or assassination attempt," Periapt said, though he was showing some signs of boredom, "there is generally a point where the first strong voice to be heard will be the one that is followed. If that voice is also that of the Prince-Consort, who better to follow?"

Someone who isn't her murderer? Andie thought, her blood running cold at all of this.

But she didn't say it aloud.

"Well, Solon was fairly sure that under the right circumstances he could arrange that it would all fall into place," the fox said. "Personally the cats and I think he's being far too overconfident about all this. Still—"

"Still," Peri put in, "he has The Tradition behind him. It is quite the classic story, really. The trusted Adviser who really intends to usurp the throne…"

"But what is really funny is the Queen," the fox said with relish, the tip of his tail swishing back and forth. "She intends to do away with him, as well. Or so the cats tell me. She thinks he is getting arrogant and dangerous."

"Which of course, he is," Andie murmured.

"And she wants to be rid of him as soon as he is no longer useful—the cats said, anyway. She is going to replace him with someone younger." The fox opened his mouth in a silent laugh.

Andie was feeling rather sick at this point. This was a side of her mother she had not expected. She knew, of course, that Cassiopeia was calculating, but she had not dreamed that her mother was so ruthless. She knew the Queen was manipulative. She'd never guessed just how cold-hearted.

"Let me put the pieces together here," Periapt said, sounding more alert. "The sorcerer has every intention of wedding the Queen, then eliminating her, in such a way that the throne is offered to him. While the Queen, growing weary of his arrogance, fully intends to eliminate *him* at her earliest opportunity." He cocked his head as Andie swallowed. "What a charming game of double deception those two are playing on one another. If the circumstances were not what they are, it would even be worth watching them. But as things stand, too many others are likely to be hurt."

"I would say that is an understatement," said Gina into the silence.

"Now since the fox has one of my brother's scales, we can probably assume it is *the* scale and act accordingly." Peri-apt nodded graciously. "You may go, fox, and bring back the scale so that we can destroy it. That, at least, will put an end to the compulsions to go and carry off maidens, which in turn will put an end to the sacrifices."

The fox didn't require a second invitation. He was out the doorway and into the darkness in no time.

"However, I, at least, am not inclined to fly off and leave the rest of you to deal with this situation. You, young ladies, are our friends. And now it all fits into place," Peri continued. "Why the dragon, why the maidens." He turned his gaze on *her.* "Because, Princess, both Solon and your mother needed a way to be rid of you."

She felt her blood running cold. "But…why?" Solon she could understand, but her mother? Her own mother?

And yet she couldn't deny the logic of the argument. Her mother would have had to agree to having her name drawn out by lot—because if Solon was as good a Magician as the fox claimed, he could certainly ensure that the name drawn was the name he *wanted* drawn.

But her mother? "Why my mother?" she managed to get out.

"That," Peri admitted, "I cannot reason out. Though, I

am certain that she has a very good reason for it. And Solon's reason should be obvious."

She nodded. "Until I am dead he can't sit on the throne."

"So he brings a dragon to take care of getting rid of you in a public manner that leaves no blame or accusation for him to face," Peri said. "It would be difficult for anyone who is not aware he is a Mage to attach any blame to him. It is possibly useful to him to have a dragon to manipulate others, as well. Are there any enemies of his who have ceased complaining since the dragon began taking sacrifices?" Peri asked.

She thought. "As many as a half-dozen, I think."

"All of whom have daughters that might be next if they do not support him." Periapt gazed wisely at her. "Although no one could know for certain that he had any power over the lottery, would anyone dare take the chance that he did? I would imagine he has already made an example of one such family."

"That would be mine," Cleo said angrily. Her eyes flashed and she stood in a way that made Andie think it would be a very bad idea to cross her.

"And there you have it. Our key in a nutshell. A way to hold power over his enemies in the Court, a way to be rid of the Princess—and all without anyone realizing who was behind it all. It really is a brilliant plan, if you happen to be an amoral, evil beast."

Peri turned his gaze back on Andie. "Meanwhile the Queen also has you eliminated, for reasons of her own."

She nodded numbly. All this made too much sense. Far too much. And she didn't want to think about it. Her own mother wanting her dead— It made her want to retch and cry at the same time. She felt sick. She felt angry. She felt— abandoned, actually. Betrayed.

"And of course," Periapt continued, "he had to make sure that no Champion could cross the Border and ruin his plans."

"I suppose he must not have thought there might be such a thing as a female Champion," rumbled Adamant.

"No wonder my job didn't seem finished," muttered Gina.

And suddenly they were all left standing there, staring at one other, in the now-uncomfortable semidarkness. And probably wondering what they could possibly say to one another now.

CHAPTER ELEVEN

"We'll sleep on it," Peri said finally. "There is absolutely no point in trying to make further plans now, except—"

All of them turned at the sound of claws clicking on stone. A moment later, the fox appeared in the doorway, carrying the plate-size scale carefully in his teeth.

"—except to destroy that," Peri finished.

"How?" Gina asked doubtfully. "I have always been under the impression that dragon scales were nearly indestructible."

"Vinegar," Peri said serenely, and turned to Thalia. "Can you fetch the big jug of wine that went off, please?"

"You mean we've finally got a use for that wretched stuff?" Thalia exclaimed. "Oh, grand!" She edged past the prone body of Adam, who twitched his tail out of the way for her, and headed for the room that served as their pantry.

"It is pretty wretched," Cleo agreed. "Even as vinegar. But

I'm not sure—how is vinegar going to work to destroy the scale?"

"It won't destroy it, exactly," Peri said, as Thalia returned with a large, and seemingly heavy jug that sloshed. "You see, what happens is this—the vinegar dissolves something. It's the same thing that makes both bones and our scales hard. Once whatever-it-is is dissolved, then the scale will be like a big piece of wet leather. Except that when it dries again, it will be brittle and can be pounded into powder."

Gina found a stone basin that had probably once been a bird-bath or something of the sort—for a fortress, this place had once boasted a number of civilized amenities, and it was clear that this courtyard had been nothing more than a pleasant place to sit and relax. The basin was big enough to hold the scale, which Thalia took from the fox and dropped in, pouring the musty-smelling vinegar over the top until the scale was entirely immersed.

Andie wrinkled her nose. She liked the sharp taste of vinegar on things herself, but this stuff was nasty. It must have been inferior wine to begin with, and it certainly had not turned into good vinegar. She found it far more comfortable to focus on trivialities like this than on—

On the idea that her mother wanted her dead.

Every time she thought about it, it made her feel horrible.

But it might not be true. It might be a mistake. It might be that Solon had worked some sort of magic on Cassiopeia to make her acquiesce to this. Surely that had to be it. Surely her mother, her own mother, could not have wanted her dead.

Gina quickly found a slab of stone to put over the top of the basin to seal in the fumes.

Another triviality: vinegar made dragon scales fragile. And Peri had just essentially revealed that to all of them. Someday that might prove to have been a mistake. People talked. "Isn't it dangerous for you to let this secret—oh—" Andie said, and blushed, realizing in the next moment what a silly question that was.

"Yes," Peri said, his mouth gaping in a grin. "I hardly think that we are in any danger whatsoever of some dragon-hunter steeping us in bowls of vinegar to soften our scales. It will take at least one full day for that scale to become soft, perhaps more."

"Not exactly a weapon, then," said Andie, blushing again.

"Not exactly." Peri stood up and stretched, extending his wings up into the night sky. "I am for sleep. Sleep will likely bring us many more ideas of what we can do about this situation." He swiveled his head on his long neck to look at each of them in turn. "Rest assured, even if the spell on Adam is broken, I do not intend to leave until we have it all sorted and you young ladies can go home again."

Maybe sleep would give her a reason why it couldn't possibly be Cassiopeia who was involved in this. Why it had to be all Solon's idea.

"Even if he would, I wouldn't let him," Adam said, doing the same. "It may not be our fault that you're here, but we're mixed into it now, and it's our responsibility to get things put right."

And with that astonishing statement they both turned

and took the couple of steps needed to bring them to the far wall of the courtyard. The two dragons did not, as she half expected them to, fly out of the courtyard. Instead, they climbed out, in a most leisurely manner, and settled themselves, one on either side of the entrance to the main section of the fortress. As they lay down and became still, they looked like gigantic stone sculptures. The maidens gathered up their mantles and the cushions that one or two of them had brought to sit on, and made their way toward that entrance. Thalia stayed behind, taking down the torches and plunging them into a bucket of sand to extinguish them.

"Come on," Amaranth said, gesturing to the two of them. "We've already taken your things to a room. I'll show you."

As each of the girls reached the doorway, she stopped long enough to take a taper from a pile on a ledge just inside and light it at the torch in the sconce outside.

It was like walking into a cave. Unlike the open, airy Palace, this place was very closed in, with thick walls and relatively narrow passages. Made to be held in a siege, with corridors that a single determined man could defend, or so Andie reckoned. It made her feel a bit confined, but on the other hand, the solid construction had enabled the building to withstand weather and time. So she supposed she needed to be grateful for that much.

Tiny rooms opened up onto the corridor, rooms that would have been like monastic cells if each of the girls hadn't made hers comfortable in her own way and according to her own taste. As she passed, Andie got glimpses of a riot of draped fabrics like a gypsy tent in one, a tapestry loom in another, painted murals of garden scenes in a third. Finally Amaranth brought them to a pair of wide doorways opposite each other, at the point where the corridor ended in a blank wall.

"These are yours," she said, gesturing. "I put the Champion's things in the right, and the Princess's in the left." She turned and went back down the corridor, disappearing into her own open door.

Gina and Andie exchanged a glance, and Gina shrugged.

"It seems we've found a home for a while," Gina said. "And it's certainly more weather-tight than a tent in the woods. Considering how things could have turned out, this is a good situation."

A good situation…though one where she had learned some things she really wished she had not. But Gina was right. Things could have been much worse. The Wyrding Folk could have been protecting the dragons.

—*well, actually they are.*

The dragons could have been evil, or in the thrall of an evil Magician.

—*actually, that's true, too.*

Still…

Andie found herself surprised by a yawn. "Well," she said finally. "Good night."

There didn't seem much else to say.

My mother's Chief Adviser wants the throne and plotted to kill me. My mother is either a party to this or under his spell. I'm out in the howling wilderness unable to leave the company of the dragons that were going to eat me. Let's see. Have I left anything out?

But Gina actually cracked a smile. "We've come out of this very well so far," she pointed out. "Think about it. We didn't actually need to fight the dragons. We've come a long way to understanding just what mischief is going on here in your Kingdom. Now that we know, we can see what we can do about it. That's plenty for one night, I think."

And with that, she turned and went into her little room. It seemed that although doors had long since rotted and fallen away, someone had taken the trouble to fix a fall of canvas as a curtain on the inside, for shortly after Gina entered, a thick piece of cloth fell across the doorway, giving her privacy of a sort.

Andie turned in to her own room. As she pulled canvas across her own door and turned to see what awaited her, the candle revealed more than she would have thought. She hadn't expected a real bed or furniture, so she wasn't disappointed. But she was pleased, even delighted, to see a fat mattress, presumably stuffed with some kind of plant material, on the floor, her bedroll waiting atop it. There was also a pile of flat cushions next to the bed, and beside them, a stack of simple tunics and dresses like those the others wore.

There was a stone shelf built into the wall; she dripped a little candle wax on it and stuck her taper into it in lieu of a sconce. The more she looked at that bed, the more she wanted to be in it, sleeping. Anything else could wait.

Including, or perhaps especially, troubling thoughts about the Queen.

With the pallet unrolled on the bed, and one of the flat cushions to serve as a pillow, she blew out the candle, got into the bed by feel, and despite all the questions she was trying not to think about, fell deeply and soundly asleep.

Morning brought no real light into the rooms. Andie only woke because she heard voices and the sound of footsteps in the corridor. When she started to get up, however, her arms hurt so much that she lay back down with a groan.

Which immediately brought a response. Someone shoved the curtain aside and poked her head in the room. "Are you ill?" asked someone that she could not immediately identify.

"My arms hurt," she said, feeling as if she ought to be apologizing. "All that water-carrying yesterday..."

"Ah." The head vanished, then returned. "Stay in bed and sleep a bit longer. We forgot you wouldn't be used to that sort of work. We'll sort out something for you to do that doesn't involve hauling heavy things about. At least until you get accustomed to doing things that involve a lot of labor."

"I—" she began, but the head was gone again. She had been going to say that she wanted to do her share of the work, but evidently that was a given here.

Well, that wasn't so bad...she'd been taking care of herself all through the journey so far. This was just an extension of the chores she had already been undertaking for herself.

Then again, she had never exactly been the sort of Princess that the Queen would have preferred, what with climbing trees and taking meals to Guards and all. *Enough that your mother doesn't think of you as her daughter? Enough that your mother would be glad to be rid of such an embarrassment?*

She pushed the horrid thoughts away and concentrated on seeking the position in which her arms hurt the least.

Once she got her sore arms arranged in a configuration where they actually didn't hurt she found herself drifting back off to sleep. And it was good not to be waking up before the sun even crested the horizon in order to get on the road as quickly as possible.

Some unknown time later, more footsteps awoke her and she bit back another groan as someone else poked her head into the room.

"Can you wash dishes?" It was Cleo's voice.

Can I wash dishes? Does she mean, "Do you know how?" or "Are you able to?" Well, in both cases she could. "Yes," she replied, grateful to be able to say yes to something. It was galling to know that she must appear to be a total burden, and incompetent to these other girls.

Granted, there were others who had also had servants and had never needed to do work themselves. But they had been here a while, and by now probably were as good or better at ordinary tasks as the girls who'd been taking care of themselves and their families all their lives.

"I mean *now*—are your arms too sore to wash dishes today?" Cleo persisted. "I do need to know this right now."

"No," she answered honestly. "This is nothing more than strain, and strain gets better if you warm your limbs up. If I just get up and get moving this will ease off—"

"Yes, but it's hardly fair to ask you to do work you aren't

physically ready to do," Cleo said, with a reasonableness that she actually hadn't expected from the girl. "So we all decided there won't be any woodcutting or water-carrying for you for a while. But if you're up to washing dishes as your regular chore—then that will be fine. It will be better than fine with me—it's mine, and I hate it. If you'll take that, I can take weeding the garden, which is not my favorite but it's better than washing dishes."

Her mother would have a fainting spell if she could hear her daughter planning to wash dishes like a servant.

Her mother…

She shoved the thought away.

"You need to get up now, though," Cleo was saying. "Or you won't get any breakfast."

"Then I'll gladly take your place," Andie replied. "I do know how to wash dishes and I can do that after breakfast. And I'm getting up now, right this minute."

She rolled out of the bed with some little difficulty, caused at least in part by trying to save her arms as much as possible. She didn't ever remember anything ever hurting this much. But she did remember what it was like when she'd first started taking dance lessons and using muscles that had never gotten that kind of exercise before. And she remembered very well what she'd had to do then.

Move them.

Once she got out of bed she slowly worked and stretched her arms until the stiffness was gone and they didn't actually scream at her when she moved them. She changed into a loose sleeveless gown with a sleeved tunic over it, and went out to join the rest of the world.

The rest of the world was finishing a simple breakfast of flatbread, honey and yogurt. Gina greeted her by finishing the last bite of her own food, grabbing her wrist and slathering both Andie's arms with liniment from a stoppered jar she'd had at her side. It smelled of sharp herbs, but wasn't unpleasant, and Andie felt it start to go to work almost immediately, warming and loosening the muscles further, easing the aches.

"What's good for the outside of a horse is usually good for the outside of a man," Gina said with a grin. "Or a woman. I'd been saving this stuff because Godmother Elena makes it and puts magic into it, but I figured you'd earned a dose this morning."

"Thanks," Andie said gratefully. She decided at that moment that she wanted Gina for a friend…if Gina wasn't already a friend.

She rather hoped that the Champion was. The more she thought about it, the more she hoped. Really, Gina had been very nice to someone that she'd had no real reason to like. After all, if it wasn't for Andie, where would she be now?

On some other uncomfortable Quest?

Well, maybe. Or maybe still at the Chapter-House.

And Andie was the one who had thrust herself on a reluctant Gina. The Champion had no reason to be happy about that.

But she said herself that having me along made getting around the countryside easier.

Still, when it came right down to it, Andie had been an inconvenience. Yet Gina had never made things uncomfortable for Andie. And once she'd been revealed as being another girl—

I'd really like her for a friend. She looked around at the other young women clustered about the makeshift table, which looked as if someone had taken a slab of the fallen stone of the fortress walls and set it on four stumpy columns.

Actually, someone probably had—that someone being one of the dragons.

I'd like to have all of them for friends, she found herself deciding in surprise. Uncommon trial and hardship, danger and uncertainty had brought them together, but they were making the most of it, and even seemed to be finding ways to enjoy themselves. They'd come to some sort of understanding, it seemed, because she honestly couldn't tell any differences of rank among them by the way they behaved toward one another.

Even as she thought that, she took a place on a stone bench and the one nearest her passed her the plate of flatbread with no deference or other acknowledgment of rank. Just simple politeness. "Sorry we don't have any fruit," Amaranth said apologetically. "Everything is either green or gone."

Andie spread yogurt over the flatbread and drizzled on honey. "This is good!" she said around a mouthful. "This is fine." And in fact, it was. It was—

It was the first time in her entire life that she had sat down at a table with girls her own age that weren't her mother's handmaidens and ladies. The first time she had sat down with girls who weren't either ignoring her as the unimportant Princess or giving her false deference.

The first time she had sat down with girls who spoke to her as if they were speaking to another human being.

It was amazing. It was more than amazing. It was eye-opening.

It was wonderful.

She listened to them banter and tease each other, wonder what on earth Peri and Adam were going to do today—evidently the word was in the wind that they were "up to something" this morning—trade off on chores and other things, and then turn and ask her or Gina a question or two. Gina fascinated them—small wonder, most of them had never seen a female Warrior before, while Andie'd had them around her all her life. They wanted to know about the Chapter, the Chapter-House and, most of all, about Godmother Elena.

Finally the last bite was gone and the girls dispersed to their various chores. Gina went out hunting again; evidently none of the other girls had ever taken up the bow, and meat tended to be rather scarce except when the dragons brought it in. That left Cleo and Andie alone with the table and the dirty dishes.

There weren't a lot of dishes; the cups from which they had drunk their herbal tisane, the plates that had held the flatbread, the bowl that contained the yogurt and two horn spoons. When the last of the girls was gone, taking the leftovers back to the kitchen with her, Cleo gathered up the lot in a big, flat basket. "I'll show you where to go," she said, and led the way down into the valley.

They went farther downstream from the place where Andie had fetched the water yesterday, which only made sense, since you wouldn't want to drink water in which you'd just washed things. Cleo stopped at a spot where there was a shallow ledge running off into the stream. "Here," she said, putting the basket down and pointing at a patch of coarse reeds growing in the mud where the stone shelf ended. "Grab a handful of horsetail there and scrub everything out twice."

She sauntered back up the trail. Andie tentatively grasped about half a handful of horsetail and tugged. She recognized it from her botany lessons and from the fact that some of it grew in and around the ornamental ponds at the Palace. But she'd never actually had any of it in her hands before.

She couldn't imagine why Cleo found this chore so onerous. It was pleasant down here in the valley, with birds singing in the trees overhead, the gurgling of the stream around her, and her spot nicely shaded from the hot sun. Oh, her knees started to ache after a while, kneeling on the hard stone, but it wasn't that bad, and anyway, she could take a break by sitting cross-legged, or sprawling on the stone, and listening to the forest for a while.

The task didn't take long. And though the walk back was somewhat difficult up a fairly steep path as it was, and though the dishes were both heavy and awkward, she found she didn't mind in the least. She had actually washed a full set of meal dishes! That was something altogether novel in her life—something *other* people did. And perhaps today she would also learn how to wash clothing, as well.

Perhaps for anyone else, the day would have been one of drudgery and boredom, but this was all new to her. People in her position never learned how to wash dishes, or to cook, or to do any of the myriad of things she was learning to do.

She helped with lunch preparations, slicing up mushrooms after cleaning them, stacking finished flatbreads with a dusting of flour between them so that they didn't stick. She had never seen anyone make flatbreads before. It was fascinating. She longed to try it herself, but didn't want to ask, because she knew very well she would ruin her first attempts and she had the feeling that there simply wasn't food to "waste."

Luncheon was like breakfast had been, except that more of the girls talked to her this time. They seemed relieved when she would say, of this or that task, "I don't know how, but if you could show me, I'll try."

Another of the girls, Helena, was perfectly happy to teach her how to wash clothing, and they spent the afternoon down by another set of rocks, pounding and scrubbing at their garments until they got almost all of stains and dirt out, then spreading them on the bushes to dry.

"Generally," Helena said, as she scrubbed vigorously at a stain, "each of us washes her own clothing unless someone asks us to do hers. That's only smart, really—the things we do will put stains in clothing and you feel bad if you can't get them out of someone else's, but worse if they give you a look because you didn't."

Andie had to laugh at that. Out of a sense of gratitude, Andie had taken Gina's clothing down with her. The only real problem was that the padded tunic and trews that went under the armor were unbelievably heavy when she hauled them up out of the stream, and though she tried hard to squeeze the water out of them, it was clear they were going to take forever to dry.

"Don't put those in the direct sun," Helena said. "If you do, they'll dry stiff. She'll never be able to get them back on. They'll be like slabs of wood."

"I don't know how I'm to get them to dry at all, otherwise," Andie replied.

Helena pondered the problem.

"Let's try pressing some of the water out with rocks." The svelte, dark-haired beauty's idea sounded feasible.

They spread the garments flat on an expanse of rock shelf, then the two of them piled clean rocks on top of the garments, and before they had heaped up too much, there was already water running from under the pile. Encouraged, they continued to pile up stones until there was no more sign of squeezed-out water. Tumbling the rocks aside, Andie picked up the tunic. It was much lighter, and barely damp.

With that problem solved, they left the clothes drying—who was here to steal them, after all?—and trudged up to the fortress.

Only to discover Gina waiting for them at the top of the trail. "The dragons want another conference," she said. "We're meeting in the courtyard. I think—" She hesitated. "I think they want us all to do something about the situation in Acadia."

Andie looked at her, round-eyed. "Do you think we actually can?" she asked doubtfully. "You're the only Warrior. Where would we get an army?"

Gina shrugged. "Let's hear what they have to say first."

Once again, Andie found herself in the ruined courtyard with the two dragons reclining in the middle and all their former "victims" arrayed along the edges. And now the thoughts that she had been trying to keep out of her mind all day came charging to the fore again.

And with them the distress that she had tried to hide. Because perhaps it wasn't as bad as it had appeared last night. Perhaps the dragons, after talking more with the fox, had decided that Cassiopeia was not to blame, that she had been under some sort of spell. That she still was. That it was all Solon's fault. Andie could readily believe it was all Solon's fault.

"My brother and I have been having a discussion," said Peri, when Helena and Andie had taken seats on a couple of fallen columns, and Gina had taken up a position, leaning with crossed arms against what was left of a wall. "This situation in your land, Princess, is intolerable."

She grimaced. "Yes, but—"

"I wish to ask you some questions, please," Peri continued. "I keep a detailed chronicle of the information I receive when I negotiate our trades with the Wyrding Folk. I went back over it today, looking for some clues. Now, how familiar are you with the arrangements between the traders and the Crown?"

"Fairly," she replied, nonplussed. What could that have to do with anything they'd been discussing?

He nodded with evident satisfaction. "The Wyrding Folk seem to be under the impression that most of the wealth of your Crown comes from fees and taxes on those traders who use your port, which is the only safe anchorage for quite some ways up and down the coastline." He peered keenly down his long nose at her.

"That's quite accurate, to a point," she replied thoughtfully. "Though, there is another source of income that no one really likes to talk about, and that is the income from wrecks. The Queen gets one-third of everything that is gleaned off the shoreline after a wreck. Unless, of course, it's shoreline belonging to the Crown—then she gets all of it."

Peri blinked. His eyes held a furtive greenish light in their depths. Or was that only the effect of the sun? "Now that," he said, "is interesting. So. If, say, the weather along the shores of Acadia began to worsen, the Queen would benefit no matter what. Those traders seeking to avoid the port and the taxes and fees by landing somewhere and smuggling their goods in would suddenly find they were losing ships to storms. The Queen would profit by what washed ashore, and profit again when these traders elected to stop trying to avoid the taxes. True?"

"Well," Andie replied. "Yes."

She was beginning to feel sick again. She did not like where this was going. Not at all. Because—

Because it was beginning to look as if either Solon had gotten complete control over everything her mother said and did, like a puppeteer, or—

—her mother was complicit in the whole dragon business.

Including trying to kill her own daughter.

Because Solon himself did not have nearly as much to do with the trade negotiations as Cassiopeia did. They bored him, for one thing, or so he said. For another, the Queen liked to have them firmly and completely under *her* control. And hers alone.

"The Wyrding Folk tell me that the weather has, in fact, worsened significantly. So much so that the current storms outmatch anything in their memories and records."

Since this seemed to be a statement and not a question, Andie simply nodded.

"So, can you tell me if the Queen has been renegotiating her arrangements with the traders of late?"

Andie's mouth dropped open at that question. Suddenly she was putting together a great many answers in her own mind that were making her even sicker at heart than she had been before this.

No, she moaned in her mind. *Oh no, please not...* But her teacher in logic had been ruthless, and if there was one thing he had taught her it was that a question or a train of thought must be pursued to its likeliest conclusion, no matter how unpleasant.

Except that the word *unpleasant* was not nearly strong enough.

"Yes...she's raising the port fees. But—" she shook her head "—there's more, far more to it than that. This bad weather is doing some awful things to the fisherfolk," she continued, feeling more ill with every word. "And to the farmers and herdsmen along the coastline. The fishermen are not able to go out as often, and people are losing crops and livestock."

"But the profit to the Queen from her agrarian folk and fisherfolk is minimal, compared to that from the traders, is it not so?" Peri said in veiled triumph. His head was up, and his cheek-frills fanned.

Andie bit her lip. She was seeing more than she wanted to see. "Much less."

"And if the Queen is aware that her Adviser is a Magician—"

"Oh, she knows," the fox piped up, from where he was curled, quite comfortably, in Cleo's lap. "She counts on it. He does things to people that she wants to give way to her. I don't know what else he does, but I know he does that. I've listened to her give the orders, and I've even seen her watch while he does the magic."

"Did you ever see him work weather magic?" Peri asked with great care, clearly enunciating every word.

"Weather magic?" The fox's ears flattened a moment as he concentrated, then his ears came up again. "Yes. Yes, at least once."

Peri's eyes blazed. "One of the most common magical workings is weather magic," he said with a certain grim elation. "Clearly he knows how to do it. If he is manipulating the weather along the coast—"

"At her orders," Andie said, feeling dizzy, because she knew in her heart that Solon must be doing just that. Too many pieces were falling into place now for her to be able to pretend that the Queen was Solon's puppet. All the reports she had written. Line after line that had proved to her mother that her own daughter was too dangerous and too intelligent—

"And now I think I know why she wanted to be rid of me. I—I pointed this out to her. Told her how the weather was worsening and how the farmers and fishermen were suffering because of it. And I saw the records of the gleanings from the wrecks—they've easily doubled in the past decade. Easily."

And she felt horrible. Because while things were hard for the farmers, herders, and fishermen, no one on shore had died. *But men had died in those wrecks.* Many men. And her mother knew that.

With a growing sense of horror she recalled the look on her mother's face whenever the tallies from wrecks were brought in.

Satisfaction.

Andie had dismissed that then, although it had made her uneasy. She could not dismiss it now. It had been bad enough to think that her mother felt satisfaction over something that had cost the deaths of innocent sailors and traders, but the Queen could perhaps be excused for not thinking of that at the time, and seeing only the revenue. They were not, after all, *her* sailors. She would not see the roster of the lost. No widows would petition her for some form of pension.

But thinking—*knowing*—that the Queen had willfully allowed the storms to be summoned that sank those ships, and had only smiled when the fruits of that crime were brought to her doorstep—that was a different matter.

That was murder. Cold-blooded murder.

And that was something terrible to contemplate. So terrible that it was all she could do to sit there and let the debate go on around her as her mind went over the pattern of deception and nightmare that Cassiopeia had woven into the tapestry that was Acadia.

The Queen of Acadia had plotted the deaths of innocents whose only crime was that they were following the orders of others who were attempting to evade onerous taxes. And in fact—since Cassiopeia had the sailing schedules for all the ships coming into and out of the harbor…

Well, it was entirely possible she had even plotted the destruction of complete innocents—those who had paid their duties and taxes, and who just happened to have valuable cargo aboard that would float. What next?

Anyone and anything that gets in her way. *Like me.*

Andie sat there in a daze. Once in a while Peri would ask her a question and she would reply with something—it hardly mattered what, since he seemed satisfied with whatever answer he got. It was just so hard to think that all this time, the Queen had been—

"Very well," Adam boomed, startling her. "I don't think any of us have to debate this any longer. The Queen of Acadia is unfit to rule. Her Adviser may or may not be the cause of her current behavior—the fox says not, and I am inclined to believe the beast—but there is no doubt that she has abandoned the responsibility of a monarch to care for her people first, last and always."

Reluctantly Andie looked up and nodded. Peri sighed gustily.

Adam glanced at him and snorted. "You know very well where this is going."

"Yes," Peri said with resignation. "I do."

Adam stood up to his full height and fanned his wings. "It is our duty as the descendants of the line of Sardonyx and Jasper, the first Dragons of the Light, to combat injustice and tyranny where we find it. Ladies, our course is clear. We must remove the Queen of Acadia from her throne."

Gina grinned. But Andie felt as if she had just turned to stone.

"We are going to war. Who goes with us?" Adam demanded.

There was stunned silence. "You and what army?" asked Cleo, the first to break it.

Adam, surprisingly, laughed. "Peri and I *are* an army," he pointed out. "But I have been flying over the capital quite a bit now, and I have to say that it would not really take an 'army' as such to get into the Palace. We don't need to lay siege to the city. In fact, we don't really want to. What we need is to get into the Palace and take the Queen and Solon. That doesn't require a very large force. In fact, with Peri and myself flying people in, it could be done with as few as a dozen, maybe two."

Gina had taken out a knife and was studiously sharpening it. At that, she looked up and directly into Adam's eyes. "I'm a Champion," she said shortly. "This is something no Champion could turn his or her back on. You have me."

"Ha!" he said, and that is when Thalia stood up.

"This is our land," she said. "And if that isn't enough, we've been made victims, too. I don't know if you can turn me into a real fighter quickly enough, but you have me."

"And me!" exclaimed Helena, jumping to her feet, shortly followed by all the rest.

That left only Andie, who felt herself flush and looked at her feet as all eyes came to rest on her. The silence grew heavier and more uncomfortable with every passing moment. It was Gina who broke it.

"Princess, we understand, she's your mother. You—"

"Actually," Andie said, looking up, her mouth twisted in a grimace, "you don't understand. Not at all."

"We probably don't," said Peri.

"This—this is—horrible," she managed to choke out. "What she's done, the innocent lives she's taken the—I can't even begin—" She faltered to a stop. She stared at her feet. The silence was thick enough to cut. *I have to do something. This is my bloodline they're talking about. I have a responsibility, too....*

There was just one rather large problem. "Without these—" she took the lenses off and flourished them, bitterly "—I'm blind. Even if you could actually train me to do some kind of fighting, which I frankly doubt, the first person that breaks these things turns me from an asset into a liability. A hostage. I'd like to help you, but I'm useless to you."

She had no idea until the words were out of her mouth how much she meant them—nor how badly they hurt. But they did. Once again, she was useless. She had spent her entire life being useless, it seemed. Nothing she was good at made any real difference to anyone.

"But, Andromeda—" Peri exclaimed. "You are the *most* important person in this scheme!"

"I—what?" she said. "You must be joking."

Peri shook his massive head. "On the contrary. You are the only person here who has actually been inside the Palace. You know everything there is to know about it. Without that, we can't even begin to mount an attack, now, can we?"

"At least not the kind of attack we can manage with as few people as we have, and as untrained or half trained," Adam agreed. "You are the key to our plan."

Of all the things she had heard today this was the most astonishing. She was important. She was vital. She who had never been anything to anyone—

"Besides," Gina said with a grin, "I can teach you to use something that you won't have to get in close to use. A sling. Believe me, I've seen a good sling-man take down seasoned fighters many a time."

Andie raised her chin and looked into Peri's eyes. "Then you have me," she said, but could not help adding, "for what it's worth."

CHAPTER TWELVE

The next day, she went to work with Peri in the "library," which was nothing more than the big, dry room—probably a former barracks room—where he kept his book hoard. There were no shelves; books were stacked atop one another in piles around the walls, by category, and scrolls were stuck into the necks of wide-mouthed jars. Light came from slit-windows—which had probably been arrow-slits—and candles and lamps placed carefully away from the piles of books and jars of scrolls. Now she discovered just how Peri was able to write things.

He spoke.

He lay on the floor of the room with an open, blank book in front of him. She watched in fascination as he talked and words appeared on the pages. This, really, was the first overt instance of magic that she had ever seen, or at least, magic that looked like magic. He couldn't correct so much as a single word after it was written, though, so he had to be very careful about how he phrased things.

She, however, was having to use an old-fashioned quill and ink that she'd made herself. Squid and octopus ink was what she'd used at home, but they were far from the coast and the Wyrding Folk that Peri traded with were not literate. After consulting with one of the books in his hoard, Peri gave her a recipe involving soot, water and the white of an egg and sent her off to concoct it. It seemed to work well enough for now, and Gina went out and brought down a goose for quills.

The exterior of the Palace was easy enough to conjure up in her mind's eye, and she had help. Adamant had flown over it many times, and she had stood on the lookout cliff above at least once every few days for most of her life. Between the two of them, they soon had virtually every stone, bush and entrance plotted well enough to have reconstructed the Palace on the spot.

At least from the outside. Now came the hard part. She had to pummel her memory to reconstruct as much of the inside as she could remember. And of course, there were places, like Solon's quarters, that she had never been inside. She could guess what they might look like, but she didn't know.

Nor did she know how many more secret passageways there might be aside from the one that the fox knew about. She'd never actually measured the rooms; it had never occurred to her to do so. Frustratingly, there was more that she didn't know than that she did know. She took a break at midday only long enough to eat and wash the dishes before continuing until she had a headache from concentrating so hard.

"Enough," Peri said, looking at her with concern. "You're thinking too hard. You are never going to remember details now if you don't relax."

"I know but—"

"We do not need this map tomorrow. We will not even need it in the next week. Or even month. You have time." He brought his head down close to hers, and his eyes, quite literally as large as plates, really did have a soft, green glow at the bottom of them. "You have time," he repeated quietly.

"I know but—" She laughed weakly as she realized that all the arguments that she was going to use were ones she herself would reject. She knew he was right. She knew her emotions were clouding her judgment. She knew all that, and her emotions were *still* clouding her judgment.

"This is horrible," she said with a sigh, carefully sealing the tiny vial of ink with a ball of wax, cleaning the quill and putting the map aside to dry thoroughly.

"Then take your mind off it, for just a little while," Peri coaxed. "Trust me, this will be a good thing. You'll be able to think much more clearly. The memories will drift to the top of your mind instead of staying stubbornly at the bottom."

"All right." She looked at him and asked the first thing that popped into her head. "Who are Jasper and Sardonyx?"

He chuckled, the sound deep in his chest. "Trust Adam

to invoke them! He is very proud that they are in our lineage. Jasper and Sardonyx were a mated pair of dragons that aided a Godmother—a true 'Fairy' Godmother, actually—and decided that they so enjoyed the feeling of making things happen for good that they would keep doing so. They became the progenitors of the line known as the Dragons of the Light, although I can assure you that they did not name themselves that. It is one of the Draconic Warrior lines. Our mother, Serpentine, is half Bookwyrm and half Warrior, and takes largely after the Warrior side. Last I heard from her, she had attached herself to a kind of Champion-Chapter on the other side of the ocean." He sighed wistfully. "Dragons need a lot of territory, you see. She and father were only mated for a season, just to have offspring. Once Adam and I reached adulthood there was no reason for her to remain on this continent any longer."

"Is that what all dragons do?" she asked. It would make sense, given what he said about needing a lot of territory.

"Not all. Some take mates for life. But it's rare to find a mate that shares your interests that isn't also in your bloodline." He chuckled. "You think humans have trouble! There are fewer of us than you by far, and we live longer than you. Not as long as the Fair Folk, but longer than you. So if you're going to take a mate for life you really want it to be someone you can talk to who isn't also your cousin, a child, or more suited to your grandfather, and that's pretty rare."

She nodded. "So, being a Bookwyrm is less dangerous, I would think?"

He sighed pensively and let his eyes roam over his collection. It really was quite impressive. The Great Library was probably smaller.

"Yes and no. Your average iron-thewed barbarian doesn't come after us, but the people that do are generally quite sophisticated, quite powerful, quite ruthless, and have the wherewithal to purchase top-notch help. They know exactly what they're looking for, they know if we have it, and even though normally I would be inclined to just let them have it, or at least borrow it, they're generally the sort of nasty pieces of work that as a Dragon of the Light, I have to make sure they *don't* get their hands on it." He sighed. "That's why I collect history books for the most part, and try not to let any magic books sneak in."

"History?" she perked up. "What kind of history?"

"By preference, historians who are aware that The Tradition exists and can analyze why events happened in the light of that." He swiveled his head on his long neck and extracted a book neatly from the top quarter of a pile. "Arthur Ventus, for instance."

She could hardly believe it. "You have Ventus? Which history?"

"*Tedious and Long-winded History of the Portaian War,*" he said, and laughed. "You have to admire a man who doesn't beat around the bush when it comes to his work."

"True, true," she agreed, and knew she was getting a greedy look on her face. "I haven't read that one—and I love Ventus."

"Well, I have more—this is just the one I picked off the top of the pile." He handed it to her. "Be careful with it, it's quite rare. Just not the sort of rare that gets Magicians with impressive staffs and hordes of demonic minions interested in me."

She took it carefully, and set it down on a stone shelf near the door so she wouldn't forget it. "How do you end up getting these things, anyway?" she asked curiously. "I mean, they're not the sort of items that end up in tombs and whatnot."

"No, but they are the sort of things that end up on the auction block," he said, surprisingly. "I buy them, mostly. Adam and I will go out on treasure hunts, sell most of the baubles, then I'll send the money to one of my human agents when I know of interesting volumes for sale." He bared his teeth in what she figured was a large draconic grin. "That simple, really. And relatively painless, except for the bauble-collecting part. We've always lived on the coastline, though, so we've made it a practice of robbing pirates. That's quite painless."

"Even more intriguing," she said aloud. "How can robbing pirates be painless?"

"Because dragons can smell treasure," he explained. "The bigger the hoard, the easier it is to smell. Unless it's something small but incredibly valuable—that sort of thing gives off its own kind of scent. So we just wait for them to bury the ill-gotten gains, then we move in, dig it up and carry it off. Painless."

She had to laugh at that.

"So tell me, where did you get those lenses?" he asked, while she was still chuckling.

"Ah, that is a long story," she replied, and launched into it.

* * *

"Armor," said Gina. "The garbage you have them wearing will not do. You've seen how my armor looks. Everything fits, and fits well. Badly fitting armor is worse than none. I don't suppose you know any dwarves?"

"New armor—right—uh—dwarves?" Adam said, taken aback. "I do, but what does that—"

"Dwarves make the best armor. Everyone thinks it's the Elves, but the Elves are only putting ornament on top of Dwarven-made suits. We don't need filigree and chasing. Just good solid pieces that will go on well, stay on, and be light enough that these girls won't be laboring under the weight of it." She tossed a helm in the discard pile; so far she had not found a single piece that was worth keeping. "This did all right to impress some country lad with his mother's best kettle on his head, but not a trained fighter."

"So it didn't impress you, then?" The poor dragon sounded terribly disappointed.

She decided not to laugh. This was, after all, a fellow fighter. Not a Champion, perhaps, but worthy of her respect. He had done his best with what he had at hand.

Actually, he had really outdone himself, all things considered. He wasn't even human, and he had managed to make a lot of untrained girls look moderately competent to the untrained eye.

"Adamant—" she began.

"Adam. Please," he said, bringing his head down to her level. At that moment she marveled at how human he acted and sounded. Really quite amazing when you thought about it.

"Adam. You did a fine job with what you had. No book of your brother's would ever have been able to help you make a gaggle of girls into real fighters. Only someone like me can do that."

And here she smiled, because this was one of the best weapons in a Champion's arsenal. And it was one of the least known. It did turn up in The Tradition, oh my, yes, but somehow, like The Tradition of the female Champion, the wrongdoers always seemed to overlook it.

"Why you?" he asked.

"Actually—let's get all the girls together. I'd like them to hear this. Down at the arena, I think."

The spot she had chosen as the training field, which she had dubbed "the arena," was a flat-bottomed grassy bowl. It was just the right size for group exercises and not so big that girls sitting on the hillside would have any trouble seeing or hearing what was going on below. When she had all of them arrayed on the shaded slope—bibble-babbling as she pretty much expected they would be—she went to parade-rest position and cleared her throat in that way that only someone trained by a competent sergeant-major could.

She got instant silence, as she had expected she would.

Adam sat on the floor of the bowl beside her, looking down at her expectantly, which didn't hurt.

"Now," she said. "We lot are about to invoke a very powerful Traditional path for our own benefit. We are about to become the Ragged Company."

"The what?" asked Cleo, puzzled. But Thalia, surprisingly enough, clapped both hands to her mouth, her eyes going round.

"You might know it as the Rebel Companions, Cleo," Gina said, and looked around. Cleo shook her head, and only Helena and another girl, Dita, looked as if they recognized the reference. Well, there probably hadn't been anything like outright rebellion in this Kingdom for a very long time, and it didn't look or sound as if they got much news from the outside world, either.

"The original tale goes like this. In a small Kingdom much like this one, the monarch fell ill and died, the rightful heir, a baby, disappeared, and affairs were taken over by the Seneschal, who was, as you might expect, a very bad man. He taxed everything in sight, oppressed the poor, so forth and so on—" She waved her hand to indicate the usual thing. "However, he also went further. He had the nobles arrested, all in a single night, and their estates confiscated on various causes. He put his own men in their place, so that the nobles would not be able to topple him. Now there was no one that could effectively oppose him."

"Except?" prompted Cleo.

Gina nodded. "Except. There was one noble, and a fine old Warrior he allegedly was, too, who had gone into the wilderness to become a holy hermit. The Seneschal assumed he was dead, or else had forgotten about him. But he got wind of what was happening, and he gathered up his arms and armor, donned them and went out to find out what exactly was going on. In the tale he has many adventures, and one by one he collects a band of untrained peasants, traveling entertainers and assorted riffraff, turns them into a small army, infiltrates the Castle with them, kills the Seneschal and conjures up the baby and puts it on the throne."

"Oh! Now I recognize that," said Amaranth. "That's Rob-bing John's Army." And Adam nodded. The rest still looked blank. All the better. If *they* didn't know it, Solon probably wouldn't, either.

"Now, we Champions know the truth of the first tale," Gina continued. "Yes, there was a Hermit Warrior, the King's former war-leader. Yes, he did get wind of what was happening and come to start some trouble. But his army was not a lot of untrained peasants, because even the clever-est villain is going to have some people escape his net. A substantial core group of nobles and their bodyguards and retinues escaped to join the hermit, and the few peasants who also joined up had all been trained fighters them-selves, usually serving in one or another of the nobles' mili-tia. And, I'm sorry to say, the 'rightful heir' was a random infant of the right age and looks. It hardly mattered, since the wee mite was immediately married while still in dia-pers to our old hermit, making him King. History says nothing more of the child, but the line continues to this day, and history does record that he was a just, honorable and fairly kind-hearted soul, so one assumes that she was happy, or at least as happy as royal heirs in such a situation can be."

Amaranth looked disappointed.

Gina smiled. "That was the *first* tale," she said. "And it served the nobles' purpose to have it spread about that the pure-minded peasantry had risen up on their own and brought down the evil Seneschal. Thus the Traditional path was begun. The tale spread, changed a little, grew in the telling. And the *next* Ragged Company that arose really was composed half-and-half of trained and untrained peasants, and with clever leadership and the help of The Tradition along the way, they, too, destroyed their evil Seneschal and put the rightful heir back on the throne. And again the tale spread and grew, and the third time—in the Rebel Companions—all but the officers were untrained. The fourth time—which is, I believe, Robbing John—only the leader had any training at all. By now The Tradition is highly in favor of an army of untrained peasantry with only the leader knowing anything about fighting. And this is where we are now."

Cleo pondered this and raised her hand. "Are we better or worse off being girls?" she asked, tossing her hair back over her shoulder. "I mean, should we all start pretending to be boys?"

"My guess would be better off," Gina replied after a moment of thought. "It's clear that The Tradition is favoring an army made up of unlikely heroes. So the more unlikely we are, the more likely it is that we'll get Traditional luck in force behind us."

"Maybe we should all be hunchbacks or something, too," Dita said from their rear, prompting giggles.

"I wouldn't go that far," Gina replied. "But it's pretty clear that the more we invoke the Traditional path, the better off we will be. So those of you who have noble blood, I would like you to renounce it and swear blood-sisterhood to the band."

A couple looked reluctant for a moment or two, but the rest, some of whom were exceedingly angry with their families for giving them up, readily agreed. Then there was some chaotic nonsense and a little girlish squealing over having to extract a bit of blood to mingle with the others, during which both Adam and Gina stood by impassively until they had all settled again.

"Now," said Gina with a grim smile. "I am going to prove to you that this has already worked."

She crooked her finger and summoned Dita, possibly the least likely fighter of them all, from the back of the group. She picked up one of the two fighting staves she had at her feet, and handed it to the girl, who held it uncertainly. Then she herself took the second stave, looked off nonchalantly into the distance, then suddenly whirled and executed a lightning three-strike attack on the girl, holding nothing back.

The others gasped, squealed or screamed. Dita herself yelped.

But her hands moved surely and of themselves. *Crack, crack, crack.* All three attacks were met. And countered.

Gina grounded the staff and went back to parade-rest with it tucked over her shoulder. Dita stared at her hands, dumbfounded.

"Now, that will only work if you are attacked without any warning," Gina said. "And with an audience. However, you will find yourselves picking up fighting skills at a rate that would make most commanding officers weep with envy. Your real job will be to get yourselves into good fighting condition so that you can use those skills. I trust I make myself clear?"

"Perfectly," Adam rumbled. And turned an eye with a wicked glint in it on the girls. "Exercises, ladies. Strength and flexibility training. Twice a day, at dawn and at dusk."

Gina smiled. She liked the way Adam thought. "We'll start out training with staves. You're less likely to get damaged, and they're easy to replace. Shockingly versatile to use, too, and invoking Robbing John's Tradition, as well. Meanwhile Adam here will be getting you proper armor and arms. And they will fit well and look like garbage."

Some of the girls' mouths dropped open, as Gina continued. "This will be armor that would make a cat laugh. You will all look as if you'd dug the stuff up out of the backyard. This will be the *Ragged Company*, remember. We need to invoke The Tradition. If you look like a lot of hardy warmaidens, shining and beautiful, you'll lose. If you look like a disorganized gaggle of girls who didn't have brothers to take the family armor, you will win."

Actually, it was by no means certain that this was the truth. There were plenty of "Ragged Companies" that had gone down into the obscurity of failure. But they hadn't had three key things that Gina was pretty certain were going to make the difference.

They hadn't had a Champion leading them.

They hadn't had a Champion trained by a Godmother planning their moves and their appearance.

And they hadn't had dragons.

"All right, ladies, you know what our plan is. You're dismissed to take care of community business, but from now on, you're each going to have to decide just how fit you are and how much extra time you are going to want to devote to training to make yourselves fitter. This, of course, is going to be as well as the morning and evening exercises and the afternoon weapon-work." Gina nodded as a couple of the girls sighed in resignation. Still. They had volunteered. They could unvolunteer at any time. Gina did not want any reluctant fighters on her side.

The group broke up, and Adam brought his head back down to Gina's level. "How much of that was true-talk and how much was morale building?" he asked quietly.

She shrugged. "Most of it is true. Glass Mountain Champions study The Tradition quite extensively, because Godmother Elena and Grand Master Alexander send us out on some rather complicated missions. If there are any Champions in the world that are good at manipulating The Tradition, it's us. Now the question of just exactly how much this is going to make a difference remains to be seen. You and I have to come up with good strategy. I think we can do this. The way that the Palace itself is situated plays to our advantage. The fact that the Princess is known to most of the Guards there plays to our advantage. The isolation of the Palace plays to our advantage."

Adam nodded, eyes glowing with enthusiasm.

She shrugged. "Now, can you get me Dwarven armor that looks as if it's been dragged through hell?"

He pondered that for a moment. "Well, I can get you Dwarven armor, and we have more than enough to pay for it, but they're pretty peculiar about pride-in-workmanship, and getting them to do something that looks bad—I don't know."

Gina smiled. "You just get the Armor Master up here and leave that to me."

They had a visitor. An Armor Master of a Wyrding Dwarf clan. Andie was playing the Princess, which was, evidently, a Traditional role that needed to be invoked occasionally—like today—in order to keep the good luck flowing.

So today, when they had a visitor, the rightful-heir part of the story needed to be displayed. Andie was gowned in the one white sacrificial dress that had survived intact, with a gold belt, a gold circlet and a gold collar from Adam's hoard making her look regal. She felt like an idiot, but evidently the Dwarf was impressed.

The visitor was a female Armor Master, which was something of a shock. There were rumors that female Dwarves didn't exist, that there were never more than one or two, that there was no way of telling them from the males because both sexes had beards.

It didn't appear that any of that was true.

The lady in question was sturdy, short and fairly rough-hewn; you would expect that of a Dwarf. She was also unmistakably female, beardless and very much in charge of her entourage.

Andie's role here was to be silent and serene. The former was easy; the latter she could fake. Apparently, according to Periapt, Dwarven rulers never said anything themselves. They let their underlings do all the talking. So she, flanked by Peri on the left, sat on an improvised throne, while the Armor Master, flanked by a swarthy dwarf with an ax almost as big as he was, sat on a section of column. Two younger Dwarves, with much shorter beards than the swarthy one, negotiated with Adam and Gina.

A price was agreed on. All of the girls were brought in and measured meticulously. Several "adjustable" sets of armor were added to the list, because it did not appear that destroying the scale was having any effect on the spell binding Adam to carry off the sacrificial virgins.

Now, finally, the subject of "appearance" came up, and Andie braced herself.

"Gold-washed, or silver-washed?" the elder of the two negotiators asked. "With these lovely ladies, I would personally recommend gold-washed armor—it will set their—"

"Actually—" Gina said, with a note of apology in her voice, "neither. We want it to look like this, more or less—"

And with that, she laid out a set of shabby armor. A mail-coat that was tarnished and even rusted in places, with ragged edges to the hems, as if the armorer had gotten tired of weaving in links and had just given up. A helmet dinged and dented. Bracers and greaves that had clearly seen better days.

The four Dwarves stared. The two youngest went absolutely round-eyed. The Armor Master's guard made as if to draw his ax.

But it was the Armor Master herself whose reaction was the most unexpected.

She rose out of her seat, bristling, outrage in every line of her. "Impossible!" she shouted. "Out of the question! We are masters of the craft! What do you take us for?"

Adam looked nonplussed and diffident, but Gina simply raised an eyebrow.

"I beg your pardon," she said politely. "I was under the impression that you were masters of the craft. I'm sorry you can't manage to give us the sort of armor we need. Have you any recommendations on who could?"

All four Dwarves stopped. Just stopped. No movement, hardly any breathing, nothing to show that they were even alive at that moment.

The Armor Master gave Gina a look that could have blistered paint, but asked, with icy politeness, "This is not what Dwarven armor should look like."

"But it is what the armor of a Ragged Company should look like," Gina replied, just as politely. "We are not only needing the best possible protection, we need to invoke the aid of a powerful Traditional path."

There was a long silence. A very long silence. And then, "Ah. I see," said the Armor Master. She sat down again, then leaned over and pondered the pathetic armor laid out in front of her.

"This is quite a challenge," Gina said casually. "Something that would take a great deal of finesse. Every suit must be slightly different. Suits that all had the same apparent flaws would be recognized immediately for a ruse. And it is going to be an even greater challenge to create those apparent flaws without weakening the armor. Anyone can make beautiful armor. It will take a true master to make these."

The Armor Master stroked her chin. "True, true," she muttered. "A challenge. Quite a challenge."

"We wouldn't ask just anyone," Adam said helpfully.

"Hmm." The Dwarf ignored him. Finally she nodded brusquely. "We can do this."

"I rather thought you could," chuckled Gina. "Shall we conclude our negotiations, then?"

The Dwarves departed with their measurements, their instructions and their fees. Andie divested herself of circlet, necklet, belt, bracelets and rings with a sigh of relief, turning them all over to Peri to be put back in the hoard. "That was cleverly handled," she said to Gina in a voice full of admiration. "Very clever. I don't think I would have thought of that appeal to their vanity."

"Oh, you would have, and I've had the advantage of dealing with a Dwarf or two before."

"Still. I'm glad I didn't have to."

Gina just grinned. So did Adam. "I will admit," the dragon said playfully, "that I was seriously wondering about your sanity there for a moment."

"Only a moment? I'm the leader of this herd of cats," she responded. "I doubt my sanity every day."

Andie went back to her room to change, carefully folding up the sacrificial gown and putting it away. They might need it again another day. Actually, they probably *would* need it again another day.

Nevertheless, it was not a role nor an image Andie was particularly comfortable with. Too much of a figurehead. Too much like the role that she thought her mother might be playing.

In the past few days she had been wavering back and forth between certainty that her mother was the puppet in the hands of Solon and certainty that her mother was equally guilty. And when she actually thought about it, she had to admit to herself that when she was certain that it was the former, it was because that was what she wanted to believe—and when it was the latter, it was because that was what logic told her.

But there was more than enough to think about and more than enough to do without brooding on something she couldn't change and something that would not affect her anyway.

While the other girls learned the sword, she was learning the sling, and evidently, The Tradition strongly approved of her taking up this ancient Acadian shepherd's weapon, because she could put a lead bullet through the eye-slit of one of those old helms at sixty paces.

She and Peri were also busily engaged in a search of history books as well as those one might lump under the category of "lore" for more ways of manipulating The Tradition to their own ends. So far the prospects for both a peasant army and an all-female army looked quite good. Granted, there had never actually been an all-female army before, but there had been a Unicorn army, a wing of a full dozen dragons, innumerable instances of Gryphons, Hippogriffs, and other creatures forming something like an army—and doing well, too.

Speaking of which… "Have you spoken to the Unicorns yet?" she asked Peri.

He dropped his head a foot. "No," he replied. "Actually—no, I haven't."

She sighed. "You know that someone is going to have to. And you know that they are too busy serving up adoration to pay much attention to anything I tell them."

His head dropped another foot. "I know," he said glumly. "But…but I hate making them unhappy!"

"If you can tell me how we could possibly bring Unicorns into the Palace, I would like to hear this plan," she replied.

"Honestly, I would very much like to add them to the invading force. But I can't see any way of getting them *to* the Palace, much less *through* the Palace."

"But they look so dejected when you tell them they can't do something!" he said. "It's a heartbreak for them!"

She considered the options. "Well, how about this. Tell them they can join our forces but only if they can get to the Palace on their own."

He perked up. "That is an excellent solution. I doubt very much that any of them will even think about it, much less plan it. Their attention span is usually dependent on whether or not a butterfly is passing. I will go talk to them."

She smiled warmly at him. "Thank you. I hate disappointing them, too."

But not too much.

CHAPTER THIRTEEN

Solon sprawled in his favorite chair, stared at the flame of the lamp on the table in front of him and brooded. The fox had vanished. Had not returned at all and there was no sign that it ever would. Solon was furious. He had tried tracking the beast, but for some reason the geas it was under had been negated.

How that could happen, he could not imagine. Unless…

The fox was in the Wyrding Lands and any number of things could have happened to it. It could have been caught and eaten. It could have attracted the attention of a Magician of some kind, witch or hedge-wizard, and the geas could have been broken in that way. A witch or a hedge-wizard should not have been able to do so, but it was the Wyrding Lands and the Wyrding Others had powers inherent to their nature that were not altogether predictable.

Likeliest, though, was that the foul thing had gotten itself eaten. It would be ironic in the extreme if it had been eaten by his dragon.

Which might be exactly what had happened. If the dragon had sensed the fox carrying around that scale he'd given it— The more he thought about it, the likelier that scenario seemed.

At least he knew that the dragon was still alive. The charm remained warm. It had shown up precisely when it should have done to take the next two sacrifices, so there was no need to worry yet.

He had sent some nonspecific curses aimed at Andromeda, but they had neither rebounded nor struck home. They probably were too nonspecific. They had probably faded as such things did when they did not find a target.

But the Queen was demanding an answer. And he did not have one to give her.

Damn fox! Why could it not have—

Then he smiled. The Queen was no Magician, and he was the only decent Magician she knew. He could tell her whatever he chose, and she would never know one way or another. He rose, smoothed down his robes and moved into his bedroom.

It was an austere place, except for the not-too-obvious comforts of silken sheets and luxurious goose-down mattress and pillows. She never came here; he always came to her, like a supplicant. That was how she liked things, but so did he. He did not want her here. She would be an intruder, impinging on his privacy. She would want to change the stark, white walls with lush murals, want to pile the bed high with pillows, want layers of gauzy drapes instead of the heavy damask, and flowers, flowers everywhere. He wanted only the occasional scent of bitter incense, aloes and myrrh. No flowers. No sweetness. Not even much sensuality, actually. Nothing overt.

She was everything overt, and becoming more so as she grew older. He craved a simpler style.

Well, perhaps he would not need to put up with her for much longer. For now, though, she was expecting him and it didn't do to keep her waiting.

He thumbed the hidden catch on the headboard of the bed, and the entire section of wall, headboard and all, moved slightly outward with a *click*, showing the outline of the hidden door-panel. He shoved on the bed, which slid sideways on hidden wheels, taking the headboard and the wall with it. After slipping into the passageway he tugged on the handle built into the panel on that side. Bed, headboard and wall moved back in place, and he pulled them shut.

The passage was black, stuffy and narrow, but he didn't need a light. It ended in only one place: the Queen's bedroom. Who had built it? Why? It had to have been installed when the Palace itself was built, and probably for the oldest of reasons, for the same (almost) reason he used it—to visit a lover.

Or perhaps not. It might have been for escape...

He felt his way along the passageway until his hands encountered the blank wall of the end; the latch and the handle were at waist height. He triggered the latch release and pushed a little, then tugged sideways. One good thing about

Cassiopeia's penchant for draperies and arras everywhere was that they hid her side of the secret passage, which was not built into the headboard of a bed. He squeezed through the gap, leaving it open as always. If he had to leave in a hurry because of an emergency or the unexpected arrival of a servant…

She was alone, lounging luxuriously on a pile of cushions. He surveyed her with a false and foolish smile on his face. But behind his smile of infatuation he surveyed her coldly.

Aging. Definitely aging—hints of a wrinkle there, a sag here; breasts that were no longer pert; the signs of a little more chin than she should have… Age did not treat women well. It gave men dignity, but it left women with signs of wear.

She looked up. "Have you—?"

"Yes. News, my Queen. They are both disposed of."

Relief suffused her features. "The dragon?"

He shook his head. "The Wyrding Others. Some sort of monster, possibly a Hydra, possibly a Chimera," he said, lying fluently. "My informant could only convey an appalling number of heads and teeth, and an ambush on the road."

She laughed. And though he was in agreement with her about the need to eliminate Andromeda, still, there was something sickening about the fact that this woman was laughing about the death of her own daughter.

"One less trouble to worry about. What chance that anyone will ever find remains? I might be forced to act if they do."

"None," he lied again. Or—well, this wasn't a lie; no one would find remains because there were no remains to be found. "The thing came back several times to drag everything to its den. No one will ever find anything."

Unholy joy. That was certainly the right description for her expression. And as he joined her in her bed, he wondered how long it would be before he could be wed to her, then rid of her.

The Queen watched the hidden door close behind Solon, and wondered how long it would be before she could afford to be rid of him.

The problem was that he was a Magician, and they were always tricky to eliminate. She sank back among her pillows and considered her options.

There was poison, but Wizards were notoriously suspicious of their food and drink and Solon was no exception to that rule. He examined every bite and sip, never ate anything in public that did not derive from a common platter, never ate or drank anything in her presence that did not come from a source they shared. For all she knew he never ate or drank anything in private that he had not prepared with his own hands. So poison was probably not an option.

There was the possibility of doing it with her own hands. That had the advantage that she could always claim he had tried to take advantage of her, or better still, that she had discovered he was the one who had summoned the dragon. That was better still, because it was the truth, and one misleading truth was better and more effective than a hundred lies. So that was a possibility. The only problem was that so far she had not seen him in a single unguarded moment for as long as she had known him. Not even in bed. Especially not in bed.

So that left getting someone else to do it.

The best would be to have someone discover he was the summoner of the dragon. Then she could easily condemn him as a traitor and have him put to death.

The problem with that particular scenario was that he would implicate her, as well. And while as the Queen she could have him silenced, one way or another, there would always be doubts. And without him to hold the Border against interfering interlopers like Champions and Godmothers, the next thing she knew there would be someone calling her to account.

So that was probably not viable.

She turned over on her stomach and rested her chin on her arms, thinking. Getting one of her Guard simply to kill him probably would not work, either. He was much, much too clever to be caught doing anything egregious. No one would believe her if he was found here and she claimed he had forced his way in, and unless he was killed on the spot—not likely—the same problem arose as with denouncing him. He would talk. Word would spread. The jealous-lover scenario was also not a good choice, tempting though it was. Not unless she could find someone who was both hopelessly naive and much more powerful than he was.

She had to laugh at that idea. Powerful wizards of whatever ilk did not get that way by being naive. She might be able to find someone, but it was a certainty that she would only trade one problem for another.

Irritating. Very irritating.

And none of this had to happen, that was the most irritating part of all. If that tedious husband of hers had just had the grace to die by himself— It wasn't as if he had been doing anything remotely useful with his life. If he had been a great King and Warrior, he would have conquered the Wyrding Others and gotten back all that valuable property for the Crown. The timber in there was amazing, so the shipwrights said. Acadia could have exported it, even started shipbuilding trades here. She frowned. It just gave her a headache. All that timber waiting to be exploited and no one touching it. And for what? So the trees could grow to a size too big to support their own weight, fall over and die. What good did that do?

And who knew what else was in those mountains? Gold and silver surely; there were Dwarves in there, and everyone knew that Dwarves went where the gold and silver and gems were. All that could have belonged to the Crown, too, if her husband had just done his duty by her and his country. Treaties weren't worth a feather. But if he had really needed an excuse, there was a ready enough one in that the Treaty Lands were simply packed with dangerous creatures that the so-called "good" ones were protecting. If those Wyrding Others were so "good," so benign, then why hadn't they been turning in the "bad" ones? That alone was sufficient reason to invade the Treaty Lands.

As it was, he had to be gotten out of the way so she would have a freer hand in controlling these people. Without a Warrior-King, she was going to have to hire mercenaries to take over the Treaty Lands, and he simply would have put up too many objections to the kinds of taxes needed to pay for something like that. And it wasn't as if she'd raised taxes all at once. A little here, a little there—people learned to cope, learned to work a little harder. Those that couldn't, well, they had to give way to those that could.

Couldn't they see how she was going to make them all prosperous? It really was annoying how ignorant they were.

She stared at the flame of her scented oil lamp and pondered the puzzle. It certainly was obvious God put some people in the seats of power. Most people were too stupid even to know what was good for them. It required those who were superior by birth and by native cleverness to be the shepherds over these sheep.

People like Cassiopeia.

Take the storms she'd had Solon create. If people had simply been law-abiding and hadn't persisted in trying to evade the port taxes, she wouldn't have needed to have Solon work nasty weather magic on the coastline. It was too bad about the farmers and herdsmen living there, and the fishermen, but the fishermen were probably all smugglers themselves, and the farmers would be able to relocate to much better situations once she had the Treaty Lands under control.

It was all about control. Everything would be so much better once she had it all under control.

Even the dragon... If people didn't have the sense to understand that she knew exactly what needed to be done to make Acadia into a Kingdom both envied and respected, then they would have to reap the fruits of their ignorance. Once someone had lost a daughter to the dragon, he became remarkably cooperative. It was too bad that those girls all had to die because their fathers were fools, but unfortunately, one could not make a pigeon pie without squab dying.

She caught herself frowning more deeply, and with a sigh, forced herself to stop. Frowning made wrinkles. This was not sorting out how to be rid of Solon, either.

Perhaps it would be best to turn to the professionals. Using a hired killer presented a number of advantages. He would not ask questions. He would not make demands past his fee. And above all, he would get the job done.

The more she thought about it, the better she liked the idea, in fact. A hired professional would know how to remove a Wizard and have the right tools for the job. There would be no accidents. No, this was a good idea, a very good idea. He would be expensive—well, a couple of shipwrecks would pay for that. But there was certainly no one in Acadia who could do the job properly, so she would have to look outside the country.

If she put things in motion to find her assassin now, by the time Solon became truly unbearable, she would have the man.

She smiled to herself and snuggled down more comfortably among her cushions. She would get the search started tomorrow. This would take some careful work—indirect of course, but Solon was not the only person of negotiable nature she employed. That was another trick, really—learning how to play such creatures off against one another. But superior intelligence and breeding would always tell.

* * *

Andie was no longer in charge of washing dishes. In fact, Andie was no longer relegated to doing any "chores" as such, unless she had the time and wanted to. The two new girls had been more than happy to take over from her so that she could help Peri in the one area where he and she outshone everyone else.

"My friend and companion, the lore-scholar," Gina called her, and with some truth. She and Peri were searching through his books looking for every scrap of Traditional magic that might be invoked on their behalf. And for tactics that might help the tiny "army" invade the Palace with no casualties.

So far, the going had been slow. A pity, but there it was. Gina was much more versed in Traditional paths as applied to the art of war than Peri or Andie were. Still, it was worth searching for, and in the process they had found one or two useful bits of information.

That the best time to stage this invasion would be right before the Watch changed, because the men on duty would be tired and thinking of dinner and bed, and not looking for trouble.

That it would be best if the Princess went in with the first of the invaders and showed the Guards who she was, because it was just possible she might be able to turn one or more to their side. Or, if she couldn't turn them, frighten them, as they would certainly think they were seeing a spirit.

That the first place they should take was the lookout point, which Adam had thought to leave for last. But according to the strategist in whose book Peri had found this gem, taking the lookout point meant they would have a secure staging area and a place to fall back to that they could hold if the entire plan went sour.

This had seemed like a very good idea to Andie, and Adam and Gina had both agreed.

At the moment she and Peri were literally curled up together. He was coiled like a giant cat in the center of the library, and she was tucked in among his legs while they both read the book she was holding. Her back rested on his shoulder, and his neck was arched so that his head was down beside hers.

"I really enjoy reading Aldo Natharn's work," she was saying wistfully. "He has a great turn of phrase."

"He's very witty," Peri agreed, sounding just as wistful. "I only wish there was more substance there."

"Exactly. We must have read ten pages already, and while we've had quite a few chuckles, we haven't actually learned anything." She sighed and closed the book as Peri nodded, and touched her shoulder affectionately with his muzzle.

"We'll have to put him aside as an entertaining gossip and chase some other hare," Peri agreed. "But—"

Andie laughed and patted his nose. "I'll put him on the pile for later."

She got up and moved over to a small pile of books isolated from the rest. These were volumes they had both found particularly entertaining. Not at all relevant, but so entertaining that they knew they were going to want to go back to them when all this had concluded.

She picked up another book from the stack, settled into the embrace of his coiled body, opened it at the beginning, and they both began to read.

This had to be the most curious situation in all of her life. Not that she had a great deal to compare it to, of course, living, as she had, quite a sheltered existence. But if anyone had ever had a friend quite like Periapt, she had yet to read about it.

The most peculiar thing was the feeling, the conviction, that here was someone she had been looking for as a friend and companion her entire life.

When they were talking and she wasn't actually looking at him—in the dark, say, when they would go up to the top of the tower to rest their eyes and look at the stars—she never, ever even *thought* about the fact that he was a dragon. In fact, if she was reading a book with him and he would say something aloud, she would get a kind of shock to her system when she looked up and saw, not a person, but a huge, dusky-emerald dragon head.

The shock was getting worse, too, not better, every time she looked up and didn't see the studious young man she expected to see.

After the first two or three pages, it became obvious that there was going to be nothing in this volume that was at all useful to the would-be fighters. Just as she thought that, Peri's voice in her ear said virtually the same thing.

"Another edition of 'Lives of the Rich and Famous and I'm Their Sycophant,'" Peri said in disgust. "At least the last one was amusing! This fellow is just a boot-licker."

She sighed. "Sad but true." She handed the book to Peri, who took it carefully between two blunted talons and placed it atop the "reject" pile. "My eyes hurt," she said plaintively, as he surveyed the stacks of books they hadn't read yet.

"Then by all means, we will save your eyes for a bit," Peri said, with a chuckle that rumbled inside his chest. He put his head down along his folded forelegs and looked up at her with an amused expression.

"What are you thinking about?" he asked.

"That I've never known anyone it was easier to be— friends with," she said, hesitating a moment over the "friend" part. Because it felt as if their relationship was unfolding into something a great deal warmer than mere friendship.

"It's odd, isn't it?" he responded. "Except for my brother, I've never been as comfortable around any dragon as I am around you. I don't quite know how to fathom it."

"Then let's not," she said instantly, not wanting to spoil anything. "All right?"

He laughed. "One can certainly analyze things until they are no longer enjoyable. I bow to your wisdom. I am just happy to enjoy your company."

She felt warm and tingly in a pleasant sort of way as he looked down at her with those glowing dark-emerald eyes. Feeling greatly daring, she reached out and scratched the soft skin under his chin.

He sighed. "Oh, glory. That feels lovely. Don't stop doing that for the next thirty years or so. Take more time if you need it."

She laughed, but kept scratching.

"I wish there was something I could do for you that felt as good," he said, in a voice rich with content.

"You already are," she said. "You're very comfortable to sit on."

He laughed again, this time with a note of self-mockery. "I shall be sure to add that to my list of virtues. 'Makes a comfortable chair.' I am sure the Great Dragon at the gates of Paradise will find that ample reason to let me in straight-away. And the rest of my clan will surely inscribe it on my memorial wall."

She blinked. "Dragons believe in Paradise?" she said, surprised.

"Of course they do, silly goose," Peri replied, with an-other affectionate brush of his nose on her shoulder. "And so do Centaurs and Nymphs, Unicorns and Dryads, Sylphs and Merfolk—really every intelligent creature." He glanced over at the corner, where the fox was curled up on a flat cushion. "Even foxes, I suppose."

"My Paradise has chickens in it," the fox said medita-tively. "Chickens as far as the eye can see. Chickens that are too fat to fly. And a pretty little vixen to share them with," he added.

"There," Peri said, with a chuckle. "Every creature that knows it is mortal has some hope for something good on the other side of death. And every vision of Paradise is dif-ferent. And, I suppose, they can all be true."

That idea just made her head spin, so she changed the subject. She recalled how he had said that except for some siblings and mated pairs, dragons rarely spent any time to-gether. "If you can't share the same territory, how can you be friends with other dragons?" she asked doubtfully.

"Oh, we can, just not in the same way that humans are," he replied. "And to tell the truth, Adam and I are rather dif-ferent in that regard. We like the company of other dragons, when we can get it, and that of other thinking creatures, too."

"Does that include me?" asked the fox.

Peri regarded the little beast steadily. "Let's just say I haven't made up my mind and leave it go at that," he said.

"Oh, you will," the fox said cheerfully. "I grow on you. Before long you'll be counting yourself as one of my legion of admirers."

Peri made a quiet gagging sound, and Andie giggled.

"To get back to the original subject, most dragons prefer to be friends at a distance. Occasionally meet where the edges of our territories join—that sort of thing. Chat, exchange news, perhaps play a round of the riddle game, then go our separate ways. Most dragons are rather hermit-like, but Adamant and I are different—we really *like* being around other creatures. That's why we stayed together after we were deemed to be adults. It just seemed too lonely otherwise." He sounded wistful, and Andie kept scratching, softly under his chin. "At any rate, there is an exception to this, and that is the Conclave that is held every five years. All dragons on this continent come together at Windhover Mountain in the Kingdom of Lavereine. The Godmother there is a particular friend of dragons, and she makes sure that everyone gets properly fed so that we don't make enemies while hunting the place dry."

"What do you do there?" she asked, fascinated.

"Socialize, exchange news, play games, hold contests, show off children, tell tall tales, deal with any important issues that have cropped up regarding Dragonkind, find mates…" He chuckled. "Not necessarily in that order. All dragons on every continent have Conclaves every five years, always in the same safe place. Or at least, the Dragons of Light do. I don't know about the Dragons of Darkness."

"Oh, they probably do," said the fox. "Where else are they going to be able to complain about all of you?"

Peri gave the fox a penetrating glance. "You are altogether too sharp," he said.

"I told you that you would become one of my legion of admirers," said the fox complacently.

"Don't count on it," Peri growled under his breath.

"Do you make laws there?" she asked the dragon curiously.

"Well—no, actually," he said, with that peculiar duck of his shoulders she now knew meant he was embarrassed. "Dragons don't much care for laws, even among the Dragons of Light. But then again, we live so far apart from one another, it's hard to imagine how we could enforce laws on each other."

"You don't need laws!" the fox said cheerfully from his corner. "What on earth do you need laws for? They just get in the way."

"Anarchist," Peri mumbled. "Anyway, we're expected to take a mate and raise exactly two offspring in our lifetimes. You can have more than two, but you're expected to have a pair. Your pairing generally lasts as long as the children are sub-adult, then breaks apart. But just because it's a pairing—well, you see, there are pairings…and pairings. Our mother and father, for instance, rarely saw one another except when he was doing his share of the hunting." He sighed. "I envy humans that closeness they all seem to have."

"It does seem as if you dragons must spend a lot of time being lonely," she ventured.

He chuckled ruefully. "Most like being solitary. I know Father did, and really, so did Mother. It's Adam and I that are the odd creatures out. It's not unheard of for dragons to prefer company over solitude, but it's not usual, either."

"You know," Andie said after a while, "you ought to get a Godmother or a Chapter-House to take you two on. You would never have to worry about whether you were depleting your territory again, and you would never have to do without company."

Peri tilted his head to the side and regarded her thoughtfully. "That is a very good idea. And when we've dealt with this situation, I believe I will look into it."

This situation. She shook her head. "I wish one of us was a Magician. Or we could find one. When it comes to the geas that's on Adam, none of us has any idea how to remove it."

"But we don't know who in Acadia we can trust," he pointed out.

"I wouldn't trust anyone when in comes to Magicians," the fox said resentfully. "I mean! Look what happened to me!"

"You don't appear to be injured substantially," Peri responded, looking over at the fox, whose glossy coat and round belly gave mute testimony that his sojourn among the sacrificial maidens was anything but unpleasant. In fact, he was being spoiled rotten.

"Yes, but I'm a wild thing! Born to run my prey to earth, to live by my wits, to be free! Now I'm an errand boy and a lapdog!" The fox flattened his ears and attempted to look pathetic.

"Oh, please," Peri replied, shaking his head. "Your geas is broken, you have every opportunity to run away and be free. So go do it. Shoo."

The fox sighed. "That's right. Bring logic into it."

"Thank you," said Peri. "I try."

Now, through all of this, Andie had been doing her best not to break into hysterical laughter. Peri's sense of humor was so much like her own that she felt as if she had finally found the kindred spirit she had been looking for all of her life, without knowing it.

She caught Peri's eye and they exchanged a sly glance.

"If you really want to be free that badly," she said, trying to put a helpful tone into her voice, "I can tell the other girls that you don't want to be given tidbits anymore, and Gina that you would rather be independent and not clean up the offal when she dresses game."

The fox's ears were flat to his head, his eyes big and sad. "No cheese," he moaned as if to himself. "No rabbit heads..."

"I'll go tell them now," she said, making as if to stand up.

"No!" the fox shouted, leaping to his feet. "No! Don't do that!"

"No?" she asked innocently. "But I thought—"

"I've changed my mind. I am just as free here as I am in the forest," he said firmly. "Absolutely. Positively. No doubt in my mind."

"All right, then," she said, as Peri made little strangling sounds. "As long as you're sure. I wouldn't want you to be unhappy."

"Never been happier," the fox replied. "In fact, I think I'll go tell the other girls just how happy I am to be here, how much I enjoy the company and attentions and how I never want to leave."

Peri sounded as if he was in danger of choking to death.

"Good idea," she said. "Go do that. Everyone likes to know they're appreciated."

The fox trotted off, muttering "cheese…" under his breath, and as soon as he was out the door, Peri let out a small explosion of fire and laughter.

"Hey!" she exclaimed, laughing herself, and batting at the sparks that fell on her tunic and hair, putting them out before they could cause a mischief. "I'm not fireproof!"

"Sorry, sorry," he said, and got himself back under control. "How do you fit that much ego into such a small body? He is so sure he can pull the wool over all of our eyes…."

"Well, he's *awfully* intelligent for being 'just' a fox," she pointed out. "I'm not entirely certain he isn't something supplied by The Tradition. The path required that we be told certain information at this point. The fox would know it if only it were intelligent enough, so The Tradition supplied a fable-fox for us."

Peri blinked. "Good grief. That makes altogether too much sense in context. Yes, I can see that. How did you manage to reason that one out?"

"Have you ever gone down to the henhouse and listened to the chickens?" she asked. It was not a rhetorical question.

"Uh, no, I don't believe I have," Peri replied, looking non-plussed.

"You and Adam have the inherent ability to understand the language of the beasts," she said. "And I don't. So I began to feel guilty after listening to the fox babble, wondering if the things I had been blithely eating were that—personable. I went down to the henhouse. And imagine my relief to discover that the chickens were basically saying nothing but 'hey' with various inflections."

It had been kind of funny as well as a relief. Each cluck translated directly as 'hey.' "Hey, hey, hey," one hen clucked as a greeting to another. "Hey! Hey, hey," a mother hen cautioned her chicks to follow. "Hey! Hey! Hey!" called a third, alerting the whole yard to the hawk overhead. It might just as well have been the clucks she'd have heard before she drank the blood.

"In fact, I've been all over the area down there by the stream where we wash dishes and clothing, hiding until wild things come out and say something. The birds are all calling some variations on a few themes—calling their fledglings, saying they found something to eat, calling their mate, singing just because they can, and yelling at everything and everyone to get out of their space." That had been another immense relief. Even the deer she had encountered had been not much brighter than the chickens, taking one look at her, shouting "RUN!" and following his own advice. This might actually have been intelligent behavior if there had been any other deer with him to warn.

She explained all this as Peri listened intently. "Now that you mention it," he said, "you're right. I don't ever remember any other animal behaving the way this fox does. Except the Unicorns—"

"Which are inherently magical beings, like a Sphinx," she pointed out.

"This makes a great deal of sense." He nodded. "But our poor fox! What is going to happen to him? When he goes to find a mate, all he'll find are dumb vixens that can't talk and are only interested in—"

She favored him with a look loaded with irony.

"—oh," he said after a moment. "Forget I said anything."

It was, in fact, comforting to know that The Tradition had provided them with this particular source of information. It meant that The Tradition was paying attention to them. Just as the girls were picking up weapons' skills preternaturally fast, as if each and every one of them was a natural with a blade or a bow, showed that it was happy with this Traditional path and was doing its best to keep them on it.

"So we must be doing the right things," Peri said. "That's a good sign!"

"Yes, but just remember one thing, something Gina told me." She paused. "The Tradition favors tragedy as much as it does happy endings."

He nodded somberly.

There didn't seem to be anything more that either of them could say at that point. After staring at one another for several more long moments, it was Andie who broke the silence.

"Let's get back to the books."

CHAPTER FOURTEEN

Either Gina was the most brilliant weaponry teacher in all of the Five Hundred Kingdoms, or The Tradition really liked this new version of the Ragged Company.

Now, Gina was good, quite good. And Adam was turning out to be extremely helpful as an assistant instructor. He had an excellent eye for where someone was making a mistake, and a knack for coaching them through doing it right without being able to demonstrate the actions himself.

But the likeliest explanation was that things were picking up momentum.

Most days, when she wasn't slinging stones well enough that she was adding to the larder, Andie was with Periapt, digging more deeply into his books to find every scrap that might give them a little more Traditional edge. The latest was to give their group a name, the "Sworn Sisterhood," and an oath.

Peri had very carefully worded that oath. Not once was there even a hint that the Sworn Sisterhood had pledged to fight until death, or anything equally extreme and unpleasant. That would just have been an invitation to The Tradition to kill some of them off, with noble dying speeches.

As Peri said succinctly, "Dying with a noble speech on your lips is still dead. And having a wonderful monument is not compensation for a too-early demise."

Both Gina and Andie had been in fervent agreement with him. So the oath that the maidens took was defiant, but it wasn't invoking that particular aspect of The Tradition.

"We, the Sworn Sisterhood, do solemnly vow to take back Acadia from those who are responsible for the scourge of the dragon and the tempests. We will fight them with our hands and our weapons. We will fight them with the power of our conviction. We will face the enemy without fear. We will take the enemy down and bring the enemy to justice and there is nothing that can stand in our way."

All very powerful and empowering and not one word of defeat. The "enemy" was also cleverly defined as "those who are responsible for the scourge of the dragon and the tempests" so that The Tradition could not twist this around until the maidens were locked into being the "saviors" of Acadia forever. It felt like a good, tight oath, to Andie anyway, and when they had all sworn it, she thought she "felt" something respond—although not being a Magician, she couldn't be sure.

The Sworn Sisterhood now looked very good in their drills. Andie was used to watching her Guard drilling, and the girls compared favorably with those seasoned soldiers.

Although there was no telling what they would do when
they actually got into combat.

With Peri gone for the afternoon, off to see their trading partners for more supplies, Andie was somewhat at
loose ends.

And oddly lonely.

She wandered off to watch the other girls practicing one-
on-one with Gina's oversight. They wore their full armor
now, although they did not use real swords, only weighted
wooden ones. They didn't use shields, either, somewhat to
Andie's surprise. Instead, the hand that would ordinarily
have held a shield held a knife nearly long enough to be
called a sword itself.

As she sat there, her feeling of loneliness increased. And
this was strange, because she had always been solitary, and
did not usually feel lonely when alone. But she watched
Gina with Adam and—

—and she realized that she wasn't happy being solitary
anymore.

But the person she was happiest with wasn't a person.

It was Periapt.

Being with him was like being with the perfect companion. He was clever. He was kind, at least to her—though
he had been scathing with the fox, and once or twice with
Cleo, whom he regarded as being rather too full of herself.
They found the same kinds of things funny, they enjoyed
the same sorts of books, and it was getting so that they
could finish each other's sentences. She was never happier
than when she was curled up with him, having a lively
discussion over some obscure point in a book.

In fact, simply being with him made her happy—happy in a way that no human male had ever made her feel. Maybe it was simply that he didn't take long, doubtful glances at her oculars, or act polite while all the time he was actually bored.

That realization made her feel very odd indeed. And she wasn't entirely sure what to make of it.

While she was thinking about this, Adam oozed up the hill as only a dragon could, and arranged himself on the hillside near her. "You watched your Guard practice, right?" he asked. "How do my girls compare?"

He was calling them "my girls," and she had to smile at that. "The truth is that I'm no expert, nothing like," she demurred. "I mean, they look like they know what they're doing but—but I'm used to people who use shields as well as swords."

"Well, Gina thought this would be a much better style for them, and I have to agree," he said, his eyes on the two combatants on the trampled grass in the center. "The problem with a shield is that it's heavy, and the longer fighting goes on, the heavier it seems to get. People who have never fought before either forget to bring it up in time, or are so busy hiding behind it that they forget they're supposed to be fighting. That long dagger can do almost as much as a shield can, yet it's not as heavy, and you can't hide behind it. You can only attack and continue attacking, keeping your opponent off balance as much as possible."

She nodded, now beginning to see the shape of Gina's tactics.

"Now that, combined with the fact that once the girls close in and it is going to be clear that they *are* girls, should give your Guards a bit of hesitation. And that, Princess, is where you come in." He leveled a shrewd gaze at her. "When they hesitate, you show yourself. One way or another, it's going to startle them. If they think you're dead and a spirit, good. They'll wonder why you're on the Sisterhood's side. If they think you're alive they're going to get a shock that you're on the Sisterhood's side."

"That's—that's really clever," she said.

He smiled. She could read all the dragons' expressions now, even the subtle ones. Like smiling.

"She's a Champion, but she's also a wise and thoughtful Champion. Me, I'm a kind of brute. You point me in the direction you want me to go, and I generally manage to clear a path for you."

She chuckled. "You don't give yourself enough credit."

He arched his neck, and his ruby-crystal eyes sparkled. "I do what I can. It's hard to keep up with someone like Gina, though my clan would probably have my hide for comparing myself to a mere human. But they ought to pay more attention to their own legends."

"Their own legends?" Now her curiosity was piqued. "What legends?"

"The legend of the first Bookwyrm. Didn't Peri tell you?" When she shook her head he cocked his. "I suppose he didn't think it was important. Well, it goes like this.

"There once was a Wizard who loved books more than anything. He had an enormous library, and as you might expect, he spent most of his time in it. So as a consequence he wasn't paying nearly as much attention as he should have been to the goings-on in his Kingdom. An army invaded and overthrew the King, and since this happened to be a barbarian horde that didn't have a lot of use for books or Wizards, they decided to finish the job by killing the Wizard and burning his books. He was caught entirely unaware, couldn't muster a lot of the usual defenses, and his men were pretty quickly cut down. So he did something your average powerful Wizard really shouldn't do unless the situation is entirely desperate and out of control. He cast a powerful and very open-ended spell, to transform himself into something unspecified that had the power to protect the books and to transport them to safety."

"He turned into a dragon?" she hazarded.

Adam nodded. "The first Bookwyrm. He managed to scare off the barbarians temporarily—just long enough for him to carry all the books away before they got their courage back. If the legend is true, he probably took them a short distance to get them all out, then found a more secure lair and moved them from the first spot at his leisure. But at any rate, that supposedly is why Bookwyrms like company in general, enjoy being with humans and hoard books."

At that moment he raised his head on his long neck and stared off into the distance. "And here comes Peri at last. I hope he managed to negotiate us something other than goat this time. I'm so tired of goat at this point that I'd choke down the oldest cow in Acadia."

Andie's heart leapt at the sight of the dark dot winging its way toward them.

* * *

"What are you thinking?" Peri asked curiously, breaking into her reverie.

Andie shook her head and stopped gazing into space. "A lot of things," she temporized, "but—" In desperation, because she did not want to even begin to talk about things she didn't understand herself yet, she brought up the one that was the most likely to intrigue him. "I—I'm trying to think of what I'm going to do if we really do have to depose Mo—"

—and now she couldn't bring herself to say the word "Mother."

Peri rescued her. "Queen Cassiopeia? I was under the impression that you were just going to have yourself crowned Queen. It's the usual thing." As usual she was in the "library," curled up with her back against his stomach, sitting on his folded legs. It was very comforting to be there.

The thing was, it was also beginning to feel a great deal like an embrace.

Not that she'd had a lot of experience with embraces. Once in a while as a child she had gotten a hug from someone, though not for a long while now. But—

This definitely felt like an embrace. It felt wonderful, in fact.

Was that wrong?

"Well…" she began.

"If you were going to entertain other ideas, however," he said, while she was still hesitating, "there is something I think you really ought to try for your country. No King, no Queen."

That so startled her that she lost track of the slightly disturbing thoughts she'd been having about Peri, and looked at him with both eyebrows raised. "How can you have a Kingdom with no King?" she asked.

"Well, it wouldn't be a Kingdom anymore. Just a country. And what you would do is find several people who are good leaders, then have the people of Acadia vote on which one they want." His eyes sparkled with enthusiasm. "It wouldn't work in a big Kingdom, because it would take too long to collect the votes, but Acadia is small enough you could do it."

"That," she said flatly, "is insane."

He looked terribly crestfallen. "But—there are people on the island of—"

"That's an island." She knew where he was talking about now, and the notion was quite, quite mad. "This is not only a Kingdom, it's one where it is hard to get to places outside of Ethanos. You can *fly*. It took Gina and me days to get to a village. Just how long do you think this—vote collection should go on? And how would people off in the hinterlands find out about these men? They can't afford to leave their homes just to spend a day or two listening to speeches. Should the candidates tour the countryside? That could take a year at least, and maybe longer. And it's dangerous!" She began to warm to her subject. "Unless you propose to leave the Wyrding Others out of the voting, which I do not advise, that means your candidates will have to come in here, the Wyrding Lands. Oh, that would be charming, for one or more of them to get eaten by a Chimera or carried off by a Sphinx!"

"But—" Peri said weakly.

"And seriously—aside from all of that—how can you *know* these people would be fit to rule? It could easily devolve to the best liar winning." She thought she had him there, but evidently that was the one argument he had a counter for.

"Rule-by-inheritance is hardly better," he said scornfully. "Look where it got you! The Queen is either the puppet of her Mage, or, far more likely, his co-conspirator in sending the country to ruin. She's fallen so far that she had no compunction about sending you to your death! And—"

She felt her face crumple, and tears form at the corners of her eyes.

He stopped in mid-sentence and stared. "Oh—oh my goodness, Andie—Andromeda, I'm sorry, please don't—"

She felt her stomach knot up and her throat close. All this time, and she had been trying so hard to keep it all under control. Because crying about it wasn't going to change anything.

"I didn't mean to offend you or upset you—I think you'd make a lovely Queen, really I do, the best possible—" He was babbling.

She was finding it hard to breathe. Her eyes burned and her throat and chest ached.

"And just because the Queen doesn't care about you, that doesn't mean that you aren't a wonderful, wonderful per—"

The first sob escaped her. She squeezed her eyes shut and tried to hold the next one in, but it was too strong for her, and the tears began, the strangled sobs slithering out of her control and shaking her body.

She felt him shifting himself under her and around her, rearranging himself, until she was being held in a real embrace. She opened blurring eyes to find that he had tucked her between his forelegs with his neck curled around her.

"Shhh—" he said, as she closed her eyes and threw her arms around his warm, soft, slippery neck. "I know, I know. It's all horrible. Just go ahead and cry, Andie. Go ahead and let it out. I think you've been holding it in too long."

She couldn't have stopped the flood now if she'd wanted to, and she really didn't want to. He was right. She'd been holding it in too long. She sobbed against his neck, eyes streaming and burning, throat raw and sore, chest aching. She babbled between the sobs, nothing really coherent, but just—

She'd wanted a mother. She'd wanted to make Cassiopeia proud of her so that she'd *be* that mother. Show her that even if her daughter wasn't like *her,* she was still worth something. Was useful. Could stand at the Queen's side and—

That was all she wanted.

And her mother found her so unworthy that Cassiopeia threw her away to feed a monster, like so much offal.

"Oh, Andie," Peri sighed in her ear. "Oh, my poor girl. It's Cassiopeia that's unworthy of *you.*"

But the doors were open, the floodgates were down, and she was quite, quite past rational thought now. All she could do was to cry—cry into the neck of her best friend in all the world, cry herself stupid and numb and finally exhausted, cry and cry and cry until she had nothing left, no tears, no energy, no feeling. And at last, she cried herself into sleep, right there, in the library, being cradled by a dragon.

When she woke, it was with a start, in the darkness. She was surrounded by breathing, deep and murmurous. If the South Wind could breathe, it would have sounded just like this. For a moment, she was only aware that she was not in her bed, and began to panic.

But the panic quickly subsided as her sore eyes and raw throat reminded her of what had happened, and thus, where she probably was.

She felt utterly drained, too weary to move, but she put out a hand and encountered a surface smooth and covered with scales, and then she knew where she was. And that Peri, rather than disturb her, had curled up comfortingly around her.

She listened to him breathing, telling herself that she was going to get up and go back to her proper bed any moment now. Any moment. Yes, any moment now…

And she fell back to sleep, still promising.

"I never meant to upset you." The voice came out of the darkness, from every direction and none, just like the breathing.

"I know you didn't," she replied. The darkness was very comforting, actually. You couldn't see, but you also couldn't be seen. Right this moment it was a good place to be.

"You'll make a fine Queen. You have everything you need to be a great ruler. And besides, The Tradition probably won't stand for anything but a monarchy anyway. We're the Five Hundred Kingdoms, right? You can't have a Kingdom without a King or Queen, or both, on a throne."

"Yes, but..." She felt an aching in her chest that had nothing to do with the grief that had made her cry herself into exhaustion. "It's the 'both' part that..."

The pain went from a dull ache to a stab, and she knew why. Assume that everything went beautifully and they won. She, Andie, would take the crown. And there she would be, with her heroic Sworn Sisterhood around her, in triumph.

Except that the Sworn Sisterhood was only "sworn" for as long as it took to put her on that throne. They would all go their separate ways—and properly, of course, because they'd had their lives interrupted and it was only fair and right that they be able to resume them.

Gina would go back to the Chapter-House of Glass Mountain. She was far too young to retire, and one small Kingdom could never hold a Champion for long.

And Peri would go, too. Adam would certainly want to return home again—wherever home was—and Peri would go with him. They were inseparable, and that was right and proper.

And there she would be.

Alone.

Oh, there were some people she could trust, of course, but—

But.

She would either wed, or not. But in either case—she would still be alone. If she wed, it would be for the sake of an alliance and an heir. It would all be very clear-cut and contractual. If she was lucky, her Prince-Consort would at least have one or two things in common with her—

But not share the enjoyment of the same sort of jokes. Not to read a passage from a book aloud because the language was so beautiful and have the other person nod and smile, agreeing with you completely...

Or she would not marry, and spend the rest of her life searching for someone with the right dynastic bloodline to put on the throne when she was gone, and do so alone.

And none of this could she, dared she, say.

"So you'll have a contest for your hand in marriage—very Traditional, that—" the voice said, *"and some handsome prince will win it, and you'll get married and live happily ever after."*

"But I don't want a handsome prince! I want—"

"—Andie—"

"—I want a kind, great-hearted, witty—"

"Andie!"

The urgent whisper, the hand on the shoulder shaking her—these finally hauled her up, reluctantly, into wakefulness.

Gina, of course. Bending over her, with a lamp in hand. "I saw you weren't in your bed and I got worried," she whispered. "First place I looked was here, since you spend all your time over here. And here you are."

If she noted Andie's tear-streaked face and red eyes, she didn't say anything about it. Just—

"Come on, Andie. If you sleep here much longer you'll get a cramp."

Insistent tugging on her arm—when had Gina taken her arm?—got her to rise, and they stumbled out into the dark together, leaving Peri alone.

She returned to her own cold, lonely bed, and lay there for a long time, wishing she was bold enough to go back to the library and sleep in the dragon's embrace.

There had been no sign of the Champion, nor of the Princess, and the dragon continued to come for the virgins just as if the Champion had never appeared at all. Solon began to feel that perhaps his lie had been the truth. Not the exact truth, but the Champion and Andromeda had met their ends, and not before time, either, somewhere out in the Wyrding Lands. And it did not matter if the end had come at the jaws and talons of the dragon or the claws and teeth of some other monster, so long as it had come.

This meant that he was free to concentrate on the next phase of his plan: to eliminate the Queen. But first, he had to induce her to marry him. It was the only way he would have the legitimacy to take over the throne when she met her fate.

So it was time to research something he had never, ever attempted before.

Love spells.

These were usually the provenance of what he referred to as the "ditch grubbers" of the magic world: the hedge-wizards, the village witches. Love spells were their bread-and-butter, their steady source of income. But most of them were not spells to make someone fall in love so much as predictive spells to tell you who would be your lover or wed you in the future. Only those of darker persuasions peddled love spells to call someone to your bed. That was coercion, and it was not the sort of thing that a "proper" Magician did.

Of course, virtually everything Solon did violated that unwritten code anyway, so he did not precisely care. However, it took time and concentration away from everything else he was doing. He often wished that he had another self that he could send out to deal with the day-to-day nonsense that was always cropping up. A minor problem with a merchant here, a conflict between nobles there, someone demanding his ear over some issue—it never seemed to stop coming. He hated it. He hated every moment of it. In a way he was dreadfully afraid that when he finally *did* take the throne, there would only be more of that nonsense.

Then again, when he took Cassiopeia's throne, there would be no Cassiopeia to deal with, so that would be one irritation out from under his skin.

Speaking of Cassiopeia...

He needed a powerful love spell—or more specifically, an infatuation spell—that did not require that she ingest, drink, wear or otherwise interact herself with the components of the spell. He didn't think that she was nearly as cautious about what she ate and drank and so forth as he was, but now was not the time to rest on assumptions. Since virtually every spell he looked at involved making a drink or baking a cake or anointing the object of desire with something, he was beginning to get quite frustrated, when utterly by chance he came across a scroll in his own library that he had not looked at in decades. It dealt with very primitive magic invoking the Laws of Imitation and of Contact. And it dealt with the making of images.

Now he had long since gotten past such simple and clumsy workings; in fact, he had really not done anything of the sort since first obediently reading the scroll, proving to his teacher that he could, in fact, make the ridiculous things work, and putting the scroll away.

But working with emotions was crude. Especially the baser emotions of lust and longing. And now, with his own vastly increased knowledge, he could make this magic so much more effective than the simplistic nonsense in this scroll...

The original called for a simple cloth doll made to resemble the object of desire as closely as possible. But the Law of Imitation was very clear that the more closely something resembled the original, the more effective the spell would be. And Solon had the means to make his "doll" very accurate indeed.

Using magic to create a homunculus, he had made a blank wax image; then, he had imbedded hairs, collected surreptitiously from Cassiopeia over long years, one by one into the scalp of the image and swirled the result into an approximation of her upswept hairstyle. He was actually surprised at how much of her hair he had acquired; he had made it second nature to carefully check his clothing and person for stray hairs whenever he had been around her or—most especially—after he had been in her bed. They were easily distinguished from his own by the silky texture. He had more than enough for a dozen dolls, in fact.

That done, he had taken the poppet, wrapped it in spell-inscribed silk and tucked it into the corner of the secret passageway. There, over the course of the next three days, in close proximity to the Queen, it had come to look more and more like her. By the time he had retrieved it at the end of that three days, it was identical to her in every way, but in miniature.

Now it was ready for the spell. And he could use all of his knowledge and all the Laws of Magic to set it. Not just the Laws of Imitation and Contact. Now, with fuller knowledge, he could invoke the Laws of Words of Power, of True Names, of Knowledge. He knew Cassiopeia as no one else knew her. Probably better than she knew herself. He knew her True Name, which even she did not herself know. And he had command over the Words of Power, oh my, yes.

So now the doll was lying on a square of red silk, written all over with Words of Power in his own blood-ink to bind Cassiopeia to his will. And it was naked, as it should be for spells of lust and infatuation. He anointed it with rose oil and musk, named it, took a needle made of the heart of a sparrow feather (a sparrow being a notoriously lusty bird) and plunged it into the heart of the doll.

> "Heart afire, loins aflame, only to my hand be tame. Wild with lust for me alone, to all others be as stone. I alone quench thy desire, I alone appease thy fire. Now I bind thee, now I blind thee, no love see, but only me."

A wild surge of scarlet power washed over the doll, and sank into it, to be absorbed. The wax took on a rosy hue, until it looked so like living flesh, flushed with sexual desire, that one would have to touch it to know that it was wax.

He smiled, wrapped the poppet up in the scarlet silk, tucked both carefully into an aromatic box made of sandalwood and put the box on a high shelf in the corner.

Just in time.

He heard the *click* and faint grind of the door to the secret passageway opening into his bedroom, and hurried there before she could seek him out in his workroom.

With her cheeks flushed with lust, set off by the stark black of her mourning garments, she looked infinitely more attractive than she had in months. Even years.

"I couldn't stop thinking about you today," she said huskily. "I don't know why but—we've drawn apart...."

"Work," he said smoothly. "And worries. But the dragon has taken care of all of that for us, hasn't it? And now we can concentrate on important matters."

"Yes," she breathed. "Important matters."

As she advanced on him, hips swaying, he was glad he had thought to lock the doors before he completed the spell.

"I wish I knew how you could manage to read anything at all in that," said Alexander in fascination, as Godmother Elena bent over the scrying bowl, an enormous flat-bottomed basin of stark-white glass that normally held clear water and nothing more.

Not today. This was not just any scrying bowl. This was a way for Elena to actually see the way that the magical energies of The Tradition were moving. She had only just learned how to do this, taught by another of the true "Fairy" Godmothers, one of the very first to take on that mantle.

In the bottom of the bowl was a translucent image, a kind of miniature landscape map of the Kingdom of Acadia and as much of the surrounding Kingdoms as would fit on the bottom of the bowl. Although normally one could not see the borders of a Kingdom, this time was an exception. A baleful red line, like the color of molten lava seen through a crack in the overlaying rock, delineated the entire Border of Acadia.

This was the magical energy on the boundary of the Kingdom, the spell that kept any man inclined to slay the dragon from getting inside.

The part of the landscape inside that line was obscured by something like mist. To Alexander it looked as if someone had dripped milk into the water there.

"That's the spells that are up to keep me from scrying Acadia directly," Elena said, as he tentatively dipped a finger into the water where the clouding was the heaviest. "Now there—" She indicated a portion of the map that appeared to be a spot on the coastline, where the milky color was now tinged a dirty, unpleasant gray, mingled with threads of an equally unpleasant scarlet. "That's Ethanos, the capital, and that ugly dark is the magic of The Tradition saturating the area with tragedy. The red threads are something else quite powerful that's being worked there. I'm not at all certain what it is, but it's quite sexual by the color. It's probably magic—one of the major players manipulating another of the major players."

"That's a lot of darkness," Alexander said, frowning at the bowl as the gray color deepened.

"Yes, it is, and I don't mind telling you it makes me very uneasy about all of this. It means the Magician there, whoever he or she is, has a clear understanding of how The Tradition works and has put things into motion to get it on his or her side." She frowned, too. "Now here—" she indicated a patch farther away of sunny yellow that seemed to light up the whiteness from within "—here are our people. That's Gina's color, so she is directing the opposition, and she's doing very well so far as The Tradition is concerned. Looking at the power here, there has got to be a lot of people involved. And see those tints of green, scarlet and white? Those are other major players."

"Can you tell who they are?" Alexander asked, his handsome, dark head bent over the bowl.

She sighed and placed both elbows on the table supporting the bowl. "I can't even tell if they're human or not. That part of Acadia is what is called the 'Wyrding Lands,' which were ceded by treaty to the non-humans. I can't even ask the Fair Folk because the Wyrding Others are not Elven in nature, so they are as much in the dark as I am."

Alexander nodded. By now a veteran of many campaigns, he no longer was frustrated when Elena could not give him direct information. Despite her anxiety about this situation, she had to smile fondly at him for that. He had matured so much since becoming the Commander of the Glass Mountain Chapter-House…and every day, she found new reasons to be more in love with him.

He looked up, caught her smile and answered it with one of his own. For a moment, she could feel the love between them as a network of support and affirmation binding them together. And it was a tangible force, backed by a great deal of Traditional momentum, although it was a constant battle to keep The Tradition itself from trying to find ways to test and try them.

"What *can* you tell?" he asked, turning his gaze back to the depths of the bowl.

"Generalities. Now, since she is, in fact, *not* on her way back here having slain the dragon, since she is doing something involving a goodly size number of people, and is sitting right in the middle of the Wyrding Lands, we can assume that the scenario was not at all what it was made out to be."

"Which is what we guessed was going to be the case in the first place." Alexander nodded, as Elena tucked a stray curl of hair out of the way behind her ear. "That makes perfect sense. This business of the dragon bothers me, however. I thought we knew the location of most of the Dragons of Darkness hereabouts."

"It's possible that this is a new one," Elena said carefully. "Or one from farther away than we have information or contacts. But—" She shook her head. "I would have anticipated signs of tragic Traditional power in the bowl—not just in Ethanos, but wherever this dragon has its lair. And there is nothing." It was her turn to frown at the bowl. "Not only that, but I would have expected Gina to be somewhere near that nexus of tragedy, and she's not."

She waved a hand over the bowl as some of the darkness spread out again, reaching tendrils up and down the coastline. "And look at that! It does this every so often. *Something* in there is creating tragedy along the coast. But it goes in both directions, so it can't be the dragon." She ground her teeth a little. "Sometimes I wish I was a necromancer.

At least I could ask the spirits of the dead what was going on!"

"You wouldn't want to do that, Elena."

She looked up and caught his eyes, and smiled. "You're right, of course. I wouldn't. But this is very frustrating." She twisted the stray bit of hair around her finger. "I would say, looking at the buildup of power, that something is going to break, and soon. But I cannot tell what, nor when. Only that one way or another, this is going to be over before too many days are out."

He stood up, resting the knuckles of both hands on the edge of the table. "My love, I will give you the same advice you would give me in this situation. Gina is not the only Champion we have sent out. There are others who need your attention, as well. She is both trained and intelligent. You have done all you can. Now, turn to another, and know that whatever happens in Acadia, we have done what we can."

She sighed, and cleared the vision in the bowl with a wave of her hand over the water, making it once again crystal clear. "I'm afraid we'll only really know what has happened when either the spells against my scrying clearly vanish, or darkness comes over the whole land."

"You still won't be able to do anything about it," he pointed out. "And what is more, we have the troop and the Children of the North Wind ready to take us there if the boundary protections do come down." He came around to her side of the table and clasped both her hands in his. "Trust in your training. Trust in your intelligence. And most of all, trust in the people you yourself trained to do their work."

She sighed, looked into his eyes and squeezed the hands holding hers. "Aye," she said. "You're right. You're right. Now, who else do I need to look in on this night?"

He kissed her, long and deeply, before letting go of her hands. "Sir Micahel, that we sent into Vraimont to stand as Champion to the Lady Sephira. He should be there by now, if you, of your courtesy, could look...?"

She smiled again, and took up Micahel's token of a sword in flames. Clasping it between her palms, she invoked the essence of the veteran Champion and gazed deeply into the bowl, as the clear image of the countryside of the Kingdom of Vraimont appeared. Together she and Alexander leaned over and peered into the miniature landscape.

CHAPTER FIFTEEN

It was time. Things were spiraling out of control in Acadia, and they couldn't wait any longer.

The final straw—the final sign—was that the last of the so-called virgins that Adamant had collected was nothing of the sort. Clenestra was someone from Cassiopeia's court that Andie knew by reputation. A rather…tarnished reputation to be precise, and Andie could not for a moment imagine how the girl had passed as a virgin until she calmed down and started talking to them instead of shrieking at the top of her lungs.

And at that point, Andie knew that Solon or her mother—probably both—had to be stopped. Because Clenestra made it abundantly clear that there was no possible way that her being chosen for the sacrifice was due to chance.

She made the point, in anger so vivid and raw it practically scorched as effectively as dragon-flames, that she was not and had not been for some time, a virgin. That in fact, she had gotten a half-dozen lovers to *swear* she wasn't, and still they took her away and left her for Adamant.

She knew very well why she had been chosen. It was because her mother had been a little less than flattering about Cassiopeia's increasingly open infatuation with Solon. "She called the Queen a doe in season," Clenestra said bitterly. "But it was me who paid the penalty for Mother's loose lips. It wasn't more than a day later when they came for me, and they didn't even pretend it was due to the lottery."

So the Queen and Solon were no longer attempting to hide the fact that those who were chosen to go to the dragon were not chosen by lot—they were chosen by whether or not they had offended the Queen and her Chief Adviser.

The Sisterhood knew now that if they did not act soon, they would never be able to act at all.

The next night was moon-dark. There would be no better night for their purposes.

Andie spent a long night weeping on Peri's shoulder. Not just because of what was going on back in Ethanos, but because no matter what, she was about to face changes that she didn't want to deal with.

No matter what, she was going to lose Peri. And it felt like the bottom was about to drop out of her world.

She couldn't tell him that, of course. As she sobbed into his neck, her eyes so raw she could hardly see out of them, listening to his comfort and encouragement, how could she tell him that her despair came from her loving him more deeply and more surely than she had ever loved anyone before?

"You'll be fine…." he whispered.

I'll be alone! her heart wailed.

"We'll beat this sorcerer…."

And then you and Adam will fly away forever.

"You will be a great and good Queen."

And I'll live the rest of my life at the side of some man I barely know, who I could never love half as much as I love you….

His soothing words helped not at all, and she could not tell him why.

Neither of them slept. And the next day, both dozed fitfully while Adam and Gina put the Sworn Sisterhood through the last training drill they would ever have, studied the map that Andie had created for them, and looked worried while trying not to look worried.

As the sun set, they all gathered in the arena. Peri stood at the top of the grassy bowl and looked down on all of them, a circle of torches at his feet. Andie's heart ached to see how regal and noble he looked. How like a King.

Far more like a King than she could ever look like a Queen.

She would give anything to have such a King at her side. Anything.

"It is now tyranny, open tyranny, in Ethanos," he intoned, his voice pitched to carry. "We have all, all of us been used and abused by the tyrants. There are countless others in that city who could say the same, but none of them have the courage and the conviction and the love of Acadia that

we have. We will fight these tyrants. We will take the battle into their own halls. And we will win, because we can
do nothing less. We strike for ourselves, for our homes and
for Acadia, and we will strike for the heart and kill this
tyranny it its bed."

The girls erupted into cheers, although at this point, the
cheers sounded so nervous that Andie suspected they
would have cheered almost anything.

Andie had expected a longer speech than that, but
Peri was probably a better judge of how long he could
hold a nervous audience than she was. It was going to
be hard enough on most of them as it was, waiting for
their turns to be flown in. The dragons could only take
three of them at a time, each—crammed in uncomfort-
ably on their backs in front of the wings. Gina was one
of the first six to go, of course, because they were going
to have to take the watch-post up on the top of the cliff,
and do it before the Guard there could raise any kind of
alarm.

And that was when the fox unexpectedly presented himself. "Take me," he said, staring up at Gina and Adam insistently.

Adam looked down at him. Andie expected him to ask
why—but he didn't.

"I was hoping you would volunteer," he rumbled, "but
you are a tiny thing, and I did not want to assume."

The fox pulled himself up to his full height. "I may be
small, but I can do things no one else can do. I will scout
out the Guards for you," he said. "I will lead the Sworn Sisterhood to them. I can do this. I *want* to do this."

Adam blinked down at him. Despite her distress, Andie had to smother a smile at the little fox's deadly seriousness.

"You can, and you will," Adam replied, with a little bob of his head. "And you will show all of us how even the smallest of us can be as brave as a lion."

And so, when the first lot left, it was with the fox held on Gina's lap.

Andie waited with the rest in the arena, pacing the grass nervously. Ethanos wasn't that far as the dragon flew, actually. According to Peri, the road she and Gina had been forced to take wound back and forth and around so many times that it covered ten times the straight-line distance. He and Adam had assured her that they could get all the girls into place before midnight.

Yet the time crawled by, and the longer they took, the more certain she was that something had gone horribly wrong. If Peri was hurt—worse, if Peri was dead—

"Fewmets," said a voice in the air above her, and she ducked her head as Peri backwinged down to land with a *thud* beside her.

"What—" she started to wail.

He turned his head toward her and huffed out his breath reassuringly. "There wasn't one Guard there, there were two. One watching the seaward side, and one watching the land. Adam and Gina and I had to devise a whole new strategy. We landed and clung to the cliff face just below the top. They went up the stairs and surprised the guards, then we took off and landed again with the girls and managed to subdue them." Peri shook his head like a wet dog. "Harder than I thought it would be, but no one is hurt."

She just looked at him fearfully, thinking of all the people in the Guard that were her friends.

He touched her cheek with his muzzle. "No, not even the Guards. Bumps on the heads, but no permanent damage and not a lot of blood lost. Scratches at most."

She sighed with relief and threw her arms around his neck, and he curved his neck to hold her against his chest for a moment. But a moment was all he had—the next lot had to go, and go quickly, and so he was off again.

Andie was in the last lot of five, and had to share Peri with the newest girl, Clenestra, who was going not because she knew how to fight, but because she'd be in more danger if she was left behind without the dragons to protect her from the things in the Wyrding Lands. And the flight was—strange.

She hadn't quite realized, watching from the ground, how apparently light the dragons were. She clung on for dear life as he leapt into the sky, expecting him to jerk upward with his surge of wings, only to drop back between wingbeats.

But he didn't. Once the initial surge got him into the air, he flew more like a butterfly than an eagle; it was almost as if he were weightless, and his wings were only there to propel him forward. The flight as a consequence had a curiously dreamlike quality to it, quite as if she and Peri were gliding along in the darkness between the stars—

It was spoiled only by the other girl clutching at her middle until she was practically squeezed in two.

How Peri was able to see in the dark she had no idea. She didn't even know they were near the cliff until she looked down and saw the lights of the Palace, city and harbor below them. Then it was a long, slow spiral downward, like a leaf falling from a tree, a sudden bout of buffeting as Peri backwinged to a landing, and then—they were down.

Cleo was waiting for them, but no one else. She shoved a dagger into the new girl's hand and took them to where the two Guards were tied up, unconscious, in the shelter. Neither of them looked like anyone Andie knew, but for a moment, when she saw how heavily they were sleeping, she feared the worst—

Then she caught a strong smell of wine from them.

"What…" she began.

Cleo grinned. "Helena's idea. She stood over them and made them drink until they were stupid and passed out. They should be safe enough for you to keep an eye on, Clenestra. Princess, we need you to persuade some of these fellows that they need to come over to our side. Or at least see if there is anyone you recognize among them who might recognize you. Come on—"

Peri was already gone, so she followed Cleo down the switchback stairs she knew so well, her heart pounding and the sour taste of fear in her mouth, with no idea of what to expect when she got to the bottom.

What she found was half a dozen of the Sworn Sisters holding torches, looking grim-faced and businesslike, and at least two dozen Guards trussed up like geese going to market. And one, at least, she recognized.

"Thesus!" she exclaimed, but in a whisper.

At the sound of her voice, the guard jerked his head around and stared. His face grew white. He gasped.

And he fainted.

It took some time after he had been revived to assure him that she was not a ghost nor an illusion, nor some kind of baleful spirit masquerading as Andromeda.

It was only when she reminded him how her first, clumsy set of lenses looked that he got some color back, and began to look convinced.

"You are my Princess," he said, and bent his head in homage as best he could.

She took a chance then, since there was no one there to tell her not to, and cut him loose. He shook out his muscles and went to one knee, looking up at her.

"Princess," he said gravely. "Since you—in the past weeks things have been bad, very bad. Most of the Guard has been replaced with street-sweepings and scum from the docks." He glared at some of the men who were within his range of vision. "There are a few men here whom I trust, if *you* will trust me to take them down into the city." His head was up, and his eyes were fixed on hers. "We can find the rest of the Guards that were dismissed. We can rouse our friends, and they can rouse theirs. By morning, we will have an army."

By morning, all this will be over, and if it is not, it will be too late, she thought. Well, too late for her. Perhaps not too late to save Acadia, though....

"Go," she told him. The others looked at her nervously but didn't contradict her. He cut four more men loose—

Then he and those four ruthlessly and efficiently knocked each of the others unconscious with the blow of a sword-hilt to the temple.

"That will keep them quiet, Princess," he said, then kissed her hand. "Farewell. When you see me next, you will be Queen."

He and the four with him vanished into the night.

And that, of course, was the moment when the entire Palace seemed to erupt with cries and the sound of fighting.

Chaos was not nearly a strong enough word for what was happening. People were running madly through the halls in all directions, shrieking and screaming. Some clutched belongings (or loot), some held nothing at all, some were clearly Guardsmen and just as clearly were looking for whatever they could find to steal. There were small fires burning here and there, but fortunately the Palace was mostly made of stone, which meant the fires were largely confined to draperies or furnishings. But the stench of burning filled the air, the corridors were thick with black smoke, and people were blundering into one another, fighting without even knowing who they were fighting or why.

It was a nightmare, and Andie was alone in it.

By choice.

She wanted to try to reach Cassiopeia before the others found her. If there was any chance that her mother was innocent, duped, she had to know. And if she wasn't—if she had done all these horrible things of her own free will…

Well, Andie had to know that, too. And she had learned that slung stones could kill.

Somewhere, Gina and the best of the fighters were trying to find Solon. The rest had followed the fox when he had called for help, so presumably if they hadn't reached

Gina they were at least trying to. The fox hadn't been at all clear about what exactly had gone wrong—he had babbled something about monsters and Gina needing them, and then led the rest off to Gina, probably assuming that Andie was following.

Of course, the dragons couldn't fit inside the Palace. If there truly were monsters out there, then Gina and the rest would have to lure them out to where the dragons could be of some help.

In the cacophony, Andie couldn't tell what was going on. She was just going to have to trust that Gina knew what she was doing…that she and Adam had some sort of plan in case everything went wrong…and that Peri was somehow safe.

Twice, when she saw lone Guards that stood between her and the Queen's chambers, her slingshot eliminated that obstacle, and she could only hope as she passed their prone bodies that she had only knocked them unconscious.

She had gotten in via the kitchen, and had blundered around desperately, dashing from one bit of cover to another until she found herself in a corridor she recognized. Now, with her stomach knotted in fear, her eyes burning from the smoke, she watched helplessly from behind a column while the two Guards at the door to the Queen's Chambers shoved panicking nobles and servants aside and slashed at anyone that even looked like he was going to attack. With shaking hands, she readied her sling and tucked a lead bullet in the pocket. But even if she took down one, the other would be warned and he would probably come straight for her.

They'll kill me before I can even get close.

But even as she thought that, a huge wild-eyed brute also in the uniform of the Guard appeared at the other end of the corridor and charged them.

They turned at the last minute and saw him. Andie screamed in horror and hid her face behind the column, the sound of her cry lost in the noise as anyone else who happened to be in the corridor decided it was the wrong place to be and elected to climb over or bludgeon the others with pieces of furniture.

Then, suddenly, there was silence.

At least, in the immediate vicinity.

Andie peeked around the column, and her stomach twisted. She shoved her hand against her mouth as bile burned her throat.

Half a dozen bodies at least were lying in front of the door to the Queen's Chambers—the three Guards, and whoever else had gotten mixed up in the fight and couldn't get free before they were cut down.

No…

She wanted to sit down and howl. She wanted to weep until there were no tears left in her. Most of all she wanted to run away, run far, far away from all of this until she came to a place that had never heard of Solon, Cassiopeia or Acadia.

But she did none of those, because this might be her only chance. While the corridor was still empty, she dashed down it, tried the door, found it unlocked and hurled herself inside.

She closed it behind herself, putting her back against it.

The antechamber was empty, and dark except for a single oil lamp. It looked surprisingly peaceful.

Bolt the door. No matter what's in here, what's out there is worse.

With the door bolted, she ventured carefully across the antechamber. The next room was her mother's private Audience Chamber, with the lesser throne. There was more light showing under the door, and Andie put one hand on the latch—

—only to have it jerked violently out of her hand as the door slammed open. She stood blinking in the flood of light.

Solon stood there, with her mother, disheveled and wild-eyed, beside him.

And the first thing out of her mother's mouth was a cry of outrage. "You told me she was dead! You swore to me she was dead and we would never have to think about her again! You lying fool! You wretched, useless, lying piece of scum!"

There was absolutely no doubt what Cassiopeia meant. As Andie shrank back, the Queen flung herself toward Solon, fingers crooked into talons.

Strangely, Solon did not move.

As Andie stared at both of them with the morbid fascination of someone who could not look away from hideous tragedy, Cassiopeia reached him. He twisted his torso a little to the side and caught her by the hair as she stumbled past him. Jerked off her feet, she landed heavily on her knees as he drew a knife from the belt of his robe. He pointed it at Andie, who felt something like a mental blow strike her and rock her back, and then—

Andie's sling dropped from her hands. Time slowed to a snail's pace and she tried to breathe through the choking clouds of fear, as Solon raised the knife, shouted something incomprehensible—

—and slashed the blade across the Queen's throat.

A shriek burst from Andie's mouth when Cassiopeia's blood fountained from her wound, splattering Solon with crimson gore. Most horrible of all was his expression.

Complete indifference.

And then—he burst into flame.

Andie screamed again and flung up an arm in a futile attempt to defend herself, as Cassiopeia's body crisped, and the throne and the draperies behind it caught fire—

—and something monstrous emerged from the flames.

She didn't get more than a glimpse of it—too many teeth, all dagger-sharp and dagger-long. Too many eyes. Horns and hooves and at least four arms, all ending in talons the dragons would envy. Eyes that burned with hatred. Eyes that had her death in them.

But now she could turn and run, and she did, stumbling toward the door as the thing lunged after her. She fumbled with the bolt and rammed the door open with her shoulder, and felt the thing's flames and smelled her own hair sizzle as she plunged into the corridor.

Screaming now, she raced down the hall and into the throne room with the creature howling behind her. As she reached the center of the room, Gina appeared, charging into the throne room from the door to the courtyard.

The Champion did not hesitate for a second; she shouldered Andie aside, sending her into the wall, as she brought up shield and sword and hit the monster with both.

It didn't even move.

A heartbeat later, the creature backhanded her with one terrible blow and Gina was flying through the air. She hit the far wall about halfway up with a tremendous *crash,* followed by a dull *thud* as her body dropped to the floor.

And did not move.

Andie's heart stopped. *Gina...*

The monster turned toward Andie again.

She wanted to run to Gina. She wanted to snatch up Gina's sword and avenge her.

And that—was stupid. She couldn't avenge Gina, she couldn't hit this thing. She had to run, and get it away from where Gina lay, so that if by some slim change Gina was still alive—

She whirled, and let her fear give her feet wings.

She ran for her life, tears of loss and horror streaming down her face and blinding her, and dashed out the door into the courtyard. She heard the thing in hot pursuit behind her, felt the swipe of its talons tearing her tunic just as she got ten steps into the open, and felt her entire body convulse in a scream of despair.

Then a huge dark shape interposed itself between her and the monster. She felt herself being brushed aside as if she were a moth. Tumbled to the cobblestones, she hit her forehead and saw stars, rolled over twice and—

—watched as Periapt pounced on the monster, seized it by the head and flung it like a terrier flinging a rat. The monster howled as it soared over the walls of the Palace, over the cliff, and vanished out of sight. And that was the last thing she saw for a long time.

"How many fingers am I holding up?"

The strange, blond-haired woman in the fancifully embroidered, amethyst-colored tunic and split riding skirt held up her hand.

"Three," said Andie, her head hurting badly enough to make her feel as if she should be going cross-eyed. "Who *are* you?"

"Elena Klovis, and I was only holding up two. Do not move." She looked up. "Periapt, see to it that she does not move. Sit on her if you must. I need to attend to my Champion."

Champion...

Andie had a flash of memory. Gina running in to face the monster alone. Gina flying through the air to hit the wall...

"*Gina!*" she called out trying to struggle to her feet.

"Don't start!" Periapt half cried, half scolded. "Adam is bad enough, he's beside himself with worry! It will be all right! It has to be all right!"

His agitated words only made her more alarmed. "What do you mean?" she wailed, blindly putting a hand out to try to lever herself up, and getting nowhere because Peri had planted a forefoot gently but firmly over her torso.

"The Champion got rather well smashed up when she hit the wall," said the fox on the other side of her, his head cocked. "The chirurgeon wasn't very helpful. But now that the Godmother is here, I don't think anyone needs to worry."

Godmother? "What Godmother?" she asked, feeling as if someone had handed her a book with half its pages missing.

But the fox was now peering over the top of her, past Peri, in the same direction as the sound of someone chanting.

"*...strong as steel and right as rain, Champion, be thyself again!*"

There was a bright flash of light, and a groan, and then Gina's voice saying clearly, "Remind me never to do anything like taking on a Demon Lord single-handedly again."

"I would," said the calm voice of the strange woman. "But you'd never listen to me. Now lie there and rest, or I will tell this other dragon to sit on *you*. I might have healed you, but you're still going to need recovery time."

A moment later, the woman was back at Andie's side. "How many fingers am I holding up?"

"Why are you asking me this? Two," Andie replied, feeling greatly relieved to have heard Gina's voice, but still horribly confused.

"It is the standard thing to ask someone who has had a blow to the head. And while I am not a healer, I have picked up a few tricks." The woman sat back on her haunches. "You would be Andromeda, I take it? Queen Andromeda now, I suppose, given what we found in the lesser throne—"

At that moment, memory came rushing back and Andie rolled over away from the woman to retch out the entire contents of her stomach. Somewhat to her shock, the stranger held her to steady her, wiped her face when she was done, then snapped her fingers. A servant in a smudged tunic and ash-streaked skirt came running.

"We're going to get this child into a bed in a moment. See that one is ready for her." Then she glanced at Periapt. "Amend that. Have a bed brought here."

The servant bobbed a curtsy. "Yes, Godmother," she said.

"Now. In a moment, I am going to work a healing magic on you. It will put you to sleep for a while. The magics that heal cracks on the head tend to do that—I don't know why, so don't bother to ask."

"But—" said Andie.

"No 'buts' and no objections, thank you very much," said the stranger. "Now, look right here—"

And once again, the world went away.

The courtyard was very crowded, but there was nowhere else they could all go where the dragons would fit. Andie was just as pleased. She didn't want to be in the throne room; didn't want to be reminded that she was Queen, in name if not yet crowned. She just wanted to be Andie for a little longer.

All of the introductions had been made, so now Andie knew that that handsome man in fine plate-armor was Champion Alexander, the Grand Master of the Glass Mountain Chapter-House. She knew that the strange woman was Godmother Elena, and that both of them had been waiting for days, waiting for the nasty magic that Solon had put on the Border to come down.

"You would think," the Godmother had said in disgust, "that a nasty little insect like this Solon would never be powerful enough to prevent a Godmother from crossing his barrier. But unfortunately, you would be wrong. He had so much Traditional force behind his curse that I don't think even one of the Fair Folk could have broken the barrier."

"It would have been interesting to see one try, though," Alexander had replied. "And you have to admit that they, too, would have satisfied the 'no man' part of the binding."

The Godmother had just shaken her head.

It was a good thing that they had been waiting on the spot and had arrived when they did, because Gina had had a narrow escape. No one was actually telling Andie anything, but she'd overheard murmurs of "broke every bone in her body," and it was very difficult not to relive that moment when she'd seen her friend hit that wall.

There was no sign of Solon. There was, however, something that might have been a terribly burned human body at the bottom of a pit about where the Demon Lord would have landed when Peri threw him.

Most of the old members of the Guard were back on duty. The new replacements had, for the most part, vanished. A fair number of valuables had vanished with them, but at this point, Andie was counting the cost as minimal.

Most of the Sworn Sisterhood had been reunited with their families. Those that had not—who, in fact, had decided that they wanted as little to do with their families as possible—were planning on joining the Guard.

"Well," said the Godmother, surveying the courtyard, with its contingent of two dragons, one Princess, a handful of Champions, and as many members of the Court as could crowd in there. "It looks to me as if we are all set for a happy—"

But she never got a chance to finish that sentence, because Andie burst into tears.

"It's not a happy ending!" she wept, as Elena stared at her, dumbfounded. "It will never be a happy ending! How can I possibly have a happy ending when I am going to have to spend the rest of my life without the creature I love?"

Elena blinked at her, as did virtually everyone else in the courtyard.

"You did say 'creature,' am I correct?" Elena asked cautiously. "And you do mean—"

But she had already run across the courtyard and flung herself at Peri's neck, wrapping both arms around it. "I mean I am in love with Periapt," she cried, sobbing. "And I don't care who knows it! He's clever, he's wise, he's kind and gentle, he's noble—"

And to her shock and amazement, Peri let out a bellow that sounded positively heartbroken.

"I will never love anyone but you!" he cried. "I swear, I will never take a mate if it can't be you, and I don't care if they exile me from the clan forever for that. Let them exile me!" He shook his head violently as he looked down at her. "If only you could be a dragon, or make me human!" he cried, curving his neck around her and holding her close.

Andie wept on, consumed with despair. "I will never, ever, ever find someone I love as much as you."

"Well, isn't this a pretty puzzle," Elena said. "Now under normal circumstances, I would have said you were asking the impossible. But this isn't normal. For one thing, the line of the Bookwyrms does lend itself to transformative magic. For another, there's enough Traditional power around you two star-crossed lovers to do it. But someone else would have to become a dragon. There has to be balance in these things. And who would want to become a dragon?"

There was silence again, but this time it was broken by an entirely unexpected source.

"Oh?" said Gina, with a significant look at Adamant. "I can think of one person."

They all turned to look at her, dumbfounded. Except for Adamant, who looked desperate and gratified. "You would?" he cried. "You really would?"

"Well, why not?" she asked. "I already spend most of my time in armor anyway. Besides, I, uh—" She looked at Adamant and blushed. "We—uh—make a good—uh—team, Adam and I. I should think dragons would make good Champions."

She shuffled her feet and looked down at them, flushing crimson. "He's a real charmer. I—uh—can understand why Andie is so in love with his brother. 'Cause—I never met anyone—I wanted to spend the rest of my life with—before I met Adam."

"Really?" The heat coming off Adamant proved he was performing the draconic equivalent of blushing and was doing so just as hard. "Gina—you're—you'd—I'd—" The big, confident dragon was gone and in his place was—

Well, he looked and sounded for all the world like a lovelorn adolescent. In a tiny voice he said, "I think I love you, too. If love is never wanting to be away from you. Ever. For as long as I live."

The stunned silence that settled over the courtyard was finally broken by laughter.

"Oh my!" Elena chortled, looking from one to another of them as if she could not quite believe her luck. "Well, that would certainly give us all the happy-ending Traditional force I would need!"

"You would?" asked Adamant.

"You could?" asked Andie.

The Godmother rubbed her hands together and looked absolutely gleeful. "This is the sort of spell that you only get to cast once in a lifetime. No self-respecting Godmother would ever miss the chance to enter the Books of the Tradition with that kind of magic to her credit." She rolled up her sleeves and took the wand from her belt.

She waved it once in the air—and suddenly everything in the courtyard glowed with a pure white light. Even the air itself suddenly seemed to be full of a glowing mist. The Godmother nodded happily. "All right, I would like Peri and Gina to stand right—" she moved around the courtyard until she could get the right spot "—here, I think."

She began cutting glyphs in the air with her wand. The signs glowed, and she filled the air with them, working her way around and around the dragon and the human, until she had formed a kind of wall of glyphs that it was impossible to see through.

There was a sort of musical hum in the air, as if what she was doing was attracting yet more power. Finally she stopped, and held up the wand.

"When love is more than form and face
When love sees past the bone and skin
When love fears not but to embrace

And seeks the soul that lies within
When truest hearts seek hearts so true
Brave any danger, and the storm
Then outward semblance be made new
Then love's own magic shall transform!"

The circle of glyphs shrank around Peri and Gina, growing brighter by the moment. It collapsed in on them, until they were enclosed in a shining ball of light that began to rise from the courtyard until it hung about roof-height in midair.

Then it split into two glowing spheres, one amber-colored and one green. The spheres began to spin, and then to circle each other as if they were connected on a common axis. Faster and faster they spun, growing brighter and harder to look at, the two colors blurring together.

Until once again they formed a single sphere of white light.

Slowly the sphere drifted back down to the stones of the courtyard. And the light began to fade.

And at last, where there had been a dusky green dragon and an armored human—there was now, an armored human and a dusky green dragon.

Andie stared, and began to feel tears of disappointment well up. It hadn't worked. It hadn't worked after all—

The dragon held up a forefoot and examined the talons.

"First things first," the dragon said in Gina's voice. "I have *got* to get these sharpened."

And the human pulled off the helm to reveal a very masculine face with a slightly woebegone expression. "It would be nice," said Periapt, "if someone would help me out of this armor. It seems to be rather too tight in a couple of very uncomfortable places."

EPILOGUE

This would probably go down in the annals of the God-mothers of the Five Hundred Kingdoms as the oddest double wedding of all time.

It had to be held outdoors, and not just because one of the couples was a pair of dragons, but because at least thirty more dragons *and* a goodly number of large representatives from the Wyrding Others insisted on attending.

The ceremony itself was a bit odd, as well, since it was conducted not by any religious authority, but by a God-mother. Some were scandalized by this, but most folk seemed to take it in stride. After all, it wasn't every day that the first pair of Dragon Champions *ever* also got married.

In fact, they so eclipsed the human couple that a great many people even forgot that it was supposed to *be* a double wedding.

That suited the human couple in question perfectly. Queen Andromeda still wasn't used to being in the public eye for most of her waking hours. And as for her new husband, Loremaster Periapt, the Prince-Consort was always happier in a library keeping quietly out of the way. Though, his researches had already begun to benefit the people of Acadia. He had opened negotiations with the Wyrding Others to allow selected harvesting of trees from their forest— the great giants were known to fall from time to time, and all were agreed that there was no point in allowing the wood to rot. And there were other stands that needed to be thinned. With the Dryads directing the thinning, the forest would rejoice in a healthy renewal, and the timber would find any number of homes. Peri had more such schemes in mind—

—but not today.

He and Andie waited on the walls for the dragons to depart. It was, after all, rather difficult to keep them fed in the city, and everyone tacitly agreed that the sooner they could move on and feed themselves with hunting, the better.

Finally, the two appeared on the Watch-Cliff above the Palace. As one, they dove from the cliff, side by side, opening their wings with a *snap* at the last minute and shooting over Andie's and Peri's heads. As the royal couple waved excitedly like a couple of children, the dragons waggled their wings in farewell, and shot up and over the mountains, heading first for the Chapter-House of Glass Mountain and then—

Well, if they had a destination, they hadn't told anybody. Not even Godmother Elena.

"Where do you think they'll honeymoon?" Andie asked Peri as the two dragons flew off together.

"Hmm," Periapt said, and raised an eyebrow. "Well, no matter what, I know one thing it will be."

"Which is?" Andie asked him, as he put his arm around her waist and held her close.

He laughed. "Someplace—fireproof!"

* * * * *

Coming next year is FORTUNE'S FOOL—the next
TALE OF THE FIVE HUNDRED KINGDOMS
from Mercedes Lackey!